Cover Design by Brittany Evans

Edited by Represent Publishing

THE EDGE OF HOPE

THE EDGE OF HOPE

TRENA CANNON

Represent
Publishing

For my husband, Chad, whose support and love is never ending.

TRIGGER WARNINGS

Mental Illness
Abuse
Prison
Violence
Crime
Alcohol
Language

WHAT WAS THEN

1

I'm in a full-blown panic. They're coming. I have to hurry. With a quick scan of my room, I ignore my parents' boots striking along the hardwood flooring and face the closet door. No. That makes too much noise. They'll hear it open for sure. I spin in a tight circle, hugging the basket close to my chest, and stop at my writing desk. Not under there. They'll see it poking out. I lean back slightly, peering out my bedroom door, and the shadows grow larger, nearly filling the hallway.

I have no other option. It has to be under the bed. The worst possible place. That's how I was caught last time. But if I hide it anywhere else, they'll hear me. They'll ask questions and I'll be caught yet again. And this time, I'll receive more than a tongue lashing. Not that I'd receive the switch. Papa and Father don't believe in that kind of punishment. But being locked in the house with nothing to do, except practice voice lessons or my stitch work, well, that's like death itself. I would just die if I couldn't see Mable for a whole week.

With careful steps, I shove the basket under my bed, and then practically throw myself onto the mattress. As I pull the covers up to my chin, my tummy knots with excitement and fear, like there are two strands of rope battling each other for victory. Papa and Father enter my bedroom and my heart pounds out of control. Please don't notice anything off. Like my dress, shoved under the blanket and wadded at my feet.

"Good night, Peanut," Father says, moving closer to the bed. He kicks the basket and fear gets a cheap shot. My heart nearly explodes when I hear it slightly slide under my bed. *Please don't look under the bed.* Thankfully, he doesn't. He tucks the covers under me, snug as a bug, and I swallow the fear down. Just like Mable has told me to do many times when we are up to no good.

"Good night," I say, hoping he can't hear my blood pumping fast and hard.

"Don't let the bedbugs bite." He kisses my forehead and then makes room for Papa. Our nightly ritual.

"But if they do, I'll grab a shoe and beat them black and blue," Papa says playfully. He bends, brushing my ink-black hair out of my eyes. "Buenas noches, Mija."

"Good night, Papa."

He reaches for the candle on my nightstand and when he turns, moving closer to the open window above my writing desk, my chest tightens. Fear is about to win as it tugs harder on the cord.

"Are you sure you want this window open? There's a chill tonight."

"Sí, Papa, I'm sure."

Please don't shut it. Otherwise, I'll never get it back open without you hearing it, and then how will we sneak out?

"Okay then." Papa turns back to me. "But if you get too cold, come get me and I'll close it."

"Gracias."

"Mmhmm." He scans the room like he's searching for something out of place, and I hope with all my might I was careful this time. Papa is the one I have to worry about. He's always suspicious of me, especially when Ford is visiting. He's my cousin and when he visits, mine and Mable's trouble making doubles. The three of us are forever in trouble, and that's why tonight is so important. Ford's parents will be here in three days to take him back home.

"Good night, Papa," I say, and roll onto my side, facing the wall.

"Buenas noches."

When I hear his boots heading upstairs for the spare room Ford is in, I brave a peek over my shoulder. That was a close one. I roll toward the window, tucking my hands under my cheek, and return the moon's full smile. For we both know tonight will be a night to remember. A yawn pulls at my throat, and I stretch my eyes, forcing myself to stay awake. I can't go to sleep. Too much depends on it.

Out the window, a star shoots across the sky, and I close my eyes. *I wish I may. I wish I might. I wish upon this star tonight.* I squeeze them harder. *I wish that I could be a real Natural.* Another yawn forces its way out and I stretch my eyes wide again. But the crickets and bullfrogs playing outside are like a lullaby, lulling me to sleep, and my eyes close heavy with slumber.

A drop of water lands on my forehead like it's dripping from the ceiling and my eyes pop open, wide and alert. Dang it. I fell asleep. I shift and see Mable standing above me, hunched over, and bracing herself on her knees, with a long string of drool hanging from her mouth. She sucks her slobber back in with a giggle.

"Eww, Mable," I quietly say and wipe at my forehead.

"Yeah, well, I knew you'd fall asleep. Ya always do." She smiles.

"Come on, we have to go. Cotton Wayne and Alex are waiting for us," my cousin says, full of irritation. He's standing by the open window, sporting a fresh black eye. Ford is a year older than us and since he starts sixth year at the end of the season, he thinks he knows everything. Luckily, he only visits during the summer seasons. As Mable would say, thankfully he'll be gone soon so we don't have to listen to how wrong we are all the time. And Mable, she doesn't like to be told when she's wrong, even when she is, which is why she clocked him good last night.

She jumps off the bed and lands on her bare feet, quiet as a mouse. "Where'd ya put it this time?"

"It's under the bed." I'm not as quiet, nor am I as sneaky as Mable, so I have to creep off the squeaky mattress. I pull back the covers and, in my sleep, I managed to lose my dress. It isn't wadded at the end of the bed, and it isn't on the floor. Where is it? "Mable, can you help me find my dress, please?"

"Why?" She carefully pulls the basket out and looks up at me with a scrunched face. "I ain't wearing one. Just wear your nightdress like me."

I grimace and she straightens, jabbing a fist into her hip, knocking the wooden sword tucked into her belt askew.

"Ain't nobody that matters gonna see us out this late," she says, and then adjusts her sword back in place.

"Come on," Ford whines and, in his haste, he grabs the basket with more force than needed, and the jars inside knock against each other. We all freeze in place, waiting for my parents to rush into my room and demand answers. But we've been here before, and if they don't come in within the next five seconds, we're good. I count to five, mentally and with my fingers, and when neither of my parents enter, I swallow the fear down and move closer to my writing desk. Mable goes first. Like I said, she's quieter and if, for some reason, my counting was off, at least she'll get away because Mable's momma does use the switch. Ford goes next, nearly as quiet as her.

I step onto the wooden slab, and it rocks slightly. I hold my breath and my footing with a quick, scary glance at the door. I listen for footsteps or whispers from down the hall and count to five again, waiting. And when nothing happens, I slip out the window with excitement, winning the battle.

Once we're free, I pull out the jars of lightning bugs and hand them out to guide our way toward our secret spot. Not that our spot is a secret. There is a trail, but when you're out at this time of night, it's top, top-secret. Father calls it the devil's hour, but I call it the magical hour. It's the only time you can dance with the lightning bugs and pretend they're fairies.

Once we're deeper into the woods, Mable and I skip through the tall grass, while Ford paces himself behind us, weaving in and out of the trees and jumping over fallen branches. He's being careful not to get too close, and I don't blame him. Mable likes to tease him something awful.

Mable slows her steps, and I join her. "Hey Ford?" she

says over her shoulder. "How's that black eye treating ya?" She laughs.

"You're not as funny as you think you are, Mable. How would you like it if I gave you one?"

She spins on her heel, walking backward with a lopsided grin. "Am so, and I don't reckon I'd like it at all." Her grin spreads into a wide smile. "But then again, you'd have to be tough enough to land a punch and there ain't a fella around these parts that can. Which leaves you out." She sticks her tongue out at him, and of course, Ford scoffs. He's forever scoffing at one of us.

A tree branch snaps nearby, and we rush behind a wide tree, hunkering beneath the hanging moss; but to us, it's the wizard's beard. And with his protection, we hide from Alex.

We aren't sure of his age because he doesn't know his numbers, and he doesn't have any parents to ask. He usually stays down by the docks with the other orphans when we are at home, but we always meet up so we can sneak him food. Because with us being what the new world calls a Spoon, and Alex a Forgotten, we aren't allowed to speak to him. Spoons and Forgotten aren't allowed to mix. It's like a real law and everything. It's one of the reasons being out this late, and with Alex, is so scary. But we've never been too keen on following that law and we've broken it many times. In secret, of course.

"Mable? Tippy?" Alex runs a hand through his long, sun-bleached hair. "Ford?"

"Wanna scare the jeepers outta him?" Mable asks over my shoulder.

"Heck yeah." I grin.

"On three?" Ford raises his hand, counting to three, and then we burst into the clearing with fierce battle cries. Alex screams like a girl, hopping up and down like he's running in place, and I nearly fall over laughing.

"You almost jumped out of your trousers," Mable giggles.

"Nuh-uh," Alex argues. "I knew ye be der the whole time."

"Right," Mable taunts, tossing her long, box braids over her shoulder.

"I did," he huffs, shoving her backward.

"Oh yeah, ya wanna go," Mable chuckles with a shove of her own.

"Aye," Alex giggles. "An' ye going down this time."

They start to circle each other in a playful altercation, pushing and shoving. With that scream being as loud as it was, we need to move. And fast. I reach for Mable's hand. "Let's go before we're caught." I lead them farther into the woods and straight to our secret spot. Where a weeping willow overlooks our island, Capra Horn.

"Hey, what took y'all so long?" Cotton Wayne asks with annoyance. He's sitting on a dead log, twisting a lock of black hair down the center of his forehead. He's the same age as us, eleven, and Ford's best friend when he visits.

"Why do you think? Tiptoe, here, fell asleep." Ford faces me with a sour look. "Again."

Mable moves between us, facing Ford. "Leave her be or I'll give ya another what for," she says with a raised fist.

"Whatever," Ford sneers with a dismissive wave.

I lower my basket near the tree's trunk, right under our initials carved into its bark. Mine, Ford, Mable, and Cotton Wayne's. And tonight, Alex will join our mark. He will become the fifth DV8R in our group. I reach inside the basket for Alex's dinner while Ford pulls out a blanket. Of course, Mable drops into the dirt before he can lay it out.

Not that I'm surprised. She's never been very ladylike. It's one of the things I love most about her. She's the only girl I know that doesn't seem to care what others think or say about her. Everyone sits down, forming a tight circle. The same way we did two years ago when Ford formed the DV8Rs.

"Before we begin the ritual, we must tell the tale of how the world was shaped," Ford says. He reaches for the lightning bugs and places one of the jars in the middle of us as Mable puts her father's pocketknife next to the jar. We have to set the mood just as Ford did when he made us go through the ritual.

Ford leans forward slightly. "In 2104, Mankind witnessed the first of many natural disasters that ripped the world apart. Tornadoes. Earthquakes. Volcanoes. Sinkholes. You name it, Mother Nature threw her best at all creation, but that's not what set the world back." He shakes his head. "It was the hurricanes and tsunamis that hit afterward that shaped our new world. Mankind could not escape the disastrous penalties of climate change. All they could do was watch as the ocean swallowed most of the land, creating small islands that now dot the world map."

"And with no law," Cotton Wayne begins, loosely hugging his knees, "folks were fighting over everything. Food. Land. Even water. It wasn't until years later when settlements and laws were formed. General stores started popping up, spreading into other kinds of trade. Leather shops, tailors, and even barber shops were built, hoping folks would flock and give coins. But with no way to travel but by ship, traveling was hard. The ocean was and still is a tough sail."

Mable leans close to Alex. "Unless ya belong to the sea. Argh," she says in her best pirate voice.

A pang of guilt shoots through me because Alex used to be a cabin boy until he was marooned for stealing a loaf of bread from his captain.

"And with more pirates than islanders, lawmen were unable to stop them from raiding," Ford says. "All they could do was not stand in their way or fight back when they attacked. Sheriffs allowed pirates to ransack homes and trade stations, taking what they wanted. In return, pirates never harmed the islanders. Not because they actually cared." His voice squeaks and he shoots Mable a threatening look. All summer, his voice has been changing, and she has teased him ruthlessly. I hold my breath, waiting for the insult to come, but she doesn't say anything. Instead, she presses her lips into a thin line and looks away, drumming her fingers on her knees. Ford eyes her a moment and then clears his throat before continuing.

"They needed our farmers, carpenters, and blacksmiths in order to survive at sea, and for many years, it worked. People worked hard, continued with their everyday life, never truly fearing pirates. It wasn't until years later when ammo became almost nonexistent. That's when islanders started to fear them. Since there weren't enough islanders breaking the law and becoming prisoners to work the mines, the Pirate Commodore demanded a new treaty. The islanders were no longer allowed to help the orphans."

Mable squints one eye and makes a hook with her index finger. "Don't be feeding, sheltering, or caring for 'em. Leave 'em hungry and scared, so they're easier to catch when we storm the shores. We'll take the strong and give the weak to the mining caves like prisoners." She spits in the dirt, just like a boy.

"Except there was one clan that refused this treaty, the Naturals," I say. "But no one knew why they refused or which side they stood with. Pirates or Spoons." I lean close to Alex. "Because the very next night, after the treaty was created, they disappeared."

Mable nudges Alex's knee. "Some say, the Commodore and her crew attacked, sinking their ship with the entire crew with it. And now, they're like these magical beings, hiding below sea and when the moon appears," she looks up, "they say, they surface, bringing a war against everyone, especially Spoons." She grabs Alex by the shoulders. "They grab the Forgotten, forcing them into gruesome brawls, tossing the losers overboard."

"But the rumor we believe," Ford begins, "their ship was never attacked, but they do travel underwater in a massive ship, traveling all over the world. They help with food and medicine and whatever else the island may need." He looks right at Alex. "But most importantly, they help the orphans. They give them a choice. They ask if they want to join their crew and become heroes like them. Or go live in a magical world where food is plentiful, and the old technology thrives." His voice squeaks and his cheeks turn a reddish-brown as he clears his throat again.

"And best of all," I say, "it doesn't matter if you're weak or strong, or even your age. Everyone is welcome. Just like our group."

"An' ye think these folks be real?" Alex chuckles. "Bag yer face," he says with a dismissive wave.

"Yes. I've seen one. Up close and everything," Ford admits. "And they aren't at all like the Pirates say. They're good people." He reaches for the pocketknife. "So, would you like to join? Do you want to become—"

"Shush," Cotton Wayne tells Ford and turns his ear to the rustling behind us. "Do you hear that?"

"What it be?" Alex asks, shifting to sit on his heels.

"The sound of victory!" Mable soars to her feet, drawing her wooden sword. "We are the DV8Rs and there ain't nothing we can't defeat." She points her sword toward the bushes. "Dragon's attack!" she commands and darts into the bushes.

"What an idiot," Ford says with a hard eye roll, closing the pocketknife.

"Don't be cross because you don't have an imagination," I tell him and reach for the jar in front of me.

"Aye, don't be heavy," Alex agrees, jumping to his feet. He bends for a long stick and waves his pretend staff high above his head. "Ghouls, storm!" He makes a whooshing sound, casting his spells, and follows Mable.

"But what about the ceremony?" Ford whines, slinging his hand out, gesturing to the middle of the blanket.

"It's not a big deal, Ford." Cotton Wayne hugs his knees closer to his chest. "We still have two more days. We can always do it tomorrow night."

"I guess." Ford shrugs and then points into the bushes. "But those two better take this serious tomorrow, or I'm kicking them both out."

Now, it's my turn to scoff at him. Ford's never been able to tell Mable what to do. She goes, says, and does whatever she wants.

"What?" Ford says, turning those fierce brown eyes at me. "You don't think I will."

"I think if you tell her what to do, you will be returning home with two black eyes." I grin, twisting off the lid and freeing my fairies.

Ford opens his mouth to argue, and the town bells scream in warning.

"It's a raid," Cotton Wayne says, pushing to his feet.

My heart slams against my chest so hard, pain radiates

under my armpits. "We have to find the Forgotten before the Pirates do." I soar to my feet, standing with Cotton Wayne. "We have to save Alex."

"Tippy, wait," Ford says, latching onto my arm as he stands with us.

"Why? We're the DV8Rs. This is what we do." I jerk my arm free and rush headfirst into the night.

CAUGHT IN A WOLVES' DEN

Six years later

Hope is a powerful word. One with so much weight, it can drive desperation into any soul and force them to hold on just one more day. But my hope is dwindling like a dandelion swaying in the breeze and the last seed is struggling for life. I fear without it, I'll fade into the shadows and join the exhausted. It's why I continue on like a tired soldier, shuffling to his next battlefield. Except I'm not a soldier, I'm a prisoner and my battlefields are mining caverns.

"File in line and move forward," a guard orders.

Some say we are a tall tale. A myth even. That the crimes we committed that night never happened. And when we hear the older prisoners retell our story to the smaller ones, we don't stand and say it's true. Nor do we admit it was us. Instead, I often wonder to myself: If I had known the outcome of that night, would I have chosen the same fate? Would I have risked everything to save the Forgotten? To save Alex.

"Keep moving!" another guard demands.

I inch forward, nearly pressed against the prisoner in front of me with fear searing the back of my throat. It's been a long day. One I should be thankful for since we haven't drilled today, but I'm not. The unknown of what is happening replaces any gratitude. Last night, it was Mable's turn to keep watch and why I allowed myself to sleep. But now, I'm thinking that wasn't the best decision because I have no idea where we are or how we ended up in the hands of a new warden.

Was our cavern attacked?

If so, how? Our warden was the most powerful man around. He was strict and forceful with his prisoners, including his guards. He obeyed the Commodore's law to the T, and no one had ever escaped or been able to penetrate his cavern. So, knowing an attack like that happened, even if Mable fell asleep, wouldn't one of us have awoken at some point before now? How did this new warden and his guards transfer all these prisoners to a ship, and we do not remember any of it?

The line comes to a stop and the tight air hums with chatter from the other prisoners, and I want to look up too. I want to see what our new post looks like. Perhaps get a sense of what really happened and where we are. But I've felt the end of a strap before and since, I've not lifted my chin or faced the warden or his guards. Instead, I secretly glide a fingertip along the smooth metal coat painted on the wall next to me, with hope swelling in my throat. Maybe we won't be mining. Perhaps our new warden wants us for a different reason. I run all four fingers against the cool surface, yearning for a new position, possibly one outside. But I know that's a fruitless dream. All positions are mining ones. Sulfur. Gold. Silver. Coal. And I swallow the desire down in a hard gulp. Wherever they are taking us, it won't be good.

"Name?" a female voice asks me.

I jerk my hand back with a chill crawling along my skin. Not that I'm scared of touching something that isn't mine, although a small part of fear pricks my skin because of that very thing. No, it's because they've never asked for our names before. Maybe I didn't hear her correctly. I start to lift my eyes, but the very thought of being punished has me pressing my chin closer to my chest. Instead, I do what all guards want; I keep my head down with my mouth shut and unwillingly stretch my arm out. And it shakes uncontrollably as I prepare for my new brand.

"Whoa! How many times have you been sentenced?" the female asks, and she sounds young. More like my age than a guard. And again, I force myself not to look.

"Eight," I hear behind me, and I know it's Alex. He's been our constant ever since Mable and I were sentenced. Alex is the one that taught us all about the Forgotten rules. The same way we taught him the Spoon rules when he first arrived at Capra Horn.

"We be—" he begins.

"It doesn't matter. Owl!" she calls. "Come look at this one's arm. At all these brands."

I fidget in place with beads of sweat forming on my upper lip because all that's ever mattered before is: Can we still drill? Black boots stop inches in front of my toes and my heart races out of control, fearful of what is about to happen. Will he stomp on my foot? Punch me in the gut? Or use the strap? After all, these are new guards, and the new ones are the worst. They like to enforce their power straight away. I clutch my cold hands together in front of my belly to stop a mean fist. Curl my toes under in case those boots come down on me. And silently pray this guard doesn't use the strap.

"Yeah, so?"

"So," the female stresses, "look at her. She's already cowering. She's weak and won't last."

"I know. That's what I thought too, but check this out."

Before I can prepare myself, fingers plow into my matted hair, and I stumble forward. I know I shouldn't look, but I want to know the face that will be swinging the strap against our backsides. And like instinct, my eyes fill with hatred the second I lock onto him.

"See that look? That's the fire we're looking for."

"Yes, but can she learn?" a voice calls nearby.

I skim the crowd, and my eyes grow wide. The warden's guards are young, all ranging from fourteen to eighteen years of age. How is it possible they overpowered our previous warden and all his men? Not only that, but they are dressed in the most outlandish clothing. The females aren't wearing bell-shaped dresses sewed together with lace or silk. They aren't even fashioning a beaded collar or a fan. Instead, they are dressed like the males. Faded trousers with rips and holes torn through the material, and their short-sleeved shirts have strange images painted on the front. But what has me flabbergasted is the females are shouting out orders among the males as if they are equal. The only time a female is allowed this type of freedom is because they are pirates. Are we no longer prisoners in the mining caverns? Have we been captured by pirates?

Before I can think more on it or even study their actions, the male in front of me inches closer, tightening his grip on my hair, and forces my eyes back on him.

"Well, Pup, can you learn?" I lift my chin higher, as if daring him to swing on me, and his lips curl into a mean snarl. "Oh," he chuckles angrily. "I do hope you are in my group, Pup."

"Leave her alone," the female guard says, pulling on the male's shoulder. He glares at me for a moment, sucking air through his teeth, and then flashes an evil grin before releasing me. I inch back in line with a sick feeling settling in my gut as he strides back into the crowd. He doesn't look at all like a guard. All the guards I've seen are dirty and smell awful, just like us, the prisoners. But this one looked more like a warden, clean. He even smelled like soap.

"Hey, eyes on me." I turn my attention back to the teenage girl and she starts to reach for my wrist, but then stops. "If you bite me, I will end you. Got it?" she threatens.

I lower my head with a nod because even if I wanted to speak, Mable has forbidden me to since day one. She says I don't have the same slurred speech as the other prisoners do. Nor do I have the Forgotten language down and one wrong word, and they would know I am not like them. That I am a Spoon, and everyone hates a Spoon. Even other Spoons, where each one desperately tries to outdo the other, proving they are the better Spoon. Whereas Mable refused all her tutoring on how to become a proper lady. She was forever sneaking out to spend time with Alex and the other orphans. Her speech is a mix of Forgotten with a deep southern drawl.

"Now, what's your name?" the teenage girl asks me.

Alex squeezes my shoulder and tells her my name. Not Tippy Lopez, mind you, but what the other prisoners call me: Mute. He says no one can ever know our real names because what happened to us is legendary. No child Spoon has ever been punished like us and, word has it, folks from all over are searching for us. And not the decent kind either. It's why I go by Mute and Mable goes by her middle name, Lou.

The female guard snaps a strange-looking bracelet onto my wrist and shoves me forward, calling, "Next."

I shuffle ahead, forcing my fingers under the cuff, but it's no use. It's made out of a strong substance like metal, except it doesn't look or feel like metal. It's soft and flexible with the top, black and shiny like glass. But like any restraint, given enough time and privacy, one can remove it. I've seen it before. That's the easy part. The hard part is not being seen during the so-called escape. One I have not seen executed successfully.

A presence over my shoulder pulls me from my thoughts and I stop breathing, squeezing my eyes shut, and prepare for the blow. Except punishment for trying to remove my bracelet doesn't come. Instead, a hot breath warms my ear.

"No need to keep your head down, Pup. You'll be safe here. No one will ever hurt you again unless you allow it."

I cut my eyes upward, but whomever it was is gone. With a heavy intake of breath, I steal a glance at my surroundings and my jaw nearly drops in understanding. I can see why everyone is whispering in wonder. Everything in here seems as if it's from another world. What kind of ship is this? It looks more like a huge metal box than a ship. I lean to the left, around the prisoners in front of me, and there's a long narrow corridor with handrails. I press my fingers to my lips as my eyes dart from the oval-shaped doorway to the guard standing nearby.

He's tapping a finger onto something fastened to his forearm; not at all concerned with us. And I take the opportunity to study the orange balls above him. How are they working? There's no candle illuminating them. Nor is there a gas lamp nearby. I lift my chin higher, to my right, and see more. The mysteriousness of them has me lifting my arm, but before I can muster the courage to touch one, I feel my wrist vibrate. I glance down and the top of my bracelet has a small blinking heart.

A coldness flutters in my chest and I slap a hand over the top of my bracelet, skimming the line and then focus on the guard watching the door. What is this thing? I peek under my hand and the heart is blinking faster. It's almost as if it's in tune with my own. Alex nudges me forward, and I follow the long line of prisoners until we come to another stop. I go back to inspecting this strange device and hear the familiar sound of bugs flying nearby. I try ignoring it, but the buzzing sound is getting closer. I swat at the air, hoping to shoo it away before it can sting me, and Alex leans close.

"That ain't hornets hovering near ye," he says and then clears the mucus from his throat. "That be some kind of strange cutter. Don't ye know where we be?"

I shake my head because it doesn't matter where we are. All that matters is finishing our ten-year sentence and if all goes well, Lou will go live with her grandmother. And I'll go live with Ford's parents and hopefully they'll take Alex in with me. After all, Ford was friends with Alex, too.

"We be on the Natural's ship," he says.

Sweat prickles my scalp because everything I thought about the Naturals is wrong. They aren't good like Ford said. Just the thought of being on their ship makes my entire body vibrate. One of the caverns we were transferred to a few years ago was attacked by the Naturals before we arrived. And from what the guards said, they're worse than pirates. They attacked everyone, stealing the small children in the dead of night, killing anyone that got in their way. I turn slightly and face Lou and Alex.

"Relax. If we stick together, we be right," Alex says.

"Ya don't know that," Lou whispers, lifting onto her toes with her brown eyes focused behind me. "If the rumors be right, and they be looking for the strongest, then we might be in real trouble here."

"So, what we do then?" Alex asks Lou. "Ye want us to still play our parts?"

"Yeah," she says, lowering herself, and Alex's face falls. He hates playing his part, just as I hate playing mine. Lou lifts her chin at me. "We be moving."

I turn back around with a hard swallow and there's no longer a line. Where did the other prisoners go?

"Let's go, Pup," a teenage boy says with a quick and forceful gesture. I wet my lips at the strange device he's holding and the clumps of hair at his feet. Extreme fear courses through me as I force my footing forward. Before I even stop, he grabs a handful of my hair, and my head instantly vibrates and tingles as the loud contraption runs along my scalp. Long strands of black hair fall at my feet, and I catch a clump, rolling it between my fingers. Traces of sulfur weaved through my hair stains my fingertips yellow. It's the same color as my father's hair and a memory of him brushing my hair while he taught me how to braid haunts me.

Tears fill my heart before they pool under my eyes because my parents are always with me, slipping in and out of my thoughts like spirits that cannot find their way. But what I did that night blankets me with shame, and any fear I have is quickly replaced with guilt. It's my fault Papa and Father died that night, so whatever becomes of me here, I deserve. With a thick throat, I brush the ringlets off my palm and force the ghost away.

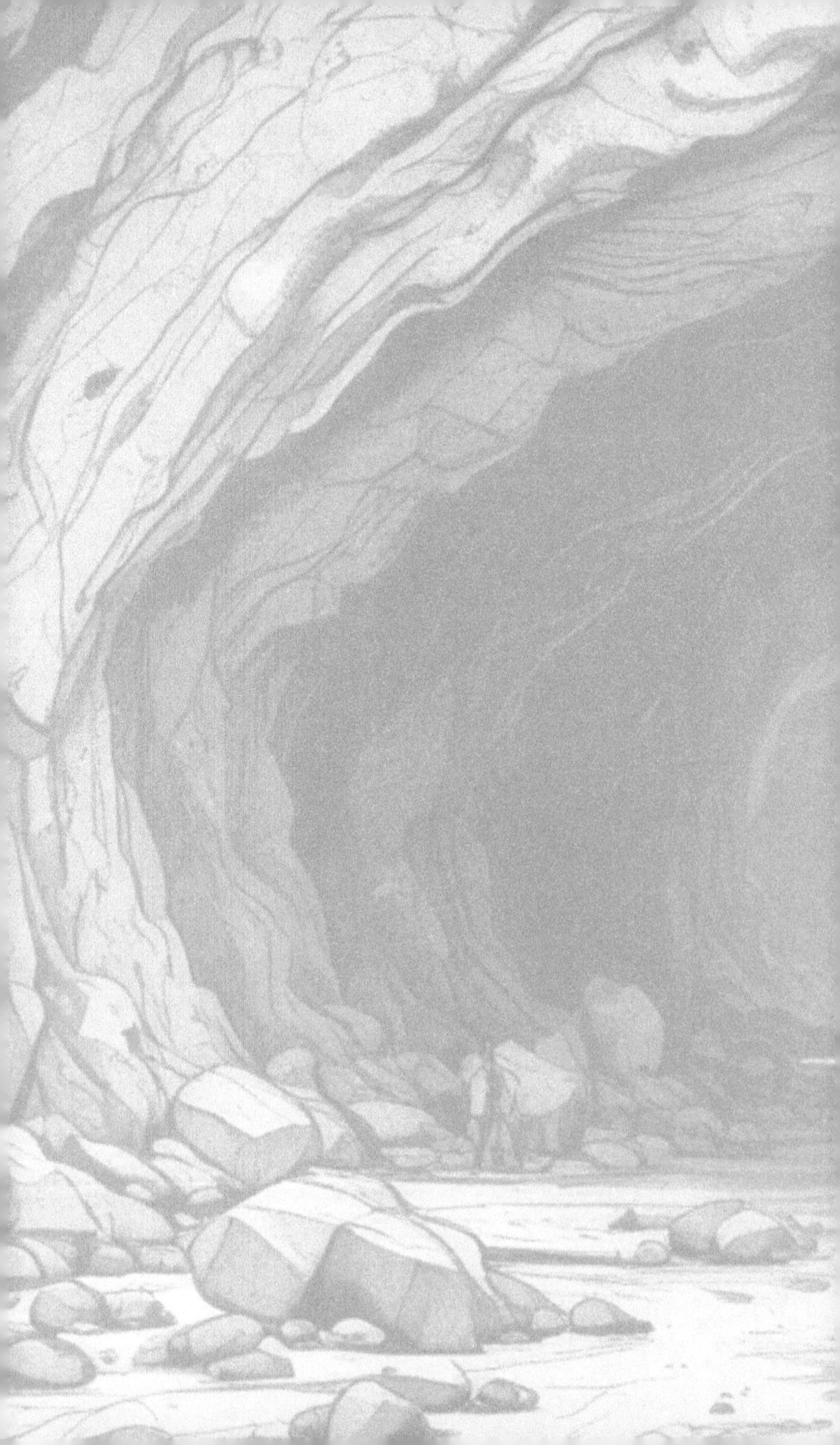

MARK THE LINE AND WE SHALL WALK IT

/ / /

"Females to the right," the teenager instructs me, nudging my shoulder forward. I look behind me and Lou is smoothing her unruly hair down. I can see her nervousness. I'm not in love with the idea of having my head shaved either. As young girls, we were taught our hair is our beauty and not once has our hair ever been cut until now. I run a hand along my bald scalp and do as instructed, and a hand clamps onto my shoulder, stopping me.

"Hold up, you'll need this before you go in there."

I stare at the pile of garments shoved against my chest and inhale the strong cleanser weaved into the fabric. I've not had a clean dress in years and the very thought of finally having a dress that fits has my chin dropping in a trembling fit. The line moves again, and we step into another room with a teenager guarding the doorway. We walk farther inside, where another teenager guides us closer to a bench shoved against the wall.

"Remove your clothes and then stand here." She walks to the center of the room. "Pick a spot and wash yourself. You have five minutes."

She walks back to the doorway, where the other guard is, and I can't help but wonder how. There is no washing tub. I search the room as everyone begins removing their garments and I stop looking. I'm frozen in place. I thought it was improper to wear only my bloomers and nightdress when I was sentenced. Not to mention how they cling to me like a second skin now. But this, to bathe alongside all these girls, is just indecent. On top of that, I don't see any of the prisoners from our cavern, except Lou. Where did the other prisoners go? And where did these new prisoners come from? How many mining caverns did they conquer?

A tall prisoner turns her attention to me. "Ain't ya gonna be washing?" I hug the garments closer to my chest with a slight shake of my head. "Why? Ain't no fellas be here." She pulls her top over her head, and I avert my eyes, completely mortified. "An' by the smell of it, ya be needing it more than us."

I wince at her statement, but I know she's right. I've had the stench of soil on me for years. It's a scent I have grown accustomed to.

Lou tugs on my arm. "Ya know we gotta or we'll get the strap, right?" She's right, and with a deep inhale, I lower my garments onto the bench and hesitantly join her in undressing. I cover myself the best I can and follow her and the other girls onto the cold metal flooring in the center of the room. With my shoulders hunkered, nearly bent over, I search the area for the washing tub again. Will they be bringing one in? If so, will we be using the same tub and water? Perhaps I have made a grave mistake in joining them.

I look over at Lou, standing next to me, and then hear, "Look here."

It's one of the prisoners and she's pointing at one of the six steel rods sticking out on both sides of the walls. Everyone moves closer to them. Even me. I stand under the one with water dripping out of it and I peek up at the small holes punctured in the middle. And then to the bar of soap nestled on a metal lip right under the rod. This must be how they bathe, but how does it work? And then I remember my father talking to the owner of the dry goods store about a new contraption folks are installing inside their homes. A new way to bathe, he'd said. I scan the area, around all the girls, searching for the lever to pump the water out, but there isn't one. I turn back to the rod and just as I lift my chin to examine it again, warm water sputters onto my face.

The room squeals with delight, and I smile so big, I think for sure my lips will split wide open. I reach for the frothy bar of soap, and the humiliation of anyone seeing my lady parts disappears while I scrub myself clean. And before I know it, I'm standing under the lingering drops, inhaling a deep, disappointing breath as a humming sound resonates. I open my eyes to a second rod, just below the first one, and it's zooming out of the wall. My eyes grow wide with interest, and I lean closer just as white dust hits me square in the face, forcing a loud cough out of me. I stumble away from the source as a strange voice from above orders, "Please exit."

"What the hell? What be this powder stuff?" the tall prisoner grouches.

"Yeah, and why my skin be burning?" her friend joins.

I hurry toward my new attire, hoping their punishment for speaking out doesn't land on me. But instead of a leather strap swinging wildly nearby, the teenager guarding the door answers in a strong voice. "It's for lice. Now get moving."

I pull the scratchy long-sleeved white blouse over my head and when I reach for my matching skirt, my head snaps up in a grimace. They gave me the wrong attire. This is for boys. With a quick glance at the other girls, I notice they are wearing the same trousers, except they don't seem to be concerned about it. I wet my lips and face Lou. Her smile is wide and proud as she pulls her trousers over her hips.

"These be clean, yeah?" She stretches the waistband out, allowing them to snap back in place, and I can't help but return her smile. She feels right at home in them. For once, I completely understand how she has felt her entire life. Always wearing a dress and feeling out of place in it.

"Let's go, pups!" the teenager orders again but with more urgency in her voice this time. I glance down at the trousers and know there's nothing I can do unless I want to squeeze back into my undergarments. And honestly, I don't think I could even if I were asked to. I pull the trousers over my hips and slide my feet into these strange, cushiony slippers and follow everyone into the next room.

I shift on my feet behind Lou as the boys blend in with us and I look for Alex. *Where is he?* The line moves and I see a group of teenage Naturals on both sides of us in a long line. Each one is holding a strange-looking pistol. But instead of a barrel that holds ammo, these have clear cylinders with liquid inside them. And if Ford's stories are correct, those pistols carry the type of medicine only the Naturals have. The type that can heal us from our coughing fits. But if they truly are looking for the strongest, then why are they allowing us to have a cure?

As if reading my thoughts, Lou turns and says, "If they

be giving us shots, then maybe we still got a chance. Maybe they ain't like the guards said. Maybe they be like Ford said."

I give another nod and lift onto my toes, hopeful she's right. *Where the heck is Alex? I do hope he isn't in trouble.* For the past few years, the three of us have not been separated for more than a few hours. And if by chance it was a day or two, we at least knew where they were. The punishing box. The very thought of losing him now makes my skin crawl like the devil himself is breathing on me. And no matter where I look, his hot breath follows.

Lou grabs my arm. "Don't be frettin'. We'll find him," she says.

I turn back, rubbing at my brow with a quick nod and fidget in place as I wait in line.

After we receive all our injections, we enter a small circular room with a ladder leading upward. Lou goes first. She always goes first in case there's a threat nearby. I step into the closet-like space and goosebumps ripple across my skin. I lift my chin to the burnt-orange sky and the pain deep behind my eyes is welcomed. I haven't seen daylight or felt fresh air in so long. I bask in it, and allow the salty atmosphere to tease me with freedom.

"Do you need help, Pup?"

I open my eyes and there's a shadow looming over me. With a slight shake of my head, I rub my sweaty palms down the front of my trousers and then begin to climb. But when I reach the landing, I shiver with a coldness I've never felt before. We've had winters back home, but nothing like this. Not where the air instantly freezes your nose hairs and slices your throat with an iciness.

With my teeth chattering uncontrollably, I hug myself as everyone walks along a wide, lengthy dock, stretching toward the mouth of a cavern. And fear doesn't just sting the back of my throat, it coats it. The entrance is nothing like the mining caverns we've worked in. It isn't formed with dirt and wood. This one looks like the actual mouth of what used to be a massive beast. A large skull is positioned at the top of the opening with even larger fangs stretched and digging into the earth. With what appears to be torn cloth and large branches and sticks wedged between its bone structure. So, whatever is in there is very important. Otherwise, they wouldn't be trying to scare off potential traders. I cut my gaze behind me, and before I can take in the rest of my surroundings or even the ship I'm standing on, I slam my eyes shut with a silent wail. My eyes are on fire like someone just poured cleanser in them.

"Sorry, I forgot you might not have seen daylight in years."

Before I know it, the shadowy figure lifts me off the ground and carries me forward. Moments later, when my feet touch solid ground, I press my palms into my eye sockets, and they immediately start watering. I blink my vision clear, and my shoulders tighten. I'm standing between the animal's large fangs and from the looks of it, they are made out of smaller bones, formed into one large fang. I turn and Lou is standing to my right, and relief washes over me. Especially when a Natural walks toward us with Alex draped over his shoulder. He stops, dropping Alex next to me and when the Natural straightens, he leans close to Lou with malice plastered on his face.

"I heard you took a bite out of, Elk. Not so tough now, are you?" he asks and reaches out, wiping away one of her watery tears with his thumb. But she isn't crying in the way he thinks, and Lou being Lou, she needed to show it. She snapped at him like a rabid dog, and he drew his fist back with a snarl. His fist hovers mid-air. Why? In the caverns, that big fist would have already made contact. What is he waiting for?

"She's testing you."

I pull my eyes off of him and see another Natural striding toward us.

"What?" the one in front of Lou asks.

"She wants to know how far she can go before you beat her," the other Natural replies, stopping next to the one in front of Lou. He balances his elbow on his friend's shoulder. "Right now, all she knows is she can look at us without being beaten."

"Jesus, Pika, she isn't a dog."

"No, but she's been treated worse than one, probably her entire life. This is why drillers like her don't belong here. They should just fail her now and save themselves a lot of trouble."

Before I can stop him, Alex lurches into the evening light and shields his eyes. "No. We can be learning. Please, ju-just give us a chance."

"What's going on? Why are we not moving forward?"

I lean to my left again, searching for the voice, and when I see him, my knees almost buckle at the majestic white wolf moving through the crowd. Images of the ghost story—The Wolfman—flash before me, and my stomach drops.

"Apparently this one wants to know where her place is," the Natural states with a thumb pointed at Lou.

Fear crawls along my back as The Wolfman skulks closer to us. I want to step away. Run and cower, but I can't force my heavy limbs to move. All I can do is watch as he moves even closer, stopping in front of Lou like he's the one in charge. I study his headdress and then lower, and finally see his eyes nestled under the disguise. His left eye is a dark brown, nearly black, and his right is a pale brown. But that's not what sends tremors down my back. It's the clean, swift scars carved around the pale eye that nearly buckles me. How did that happen? Was it here? From these people. I glance up at the bones formed into a larger one. Are those human?

"You want to know your place, Pup?" I turn back and the Wolfman is smiling. But it isn't a welcoming one. It's the kind I've seen many times. And I instantly know this is the one we need to fear the most. He raises his fist and Lou stands taller, bracing for the impact, but it doesn't come. Instead, he points over her shoulder. "It's in the fucking line!" he roars.

He shoves by me, and I inhale deeply, glancing down the long dock and there are more of those animal-like head-dresses moving toward us. Except they aren't like the Wolf-man. Each one is wearing a different type of animal. And when the last one brushes by to enter the cavern, a younger Natural, not wearing a headdress, maybe fourteen, stops near me and climbs to the top of the dead beast. He lifts some sort of bone curved object to his lips, aiming it skyward, and within seconds, the sound of a horn pene-trates the air in an eerie echo.

Movement catches my attention down the dock and the metal ship we were on is now gurgling and spitting water like it's sinking. I grab hold of Alex's arm with frightful eyes. This must be the ghost ship Ford spoke of in his stories. I can't recall what he named it; all I remember is he said it moves underwater. It's how they can maneuver from place to place and never be seen.

"We be moving." Lou tugs on my arm, and I turn around to follow her inside the most terrifying cavern I've ever seen. I steady myself, forcing my limbs forward, and, with each step, the cavern grows darker and darker. Lou reaches for my hand as I feel for Alex's behind me. We give a quick squeeze, for we know what a dark cavern like this one means. There's only one way out. With it pitch-black, you'd never find the exit, unless you're a guard or the warden holding the lantern.

The line turns right and, in the distance, there is a green pulsating glow. It's not nearly as dark now and the tunnel isn't formed by digging large holes out of the dirt. I sidestep to my left, gliding my fingers along the side, and there's a rough texture to the walls with all sorts of animals painted on them. We turn left and I keep contact with the wall, memorizing every step, turn, and painted animal. But the deeper into the tunnel we go, strange noises are heard, and I nearly falter, losing count. It's almost as if the animals painted on the walls are coming to life the farther inside we go.

"Stay close, yeah?" Alex says, pulling me back in line.

We finally enter the interior of their homeland and I lift a hand, blocking the brightness of the room. It's massive and completely empty, with a sadness to it. That even the murmurs playing off the walls have a tearful echo as they direct us into four long rows. Once everyone is fully inside and lined up as instructed, they tell us to sit. I squint at the harshness, trying to adjust my vision. Are we still inside a cave? I lift my chin, looking around and Lou nudges me, offering me a stack of wooden bowls. I take one and turn to Alex, offering him the same small stack.

"Eyes on me!" a voice booms. "My name is Yak."

I cut my eyes forward and a tall, dark-headed gentleman is striding into the room, quick and efficient. He looks maybe mid-thirties and the first adult I've seen. I know without having to ask, this is their leader. He stops near the first row of prisoners and my stomach churns. I've been in a lot of different mining caverns and, in my experience, wardens that look like him are usually the worst. Neatly groomed, perfect posture, and an air that radiates superiority and impatience. I look over at Lou and the long-jagged scar on her left cheek is because of men like him. When they allow their anger to get the best of them and they lose control of the strap.

"This is your lifeline," their leader says, and raises a bowl high in the air. "Without this, you fail." He tosses the bowl to someone standing by an open door and addresses us again. "While you are here, you will go through four phases to prove your worth. You may out smart, even sabotage your opponents to gain your spot, but there is no fighting in my house, unless I say otherwise. If you are caught, you will fail." He gestures to five Naturals to our right. The ones wearing the headdresses. "The Naturals standing at the front of your row are your trainers. You will do as they say, how they say, and when. Or you will?" He cups his ear.

"Fail!" the trainers against the wall roar.

"Let the competition begin!" their leader hollers.

"Hooray!" the trainers boom, and the room bellows with excitement, and not just from the Naturals, but everyone here. I shift uncomfortably between Lou and Alex because I don't believe everyone here is a prisoner. I scan the room, twisting my bracelet continuously as the realization slowly sinks in. Everyone sitting on the floor with us is a true Forgotten, not prisoners. And from the looks of it, they want to be here. They don't even look scared. Why?

"Now, please stand and follow your trainer to your quarters."

I push to my feet and the trainers shove their headdresses off to where the animal's head now hangs on their backs. And although they aren't much older than my seventeen, I know each one of them will be just as callous as any guard or warden we've known.

My eyes follow the Wolfman as he starts forward and then he stops, slicing his eyes onto me as if he could sense me watching him. I instantly drop my chin and inch closer to Lou with my stomach forming knots. I shouldn't have looked at him. Not for that long, anyway. If I'm not careful, I will fail before we even begin. I must remember my place and where I am. This isn't the mining caverns where mistakes are forgiven with punishment. These people are the Naturals. The sworn enemy to all Spoons, and Lou and I are trapped inside the belly of their homeland. Lou grabs my hand before following the others, and I turn slightly, reaching for Alex's.

MAYBE, SHE OUGHT'VE KEPT HER HANDS TO HERSELF

////

My row turns into a smaller room, and I glance over my shoulder, watching the other lines of Forgotten entering different doorways. From what I can see, it seems as if there will be four rooms filled with us, and my stomach flips upside down. *Why are they separating us?* In the mining caverns, they kept us together, so we were easier to watch and control.

Once inside our room, it instantly resonates with chatter as everyone groups up with the ones they knew before landing here. I glance at the large painting on the back wall and the only color on it is black. Except, it isn't coarse from brush strokes. It looks smooth and shiny, almost mirror-like. Below it is a medium-sized rectangular box and attached to the top is a small, thick, odd-looking hook. It's the strangest thing I've ever seen. I pull Lou closer, guiding her toward it, hoping she'll know what it is. After all, she has spent more time walking the caverns than us. Not that she had more freedom, but because she was forever breaking the rules and sent to the punishing box. Before I can guide her closer and gesture to it, a demanding voice stops me.

"Eyes on me!" I whip my head around and our trainer is standing at the front of the room. "Line up!"

I shuffle into the center of the room as everyone forms into two rows. I peek over my shoulder, wishing we were in the back, but before I can move and be somewhere unseen, the trainer's voice controls the room.

"My name is Bear, and you will address me as such. Not hey, or yo, but Bear." He begins to pace in front of us with his hands behind his back and I watch his every move. "Each morning you will clear your bedding, and when I say line up, you will do so with your back straight, arms at your sides, and head forward." He stops for a moment, eyeing the front row, and his gaze lands on the tall teenager standing next to me. And this Forgotten must have been the top dog where he's from because the only time a Forgotten is that big is because they eat first and more than the others. Bear arches a golden-brown eyebrow at him and then begins pacing again.

"While you are here, I will replace your fear and hatred with honor, strength, and confidence." He pivots and faces us with a thumb over his shoulder. "Behind me, you will notice a bell. Only ring it if you want to quit, but in doing so, your chance of joining us ends at the door."

Out of nowhere, Bear marches toward me but stops in front of the Forgotten next to me. "Did you just roll your eyes?" When the boy snickers, Bear leans even closer, towering over the boy. His face is relaxed but his pale gray eyes are full of bitterness, like an evil spirit pulled the soul and color right out of them. "Are you not scared of me?" Bear asks.

"Nope."

Bear flaps his cloak back and draws a strange, bulky pistol from his hip, and when he presses it against the boy's temple, my throat tightens. "How about now, Pup?"

The Forgotten steps back with another snicker. "Not even a lil'. And my name be Christopher, not Pup."

"I don't give a shit what your name is. We have gathered seventy-eight Forgotten in the last six months, and since we only need three of you, there is no need for me to learn your name."

I peek up, and the boy's mouth tugs into a smug grin, and I inch closer to Lou. *Why is he provoking him?*

"Welp, I'll be one of those three that be makin' it. You'll be remembering my name."

"Is that so?" Bear steps away from Christopher, scanning the row for a moment and then responds, "This is not a game. I am hard, but fair. And when you start to hate me, and you will, just remember, no one is coming to save you." He aims the pistol at Christopher and stares right at me as he pulls the hammer back. The pistol makes a weird noise, like it's humming to life, and my heart slams against my chest. *What kind of weapon is that?* It looks just like a pistol, but I've never heard one make that kind of sound.

Before I can think more on it, Bear bellows with a loud and demanding voice, "I am your savior!" His pistol pops, creating a sound similar to glass shattering, and I flinch with fear running down my legs.

The room thunders in fright while I force myself not to look. Not to watch the life drain out of the boy's eyes, but he fell at my feet in a trembling fit. I curl my toes away from him, fearful of what may happen if he makes contact with me.

Once Christopher stops shaking, Bear grabs a hold of

his ankle. "Phase one has begun," Bear says, dragging Christopher out of the room.

Seconds after Bear leaves, the door slides shut, and the room buzzes with movement once again. I rub the back of my shaved head, because just like any place, especially in the Forgotten World, when the top dog falls, another one emerges. I start toward the table with bedding stacked on top of it and, right on cue, a girl's voice cuts over the others as she calls out her rules about not touching anything. She painfully grabs my arm, jerking me around to face her. She's short and thin with dark blue eyes.

"Whoa! She be wobbled," Lou says and gives me a slight nod. And I know what that means. What she wants from me. I must continue acting like I teeter between reality and a fictional world. The same way I did in the mining caverns. Most people won't have anything to do with a wobbler, in fear of what the lunatic may do. But it isn't fair I get to play the weak one and not her. But she says she is stronger than me and can handle it. And she is. Once she learned prison law, and Alex helped her with the Forgotten rules, she started taking our punishments, along with the smaller prisoners. In the caverns, Lou protected everyone that needed it. She was the top dog. Lou is the reason we are still alive. I'm not so sure the three of us would still be here if I were the protector.

Our top dog looks me up and down and I disgracefully lower my eyes as she snorts at me for wetting myself when Christopher died.

"Fine." She turns to address the others. "But everyone else, leave shit alone unless you wanna be ending up like Christopher. I be like Bear. I be hard, but fair." She walks over to the table. "I'll be passing out these."

Of course, she doesn't give me anything. Not that I

mind. My brain is working overtime. *How are we going to survive this place?* I walk over to the back corner with my head lowered. Not because I have to keep my eyes down, but because my heart aches with real fear for everyone here. Christopher wasn't the first to die at my feet and I know without a doubt, he won't be the last. Not in this place.

When the lanterns hanging above us go out, I lower myself to the floor. I don't know how or who turned them out, but it's pitch black in here. I feel like I did the first day I became a prisoner. All the way down to lying in my soiled clothes with no means of cleaning myself. The only real difference between then and now is the walls. Instead of dirt and grime, I'm surrounded by clean white ones and there are no bars holding us inside, but I'd wager my life there's a lock on the door.

I rest between Alex and Lou for what feels like hours, with my brain spinning on every possible outcome of staying here. I can't sleep. This place is worse than the mining caverns. At least there, we had a chance of finishing our ten-year sentence. Not that we would have a life afterward. If a Spoon breaks the law and is sentenced, most don't survive that long in the caverns. And the ones that do aren't accepted back into the Spoon world. They become vagrants, older Forgotten if you will, and end up breaking the law, yet again, and sent right back into the mining caverns with a new sentence. My only hope is Ford's family, but there's no guarantee my aunt and uncle will take me in with Alex in tow, and I won't leave him behind. And even if they do take us both in, there's no assurance they will allow us to stay. Not if they find out about some of the stuff we've done in the caverns.

The sound of a bowl skidding across the floor perks my ears and I sit straight up. *Is someone quarreling over a bowl?* I strain my eyes to my left, trying to see in the dark and then back at the hot air and grunting to my left. *Is that Alex?* The bowl skids again, and I feel Lou on the other side of me push to her feet. Seconds later, I squint at the intense lanterns flooding the room and my stomach drops as their leader marches toward us. Straight for Lou. He yanks Lou off the bigger boy and slams her against the wall with her arms pinned behind her back.

"What's going on?" he asks Lou.

The bigger Forgotten that was tussling with Alex tugs his shirt in place and glares at Lou. "Nothing," he snarls.

"Were you trying to steal his bowl?" their leader asks Lou.

"No. She be stopping him from taking mine," Alex admits, and it takes everything I have not run to their defense.

Their leader releases Lou and faces her with annoyance. "Do not interfere with the process. This is how we weed out the rejects," he says and starts for the door.

Our top dog glares at Alex and Lou, and I rush to their side just as the sound of glass shatters behind us. The same sound we heard before Christopher died and before I can fully turn around, the room echoes with fear for the second time in one day. Most everyone here is like us, huddling together and clinging to their group as the boy is dragged out of the room just like Christopher was.

I turn to Lou with a coppery taste, and she pulls my fingers away from my lips. "Don't be frettin'. I ain't gonna let anyone be hurting ya."

"And that be it," Alex snaps.

"But what if—"

"No," Alex nearly squeals, moving into her personal space. "We can't be helping others here. This ain't the pits. Here, it be for themselves. We ain't taking top dog. Not here."

"Fine," Lou says through her teeth and brushes past Alex.

I squeeze my eyes shut, forcing the fear down, and Alex touches my arm.

"Ye be right?" he asks me.

I open my eyes with a slight nod and follow Lou back to our spot, refusing to look at the other Forgotten. *How are we going to survive this place?* If there are four phases with only three making to the end, how will we be on that list? We haven't even fully finished day one and we're already down two Forgotten.

I lower myself next to Lou with a sour taste forming in the back of my throat. Alex is right. We can't worry about the others. Not here.

IT'S CLEAR THESE PEOPLE ARE NOT FROM OUR WORLD

After a few hours of tossing and turning, the lanterns come on and Alex stirs next to me, but not enough that he wakes up. And neither does Lou. No one really does, so I study the white balls glaring down at me. Once I understand them and what they are, a smile slides across my lips. I think of Ford and how amazed he would have been if he saw this place. I can even see his face, eyes bright and all smiles. *They have the old technology, Tiptoe. They have electricity.* Then his dark brown eyes turn wide and frightful as the night I was sentenced creeps in. I sling Alex's blanket off and sit up in anger. No matter what happy image or memory I conjure of my family, that night returns, ruining any moment I had with them.

"Grubs here!" someone calls, and my eyes are drawn to a Natural pushing a cart into the room. It's one of the younger ones that helped with cutting our hair and I instantly rub a hand along my scalp.

"Food?" I hear next to me.

I glance to my right, and Lou isn't beside me. Instead, there's a Forgotten in her spot. She looks the same age as me, but bigger. Meatier. She sits all the way up, stretching, and from the looks of it, she might be the biggest one here now. I slowly pull the corner of Alex's blanket off her knee while she cleans the sleep from her eyes, hoping she doesn't feel it or see it. If she plans on taking the top dog position, I don't want to be on her bad side by not sharing our blanket. I don't need her targeting me because she thinks I'm the weakest one here. Not only that, but I don't remember seeing her with us yesterday. *Where did she come from?* I look over my shoulder and Lou is stirring awake behind me.

"How ye be hungry?" Alex asks. "I be full of that ivy they give."

"The what?" Lou snorts, sitting fully up.

"The ivy," he repeats.

"Yeah, I be hearing ya. I just don't know what an ivy be, or remember chewing it." Lou scoots closer.

"It ain't something ye chew." Alex giggles. "It be something they stick in yer hand. Like those skin pricks they give us yesterday. It happened while everyone be asleep on the ship."

"Hold up, are ya saying while we be sleeping, they gave us a shot in our hand that be feeding us? Bag your face." Lou chuckles with a dismissive wave.

"No, really. That be what I overheard when they stick ye. They say, at least ye won't be starving no mores. And we be on the ship a long time. Every time I wake, there be more Forgotten, and then they'd stick ye again, an' out ye'd go and then they'd do us. I don't know how long we be on the ship, but long enough we ain't looking the same," he says, scanning the room.

I pull my knees into my chest, and it dawns on me. I'm not hungry either? I'm not even dizzy. I actually have energy for once. Is that why? I sit up taller and skim the room; no one is rushing to the cart, pushing and shoving for food. Instead, they're slowly lifting to their feet and moving toward it. In the mining caverns, everyone raced to be the first in line because sometimes there wasn't enough food for everyone.

"Either way, let's get some grub. Who knows when they'll be feeding us again. Yeah?" Lou voices.

"Yep," Alex voices, soaring to his feet.

As they move toward the food cart, I watch the room, trying to get a sense of the others. And it's just like in the mining caverns, a mix of nationality and age, with a lot of different dialects. Thankfully, we know nearly all of them. You don't spend as much time in the caverns as we have and not pick up on most of them. Standing in line, some are small like Alex, some are older like me and Lou. A few are loud, looking for attention, but most are quiet, hoping not to be seen. And as I'm scanning the room, my eyes land on the girl next to me. She smiles, wide and full, and I blink with surprise.

She has all her teeth. And pretty ones. How? Every Forgotten I know has the same rotten teeth as me. Black and broken, with some missing. I give a forced, empty smile and quickly look away, and she jumps to her feet. She folds her blanket and then walks it over to the empty table. When she turns around, she looks at me and gestures her head at the table. *Why? Oh, that's right. Bear said for us to clear our bedding each morning.* And for the first time since our sentence, I make a choice of my own, without secretly asking Lou. I give the girl a slight nod and do the same before lining up behind her for my daily meal.

When I return with my bowl heaping full, a boy sitting close to Lou asks me, "Why'd ye wait so long?"

I nearly falter as I sit next to Alex. The boy looks about my age, maybe a year younger. He has dark red eyebrows and the same green eyes as Alex. In fact, he has the same accent as Alex, like they are throwing away the last letter in every word.

"Mute don't eat till everyone has," Alex replies.

The boy scrunches his round face, asking, "Why?"

"Cos if there ain't enough grub, she go hungry."

"That be brain rot," the boy says, shaking his head.

I sit up straighter with the realization that he's from a pirate crew, too. Or at least he was. It's why his accent is like Alex's.

"Cos," Alex begins with irritation laced in his voice. "We be seeing a lot of kids die from hunger and we don't wanna be seeing it again."

"So, it be top dog stuff?" the boy asks. He sets his bowl down and turns fully around, pulling his knee into his chest. "So ye gonna be taking top dog, huh?"

Alex snorts loudly, "Naw." He lifts his chin at the girl that is now our top dog. "We gonna be letting her keep it. Why, ye want it?"

"Nah, but we ain't wanting her to be having it either," he says, gesturing his head at the group next to him. "Was just wondering in case ye needed help." The boy throws a thumb into his chest. "Hutch."

"Alex," he says, and before he can introduce us, Lou stands with her fists curled in disgust. I look in the direction she's staring. Across the room, the smaller kids are giving half their food to our top dog. Lou steps around me, and the girl sitting next to me makes a grab at Lou's trousers.

"No need to quarrel. There are better ways to stop that."

Lou stops immediately with her eyes locked on me. We both know what the girl with nice teeth is just by using the word "quarrel". That's a Spoon word. If the others hear her speak, she'll not see tomorrow. And that's if the Naturals don't hear her speak first. There's no telling what . . . and then it hits me. The Naturals speak just like a Spoon. *How?* I shake my head. It doesn't matter. The Naturals aren't locked in this room with us. They can speak however they choose. But the girl next to me, well . . . and then my stomach twists in disgust. A Spoon like her would have never made it in the Forgotten world. She must be someone the Naturals planted here to spy on us. And knowing this, I'm not sure if I can trust her. Perhaps I shouldn't be making my own choices after all. I mean, I did just trust a snitch. I need to be more careful and keep an eye on her.

Hutch angles his head with a, "Hmm," staring at the snitch and then turns back to his group. Did he pick up on it, too? Is he telling his group what she is? Lou moves back to her spot and Alex motions for me to scoot closer to them. I don't disagree with him. We should stay away from her.

I shift slightly to where my back is sort of to her and pinch off a hunk of oats mushed together, known as slop. And my fingers halt mid-air when Bear enters the room. He strides, quick and confident, to the Natural serving food, and he looks different today without his headdress and cloak, but his attire is still just as strange. I mean, I understand they dress differently, but if these people truly are the Naturals and they have all this equipment and skill, then why do his clothes not fit him properly? Can they not make him new ones where his undergarments aren't longer than his short pants? Which, by the way, his long johns don't even reach his ankles. They are tight and only reach his calves. And perhaps a shirt that isn't skintight.

I shove the tasteless slop in my mouth and cock my head. Although, the length of his sleeves is right, and his belly isn't showing. Maybe they only have one size, and since he is the bulkiest trainer here, it fits like a second skin. I mean, his arms alone look like he has muscles on top of muscles. Furthermore, why is his hair so long and neatly pulled back into a bun? The only time a male has long hair is because they are a Forgotten.

His stance shifts slightly, and I see a tattoo on his left ankle. It has five lines, like a verse or something, but I can't read what it says. He's too far away. Plus, I think it's written in another language. Alex jabs me in the knee, and I realize I've been staring at Bear for far too long. I lift my gaze and he's staring back at me with a bitter grin. I quickly clamp my jaw shut and turn away from his hard eyes.

"Stop eating and line up!" Bear demands.

I push to my feet, shoving the rest of my breakfast into my mouth, and Lou leans close to Alex's ear. I don't know what she told him, but if we are to continue playing our parts, then she must be asking him to test these people and the situation. It's what he does, and he's good at it, too. And when he isn't testing the guards, he's making friends with the other prisoners. Alex is our snitch.

After walking over and hiding my bowl inside what I hope is our blanket, I join everyone in the middle of the room. But when I turn around to face forward, my heart drops. Alex is standing by the bell, bouncing on his toes and holding himself. "Bear, if I give, can I go pee?"

Bear turns slightly and addresses him. "You don't need to quit. Just go."

"Okay," he shrugs and then points at us. "No chicken hawks," he giggles and faces the wall.

Bear rushes toward him and grabs his arm, yanking him away from the wall. And if Lou hadn't had a tight grip on my arm, I would have lunged forward.

"Not there, idiot! In the latrine."

"Mister, I ain't knowing what that be."

"It's where you pee," Bear states and points behind us.

Everyone turns, looking over their shoulder and then back at Bear.

"What be the difference between this wall and that one?" Alex asks, and I'm grateful. I was wondering the same thing. *Where are we supposed to go?* In the caverns, we at least had buckets. *Is this what Lou was wanting him to do?* Find out where we relieve ourselves.

"Not on the wall. In the latrine," Bear hisses, pointing at the back wall, and again, everyone looks at the back wall and back at Bear.

"In where?" Alex screeches.

Bear faces us. "Who else needs to pee?" Everyone shoots their arm high in the air. "Did Rabbit not come in and show you all this last night?"

"No," the Forgotten reply.

"Follow me." Bear stops at the back wall and points at the metal box below the black portrait. "This is water. It's what you drink when you're thirsty." He presses a button on the side, and everyone gasps as the water fountain's out of the small hook. He presses another button flush with the wall, and we shuffle backward with another "whoa", as the wall slides into itself, just like the door in the front of the room. We follow him inside and there's a row of stalls to our left. He pushes one of the doors open and my eyes nearly pop out of my head.

"Why ya got an outhouse inside?" someone asks.

"It's not an outhouse. It's a toilet, and once you are done, it flushes." He waves his hand over the hole a few times and the toilet makes a loud ruckus. The water swirls and swirls until there isn't anything left and then refills with water once again. Everyone grouped together is completely flabbergasted, including myself. I repeat the word "toilet" under my breath as Bear moves toward the row of washbasins.

"This is a sink. It's where you wash your hands after you use the toilet. And this is the soap you use. And yes, every single time you use the toilet, you wash your hands."

I repeat the new words: toilet, sink, latrine, trying to memorize them as he gives us a demonstration on how to wash our hands. Something I already knew how to do, but I never had a sink where water ran freely from the wall. We had to go outside and pump the water from the well and bring the bucket of water back into the house and fill the bowl or tub with water.

After he dries his hands under the strangest contraption I've ever seen, he gestures to another entryway. As we follow him into the next room, we each have a turn, placing our hands under the loud device as air blows against our skin. Well, not everyone put their hand under it. Alex stuck his entire face under it, giggling as the air puffed out his cheeks like a blowfish. Even I smiled at that.

In the next room are two closed doors with symbols on them.

"This is where you will shower. Males to the left and females to the right." He points. "And over there is your cubbyhole. It holds all the items you will need for the next two weeks, including your athletic clothes." He gestures to himself. "It's what I am wearing. Every morning, you will change from your evening clothes, what you are wearing now, into your athletic clothes. Are we clear?"

He doesn't wait for a response. He marches over to the far wall with names printed on large squares and reads out our names. Once mine is called, I move toward my square, staring at the name "Mute" written on a small piece of parchment. He goes on and explains what electricity is and how everything here works, including how water runs freely from the pipes. But I'm eager to open my cubbyhole and hopefully, fingers crossed, they finally gave me the right attire this time.

"You have ten minutes to use the toilet and change into your day clothes," Bear tells us.

Once he leaves, I turn back to my square as everyone rushes to the other side for the toilets, including Lou and Alex. I press the button under my name, and it opens toward me like a drawer. Just like Bear demonstrated. Inside, there's all sorts of stuff, along with new garments, and my cheeks warm at the thought of changing into female attire. But, even though I'm eager to know what most of this is, I can't take it anymore. I look like Alex. I'm bouncing on my toes, wanting nothing more than to hold myself as he did. I have to pee. I grab the garments and head toward the toilets before I embarrass myself, yet again.

SOMETIMES, THOSE THAT DESERVE IT, GET THEIRS

||||/

I stand in the corner of the room where we sleep, and I don't believe they gave me the right size. Nor do I believe they know the difference between male and female garments. Once again, I am dressed in white clothing, like Bear. All the way down to our snug long johns. And this corset is nothing like I've seen before. Luckily, the female Natural, Rabbit, came in and told us what it was and showed us how to put it on. I tug at the hem of my sports bra, but when Bear enters back into the room, carrying two medium-sized stands, I stop at once. He places the stands at the front of the room a few feet apart and then turns to us.

"Eyes on me! The world doesn't owe you anything. Not a loving home. Or food in your belly. Nothing. However, there are opportunities this world may offer. And today, I offer you a grand one." He places a fist-sized rock on the left stand and a small glass block on the right one.

"Choose wisely because the one you select will seal

your fate." He points a small device at the back wall and the room rumbles with excitement as the black portrait flashes red numbers on it. "You have thirty minutes." Bear turns for the door, but then stops with a loud exhale and faces us again. "It's when those numbers turn to zero," he says with his fingers shaped into a circle.

The second Bear leaves, everyone rushes forward, into two groups, gathering around the objects. Our top dog picks up the rock, tossing it from hand to hand, while a few Forgotten examine the glass block.

"What'cha think it means?" Alex asks in a low whisper.

I shrug and notice there's something in the center of the glass block. I move toward it and peek over a girl's shoulder. It's a butterfly pressed perfectly between the glass. I look up at the portrait and the smaller numbers are ticking down at a fast rate, but the big numbers are slow and steady.

"Try throwing it. Maybe there be something in it, like the window one," someone says. Our top dog hurls the rock against the wall, and it bounces back.

"Ain't ye hammerheads ever see a rock before?" I turn slightly and it's the boy named Hutch. "Ye can't just be whacking it open like that. It be solid, ye know, like a rock." He chuckles.

"He be right." The top dog agrees and bends for the rock. "This be strong and that be beauty."

Alex shuffles closer to me. "Do ye think she be true?"

I shrug, thinking about Bear's words: "Choose your fate". I look over at where most of the Forgotten are huddled around the top dog, and I know she's right. They both represent something, but a part of me is screaming there's more to this. It cannot be this easy, and apparently, so does the snitch, because we both circle the glass block at the same time. She stops with her back to the door and her brown eyes flicker up at the numbers.

"Twenty-three minutes left," she whispers, and I glance over my shoulder. So that's their version of a clock.

"Do ye be knowing the key?" Alex asks, standing beside the snitch.

She eyes him for a moment with her mouth partly open, and I know she's trying to figure out what the word "key" means. And then one side of her lip curls in a grin. "Not yet."

Her stance shifts, and I notice her left ankle is bandaged. *Why? What happened to her? Is that why she wasn't with us yesterday?* I hug myself, pretending to cower as I move closer to Alex and look down. Her bandage has come loose at the top and peeking out are the same swirly loops as Bear's tattoo. My pulse races. *Crap. She is a snitch.* I move back over to Lou, away from her, knowing we definitely can't trust her.

"Maybe it represents death. It is dead," the snitch says quietly and then glances over at the other stand. "But the rock is not alive, so this cannot be death." She tilts her head, talking to herself. "However, the butterfly was alive at one time. It flapped its black and orange wings from flower to flower, laying . . . " she straightens with a huge smile. "This is the one," she tells us and picks her fate behind the butterfly.

"Ye sure?" Alex asks.

"Yes. Trust me, this is the one they want us to pick," she voices.

"Ya be picking beauty?" a Forgotten groans.

"Yes," the snitch responds with confidence.

"Yeah?" our top dog questions, measuring up the snitch.

"Well, ya be wrong. This be the one and since I be top dog, ya be choosing this one."

I swallow with relief because it doesn't seem as if our top dog will fall into the snitch's trap.

"Yes, you are correct; the rock is strong. However, this does not represent beauty." The snitch steps forward, flinging her arm out in front of her. "Everyone here is a Forgotten, including the trainers. Only difference is, they changed into something better, like this butterfly. Trust me, this is the correct answer."

A Forgotten standing next to the top dog scratches the back of his head. "What? I no git half those words."

The snitch looks at Alex and then back at the group, pointing at the butterfly. "This is the key they want. This did not start out as a butterfly. It started out as a . . . a . . ." she scrunches her face, "I can't remember what it's called, but it was like a worm or something before it transformed into a butterfly. They are asking us if we want to transform into something better or stay as we are."

"How's ya know this? Ya be a Spoon or something?" our top dog states. "Cos ya be sounding like one with your voice all uppity and your fancy words."

"I'm not a Spoon. I am just like you, trying to prove my worth."

"Naw, ya be a Spoon turned Forgotten," someone chuckles, but the venom behind it is more of a threat than a statement.

"Yeah, and a Spoon, a Spoon," the top dog grouches as she starts toward the snitch.

Before I can stop her, Lou rushes forward, inserting herself between them, and my bracelet vibrates against my wrist. I glance down at it and the small blinking heart is racing just as fast as my own.

"Wait!" Lou says. "I know she be a Spoon, but don't ya think, since she be one, she be knowing all the right keys. We can use her." She turns slightly, addressing everyone. "This be good."

"Move or I be going through ya," the top dog growls.

Lou inches into the top dog's personal space and my throat tightens with my bracelet vibrating even more.

"I don't care what she be or was. Right now, she be the sharpest block in the room, so she be the one I follow." Lou moves even closer, nearly nose to nose. "Now, back down or ya be losing your rank," Lou threatens.

I scan the room at everyone's reaction and stop on the snitch. She's the only one that seems amused by this. She shifts slightly, taking a defensive stance, and anchors those brown eyes onto me. I quickly avoid eye contact and look back at Lou and our top dog.

"If these phases be thinking ones, we need someone sharp to lead us. I be following the Spoon," Hutch says and walks past Lou. He takes his spot behind the butterfly and within seconds, his friends follow.

"I be good at riddles," another Forgotten admits, joining the snitch as her friends follow.

The snitch clears her throat, looking weak and innocent again. "If we act together, we can pass each phase without anyone failing, and then they must accept all of us. Not just three. Trust me, this is the one they—"

The door slides open and everyone, including the top dog, races behind the butterfly stand just as Bear enters. With annoyance stuck in the back of my throat, I join them. I stand between Alex and Lou as Bear swaggers toward us, confident and cold.

"This is a first," he says.

The hallway explodes with a devastating echo, and I

know that sound. Someone from another room has failed. It resonates again, and I flinch with my teeth clenched tight as it repeats many times, followed by loud screams. Bear stops in front of us with a smug grin plastered on his face. He settles a palm on the pistol strapped to his thigh and my heartbeat doubles. I swing my hands behind my back, trying to calm my bracelet before anyone hears the vibration. I cut my eyes at the snitch standing next to Alex with worry and fear twisting in my gut. *Are we about to join the others that failed? Was this her plan from the beginning?* Their leader did say we could outwit or sabotage others for that spot.

"It be her fault; she be making us choose this one. End her, not us," our top dog complains at the end of our row.

Bear marches toward her and stops inches in front of her. Without looking away, he asks, "Does everyone agree with her?" And silence hovers in the air. "Looks like—"

"No clean up?" a voice interrupts, and I turn my attention to the Natural by the door. It's the one with the scar. The Wolfman. Even though he's leaning against the doorframe, I can tell he's taller than Bear. He also has shoulder length hair, like Bear. Except his isn't pulled back into a low bun and it's curly, not straight.

"Not sure," Bear begins, still staring at our top dog. "I don't know if I want to fail this one or not. I mean, teamwork is ninety percent of these tests."

"Well, think faster. We have shit to do," the Wolfman voices, pushing off the frame. He shoves his hands into a thick, red sweater that has a small swirly design painted on the front. He catches my gaze, and I quickly focus back on Bear. I really need to stop watching that one or I'm going to fail, but there's something about him that scares me.

"Count yourself lucky today, Pup." Bear pivots and smiles at his friend, and our top dog mumbles something.

What? I have no idea, but whatever it was, Bear stops right in front of me with an evil grin sliding across his face. He draws his pistol so fast I barely have time to register what is about to happen. He pulls the trigger without even turning to look at her or where his pistol is aimed. It is as if he doesn't even care which one of us he kills.

Before she even falls in a trembling fit, he's walking for the door, and I want to put my hands on him. Make him pay for all the Forgotten he has killed, and not just the ones he has taken since our arrival, but for all the ones that have come before us. Except, I'm not the protector; Lou is. And I know from experience, if I tried, she would interfere and be the one punished, not me. Instead, I quiet my bracelet with a tight grip as it hums out of control.

Bear stops walking again and glances at the bracelet on his arm. It's similar to ours, except his is much larger, with the glassy top nearly covering his entire forearm. He turns slightly, looking at me, but only for a moment, and then continues forward.

"Wolf, will you grab the reject? I need to speak with Hyena."

"Sure," Wolf says. He walks into the room full of assurance and when he gets near us, he feigns a lunge at the Forgotten next to Lou with a low growl. Except Lou doesn't see it as a playful grab and before we can stop her, she draws her fist back and swings. Wolf's head snaps back with a slight stumble and when he faces her again, I can see the meanness in his one good eye as he wipes blood off his lower lip. With the quickest reflexes I've ever seen, he snatches Lou by the neck. And every sip of air I have lodges in my throat as if it were my own neck his fingers are wrapped around. He marches her toward the back wall with her toes barely scraping the floor and when he slams her against it, releasing her, I gulp for air with her.

"Know your place, Pup."

My nails dig painfully into my palms. I have to do something. She has saved Alex and I so many times, it's our turn to save her. I muster all my courage and bolt forward. I jump onto his back, wrapping my legs around his waist with my left arm gripped tightly around his neck.

"Let go!" a voice orders, but I ignore them and tighten my hold. I can't stop now. If I'm going down, and I know I am, I'm taking at least one of these monsters with me. But before I can choke the life from him, the voice yanks me off and tosses me aside like I weigh nothing. I turn, sliding down the wall next to Lou, and curl into myself, preparing for my punishment, but instead of punishing me or Lou, their leader faces Wolf.

"You know the rules."

"I was only protecting myself, Yak," Wolf hisses, brushing at his bloody lip again.

"No." Yak gestures at the small Forgotten. "She was protecting her from you. And if you truly believed your life was in danger, you should have used this." Yak yanks his pistol out of its holster and holds it up. "That's what these are for. Why do you think we have them? To protect ourselves if they attack us."

Yak spins around, turning his attention to me, and I know I can't stop a bullet. However, I can force him to face me. Make him look me in the eye before he takes my life. Something I've noticed they do not do. They won't face the Forgotten they kill, but he will face me. I scramble to my feet and plant myself right in front of him with a bravery I thought I lost a long time ago.

Except he doesn't take it like I thought. Instead, his lips

curl into a devilish grin, and he moves closer until we are sharing the same air. "I told you once before, no one will hurt you unless you allow it. And today, you allowed it. So, this one's on you, Pup." He steps back, swinging the pistol over at Wolf, and I inch backward, closer to the wall. *Is he going to shoot him? One of their own?* A cold sweat runs down my back. *Is no one safe here? Not even the trainers.*

"Yak, wait!" Wolf demands, thrusting his hands out. "You don't have to do this."

"Yes, I do. A lesson needs to be made." Yak shifts his stance slightly to address everyone in the room. "No one is above a punishment. Not even the trainers." He turns back to Wolf and pulls the trigger.

I clamp a hand over my mouth, watching the trainer flop around like a dead fish, and Yak steps into my view.

"Mind yourself, Pup," he warns.

Once Wolf's body stops trembling, he grabs his ankle, but before he drags Wolf out the door, he stops near the doorframe. He inserts a key into the wall, turning it and swiftly pulls it out. He removes a small metal box and then presses a red button that was hidden behind it. "A gift for passing the first test," he says, and the floor shifts and moves. Everyone scatters, hugging the walls as the flooring rotates and opens, allowing furniture to rise out.

Lou grabs my hand as Alex rushes to our side. "What it be?" he asks.

"Beds," Lou replies, rubbing at her neck.

CAN YOU CATCH OUR BREATH?

||||| ||

The rest of the day, everyone sits silently, waiting for Bear to return. But as time passes, and our meals come twice already, we realize it may not be until tomorrow, so everyone crawls into bed. I pick the one between Alex and Lou, and just as I am about to fall asleep, a ruckus is heard nearby. I lift onto my shoulder and it's getting louder and fiercer. *What is happening? Is there another physical altercation going on?* I sit up with my ears strained, and it sounds like there's a group of Forgotten ganging up on someone. *Is it the snitch?* I swing my legs over the edge of the cot just as Bear enters, banging on a large metal can, and the room floods with light.

"Wake up! Use the latrine and line up!"

I'm on my feet in seconds at the demand. Something I learned a long time ago. If a guard calls out orders, you do as you're told and fast, or pay the consequences. I start for the latrine and sure enough, the snitch's face is bloody, and she's holding her side. Now, I really can't talk. If the others find out I'm like her, there's no telling what they will do to me. *Heck, how far would they have gone if Bear hadn't entered and interrupted them?*

When I join everyone back in the main quarter, our beds are lowered back into the floor, and Bear is standing by the door speaking to another trainer. He points right at me, and I immediately avert my eyes, fidgeting in place. Movement catches my eye and I turn my head slightly to the snitch standing next to me. I shuffle away from her, thankful it wasn't me Bear was pointing at. At least I hope it wasn't.

"Listen up!" Bear's voice booms. "Phase one is all about transformation through body and mind. And for the next few weeks, I will push you physically and test you mentally. I will teach you basic training skills on how to strengthen your muscles. It is something we will do every day with each day harder than the last. Even after your training, you will keep your body and mind strong." He pulls a small device from his pocket and points it at the black portrait. I glance over my shoulder and the numbers are back, but they aren't counting down, not yet.

"Because once we sail for war, you will need both."

War? Is that what all this is about? Who are they at war with? Pirates? Spoons? Or both.

"So, if war is not what you want, then please feel free to ring out and someone will come in and remove you." He waits a moment and I almost laugh at his statement.

Does he really think anyone here is going to willingly die?

"Alright, let's begin." He moves to us, positioning everyone a few feet apart. Once he has everyone where he wants them, he moves back to the front of the room. "Jumping jacks," he says with a demonstration.

Lou looks at me with a lopsided grin. "Looks fun," she says and follows Bear's lead. I glance over at Alex, and he gives me a shrug before joining the others.

After what feels like hours of physical activities but has only been thirty minutes of doing push-ups and sit-ups and something called "burpees", Bear tells us to line up for our next exercise, and I can barely catch my breath. These exercises are much harder on my lungs than it ever was mining sulfur. I thought we were healed from our sickness since we haven't had coughing fits. But the more of these exercises we do, the harder it is to breathe. It makes me wonder if that was even medicine they gave to us. Plus, it seems as if my breathing is worse than Alex and Lou's. I clutch at the pain radiating on my right side and lean against the wall, gulping for air.

A long metal rod descends from the ceiling and Bear points at it. "This is called a 'pull-up bar'. When I say, 'up', I want your—"

A violent cough nearly buckles me and when I straighten, wiping at my wet eyes, Bear is no longer in the room. I scan the area, searching for him, and Alex pats my back, asking, "Ye be right?"

I give a slight nod just as Bear enters back into the room, hollering for the three of us to come forward.

"Please, we can be doing it," Alex pleads.

"I didn't ask if you could do it. I said come here."

Alex grabs my hand, helping me to the front of the room, and as we stop in front of Bear, I fall to my knees with a rattling cough. A hand massaging my back calms my breathing, but as I sit back on my heels to give Alex a silent nod, it isn't Alex squatting beside me. It's Bear. My throat hitches, sending me into another fitful cough.

"Take it easy. Try breathing small shallow breaths. In and out. Good."

When I finally catch my breath and face him, he holds up the same skin-pricking gun we received when we arrived.

"Another round should do the trick. Do you accept my help?"

My stomach knots at what Yak said the other night: "This is how we weed out the rejects." *What if this is another test? Another way to fail.* If so, it's too late. Alex and Lou are receiving theirs from another trainer. And I know I must, too. I cannot do this without them.

I turn back to Bear, and he adds, "It will be okay. This is not a test. I'm only trying to help you further yourself in the phases."

I wet my lips with a hesitant nod, hoping our death is quick and painless. But from the way the others have fallen in a trembling fit from that pistol, I don't believe it will be. After my injection, I sit on my heels, waiting for my next orders, but he isn't saying anything. Both Bear and the blond trainer are just staring at us. *Do we go back and join the others or stay here?* In the mining caverns, you didn't move or speak unless instructed, and they aren't telling us to do anything.

Alex looks at me with a shrug, and that's when the magical thing happens. My breathing is better, and my chest no longer feels like there's a belt wrapped around me. I inhale deeply with a relaxing sigh, and that's when they order us to move back to the others. Alex hooks his arm around mine, and I hear their hushed voices behind me.

"We've been here before, Bear. Are you sure this is a good idea?"

"Yes. I was able to separate myself from my brother and look at how well I turned out."

"Well, good luck with that, brother. And not just with them, but with Yak. If he finds out, he'll fail them for sure."

"Don't I know it."

I peek up at Alex and my throat tightens. *Are they talking about us? What if our friendship is what gets him, or Lou, killed? Maybe in order to save them, I need to detach myself. Not completely, just enough that Bear will believe we aren't as close as we seem.* And for the first time, I become the protector and pull away from them by squeezing between Hutch and his group. I lower my head, refusing to look at Lou and Alex, and silently ask for their understanding and forgiveness.

A GLIMPSE OF WHAT WAS

卌///

Detaching myself from Alex and Lou apparently worked. Even if it was as simple as not standing next to them sometimes, because Bear has stopped watching us like before. And the three of us have excelled in training these last few weeks. Not that the others haven't, they have. Everyone has grown in strength, even in height. Some of the Forgotten that were shorter than me when we first arrived are now taller and meatier. Not by much, but enough that Father was right.

"Exercise and eating healthy will help you grow tall and strong. One more bite, and then you can go play with Mable," Father says.

"But I hate carrots. They taste like dirt," I sulk.

"If you do not eat your carrots, then how will you defeat Mable's dragons?" he asks.

"Or me?" Papa growls, soaring out of his chair and chomping near my neck, making me squirm in my chair.
"Potro!" Father stresses.

But it isn't Father's playful tone I remember of that day. It's hoarse and fearful. It's of the night I was sentenced.

"Hey, ye be right?" Alex asks me, and I push the memory away. I nod and scan the room as we wait for everyone to finish using the latrine. Not that there are many of us left. We are now down to twelve in our room. Not because of the exercises. It was for ganging up on the snitch again. Their leader said he'd fail everyone in this room if we couldn't get along. And that evening, everyone gathered as one big group to set rules. From no one stealing bowls or bedding to no sabotaging or fighting, and most importantly, no top dog.

But where we lost most was during the swimming tests. At first, I was excited about the idea of going outside. I thought maybe we could scout the area. Perhaps see if it was even possible to escape this place. Instead, we were led into another large room with something similar to a man-made pond in the center. Those that couldn't swim or follow direct orders failed.

Hutch lost his entire group that morning, and ever since, he and Alex have become fast friends. Even Lou has been spending most of her time with Hutch. Which leaves me sitting in the corner, watching everyone else. Not that I mind; it gives me time to spy on the snitch. To make sure she doesn't do anything sketchy, and, to my surprise, she hasn't. Yet.

The following week, we were given a portrait test, and that's when we lost more. Apparently, we had to guess what the images were, but to me, it just looked like a bunch of nonsense with black paint splattered on parchment. Bear called it an "inkblot". But, since I'm not allowed to speak, or know how to write, I didn't have to take the test. Instead, he moved the portraits aside and gripped his hands on top of the table and stared at me with smugness. Like he knew some big secret about me. Little does he know, I know one about him. I've been watching him and noticed he can't hear very well out of his right ear. My advantage.

So, while I stared at him and him at me, it reminded me of a game Ford and I used to play to see which one blinked first. Of course, I always lost because I could never hold in my giggles. But this time, it wasn't a game, and I wasn't playing with my cousin. This time, it was more like two dogs demanding dominance and I refused to submit. Even when my time was up and the blond trainer poked his head in, I never looked away, and neither did Bear. We kept eye contact the entire time until, finally, I was yanked from the chair and out of the room. I wanted him to know: I saw him and how awful he was for killing a small child, younger than Alex, for not guessing the portrait correctly.

After that day, I truly believed he would fail me or, at the very least, push me to quit. But he never did. He barely even acknowledged me. And in my book, that's a win. At least that's what I thought until now. He's standing at the front of the room, grinning at me like a clever dog that just buried his favorite bone, and he's daring me to find it. His grin widens as he points at the ceiling like he's giving me a hint of where to look. I follow his finger and the ceiling folds open, revealing a massive tree log. My mouth parts and I take a step backward, bumping into someone standing behind me.

"Whatever happens, do not let go." I look over my

shoulder, but before I can figure out what the snitch means, the leader's voice controls the room.

"Line up, pups! Today is the last day of phase one," Yak says as all the trainers enter the room behind him.

Why are they not watching their own group? Did their group fail? Are we the only group left?

Yak motions for the trainers to move to the center of the room, and then points at the log as he addresses us again. "Meet Betty. She's a nasty bitch, and today, she is your test."

The log stops just above the trainers' heads with their arms raised, like they are holding it up. And my palms prickle with sweat when the chains secured to the log start spinning free.

"Pick a spot and join them," Yak orders.

I ball my hands into my shirt, wiping my palms dry, and quickly rush forward. *Crap!* Bear is in front of me. *Why did I need to pick this spot? I'd rather not be anywhere near a trainer.* I lift my arms with everyone else and his arms are bigger than my entire body. His muscular form alone terrifies me, but when the numbers blink alive on the black portrait, I'm grateful for his strength.

"The timer says five hours, and just like everything we do beyond these walls, it may seem impossible." Yak begins pacing around us. "Your mission today is to prove, no matter how impossible it may be, you are still willing to try. To push through the pain and give it your all. Even if you see your brethren fall at your feet. Prove your worth today and you shall pass."

My eyes are fixed on the numbers as if I stare at them long enough it will start to tick faster. But it doesn't, and as the minutes go by, the log becomes heavier. There's no way we can hold this up for that long, even with the trainers' help. And that's when I notice a trainer that was under the log is now following close behind Yak. The trainers are peeling away, one by one, and when Bear lets go, the log drops slightly with the bark digging into my shoulder.

Yak passes by me. "Arms up, Pup. Just because you can't reach it doesn't mean you get the luxury of standing there comfortably."

He must be speaking to Alex. He's the smallest one here now. But my eyes aren't straining behind me to know for sure, they are focused on the trainer stopping next to us. He's indigenous with high, prominent cheekbones and ink-black hair that hangs all the way down to his rear. And on top of his head is a strange-looking cap that reminds me of a sock. He catches me staring and his brown eyes pierce right through me, mean and feral, as he side-steps toward me.

"Don't look at me. Pay attention to the task at hand." I adjust my footing, and he leans close, jabbing a finger into my temple. "Focus or ring out."

I shake my head, and he moves on. But the trainer behind him, the one with blond hair and sporting a dimple in his chin, stops and addresses me, too. "Are you sure, Pup? Because from where I'm standing, you're no better than a Spoon with your head in the clouds."

I shake my head again, and the snitch in front of Lou drops to her knees.

She's still wearing that stupid bandage. *Why? Does she really think we wouldn't notice?* Well, maybe the others haven't, but I have. I know exactly what she's hiding. It's the same tattoo all the trainers have and why I truly believe she is a snitch and not a Spoon. What I don't get though, is why the others keep following her example. *Why do they trust her?* At some point, she will lead us down the wrong path.

"Get up," a Forgotten demands.

"I can't," the snitch cries. "It's too hard."

"Yeah, ya can," someone voices behind me. More Forgotten encourages her to get up. I don't know if it's because they want her strength, or if they truly care what happens to her. *And why is she pretending to be weak all of a sudden? What game is she playing?*

I shift my stance and see Bear squat next to her. "If it's too hard, Pup, just ring out and you'll have everything you've ever wanted."

"Really?" the snitch blubbers.

"Yes. All the food and comfort is just beyond that door. All you have to do is ring out."

"If that be true, then why'd they fail the others? He be double-dealing. Now, git up and help us!" someone grunts, and the snitch shakily pushes herself off the floor. But not before I see the self-satisfying grin on her lips.

The trainer that pulled my hair and asked if I could learn on the first day walks by me, saying, "Looks like you have the better group."

"Team works better than mine," the blond trainer voices.

"Yeah, I had five ring out, and no one encouraged them to stay," the one wearing the sock on his head says.

I wet my lips just as Yak stops near the front, rubbing his hands viciously together. "Well, let's see how they are with distraction, shall we?"

At first, I thought he was going to address Lou, and my heart skipped a beat, but he shuffles closer to Hutch.

"You are weak and insignificant. You'll never make it out there. Give!"

The trainers join their leader, and I flinch as spit flies from both sides of me. They are trying to find the weak link, but I refuse to play their game. Instead, I squeeze my eyes shut and go to the one place they cannot reach me. I go home.

Laughter and banter surround the campfire as Alex tosses a shrimp into his mouth. Lou's jaw drops, asking, "You didn't eat the tail, did ya?"

"Aye. Why?"

"You're not supposed to," Ford tells him with a slight giggle, digging a stick into the fire pit.

"Why? What's gonna be happening?" Alex asks with wide, frightful eyes.

I playfully nudge Ford. "You turn into a shrimp," I say with a grave face.

"But it doesn't happen until you fall asleep. You can never fall asleep now," Ford says with a quiet chuckle.

Alex straightens from the dead log. "Ain't neither, and if ye don't bag your face and stop tricking us, I'm gonna bag it for ye," he threatens.

Lou jumps to her feet, and I squeeze my eyes tighter because the memory has changed.

It's the night of the ritual, and Lou has her wooden sword drawn. "Dragon's attack!"

Before I can fully join them, the town bells scream in warning.

I shake my head, not wanting to remember the next part.

"I be jolted. Ye sure ye can be saving us?" Alex whimpers.

"Yes," I assure him. "Remember, we're the DV8Rs. We just have to make it to the bunker before they find us."

He grabs my hand, tight. "Give us yer oath, ye ain't gonna let go?"

"On my life. I'll never let go of you, Alex," I promise, squeezing his hand, and we take off through the woods.

My eyes twitch at the large leaves slapping against me like I'm still there, running for my life, because I know his does. Animals scurry and twigs snap as boots pound into the earth. The pirate's getting closer. I can hear his heavy panting and my fear is heightened to a frightening degree. I force a glance behind me and there he is. A grime-covered hand, bursting with jewels, and stretching toward me. Alex falls, pulling me down with him. I twist around, scooting on my rear as the pirate marches for us, quick and violent. He yanks me and Alex both to our feet. I'm trying to squirm and wiggle out of the death grip he has on my arm and Cotton Wayne shoots out of the bushes like a bullet.

"Let go of 'em!" he demands, punching and scream-ing, but he's no match against the burly pirate. None of us are. With a mean fist, the pirate backhands Cotton Wayne, and he falls into a heap. The pirate starts toward us again and then stops with his eyes wide. He clutches at his side and blood seeps through his fingers. He turns slightly, and Ford is standing beside him with a bloody pocketknife gripped in his hand.

"Run!" Ford screams, inching backward.

"Let go!" a shrill voice orders, and before I can shake the memory clear, I'm yanked from under the log. "What's wrong with you?" Yak rants.

I stumble sideways, into Alex, and notice no one is under the log. I glance at the device used as a clock and it's not even been an hour. They have finished the test. In fact, the log is secured by the chains again and is rising back into the ceiling. I turn to Alex with my throat raw and sore. For I will never forget the sound that tore out of Ford seconds after we ran. *Wait. Is that why he wasn't sentenced with us? I press my fingers into my lips and stare at my feet. Did Ford not get away like I thought? Did something bad happen to him? And what about Cotton Wayne?* I cup my head, squeezing. *Why can't I remember what happened to them?*

"Pup." Fingers snap, quick and loud, close to my face, and I flinch my eyes upward. "Grab your bowl and get in line," Bear tells me.

I look over at the line already formed by the door and Lou is gesturing for us to hurry. I grab my bowl and follow behind everyone as Bear escorts our room down the hallway. Once we enter the same room we arrived in on day one, I take my seat next to Lou with Alex on my right. Without the other rooms here, this area looks bigger and emptier than before, and I can't help but wonder where the other Forgotten are.

"Eyes on me!" Bear orders as two younger Naturals, maybe fifteen, enter the room and stand next to him. "Since everyone here will be moving on to the next phase, you will also be given a new lifeline. Please, pass your bowl to the end of the line." He motions for the younger Naturals to step forward. Both are dressed in snug, black trousers with white tops. "Martin will be taking your bowls, and Robin will be handing out your new lifeline." He raises a fork high in the air. "This is your lifeline now, and the same rules apply."

Once everyone is holding a fork, Bear gestures to the back wall. "Now, line up against the wall for pods."

Everyone does as Bear commands, and the floor rotates, opening just like in our quarters. Except these aren't like our beds. These look more like huge eggs and unease swims in my belly when they hatch open.

"This is where you will be staying for the evening. Pick a pod and enter," Bear tells us, and I notice the other trainers are entering the room. *Why? What's about to happen?*

"Let's go! We don't have all day," the trainer with the sock on his head hollers.

I flinch at the forceful clapping of his hands, and start forward, but Lou grabs at my shoulder. I know I should pull away. Detach from her, but when I feel her fear tremble against my blouse, I can't walk away. I look over at Alex for help and he gives a slight nod, jogging back over to us and reaches for her hand.

"This ain't the same. Ye ain't being punished," he says, slowly guiding her. He points at the one next to hers. "I be right here, yeah?"

Lou nods, and as I start to pull away for my own pod, she grabs me again. "I can't," she sniffles. "What if it be like the caves? What if we are being punished? Why else would the other trainers be here? What if—"

Alex rushes back over and grips her shoulders. "Hey, it be right. Ain't nothing bad gonna happen," he whispers.

From the corner of my eye, I see Bear moving toward us and panic swallows me whole.

"If you cannot—" Bear begins.

"She can. Just be giving us a tick," Alex stresses, and I can hear the desperation in his voice. It's low and sad, like each word physically pains him. I can't give Lou the words she needs. Even though I desperately want to. All I can do is stop Bear from reaching them, and I do. With my head down and my back to him, I sidestep into his path.

"Ye gotta do this or they'll be failing ye. And ye know I can't be going on without ye."

"There is—" Bear begins, moving closer, and I sidestep again.

"Back off!" Alex roars.

"Screw this," I hear behind me and, without warning, the sound of glass shatters. I quickly turn just as something bites into my leg. There's a small needle sticking into my thigh. It looks exactly like the type I was tutored in for needlepoint. I reach down to pull it out and a heaviness courses through me.

"No!" Alex bellows and the sound of glass is heard again.

I stumble forward, shaking my head, but my vision is starting to go. And the voices around me are jumbled but heated like someone is arguing. I grip the side of the pod for support, and out of nowhere, a hot stabbing pain ripples through me as I fall, stiff and trembling, and the world goes dark.

TWICE AS HARD

~~IIII~~ IIII

I peel my eyes open, and my mind is completely blank. I'm inside a strange-looking bed with no idea of how I arrived here. *Why? What happened?* The last thing I remember is going to bed last night. I start to lift up and feel something resting in my palm. It's a fork. *Why am I holding this and why do I have it?* I wet my lips, and the lower part of my face feels swollen. I touch my mouth and fear crawls up my back as a cold sensation needles my lips. *What did they do to me? To us?* I skim the room, looking for Alex and Lou, and they aren't here. Only Hutch.

Panic coats my throat.

"Easy." The voice startles me, and when I face him, an elderly gentleman is smiling at me. He reaches for me, and I jerk away with my heart hammering painfully in my chest. "It's okay. I'm only trying to help you out of the pod." He offers me his hand with another smile, and I hesitantly allow him to help me.

"The effects will wear off soon. Until then, try not to speak too much. No eating or chewing on your cheek or tongue until feeling returns or you can bite through them." After he helps me to my feet, he gestures at the fork in my hand. "The fork you're holding is your new lifeline. You no longer have the bowl." He pats my shoulder. "Good luck in phase two."

Phase two. When did we finish phase one? It doesn't matter. I have to get out of here. I have to find Lou and Alex.

"Let's go, pups!"

I whip my head around and the blond trainer is standing by the doorway.

"Me mouth be feeling offbeat," Hutch says, walking beside me. He looks around the room and I look at him, wondering what's wrong with his speech. It sounds like he has a mouth full of water and he's trying not to spill it as he talks. He nudges me. "The others gotta be waiting, yeah?"

I give a slight nod, hoping he's right. But with the uncertainty of this place, it could very well be possible we are the only ones left. But why? I want to talk to him. Maybe between the both of us we can figure out what happened, but I know I can't, or he'll know I'm not a Forgotten. And I've seen the way he watches the snitch. I'm not entirely sure if he was involved with her beating or not, but if he was, I don't want him turning that anger onto me. Plus, with him walking this close to me, he must trust me somewhat. And if we are the only ones left, I definitely don't want to speak now and lose that trust. I may need him.

With a heavy intake of breath, I head to the trainer, and he pushes off the doorframe, disappearing into the hallway. Hutch and I round the corner to follow, and the trainer is at the end, standing inside of a small closet with his hand oddly out in front. It's almost like he thinks the wall will collapse if he doesn't hold onto the doorframe.

As we walk down the hallway, I glance inside each doorway, but all the quarters are empty. Everyone is gone. I face forward, closer to the trainer, and the second we join him, Hutch asks, "Where be the others?"

But the trainer doesn't reply or respond in any way, and when I lean forward, I see something small hidden in his ear. *Why does he have his ears plugged? What's about to happen to us?*

He presses one of the buttons lined with numbers against the wall, and the doorframe he had his hand on slowly slides shut. The floor bounces like a spring being pulled tight, and I nearly lose my balance. Hutch grips my hand tightly and if I wasn't as scared as him, I would have brushed it away. But when the spring releases, shooting my insides into my throat, I squeeze Hutch's hand and he releases an ear-piercing scream. Just as I'm getting used to this spinning sensation in my belly, the room bounces to a stop. The closet door slides open, and I swallow the salty saliva with a deep inhale while Hutch's scream lingers to a stop.

Hutch lets go of my hand and rubs the center of his chest. "That be wicked clean," he says with a huff, and then turns with a finger pointed at me. "If anyone asks, that be ye that screamed, yeah?" he says with something similar to a chuckle, but I can't tell. His eyes are happy, but his mouth is serious.

I give a slight nod and step out of the closest with loud voices and commotion buzzing. We follow the trainer down another long hallway with only two doors on both sides of the wall. Again, four rooms.

Hutch pulls on my sleeve. "There be the other groups,"

he tells me as we pass the first door. And sure enough, the next room has Forgotten in them, too. Not as many as before, at least from what I can see, anyway.

The trainer stops at the last door on the right. "This is your new quarters and training room," he tells us, then spins on his heel to leave.

"There," Hutch points.

Lou and Alex are in the back corner with the snitch, and my heart swells into my throat. I've never been so happy to see them in all my life. Hutch moves forward, and I start to follow but stop when my foot slightly sinks into the dark flooring like it's made out of a thin bedroll. I look up, taking in our new quarters and its sort of the same as our last. There's a water fountain and a black clock in the exact same spot as our last room. But the latrine doesn't have a door closing it off; instead, there's a thick archway. And the beds aren't hidden this time. There are rows of them pushed against the left wall with more stacked on top, like they are hovering. I move closer and from the looks of them, they seem to be bolted to the wall for support. Or at least I hope so.

I make my way over to Alex and Lou, lowering myself between them and angle my head at Alex's green eyes. They are bright and happy, like he's smiling, but his lips aren't curled. Sort of like Hutch was a minute ago. He reaches up and pulls his lips apart, and my eyes instantly grow wide. His brown teeth are now white, with his broken ones fixed into a straight line. I quickly force my fingers between my lips and feel a tooth where a missing one was. I jump to my feet and race into the latrine, smiling into the mirror, but my lips don't turn upward. I look just like Alex and Hutch, no smile. I raise a shaky hand and lift my upper lip, and the second I see a glimpse of white, tears threaten.

I'll finally be able to eat and drink with no pain. *But how and when did they fix them?*

"They be nice, huh?" Alex asks, and I nod at his reflection in the mirror. "I be having some feelin' back," he says, moving closer so he can smile into the mirror. His reflection has me clamping a hand over my mouth, trying not to laugh.

"Alex, ye be looking like a wobbler." Hutch chuckles and then looks at me with a grimace. "My bad. I forgot."

"He looks like an insane person," the snitch states with a full smile. I start to ask myself why her smile isn't frozen like ours, but then I remember she already has perfect teeth. They didn't need to fix anything about her.

"That be what a wobbler means," Lou tells her.

"Wait, how ye be knowing what her word means? Ye be a Spoon, too?" Hutch asks with a scrunched face.

I slowly turn around with wide eyes, but Lou snorts like she couldn't care less she's been outed as a Spoon.

"I was," she admits.

"So, you can read and write, and you know all the lingo between Spoons and Forgotten. That's brilliant," the snitch voices.

"Hmm," Hutch grunts, and the way he's eyeing the three of us, it looks like the trust he had in us is gone. And I don't blame him. *Why did Lou have to open her big mouth and admit it?* She could have just said she learned it in the mining caverns from a guard or something.

I turn back with slow, cautious movements, knowing I'll need to keep an eye on Hutch now. Not just the snitch. And I'll have to pull Lou aside later and tell her she's getting a little too comfortable around them. In fact, so is Alex. I understand he and Hutch are both males, but why does he have to spend more time with Hutch than he does with us?

WHY DOES SHE NEED TO BE SO BOLD?

$\cancel{||||}\ \cancel{||||}$

After my morning shower, I put on my new attire, which is the same athletic gear, only a blue color instead of white now. I join the others in the main quarter and the two stands are back. The one on the left has a bowl of feathers and the one on the right has a small statue of a bird. I glance at the back wall as everyone gathers around the two stands, and the numbers are already counting down fifteen minutes. With a hard eye roll, I shuffle closer to the group. *Why do the Naturals even bother with these tests? It makes no sense at all. They act like we actually have a choice.*

"Hey, that be an eagle," Hutch announces, pointing at the fist-sized statue.

The snitch looks at him. "Are you sure?" she asks but her eyes glisten like she already knew that. Which, of course, she does. I'd be surprised if she didn't.

Hutch moves closer to the stand. "Yeah, I used to be a

cabin boy and me ol' captain had this bird inked on his arm." He grabs the small statue, inspecting it. "He say it mean power or something."

A Forgotten, standing by the bowl of feathers, points at it. "This be eagle feathers?"

"Search us? Ain't never seen a real one." Hutch shrugs.

"It ain't," another Forgotten says, standing by the feathers. He dips his hand into the bowl. "These be smaller. Soft with the end pointy like our pillows."

The snitch snaps her fingers at the feathers. "Comfort." She points at the statue. "Power."

"So, which one be the key?" Alex asks.

A tall girl with a mousy voice says, "Power. When ya wanted to give, Bear say, all the comfort ya want be beyond those doors."

And the snitch grins like she already knew that, too. Why not admit it first? This is why I don't trust her. Sometimes, she admits when she knows the answer and other times, like now, she pretends she doesn't. I slowly move behind the statue with everyone else and a lean boy with dark spiky hair steps out of line.

"Does anyone else feel like this be too calm?"

I glance at the numbers on the black portrait, and he's right. It's only been a few minutes. Maybe there's more to this. Maybe that's why the snitch looked happy. Could this be a trick and, if so, what will happen?

"Yeah, but I think that's cos there ain't a top dog to shush us," his friend adds. "Think what the Forgotten out there could be doing if there ain't a top dog holding 'em down."

"Well, aren't you the smart one of the group?"

Everyone turns in the direction of the latrine, and Bear

is standing in front of it. *Has he been here the whole time?* I mash my lips together, skimming the group, and I can tell by their expressions they are just as confused as me. I nudge Alex in the arm, and he gives me the same questioning look. Which means Bear wasn't here before. *But how did he enter without us seeing him? Or was he hidden in the corner, and no one noticed?* I pull on my bottom lip, staring at him as he walks to the front of the room. I'll need to be more cautious of him and my surroundings.

"Is this your fate?" Bear asks, and everyone nods in agreement. "Good. You are correct. Now, follow me," he says, walking out of the room.

As I step into the hallway, the sound of glass shatters and my throat tightens. I glance over my shoulder and see the other trainers dragging lifeless bodies from their quarters, and my stomach boils with anger. I ball my hands into fists and face forward, not realizing we have stopped just inside another room. I wasn't quick enough to halt myself before bumping into Lou, who bumps into Alex, shoving most of the line forward. Alex turns with a wicked grin, and Lou palms the top of his head, forcing him back around before he can sass her.

"Why are you always mean to him?" the snitch asks behind me.

Lou turns all the way around, facing both of us. "I don't want him to be getting into trouble for not paying attention. It ain't mean. It be for his own good."

"Hey, pay attention back there," Bear shouts, snapping his fingers at us.

"See," Lou stresses, wild-eyed, and then faces forward with a sour face.

"This is called a 'Mess Hall'." Bear tells us, gesturing to the row of food lined against the back wall. "You will no longer eat in your quarters. Instead, you will come here for your meals. Does everyone have their eating utensil?"

I pull my fork from my waistband and hold it up with everyone else.

"Good." He steps out of our way. "Grab a plate and load up."

We move forward, and the snitch skips the line, moving to the front. I lift onto my toes, watching her. She's telling our group something. And whatever she said, the line moans with disappointment. When she returns, she stands behind me and says, "No sugar. It will drag you down later and make you sleepy. Which, in turn, could make you fail."

I eye her as the line moves again. At least that part is true. I remember Father telling me something similar about sugar. I reach for my tray and the second it's in my hands, the snitch plops scrambled eggs onto it. I've been eating slop for so many years, my mouth waters at some of the comfort food I used to have back home.

"Always eat protein and fruit," the snitch tells me. "It will fuel your body with what it needs for the day, okay?"

I don't even look at her or reply with a nod. Instead, I sniff at the rest of the food she piles onto my plate. I have no idea what some of it is, but it smells wonderful. I turn to one of the tables scattered around the room and stop. Alex and Hutch are pushing a couple of tables together, creating a larger one. *Why?* I mean, we barely even speak to the other Forgotten in our room. *Okay, I never talk to the other Forgotten. I try to stay away from the others. Why get close to them if they might not be here tomorrow?*

Hutch sits near the end, looking right at me with a huge smile, and then pats the empty seat next to him. *Why does he want me to sit by him?* The only time he's paid me any mind was yesterday when we both woke up from those strange beds. *Are we friends now? Or is it only because he's friends with Alex and Lou?* I scan the table, searching for an empty seat, and the only one available that's near the end of the table is the one next to him. And I can't ask Alex to move. That wouldn't be fair. I start walking, and Hutch grins even more.

"I thought ye'd want this one, since it be open at the end."

I give a forced smile and a slight nod as I slide my tray onto the table, and Alex shouts out, "Blimey! What be this? It be guu–uud," he smacks, directly in front of me.

"It's turkey bacon." The snitch giggles further down the table, and my mouth parts.

Turkey bacon? I've never heard of that before, but bacon, that I've heard of, and that's usually only for the wealthy. And I mean really wealthy. Not even my parents had the coin for this type of meat, and they lived comfortably. The only meat we ever had was roast or ham, and that was only on special occasions, like a holiday. I nibble at the extravagant meat and my taste buds dance with flavor. No wonder this is only for the wealthy.

"And this," Hutch asks.

"Yogurt," the snitch chuckles again, "and next to it is a kiwi."

Bear stops at the end of the table, blocking my freedom, and sweat prickles my skin. "No donuts or cinnamon rolls? Smart," he says, sliding his plate onto the table. He drags a chair up next to Alex and gestures for him to scoot down the table. "Usually, that's the first thing snatched up." He sits directly in front of me, and my stomach churns with disgust.

"It be a test or something?" Hutch asks with a mouthful.

Bear lifts his chin at a nearby table. "See Hyena over there and how his group has all that sugar piled on their plates?" I crane my neck to see which group he's talking about and it's the trainer that wears the sock on his head. "His group won't be worth a damn by the end of the day, and some of them will fail because of it. So, yeah, I guess you can call it a test."

A chair grinding across the floor has me turning back around and when I see Lou on her feet, my heart sinks into my belly. *Please sit back down.*

"What'cha doing?" Alex asks.

"I wanna be helping the others by taking away their sugar. It ain't fair we know it can be hurting us today, and they don't. Everyone should be having the same fair shake as us, yeah?"

"Yeah," Alex agrees and then addresses Bear, "Do it be against the rules?"

"No, but it's a bad idea," Bear replies.

"How bad?" Lou asks.

"Guess you're about to find out." Bear grins with a shrug and shoves a spoonful of eggs into his mouth.

"Guess so," the snitch says and then stands with Lou, reaching for her arm. "Let's do it."

Lou, Alex, and the snitch walk over to the garbage cans, and I glance over at Hyena, the trainer. His dark eyes are locked onto them like they are his next meal, and I wet my lips as Lou continues forward. She stops at the end of Hyena's table and all the blood drains from my face as his group stops eating. They are watching Lou like she's the center of the show and all are waiting for her to begin. I cut my eyes over to the snitch and the blond trainer sitting at that group's table isn't angry at all. If anything, he's allowing the snitch to help his group. But then again, why would he not? She is one of them.

I turn back to Hyena, and he leans back in his chair with his arms folded across his chest.

"Whatever you're about to do, Pup, I suggest you not do it and return to your table," Hyena growls.

I press my fingers into my lips, desperate for her to behave, but I know she won't. It's just like in the mining caverns, always wanting to help others no matter the cost.

Lou lifts her chin higher, dragging the can closer, and Hyena shoots to his feet so fast and mean, his chair overturns behind him. But his violent and angry actions don't seem to affect Lou. Instead, she holds Hyena's stare, grabbing a sugary roll off a nearby plate as Hyena's group pushes away from the table. And I don't blame them. I'm just as scared, especially when Hyena's face turns red with his nostrils flaring. He rounds the table like an angry bull, and Lou grins like this is a game.

She heads in the opposite direction, tossing sugary treats into the can. My palms sweat with my pulse racing as Hyena jumps on the table after her, but Lou bolts forward and rushes to the next table with her grin blossoming into a full smile. She spins around, avoiding Hyena, and slams into the blond trainer, and I lift out of my chair.

"Grab her!" Hyena demands.

"Sorry, but there are no rules that say she cannot help those not in her room," the blond trainer voices, stepping out of Lou's way, and I swallow with relief. But my eyes are locked on Hyena. He looks like he's about to rip the other trainer's head off. *What's about to happen to him?* I know they aren't afraid to use their pistols on each other, and my heart betrays me. I actually feel sorry for the trainer helping Lou. Instead, I should be thankful Hyena is willing to take him out for me, giving us a better chance of escape. The fewer Naturals to fight when the time comes, the better.

Hyena starts left, around the other trainer, and from the looks of it, the blond intentionally bumps into Hyena. "Sorry," the blond chuckles and then moves right, intentionally bumping into Hyena again. "Just tell me which way you're going, brother, and I'll get out of your way?"

"Move, Fox!" Hyena demands and shoves him forcefully out of his way.

Hyena then barrels toward Lou just as Alex stumbles into his path like a fumbling idiot, and my eyes grow even wider. He grabs Alex by the scruff of the neck, tossing him aside, and I hear Hutch say, "No sugar! It be a test!"

I twist around and our entire group is on their feet, helping Lou. I turn back and Hyena is in the middle of the room with his pistol humming to life. I dig my fingers deeper into my lips with my heart seconds from exploding. The only thing that kept it from blasting was Yak inserting himself in front of Hyena.

"Do we have a problem?" he asks Hyena.

After a few silent moments, Hyena finally lowers his pistol with a snarl, and I inhale deep with relief washing over me.

"No." He spins on his heel and stops in front of Bear. "You keep her away from my group, or there will be trouble." Hyena starts back to his table, and I look over my shoulder. Yak eyes Lou a moment and walks out the door like nothing happened, carrying a block of wood in his hand like he's been whittling it.

"Hey." Alex leans close to my ear. "We need to be watching that one. From the looks of it, Hyena be the meanest one here. Meaner than Bear." And I nod in agreement.

"Pup, no one here is as mean as I am." Bear grins, sinking his teeth into an apple.

Alex slowly sits in Hutch's chair as I watch Bear. *How did he hear what Alex said?* He barely spoke enough for me to hear him. Furthermore, why did Yak save Lou and not him? If anything, he looks pleased with himself. Bear gives a slight nod to someone behind me, and when I turn my head, sure enough, the snitch nods back. I knew it. She really is a snitch. Like for real, real now.

WIN OR LOSE, SHE'LL SHOW YOU HOW

~~HHH HHH~~ I

When we return to our quarters, everyone places their forks on a nearby table. Trust has been established within our group that there is no fear of it being stolen. However, for Lou, Alex, and I fear still lingers. We know a punishment for what went down in the mess hall might come as we huddle close together. But when Bear enters, nothing happens. Nor is anything said about it. Instead, he gestures to his right.

"Take a seat over there. It's time to see who can fight and who needs work." He points at the two boys closest to him. "First one on his back, loses. The winner takes on the next one and so forth."

The two boys move to the middle of the room with their fists raised and, from what I've noticed, these two boys are friends. Close, like I am with Alex and Lou. I look over at their third friend and he's smiling like it's no big deal that his two friends are about to tussle. *Why? If it were me, I wouldn't be happy about raising my fists to Alex or Lou.* I turn my attention back to the center of the room and the first blow strikes. I wince as the blond stumbles backward with his mouth open, like he's in shock.

"Didn't know we be drawing blood," the blond says with a quick wipe at his bloody lip.

"He say first one on his back," the dark-headed boy grins and swings again.

He rapidly pops the blond in the nose three times. And I realize the blond has never been in a physical altercation before. He doesn't even know how to defend himself, and before the dark-headed boy can finish him, Bear calls, "Next." He points at Alex. "You're up."

"Against him?" Alex squeaks.

"Yes."

"Ya got this," Lou cheers.

"Right," Alex snorts, and steps forward, shaking his head. "I can tell ye right now, I be one of those that be needing help."

Ever since I could walk, my papa would spend every evening teaching me how to defend myself.

Not every gentleman is a gentleman; therefore, every lady should know how to defend herself.

After my lessons with Papa, I would race over to Lou's house with the same speech and teach her. And when Alex arrived, we taught him, and since our sentencing, we have done just that. Lou more than me and Alex, but all three of us have protected ourselves against vile men and selfish Forgotten in the mining caverns. And when you practice that much, you refine those skills. But I know Alex must continue to play his part, just like me, so he'll take the hits. He'll pretend like he's weak and not a threat to anyone.

"Everyone here needs improvement, but let's at least see how much you need."

"All of it. Ain't never been in a scrap before." He raises his fists. "Oh, wait." He looks over at me and Lou, pulling his thumbs out of his fists with another snicker, and a smile pulls at my lips. "I do member this part," and the room bellows with laughter.

"Don't be flat, I'll be easy on ya. Ya can even be having first swing. Right here," the dark-headed boy says, tapping at his cheek with a smug grin.

"Ye sure about that?" Alex grins.

"Yeah," the dark-headed boy says with another tap at his cheek. "Let's see what ya got."

Alex shrugs, then swings wildly out in front of him, and everyone grimaces as the dark-headed boy hobbles sideways, cupping his ear.

"Blimey! I thinks ye busted me hand," Alex hums, shaking his hand violently. Exactly like it was all those years ago when we taught him.

The dark-headed boy turns to Alex with a hard glare. "Yeah, well, now it be my turn."

Alex's eyes grow wide with fright, and he throws himself onto the floor. Flat on his back. "I give."

Bear shakes his head and then points behind me. "Next."

"Why me?" a lean boy asks. "That little shit just made him all kinds of heavy. I don't wanna be taking the heat."

"Then take him out first," Bear states.

"No way," the boy grouches, and I twist around, skimming the group. No one wants to go against him, but I could, and I can win too and apparently Lou thinks the same thing. At the same time, we both shoot our hands high in the air, but Bear doesn't pick me. He picks Lou.

"No dames," the dark-headed boy tells Lou.

"Excuse me?" Bear asks.

The dark-headed boy twists slightly, facing Bear. "Ain't nothing against her. She can be scrapin' someone else. I just don't scrap with dames."

Bear inches closer with his arms folded over his chest. "Refusing to fight her is the same as failing her. Out there, in war, she will go up against men twice your size. Now, you can help me by teaching her and the other females here on how to take on a man and fight like one, or you can ring out. The choice is yours."

The dark-headed boy looks back at Lou with annoyance and then waves her to him.

Lou stands and moves to the center of the room as Alex chuckles out, "Ye be in trouble now."

"No way a dame can be winning against my mate," his blond friend voices, holding a cloth against his nose.

"Wanna risk?" Alex asks with a playful grin.

"Yeah. If he wins, I be getting your pillow."

"Ye be on."

Lou rubs her palms together before planting her feet and waits for Bear to give the word to start. And when he does, the dark-headed boy swings a right hook, and she blocks it with her left forearm. He swings again, and she blocks that one and then the next. He's fast, but I know Lou and she's faster.

He kicks this time and, instead of blocking it, she grabs his ankle, pushing him backward. Now, it's her turn, and the adrenaline on her face races through my veins as if it were my own. She has the opening she needs. He stumbles backward with a wide swing, and she bends, ducking under his punch and jabs him in the gut. Then she lands a left hook and throws another punch to the gut with a clean and fast uppercut. His head rolls back, and he drops to his knees, dazed, but Lou catches him before he falls face forward and turns him onto his back.

"Told ye, Lou be a brutal scraper," Alex says with a grin.

"That may be, but let's see how you are against a bigger opponent," Bear says and calls on the biggest boy in our room. Hutch.

He steps forward and points at her with an easy grin. "Take it easy on us now. I ain't as good as ye."

"Don't fret, I'll pull my punches." She grins.

"Go," Bear tells them.

They circle each other with their fists raised, but neither making a move, and then Hutch smiles with a quick feign lunge. But Lou doesn't flinch; instead, she returns his smile and keeps her eyes on him. His open palm swings out, hard and fast, and she blocks the slap. When he does it again, Lou ducks and twists around, kicking her heel into the back of his knee. He buckles, and she jumps on his back, wrapping her arm around his neck and squeezes. Not hard, just enough to let him know he's lost.

Hutch snickers out, "Alright, dang." Lou releases him with a playful shove forward and Hutch falls on his hands. He looks over his shoulder with another chuckle. "It be like that, huh?"

"Yeah." Lou smiles and jumps on his back again, rolling him into a position that could break his arm. *When did they become friends like that?* I mean, I knew they were friends. I just didn't know they were friends like that. I thought Alex was the one close to Hutch.

"Alright, knock it off," Bear says at their tomfoolery, and Lou releases Hutch. "In the future, if your opponent has you in a hold that you cannot get out of. You may tap out with no repercussions. You will not fail. This is how we practice and how you learn. It's called 'sparring', and we will be sparring a lot during this phase."

The snitch shoots her hand in the air. "What is a tap out?"

Bear turns to Lou. "I want you to put me in the same choke hold you had him in." He kneels in front of her, and she eyes the back of his head with an evil grin, and a dropping sensation spins in my belly. He sure is putting a lot of trust in her, and I think if he truly knew her, he wouldn't. Especially when she wraps her arm around his neck with a satisfied grin. Alex straightens with concern because he knows what she can do and has done in the caverns. But the look he is giving her, she knows he is asking her not to and I hope for all of our sakes, she doesn't. At least not yet. Not until we know how to escape this place.

"If you break his neck, Pup, you will receive the same." I sit up straighter, leaning to my right as Yak strides closer, reinforcing Alex's plea. I focus back on Lou and her posture seems as if his threatening voice is nothing. Her lips curl as she pulls Bear closer and winks at Alex.

Bear taps her forearm. "Let go," Yak tells her, and Lou raises her hands with a small backward step. "Again," Yak orders, nudging Lou forward and she scratches at her cheek before pulling Bear toward her. This time, Bear taps her on the leg, and she lets go just as Yak steps around them. "It doesn't matter where you tap them, they should let go immediately." He turns his hard eyes on Lou. "You will let go immediately," he stresses, and then says to Bear, "I got it from here."

Bear jumps to his feet and begins for the door.

"And Bear?"

"Yes." He turns, thumbing his bottom lip like he is in deep thought.

"The next time this one wants to pull a stunt like that in the mess hall, stop her or it will be you that pays the price."

Bear rubs his jaw like he can already feel Yak's fist against it. And for a brief second, before he walks out the door, I thought I saw compassion in those pale gray eyes.

ABOVE ONE'S BEND

$$\cancel{||||}\ \cancel{||||}\ ||$$

The last few weeks have been grueling with all the sparring and strength training, and not to mention all the swimming lessons. But honestly, it isn't much different from the mining caverns. I still go to bed exhausted and sore all over, with someone shouting orders. The only difference is the healthy meals before each drill.

And with testing next week, I believe as long as we keep our heads down and do as we're told, we have a good chance of moving onto phase three. The sooner we get to whatever war they want to throw us in, the sooner we can escape. The only thing that worries me is Alex. He doesn't seem as determined to escape. Instead, he has spent all his free time with Hutch. And with each passing day, their bond is making it clear: he wants to stay.

I stand next to Alex, waiting for the door to open so we can go have breakfast. I hope I'm wrong about him. I don't want to risk my life fighting a war that has nothing to do with me, just to keep him safe. Even though I will. I just hate these people and everything they stand for. They are heartless and cruel. They say they are helping those that cannot help themselves, but they are no better than those they are at war against. Or they wouldn't be killing the failed Forgotten. Which, by the way, I don't understand why no one is scared of them like I am. Not even Lou is scared of them anymore.

The door opens and the second Lou and Alex are in the hallway, I quickly fall into step beside them. Most of the other Forgotten are still in the latrine, showering or dressing for the day. I peek up at Alex on our way to the mess hall with a quick glance over my shoulder. We are finally alone. This is the perfect time to ask if he has changed his mind. I start to reach for his arm and hear Hutch behind us.

"Hey, hold up," Hutch calls, and I drop my arm. No matter where we are or what we're doing, someone is always nearby. And if one leaves, another one seems to slip up from the shadows, like now.

"I heard a bunch of 'em are sneaking out tonight. Wanna join?" Hutch asks, running a hand through short auburn hair.

"How they gonna do that? The doors be locked at night," Lou scoffs. "Plus, ain't ya scared of failing?"

Alex turns, walking backward. "They ain't locked. I've sneaked out loads of times already. And they ain't gonna fail us. If they be, then Toggy and I would already be goners."

"Toggy?" Lou asks.

"Yeah, the Spoon," Hutch adds.

Wait. When did Alex and Hutch become friends with her. I mean, I know she follows us around, but I didn't know it was because they were friends with her. Furthermore, if Alex knows the doors aren't locked, why wouldn't he tell us? We could have escaped. I look over at Lou, and she isn't paying attention to me. Only Alex.

"Bear caught Toggs and us last week and all he says is get back to bed."

That's interesting. Why did Bear not fail Alex and Toggy, but he failed the others for a simple mistake or speaking out of turn? Could it be, to fail Alex, they would need to fail Toggy? I see the way all the trainers watch her. Probably to make sure their snitch is still okay.

We enter the noisy mess hall and Lou grabs a tray. "And how ya gonna get all us past Bear? Ya know he be watching us like a hawk."

Alex glances over his shoulder and then back. "Don't worry. Toggy's got that covered." He smiles. I look at Lou, rolling my eyes. Whatever this snitch has planned will probably land them in trouble. Perhaps this is her time to shine. To prove to the trainers she's a good snitch. I mean, she hasn't done anything yet, which is concerning in itself. What is she waiting for?

"Yeah, and how that be?" Lou asks.

Hutch reaches over me for his tray. "Ye shall see, Little Pup," he answers, wiggling his reddish-brown eyebrows. Hutch calling Lou, Pup, and Alex snorting with laughter only heightens my paranoia. With a deep inhale, I load my tray with sausage, eggs, a biscuit, and then grab a banana. And when I turn to our table, it isn't our normal group. It's a mix of all the rooms. Even the trainers have started sitting together at their own table.

"That's who we be meeting up with tonight," Hutch tells me before joining them at the table. *Why is he telling me this? I couldn't care less. Making new friends isn't high on my list.*

I sit at the edge of the table. My usual spot with Alex

beside me and Lou on the other side of him. The boy across from me smiles at Lou. He's big. Bigger than Hutch. He aims those hazel eyes at her and grins.

"I be hearing loads about ya," he says. "An' skinny be, ya be a brutal scraper."

I look over at the trainers' table, wondering which trainer he has.

"She be," Hutch replies with a mouthful. "Better than your bunk-face." He chuckles, and the table joins him in a hearty laugh.

"Is that so?" He grins, staring at Lou.

Now my annoyance has turned into anger. Everyone at this table is happy and excited to be here. Don't they realize we are no better than prisoners, where success means fighting in a war that will probably kill them. The Naturals chose us because they know no one will miss us or care that we have disappeared. There's no one out there searching for us.

Toggy's voice draws my eyes down the table, but I missed what she said, only that the boy in front of Alex is shaking his head and he's definitely not from our room. I might not know the names of everyone in our room, but I know their faces.

"Naw, I be talking about that one." He points his fork at Alex. "The skinny be." He digs into his food. "Ya be dead last in the ranks, and the only reason ya still be here is cos your group be protecting ya."

My eyes dart from Alex to the boy talking and, out of nowhere, Toggy's arm soars across the table so fast, I almost missed the fork jamming into the boy's hand. And if not for the ear-piercing scream slipping from the boy's mouth, I may have.

"Do you mean like that?" Toggy laughs and with a hard yank, she pulls her fork back.

The table barks with laughter and the boy jumps to his feet, holding his hand close to his chest. "Y'all's gonna be paying for this," he squeals, and then glares hard at Alex. "Specially, your bunk-face."

I glance over at the trainers' table, and they don't seem to even care what's happening over here. But then again, why would they? It isn't like they haven't hurt or killed their own share of Forgotten. A voice pulls my attention back to the table, and the bulky Forgotten in front of me is on his feet.

"Hey Caleb, at least we know that skinny be just, eh?" He sits back down, asking, "Tell me ya groups gonna be coming tonight."

"You know it," Toggy says, leaning across the table and stealing Caleb's banana.

Movement catches my eye, and Alex is on his feet, pointing his fork down the table. "Good on ya, Toggs. I be seeing ya down there."

And just like that, I have my answer. I grab my tray and walk over to the garbage cans. I know Alex better than I know myself. Alex will come to me, not anytime soon, mind you. But he'll come. Probably right before the last phase is over and he'll have a new plan. "A better plan," he'll say. One that will involve us in staying. Of course, Lou will join him. Ever since we were sentenced, those two have been thick as thieves. And the Naturals, they'll probably pretend to care, maybe even go as far as telling Alex he's part of their family. I toss my uneaten food along with my tray into the garbage can.

After all, if you don't want your captive running off or

turning on you, you must give them some sort of hope or offering. It's the same as the mining caverns; except there, the Forgotten sort of had a real chance. If they could survive the beatings and starvation, they could move up in the system after their sentence. One day, they could become what they hate and be on the other end of the leather strap. And what's a better offer than promising Alex a home. Something Lou and I could never truly give him. I start to leave the mess hall, but then turn back to the can, reaching inside for my uneaten banana before heading back to our quarters.

NO STRANGER TO YOU

~~HHH HHH~~ III

When everyone finally returns, Bear pairs us up for sparing exercises. It's one of my favorite things to do because they're only teaching me how to better defend myself against them. Not that it will matter now. I know how this will end. I glance over at Alex and Lou and swallow my hurt feelings. If I attack or escape, once we leave for their war, I will be alone in my actions. All I can do now is prepare for the biggest fight of our lives.

"Pup, you're with me today," Bear tells me, and I roll my eyes because he says it like I didn't already know that. For some reason, I've become his favorite pup to torment because he always has me paired with him. I never get to spar with the other Forgotten.

"Hey Hutch, first one to master it, wins," Lou says. Even though I'm cross with her at the moment, I can feel my lips tugging into a smile. Everything with her is a contest. It always has been.

"Yeah, and what will I be winning?" Hutch asks with a cocky grin.

"Nothing, now pay attention," Bear growls and steps onto the mat. "Today, you will learn the half-shoulder throw. I'll give a demonstration and then I want each of you to practice it." He beckons me forward and then tells me, "Throw a slow punch." I do, and he grabs my wrist, holding my arm out straight. If this were the mining caverns, I would know how to get out of this, but unfortunately it isn't, and I have to allow him to throw me.

"When your opponent strikes, block it and grab their wrist, like this, and then strike." He demonstrates, stepping close, almost sideways to me. He fakes an elbow to my ribs before pulling me onto his shoulder. "See how she is partly on my back? Now I can roll her off by twisting my upper body slightly." I hit the mat with a loud thud and his fist stops a hair away from my nose.

The first few times we spared, my instincts kicked in and I nearly broke his nose, a rib, and an arm. He had harsh words to say of course, but since, I've learned to hold back those instincts and not react every time we spar. Now that I think about it, perhaps that's why he is always picking me to spar with him. Maybe he's afraid those instincts will kick in and I'll hurt one of the other Forgotten. And knowing that shows how much the trainers don't know me or anyone here, really. For it isn't the Forgotten, I hate. Only the Naturals.

Bear straightens and then faces the group. "I want you to go slow and learn the technique first. Afterward, you can speed it up."

We practiced our combat moves for hours, and all through training, I couldn't help but wonder what I'm going to do about Alex and Lou. I can't force them to run with me and I can't leave them behind. Just the thought of it makes my chest tighten. I've never been without them. Even now, during our downtime, I feel completely isolated from them as they group up with Hutch and the other Forgotten. But I know they are still with me. I'm not alone. And since they are finding their footing with others, perhaps I should as well. I grab my water jug and walk over to Toggy.

"Hey," she says with a big smile.

I give a quick nod and slide down the wall to sit with her instead of finding a corner to sulk in. At least this way, I can keep a better eye on her. Perhaps, gain her trust and hopefully she'll slip up and reveal her true self.

At dinner, I pick at my food, trying to force myself to eat something, but my stomach is still in knots. Not because Alex and Lou want to stay, but because now they are putting themselves in danger for no real reason. Toggy told me everything and, according to her, I'm supposed to help her with the plan. Lou's suggestion, of course. I glance down the table, at everyone's excitement about sneaking out, and my gut is churning. Sneaking out is a bad idea. Even if they don't fail us, there are other punishments. Have they forgotten about all the punishments Lou has endured because she tried to save others that wanted extra food or tried to escape? Why can't they just behave and do as they're told?

Toggy stands and eyes me with a quick jerk of her head at the doorway and I push my chair out. I really don't want any part of this, but since they are dead set on going, I can't let them go alone. What if something terrible happens? I follow Toggy to the door, but before I cross through, I look over at the table where all the trainers are at. Bear is leaning toward Hyena in a hearty laugh. He looks happy. Almost approachable.

"Don't go soft on me now," Toggy puffs and yanks me through the doorway. But instead of guiding me to the right, into the trainers' quarters, she directs me back into ours. I follow her to the back wall, next to the latrine, and she stops near the water fountain.

"The trainers' rooms are locked, but check this out." She reaches behind the water fountain, and I have no idea what she did, but the water fountain moves toward me, along with part of the wall. I steal a step backward just as Toggy grabs my arm and pulls me inside a dark tunnel. "We could all sneak out this way, but I don't want anyone else to know about it." She grabs a small black cylinder off the wall and then reaches for the knob on the back of the water fountain.

Once the door is closed, the cylinder floods the secret tunnel with light, and I am completely flabbergasted. It works just like a lantern, but instead of lighting the wick, it brightens with the push of a button.

"Do you remember the first room we were in, and Bear pushed all of them buttons and things were revealed?" I pull my gaze off the closed door and follow. "Well, after that, I started searching the rooms, looking for buttons or something that looked out of place. I never found one in our last room, but this one . . . Look what I found." She disappears around the corner.

I look over my shoulder with my heart racing and quickly fall into step behind her. But when I turn right, I nearly run into her. She stopped at a fork in the tunnel. She swings the light to the right. "That way is the mess hall." She swings the light to the left. "That way is medical. It's where I lifted this," she says, holding up a vial and then shoves it back into her waistband. She swings the light back in front of her. "And this way is to the trainers' quarters." She starts forward, speaking fast and non-stop, but I'm not listening.

I have too many questions. With the first one being, how does she know all this? Especially about the vial. How did she know which vial to steal? But mostly, I just want to come out and ask her if she is one of them. If she is a Natural.

We reach the end of the tunnel, and she walks up to the wall in front of us. "Fingers crossed Alex was able to keep Bear distracted." She presses her ear against it. "It doesn't sound like anyone is in there."

As she pushes the door open, I turn, straining my ears behind me. There's a low vibrating sound coming from the darkness like metal being pounded into a blade. I wait a few seconds and, when I don't hear the noise again, I follow her. But she has moved farther inside, taking the light with her. I peer into the darkness and the hairs on the back of my neck rise at the warm air tickling my skin.

I cut my eyes over my shoulder with slow, cautious breaths and feel the same warm air brush my arm. My breath stops and I gulp a dry swallow, stretching a shaky hand behind me. My fingers pass through warm air and then cold air, like someone was standing right next to me. My muscles tense with alert movements as I back away from the source. I turn around and my heart slams against my chest at the glowing, feral eyes shimmering in the darkness. I hold my breath, watching them shimmer. The cat moves and the eyes disappear. I pat at my chest with a steady breath and the door behind me slams shut.

Toggy turns, nearly blinding me with the light. "Did you shut that?"

I lift a hand, shielding the light, and shake my head with wide eyes, wanting nothing more than to run. Something is wrong. I can feel in my bones.

"I did," a voice announces.

I squint and the gleaming white walls enhance the light. My first instinct is to run, but Bear and the blond trainer are blocking the doorway. And I can't go back the way I came; I would never find my way in the dark. Not without Toggy's help. After all, she is the one holding the light and knows the tunnels better than me. I look over at Toggy and she is standing between two beds pushed against the wall, frozen, with one hand reaching for something on a small stand with items on it. Crap.

I look back at Bear and my heart slams against my chest. He's staring right at me with his arms folded over his bulky chest, like he can't decide whether or not to fail me. *I knew it. Freaking snitch. I knew it was a trap. Why didn't I trust my gut?* Because I'm loyal and will do anything Lou and Alex ask of me. I inch backward and my thigh catches on another table with one of those black clock-like portraits on top it. I adjust my footing, slowly inching backward.

"What are you two doing in here?"

I swallow with unease as I continue farther away from the trainers. *Why aren't they failing us? What are they waiting for?*

"This," the blond replies, yanking the vial from Toggy's hand. "They were going to poison us."

Another step away from them, with Bear holding my

gaze. I'm going to have to take a chance in the tunnels. Light or not.

"No, just give you the runs," Toggy squeaks.

I reach behind me, and my fingers graze the secret door. All I need is another step, and I can bolt out of here before either of them can draw their pistols. *Just look away, Bear. Please.*

"Jesus, with this much you'd have blown our guts out," the blond sneers, and then cocks his head. "Where'd you even get this?"

My fingers fumble behind me, searching for the handle or whatever opens this door.

"I found it," Toggy mutters.

Bear marches toward me, and a river of sweat runs down my back. I turn and Bear grabs my arm, tight and forceful, and fear chokes the back of my throat. *Where is he taking me? To their leader?* My entire body goes numb; I don't even know how I'm still walking.

"Well, consider tomorrow your fun day because tomorrow is testing day," Bear says.

"What? I thought we still had another week?" Toggy complains, and I'm nearly shaking out of control.

Tears pool under my eyes. *Will I become another lesson?* My chin trembles uncontrollably and my vision blurs. *Will Alex and Lou know what happened to me? Will they even care?*

"Yeah? Well, you probably should have thought about that before you pulled this little stunt," Bear tells her. "Now, get out of here," he orders. He releases me, shoving us both forward, and a heaviness drops in my belly. *Why isn't he failing us? Me, most importantly.*

"Go on now," Bear orders.

I shuffle out of the room with my heart racing out of

control. If Alex is right and they won't fail anyone that's with her, then I should be careful during testing and not give him a reason to fail me tomorrow. But how? We step into the hallway and my muscles tense at the boy leaning against the wall. It's Caleb. The boy Toggy stabbed in the hand.

"You're going to pay for this, you little shit," Toggy tells him.

"Yeah, and what'cha gonna do about it, Spoon?" Caleb threatens, pushing off the wall and popping his knuckles. Before he can take another step closer, Toggy jabs two fingers in his throat. Caleb stumbles backward, holding the front of his neck, and my eyes widen in surprise. How does she know how to do that? Because, I know for certain, Bear hasn't taught us that. I mean, I knew from Papa, but how did she?

Bear and the blond rush out of the room at the loud gasping and Toggy moves closer, almost in front of me.

"What the hell happened?" Bear demands.

Toggy looks down at her nails like she has something stuck under the bed. "No idea," she shrugs, "he was like that when we came out."

"And you did nothing?" the blond hisses and then races down the hall.

"Oh, duh," Toggy says with a playful roll of her eyes, and then pats the boy on the shoulder. "There. There. You'll be alright."

Bear grabs the back of her shirt and tosses Toggy into me. "Get away from him, idiot."

Toggy rights herself with a lopsided grin. "Well, I'm no medic. What else am I supposed to do?"

"Go." Bear shoots a finger down the hall, at our quarters. "Now!" he says through his teeth.

My throat nearly closes at his tone. I've not seen him that cross with any of us before. Normally, he just pulls his pistol and kills what he thinks is the problem. I follow Toggy into our quarters and can't help but wonder if Toggy isn't as well liked by the Naturals as I thought. Perhaps we can use this to our advantage. After all, she hasn't done anything to hinder our goal. If anything, she has helped us significantly. Especially with this new information.

THE COST OF BAD BEHAVIOR

$\cancel{||||}\ \cancel{||||}\ ||||$

Today is testing day, and an ominous feeling crawls down my back as we shuffle inside a pitch-black room. Bear hasn't told us what to expect or even hinted at what the test will endure. However, if this test has anything to do with what we've learned so far, then I fear it might have something to do with physical altercations. Not that I'm scared we will lose. The three of us have grown in skills and have developed even more than before. What I'm scared of is Bear thinking I'm a problem.

The door slams shut behind us with a loud bang, and the silence that follows has an eerie stillness to it. I walk on my toes, searching for something, anything, but there's nothing to see; it's completely dark. I don't know how Bear even knows where he is going, but he continues forward, guiding us along like he's walked this path a hundred times.

Alex grabs a handful of my shirt and I reach behind, squeezing his wrist with reassurance as I follow close behind Hutch. A door opens on the other side of the room with light filtering behind moving shadows, and I instantly know it's another team. *Are we going to test our new skills against them?*

We come to a stop, and my mouth dries as the door slams shut with a deafening sound, and the shadows blend into the darkness. A light flickers and sizzles on, focused mainly above a large cage in the center of the room. The other team appears out of nowhere, jumping and climbing and shouting onto the cage with enthusiasm. I flinch with anger, but not because they scared me; although they did a little. It's because we are competing against the other groups. *How could I be so senseless? I should have known better.* Not only that, but this other group is acting as if they are excited and eager to do this. *Why? Do they not understand what is about to happen? That some of us, including them, may not be here tomorrow.*

Bear pulls me out of line and grabs my hand. "Forget about them and listen to me." He's wrapping a strange cloth around my knuckles. "Size matters. If they're bigger than you, bring them down fast. If they're smaller than you, stay on your feet and don't allow them behind you." He rips the cloth with his teeth and then starts wrapping my other hand.

Crap! Am I going first? Why? Bear peeks up at me from his work and grins, and my heart drops. This is my payback. This is how he will fail me. I wet my lips, skimming our group, and Toggy is heading toward us.

"Are you listening to me," Bear asks, and I look back at him with a nod. "There's only one rule. One I cannot bend, so do whatever you must, but do not lose. If you—"

Toggy leans close to my ear, interrupting Bear, and I missed what the one rule is. "There's no rule against going twice," she says with a quick glance over at Alex. "If we work together, we can dominate. Take as many rounds as you can."

My mouth parts at what she's asking of me. I'm not Lou. I'm not the best brawler. Bear rips the cloth on my other hand and then hands me one of the mouth guards we use in training. I'm not saying I wouldn't give my life for Alex. I would. A hundred times over, but why is it on me? Lou is the better brawler. It should be her. I search for Lou and Bear grips my arm, shoving me inside the cage, and animal noises roar above me.

I look up, and my pulse races at the massive group of Naturals leaning over a railing. Each one releasing what I assume is their animal voice. From growling, roaring, and grunting to high-pitched squawks and hisses. *Why hadn't I seen them when we entered? Or heard them before now? And where have they been this entire time?* There must be at least fifty of them, if not more. This place must be a lot bigger than I thought. I pull my gaze off the Naturals and look over at the other team. The Naturals must be here to watch us fail or succeed, and knowing that makes my belly sick. *How can they be so vile and heartless to use this as some sort of entertainment?*

A tall, lean girl with dark hair enters. She balls her hands into fists and muscles ripple along her forearms as she moves along the mat, slow and cautious. I shove my mouth guard in and plant my feet with a thick swallow. I don't want to hurt her, or any of them for that matter, but I also don't want to die.

She stops a few feet in front of me, bouncing on her toes with a cruel smile, and waves me to her. Instead of lunging or swinging, I remain like a statue and wait for her to come to me. "Clobber her!" someone shouts, and just like that, she draws her fist back. I duck and thrust my fist out, crashing into her belly. I land an uppercut and then a left hook, and the crowd above goes wild. She stretches her eyes, dazed, and, with no hesitation, I slam my foot into her middle. She clutches at her belly with a gasp and falls onto her rear, slamming her head onto the mat. I've won.

"Finish her!" a voice roars behind me, and I look over my shoulder. Bear is pacing outside the cage, shouting at me. "These aren't training rules, Pup. You must force her to give, or you are the one that fails," he stresses.

My stomach leaps into my throat with my pulse racing. *Is that the rule he could not bend? How can they force us against each other like this? It's inhumane.* I look back over at the girl on the mat and she's swaying, forcing herself back up. I don't want to hurt her. I turn back to Bear with my eyes pleading: Please don't make me do this.

"Finish her!" He settles his palm on his pistol and my ears ring with fear. I don't want to die. He yanks the pistol from its holster and aims it right at me. "Now!"

I ball my hands and turn back to my opponent, and all the rage I've pushed down for years finally explodes. I rush forward, diving into her, forcing her back onto the mat as I straddle her chest. My fists strike hard and fast as blood spurts from her nose and mouth and cheeks. I don't even see her anymore. All I see is my last warden, and then I hear Bear in my ear. "Stop! It's over."

I force a dry swallow and I have no idea how I ended up on the other side of the mat. Nor did I feel Bear pull me off her, but his arms are wrapped around me in a tight hold. "It's okay. You did as I told you. You did good."

I gulp for air as the crowd above cheers with more excitement and then look back at the girl lying motionless across from me. Two young Naturals enter and carry the girl out as another one hurries inside with a cloth. My chest vibrates in pain and sorrow as I watch the Natural cleaning blood off the mat. I went too far. *Did she tap out? Did she give?* I don't even have time to absorb what happened or what I've done before another opponent enters the cage.

I follow Bear toward the door, wiping my wet cheeks, and see blood smeared on my fingertips. *Is that mine or hers?* I stop at the exit and Bear motions for Alex. "Alright, Pup, you're up next."

Lou reaches through the cage, grabbing my wrist with her eyes wide and frightful. "We can't let him in there. He might not be as small as he was, but he's still smaller than the rest of us. They will destroy him. You have to go again." She squeezes my wrist until it hurts. "I ain't asking, Mute. I'm telling ya. You gotta go again."

With a deep, heavy sigh, I slam the door shut behind Bear and face my next opponent. But before the match begins, the other team's trainer enters, marching right at me. It's the one that chased Lou in the mess hall, Hyena, and an emptiness drops in my belly.

"You already won. Get out!" he demands.

"Let her fight!"

I glance up and it's their leader. *Where did he come from?*

"But she's already fought. There are rules against this."

"Just because no one ever has, doesn't mean it's a rule," Yak states.

Hyena turns to his recruit. "End her," he orders with a finger pointed at me.

The boy steps forward with his lips mashed together and I can see he's scared, but so am I. I just can't allow mine to show, nor can I lose control again. I plant my feet like before and wait. But he doesn't swing or come at me;

instead, he begins to circle me. I keep steady, only moving when he does. I can't let him get behind me.

"Swing!" someone shouts, and his eyes flicker upward. When he faces me again, his Adam's apple shoots down in a hard swallow. He's not just scared, he's terrified. Although my heart breaks for him, I can't let my emotions swim to the surface, or I will die. It's me or him. I lunge forward, and he stumbles backward with a whimper. I attack again, and he runs away from me. I turn, and he starts running around the cage in terror every time I try to attack.

"Fail!" Yak calls. I don't have time to respond or even move. His pistol pops and the boy staggers slightly, like he doesn't know what happened. But he must because he pinches a small needle embedded in his thigh. *What the heck is that? That is the strangest bullet I've ever seen. Furthermore, how was he able to pinch it out with ease?*

The boy shakes his head, muttering, "No," and then falls face first into the mat.

I glance up at the leader and then back at the boy on the mat. How does a small needle like that kill someone? I inch closer, scrutinizing the boy's trembling form, and Yak demands, "Next!"

A younger Naturals pulls me away as two Naturals pick up the boy's body. I cock my head, watching the scene, and my mouth parts. *Why is there no blood?* My brows pinch. *Was there blood when the others failed?* I cup my head with my mouth wide open. I don't think that kills them. I look over my shoulder at Lou and Alex, wanting to tell them. Or, at the very least, ask if they knew this already, but I hear the door open, and Hyena is pushing another recruit in.

I start for the exit and Lou holds the door shut. I shake my head, moving closer, and she points at the boy behind me. *I don't want to do this. Why is she asking me to? Alex is nearly as good as us.* I close my eyes with my chin trembling because she knows I will. The last time I refused her request, she was thrown into the punishing box. Ever since, I've always done what she asked of me because, deep down, I've never forgiven myself for what happened.

I take on three more opponents and before the sixth one can enter, Bear is calling me to him. I start forward, nearly drained, and I reach the door. I peek up at Lou and she shakes her head at me, and I stop.

"Don't be a dumbass. Look at that hoss. He's nearly three times your size," Bear grouches.

I peek over my shoulder and it's the boy everyone wanted to sneak out with, Jack. Hyena hands him something before shoving him inside the cage.

"Hey." I turn back to Bear. "Let someone else take him. Someone that matches his size and strength," Bear yanks Toggy to him.

"No," Lou states. "Mute can take him."

I look over at her and my heart breaks. *Why does she want me to keep going? Is she so close with the others that she wants them here instead of me?* Lou slams the door shut and something hard crashes into my back, dropping me. I stagger on my hands and knees and a foot swiftly connects with my belly, slightly lifting me upward. I roll onto my back with my vision blurred and my lungs gasping for air. I cannot catch a proper breath.

With a desperate inhale, I stretch my eyes and a fist is soaring toward me. I twist to the right and his fist connects with the mat. He tries again and I twist to the left, but this time, I wasn't fast enough. His knuckles nick the side of my temple and my head spins. I shake my vision clear and kick him between the legs, and pain sears through me like every bone in my foot is shattered.

He swings on me again and, before he can make contact, I scramble painfully out of the way. I hop on my left foot with a quick glance down and the top of my foot is split open, with blood spilling out. *Is he wearing a steel plate in his long johns?* He grunts, and I look up just in time to see him barreling at me. I pivot on my good foot, swinging my damaged foot out, colliding into his shins, and it takes everything I have not to buckle in agony.

He falls into the cage, and I know this is my chance. I push through the pain and rush forward. I know I only have a few seconds, but I need to do as much damage as I can. I punch him in the lower back, swinging left and then right, over and over as fast and as hard as I can, and then something hard strikes me in the nose.

A loud pop rings in my ears. With my eyes watering, I stumble backward, trying to shake my vision clear, but I can't. Blood is pouring from my nose and my vision is blurred yet again. Before I can stabilize myself, pain shoots through my nose with my head snapping back and my knees buckle. I'm back on hands and knees, swaying, as his foot slams into my belly again. I roll onto my side, clutching myself with my nose, screaming a song with my lungs.

I can hear the others yelling, but my brain is like seaweed wrapped around coral and I can't untangle what they're saying. All I see is a blur moving toward me. I can't let him on top of me, or I'm done. I roll to my side, trying to crawl away, but his foot slams into my back, flattening me, and I choke down another sob. He rolls me on my back and squats next to me. "Do ya give?" he asks, and the room falls silent with everyone eager for my answer.

My stomach hardens with nausea, and I stretch my eyes, clearing my vision. Above me, Yak has his pistol aimed right at me and I react. I swing my legs up and out, wrapping them around the boy's neck. He's cursing and grunting, trying to free himself, but the only thing he can punch is the lower part of me, and he is. However, I'm still at a disadvantage. The mat is under me, blocking my elbow, so I have no way of gaining power behind my punches. The only thing I can do is the one move Papa told me to never use unless my life is in danger and I am willing to live with the consequences. The same move Lou has used in the mining caverns.

Another blow hits my side and I know he's cracked a rib if not broken it. I can't take much more, or he'll be the one that kills me. I cup his jaw with my left hand, and with my right fist, I punch the back of my left hand. Before I can do it again and break his hold on me, or worse, his neck, Yak's voice fills the room.

"Fail!" I hear that gut-wrenching sound of glass shattering and I lift my eyes. Yak is holstering his pistol. *Which one of us did he fail?*

I unwrap my legs, scooting away as the boy takes a backward step. We both stare at each other, not knowing which one just failed. It can't be me. I don't feel anything, and then, out of nowhere, my body tightens with a hot searing pain rippling along my skin.

BEFORE WE FALL

卌 卌 卌

The stench of disinfectant is strong, as cold air assaults my nostrils. I shift with my eyes fluttering open and there's something on my nose. I lift my arm to pull it off and a warm palm wraps around my wrist, stopping me.

"Take it easy," Yak says with a gentle hold on my wrist.

My muscles stiffen and when I face him, I know he feels it because he quickly releases my wrist. He faces a tall, thin pole next to me and hooks a clear pouch to it. He squeezes the middle and tiny pellets appear, sinking to the bottom. They look just like the ones my papa used to use as ammo for his rifle. I reach over and grab hold of the small clear tube embedded in my arm, following it up to the pouch, and one of those small pellets drops into the tube. The pellet unfolds like it's stretching awake from a deep slumber and starts crawling along the tube. I quickly sit up, stretching my eyes wider, wondering if I'm hallucinating.

"Careful, you just woke up and you aren't healed all the way. But after this one, you'll be free to go."

I clean the sleep from my eyes and focus on the clear fluid inside it.

Yak eyes me. "How are feeling?"

I point at my forehead with a grimace. I have a headache, but everything else feels fine, like I was never in a physical altercation. My knuckles aren't sore, and my ribs and face aren't in pain, or feel swollen, either. I lift the sheet and look at my foot where I felt the skin split open, but there isn't a wound. Not even a trace of a scar. I glance over at the clear liquid. *What kind of medicine is that?*

As if reading my mind, Yak replies, "They're called 'Nanos'." He drops a nearly empty pouch onto the bed and I reach for it, inspecting the few pellets left inside it. "I'm surprised you're taking it so well. The first time I saw them, I freaked out," he smiles, "but they aren't harmful. It's what helps you heal faster." He works on the contraption next to me and I look out the open doorway as Bear stutters to a stop. He pivots and turns to me, and he has a swollen lip like he's been in a scrap, too.

"Hey, you're awake." He walks in and stops at the end of the bed, squeezing my toes like we are old friends, and I pull my knees into my chest. "It's good to have you back. I can't wait to see what you can do in phase three."

"We all are," Yak says, reaching for the empty pouch. And I can tell he's mindful not to touch me as he takes it from me.

"Yak." I look around Bear and the blond trainer is holding onto the doorframe, leaning inside. And he, too, looks like he's been in a scrap. He has redness around his left eye. "Alex is having a conniption. Can him and the others come in yet?"

Yak eyes me again as if asking for my permission, and I nod.

"Yes, they may come in."

"Thank God. That little shit is hard to handle." The blond trainer steps back and looks down the hall, whistling. Seconds later, I hear squeaking coming from down the hall. Alex stops in front of the blond and the blond gestures dramatically into the room. "You're welcome," he says sarcastically.

"I'll come back for you in about an hour," Yak says, turning for the door. "The rest of you, five minutes," he tells Alex and the others. Bear follows Yak out as Alex, Hutch, and Lou move closer to the bed.

"Hey." Lou reaches for my hand. "Thanks for helping today. I wasn't trying to be mean or anything, but I knew you could do it. You're stronger than ya think," she says, squeezing my hand.

Before I can nod or smile back, my body is jostled as Alex jumps onto the bed, drawing my attention to him. "Ye got yer bell rung real good. Between ye and Toggs, the rest of us didn't get to be showing off our new skills," he says, with his small fists swinging out in front of him. "Ye two clobbered everyone."

"And the other trainer, Hyena, he be super heavy cos he be losing his whole group except Jack. The one ye be scraping before they shoot ye," Hutch says with a wide smile, standing next to Lou. "But the best part be when all the Naturals watching above, jumped down an' blocked the younger Naturals from carrying ye out. They not let Yak fail ye. There be a big claim 'bout it, too. But Yak say he ain't failing ye, only stopping ye from ending Jack." Hutch leans closer, cupping his mouth with the back of his hand. "But what be edgy is Bear say we ain't got enough recruits and they gonna combine 'em." He looks over his shoulder and then back. "Hyena's gonna be part of our trainin' now." He straightens with a grim face.

"He be worse than Bear," Lou agrees with a long face.

"Ye tellin' us," Hutch grouches.

Interesting. It sure seems like a lot happened while I was out. How long was it? I look over at Lou and Yak enters back into the room. "Alright, everyone out," he says.

"What? It ain't be no five minutes, it be like," Alex looks at Lou, "how many be little?"

"Two." She grins.

"It be like two minutes."

"Nonetheless, you should get back to your quarters. Bear and Hyena are waiting for you."

"Dang it," Alex moans. He slides off the bed and then turns to me, hesitating. He looks like he wants to tell me something but is mindful of the others. He cuts his eyes at Yak and then back at me, wetting his lips. "Hurry back, yeah?"

I give a slight nod and settle back on the pillow as Hutch gives me the same look. *What the heck happened while I was out? Why do they look worried?* I start to reach for Lou, but she moves away from me, following the others.

Once Yak releases me from medical, I start back to our quarters, feeling better than before the test. My eyes are brighter, fully awake, and there's almost a bounce to my steps. I feel like I could take on the world. Whatever was in those pouches doubled my energy. I step inside our quarters, and everyone rushes me, talking non-stop and all at once, that I only heard a few words jumbled together into one sentence. I shake my head, mentally trying to piece them together, and Bear enters behind me.

"Alright, calm down. Let her breathe a minute before we start the next phase."

I turn around and he's smiling. It's the first time I've seen him genuinely smile at us and I notice he has a small dimple on his left cheek. "You did good today. I am proud to have you on my team. Hoorah!"

My throat tightens with a mix of emotions. I'm happy I was able to do something good for our group, but cross with myself because Bear saw me. I don't want to stand out. It's why I've kept to myself. Even when I am around the other Forgotten, I don't join them in games of rock-paper-scissors like Alex does. Nor do I do my morning exercises with anyone like Lou does. I keep to myself, hoping no one sees me, including Bear. And I thought no one had. But now, the way he's looking at me, I know he sees me. And that alone is terrifying. *Will he use me not just as a soldier, but the first one on the field? Will I be the first to die in their war?*

"Is everyone ready to begin the next phase?" Bear asks.

"Hoorah!" everyone cheers loudly, and I press my finger into my lips.

I follow behind Lou and my heart races as Bear escorts us to another room, one that is completely empty. After he tells us to stand against the wall, he disappears through the door at the opposite end of the room. I glance past Alex over to Lou with this dreadful feeling like I've been here before. And not just on the first day we arrived. But this exact moment with the same frightening fear, and my bracelet vibrates out of control. I turn my attention to the floor turning upside down with beds rising out of the flooring. They look like the ones we woke up from when they fixed our teeth. I wipe beads of sweat from my forehead with this awful feeling that something bad is about to happen. I'm going to be sick.

"Hey, ye be right?" Alex asks Lou.

I look to my left, and her face is etched with fear. She opens her mouth, but before she can answer him, Bear walks back into the room. "Eyes on me!" He's wearing a black scarf wrapped around the lower part of his face and striding toward us like he means us harm. *Why?*

"This time, we do it the easy way." He draws his hand back, tossing a small blue ball right at us. It bounces near our feet, and with each leap, purple smoke billows out of it. Within seconds, the room is clouded with purple smoke and the sound of terror is loud and clear. Screaming. Crying. Hands jabbing through the haze, grabbing onto whatever they can and clawing for help. And then everything slowly dies to a shrill, rapid breathing. I lean against the wall, stretching my vision clear. *What is happening to me? To us?* Everyone is dropping against one another in a heap.

The energy I had before is draining like someone is sucking the life force out of me. Lou falls next to Hutch and my heart leaps into my throat. I brace my hand on the wall, trying to reach her, but my knees are weakening. I will myself to stand, but all I manage to do is stagger against the wall, slowly sliding. Alex falls next to Lou with his arm stretched to her, but she's already out. I stumble toward him, trying to reach him as I know Lou can't, but instead of grabbing hold of his hand and reassuring him, he isn't alone. I fall nearly on top of him, and darkness consumes me.

AMONG THE WILLOWS

HHH HHH HHH I

I force my groggy eyes open and lift onto my elbow. This is the second time I have woken up in these strange beds and have not know how I got here. The last thing I remember is waking up in medical with a voice talking, but who? And what were they saying. I squeeze my eyes tighter and sit all the way up. Wait. Yak was there. He was explaining something to me, but what? It seemed very important. I cup my head, trying to clear the confusion, and then I remember. That's right. Nanos.

"Take it easy." I open my eyes and there's a teenage girl, maybe fourteen, standing in front of me. She lifts my arm, trying to help me get off the bed. "Go slow," she says.

I give a slight nod, scooting to the edge of the bed, and my muscles are fatigued like I've been doing hard labor all night. When I stand, my entire body screams like a thousand needles are assaulting my muscles awake. *What is wrong with me? Why am I in pain? Is this from the Nanos?*

No. It can't be. I remember leaving medical, but that's it. Something else must have happened.

"The effects from the procedure will wear off in a couple of hours. Until then, let's get you to your quarters so you can rest and let your body fully heal," she tells me.

Procedure? What does that mean? I look to my right, and Hutch is being helped by another Natural, too. I instantly turn my head, searching for Lou and Alex. When I find them among the other recruits, I inhale a deep, relaxing breath. Lou is flat on her back, still asleep, and Alex is just now waking up, like me.

"I know this is painful, but we'll be in your quarters in no time," the girl says with another kind smile.

We slowly walk to the closet that moves from level to level, wincing at every step. And once we are on the level she chose, she guides me down another long hallway, and my heart drops into my belly. There's only one trainer here; Hyena. I search behind me, hoping to find Bear nearby, but my caretaker hands me off to him. And, to my surprise, instead of growling at me or accusing me of how I shouldn't be here, he smiles at me. However, knowing the Naturals and how cruel they are, especially him, I'm not sure if his smile is genuine or a threat. Plus, with him being one of our trainers now, I worry about passing this phase. I can't show any weakness. Not around him. I straighten my shoulders, wincing silently, as he helps me inside our new quarters.

"This is where you will be staying for the next phase," he says with another smile.

But I ignore him and take in the small area, and from the looks of it, we are no longer sharing quarters. I know I should be happy, thankful even, but not knowing how Alex and Lou are faring or a way to help, if needed, replaces any kind of gratitude with anxiety.

As I'm scanning my new quarters, from the small bed against the navy-blue walls to the shower and sink across from the bed, my pulse races. If we have our own room and latrines, then that means not many passed the last phase. I start to face forward and trip over a bag on the floor. I fall onto the bed, hanging halfway off the side with pain slicing down my legs, and Hyena curses. He bends, offering me his hand, but I refuse his help by throwing his arm off me. If I can't do this myself, he might fail me. This might be another test.

"Don't be stupid. I know how much pain you're in. I've been there. Let me help you," he grouches, but I push him away again, gripping the blanket, and power through the sharp, stabbing pain. Except, all I manage to do is slide farther off the bed.

"Fine. Stay on the damn floor for all I care," he grumbles, and the door slams shut behind me.

I struggle to pull myself onto the bed once more, but the muffled voices outside the door have my head whipping around.

"You weren't in there very long. Did you even tell her what happened?"

"She wouldn't even let me help her off the floor. How am I going to explain that her body was modified?"

Modified. What does that mean? Is that what's wrong with me? I twist around on the floor and quickly start inspecting myself. But I don't see any indication that I have even had a procedure. Not like my teeth. At least then I knew something had been done. But this, there isn't even a mark on me. *How will I know what they did if I cannot see it?*

Thankfully, Bear has been my caretaker for the last few days. In fact, he's the only person I have seen. And when he isn't assisting me with my daily walks down the hallway, in regaining my strength, he is rocking on the hind legs of a chair, braiding three strands of rawhide. The only time he leaves is when I need to use the toilet or he's getting food. Even then, he brings two trays and eats with me.

At first, just the sight of him annoyed me, but now, in the last two days, he seems like a different person. When he leaves for food, he returns with messages from the others. And that alone I am grateful for, so I've been cordial with him. In return, he isn't shouting and demanding orders from me. Instead, he jokes and laughs, and when he's not braiding his rawhide or reading to me, he teaches me how to play cards and chess. All the while, he tells me stories of his time here.

Like how we share the same experience. He, too, was apprehensive of the Naturals when he first arrived. To the bonds he formed within his group and how his group was nothing like ours. His group didn't work together as one. They had smaller groups within their rooms, but each small group snitched or sabotaged the others, desperate for that spot to become a Natural. He even admitted how he used to stay awake at night, forming escape plans and when to strike. And I can't help but be drawn in like I finally found someone other than Lou and Alex that truly understands me. Not that I could talk to him, but at least he is different with me now. Cautious and considerate when speaking to me.

And now, without the demanding phases, I can feel that

sense of normalcy the others feel. Perhaps Ford was right, and these people aren't bad. Maybe they aren't the enemy, after all. They are feeding us and giving us a warm place to sleep with luxury items. They've even helped with our illnesses. But most importantly, I don't think that pistol kills. I don't know what happens to the failed Forgotten when they drag them away, but hopefully they are still alive, wherever they are.

The doorknob turns and I straighten on the bed, smoothing my bangs out of my eyes, eager for another game of chess. Except it isn't Bear that enters, it's Hyena. He slides a tray of food onto the bed.

"Today is a big day, Pup. Try and eat as much as you can, okay?" He turns to leave, and he starts to shut the door, but then pushes it wide open before walking out. I quickly push to my feet, peeking outside, and to my left, I see Alex doing the same.

"Ye right?" he asks, and I give a quick and happy nod at seeing him.

"Hey," I hear Lou say. On my right, she's looking outside her room like us. "Does this mean we be free to roam?"

Alex shrugs just as Bear steps into my view. "Are you feeling okay? Do you need something?" I shake my head, inching backward, and he adds, "You don't have to stay in your room. You can go eat with your friends." He turns his head, snapping his fingers at someone down the hallway, and then turns back to me. "Just make sure you're dressed and ready when I come back for you."

Before I can turn and reach for my tray, Alex, Lou, and Hutch are pushing by Bear and entering my room. Even Toggy joins us. We sit in a circle, eating and laughing, while Alex exaggerates his recuperating time with Hyena, that by the time we have to get ready for testing, I no longer have the urgency to run. I'm starting to feel more like the others than a prisoner. *Safe.*

I dress in the same athletic gear we've been wearing in all the phases, except now the color is brown instead of blue. I sit on the edge of the bed, and just as I'm pushing my feet into my shoes, Bear pokes his head inside the doorway with an easy grin.

"Are you ready?" he asks me.

I give a quick nod.

"Good." He smiles and throws a thumb over his shoulder. "I need you to join everyone in the hall and stand at attention, okay?"

I nod again, and he disappears around the corner. I step into the hall and squeeze into line with the others. Lou is behind me with Toggy in front.

"Hey, Mute." I look over my shoulder, and Hutch is behind Lou, leaning over her shoulder. "Ye be looking clear. And ye never look clear." He looks over his shoulder and then back at me with a wide grin. "What'cha got cookin'? I wants in."

Alex is behind Hutch and leans to his left, imitating Bear's voice. "Pay attention, Pup," and he playfully pushes Hutch forward and Hutch stumbles into Lou.

Lou turns with a lopsided grin. "Ya be trying to start something, Pup? Cos I be finishing it," she says in the same imitating voice. She pushes Hutch, and he stumbles backward into Alex.

"Ye two be making me heavy. Knock it off," Hutch bellyaches.

Lou turns all the way around. "Yeah? And what'cha gonna be doing about it," she threatens with another playful shove.

"Nothing," Alex laughs, shoving him forward.

It's the same playfulness we had in my room minutes ago, and my guard slips even lower. *Is this how the others have felt this entire time? Is this why no one was ever scared of them? And perhaps why there was so much silliness happening?*

Before Lou can push Hutch again, Bear steps out of a doorway with Jack. "Hey, knock it off or I'll come over there and finish it," he growls, and they immediately stop their tomfoolery with hushed snickers as Jack goes to the end of the line.

We follow Bear into what I assume will be our new training room. However, as we enter, the laughter stops at once. Above us, to the left, is a ledge with some kind of platform and all the Naturals, maybe fifty of them, are crowded on something similar to a wide staircase.

"This be offbeat, yeah?" Hutch voices.

"Yeah, whatever's about to happen, they've all come to watch," Lou says. "Which means this ain't gonna be good. The last time they came, it didn't end well for the other teams. An', from the looks of it, we all be one team now," she adds, and I can feel myself shrinking back into my shell.

A TERROR-FILLED MOMENT

//// //// //// //

I follow behind Toggy and see Yak at the front of the room. He signals for us to stop and form a row. And as everyone is shifting into place, I look to my left. Under the platform the Naturals are on, are three orange objects scattered on the hardwood floor. Behind Yak is a tall, thin pole with an "X" painted under it. To our right are numbers shown on the floor and they're spaced apart. One through fifteen. I look over my shoulder, and near the door we came in are two really long, white lines marked on the floor. I turn back to Yak, and he folds his arms over his chest and addresses us.

"Last week, each of you went through a painful procedure that should have turned you into the perfect soldier. If the procedure was successful, you will be as silent as a panther with the speed and reflexes of a cheetah. However, sometimes the procedure doesn't take as it should, and you may only have a portion of it. And that is why we are here today. To test your skills and see if you are 100 percent

Natural. The test you will perform today is called 'Combine Drills'." He lifts his chin. "There are four stations. Once you—"

Alex raises his hand, and Yak motions for him to lower it. "No, you will not know if you have passed or failed until the end. Please do not ask after each station. And yes, if you are not 100 percent Natural, you will fail." He gestures at the orange objects. "Now, please line up behind Hyena and Fox, and we will begin."

I follow behind Toggy, making a mental note. The blond one's name is Fox.

"Hey Fox, do you know why they're here?" Hyena asks with a thumb aimed over his shoulder, pointing at the Naturals gathered above us on the platform. He moves closer to Fox. "I mean, they never come to this test." He glances over his shoulder and then back. "They're watching us like we've done something wrong."

I cut my eyes over to Bear. He's standing at one of the tests and from the looks of it, he's just as curious as Hyena. I turn my gaze back to Hyena and press my fingers into my lips. *If he's on edge about this, then what's about to happen? Why are they here?*

"Well, I haven't done anything wrong," Fox says. He looks over his shoulder at the cluster of Naturals and then back at Hyena. "Maybe it's you they're after. You did finish the last phase with only one recruit," he says, and I can hear the jesting in his tone. Fox turns his attention onto us, clearing the happiness from his throat. "This is called a '3-Cone Drill'. It's a test to see how well you can pivot. Hyena will give you a demonstration, and then each of you will go one at a time. Let's get started."

Fox faces Hyena, who is next to a cone, and when he clicks a small metal device in his hand, calling, "Go," Hyena bolts forward. He bends next to the second cone, touching the ground, and then sprints back to us. He turns and does it again, but this time he doesn't stop at the second cone. He touches the ground at the third cone, racing back toward us. On his third time around the cones, he performs the same tasks, but does it running backward. When he finishes, Fox clicks the object in his hand and peers up at Hyena. "Are you sure you passed the first time?"

Hyena adjusts his strange cap with a grin. "Yes, and I believe your old man said I even beat your score."

"You mean, he felt sorry for your slow ass." Fox grins, and my heart skips a beat. *Old man. Is Fox not a Forgotten? Was he born here?* I look over a Bear. No, they can't all be born here. Unless he was lying to me about those stories he told me. Which is possible, but then I remember the trainer that Yak shot on our first day here. The one with the scar on his face, the Wolfman, and I don't believe all of them are. I wonder what happened to him. *If they aren't killing them, where did they take him?*

"Hurtful," Hyena chuckles and taps on his bulky bracelet. "Alright, Toggs, you're up first."

Toggy moves forward and my eyes widen slightly. She isn't a Spoon turned Forgotten. She's from here. It all makes sense now. How she knows so much about this place. The tunnels and the tests. Maybe she really isn't a snitch. I mean, she hasn't done anything to prove she is.

I look at Lou and she's pulling on her bottom lip, staring at the back of Toggy's head. "Yeah, I see it too," she says. She leans closer and whispers into my ear, "But just cos she ain't a snitch, don't mean she ain't still dangerous."

Hyena calls Hutch forward, and Lou straightens as we both pay attention. Hutch steps up to the line and just as he bends, readying himself, Fox clicks his device, and he's just as fast as Toggy. Maybe faster than Hyena. When he comes to a stop, Fox must think so too because he shows Hyena his time.

"This is how you beat my record."

Hyena taps on his bracelet with a grunt and then calls on me. I step forward, peeking up at the Naturals, and a nervousness crawls along my skin as they lean over the railing to watch. I wish I knew why they're here.

"Ready?" Fox asks.

I pull my gaze off the Naturals, shaking the tension from my arms, and notice the Naturals above me aren't whispering anymore. Their attention is focused mainly on me. *Why? I'm not the best recruit here. Lou and Hutch are.*

"Go."

I bolt forward, and after I have raced around all three cones, I move to the next test with slow, cautious steps. As fast and flexible as I was, I do believe I have the modification. I peek up at the Naturals and thankfully they aren't watching me anymore. Their attention is on Alex now.

My next test is with a trainer I've not had any interactions with until now. Thankfully. It's the one that pulled my hair and asked if I could learn when we first arrived. I don't even remember what his name is. And he looks a lot younger than I first thought. Maybe fifteen with dark, nearly black hair. I stand beside him as he taps on his bracelet, and I notice I'm taller than him now. I wonder if he remembers me. He looks up from his bracelet, locking those intense brown eyes onto me, and smiles. I don't think he does.

"This is called a 'vertical jump'." He gives me a demonstration, and he jumps so high, it seems impossible for me to match that. He steps to the side, tapping something on the back of the tall pole, and the tiny slates he moved mid-jump shifts back in place.

"Ready?"

I give a slight nod and step onto the "X" painted on the floor before pushing off on my toes. My hand hits above his mark and I land silently with a satisfied grin. *Wow. Whatever modifications they gave us are extraordinary. There isn't anything I can't do now.* A smile builds as I move to my next test and stop next to Bear. I could even take Bear out if I needed to. I bounce on my toes, waiting for him to notice me, but he isn't paying me any mind. He's tapping on his bracelet. I look over my shoulder, and Alex lands on his feet with a proud grin, turning to the trainer I was just with. "Boorah!"

"It's hoorah," the trainer corrects with a chuckle.

Alex skips toward me, making an ugly face, and I can't help but return it.

"Focus," Bear hisses and flicks me hard against my temple. I mouth, "Owe" and touch the sore spot and watch as he gives me a demonstration. When he moves out of the way, I step into his place and jump forward from a standing position, landing at the number "15" marked on the floor. I don't wait for him to say anything; I move straight to my next test.

This one Yak is in charge of. He gestures to the paint on the flooring, stretching from one end of the room to the other. "Here, you will be timed on how fast it takes you to run from here to there. Ready?" I give a quick nod, and he says, "Go."

When I get to the end, I jog over to the wall and slide down it, next to Hutch. It doesn't take long for everyone to finish. Mostly because there are only eleven of us left, and that's every recruit here, not just from our room. I skim the area and it seems as if everyone is 100 percent because no one has failed.

Yak strides toward us, telling us to stand, and a coldness flutters in my chest because the blade in his hand isn't a normal one. Not like the ones I've seen. This one is thin and sharp on both ends with no handle.

"This is a throwing knife. It is our emergency weapon. This is why you had a bowl and a fork. We call it a lifeline. As a Forgotten, you are not used to having anything to carry or protect. A lifeline forces you to remember to never leave without it. Just like your throwing knife. You carry it with you everywhere you go because one day, this might be what saves your life," he finishes, and then throws it right at us.

I cringe the second it leaves his fingers and watch as it soars through the air. When it lands between Toggy's feet, I glance up and she has her arms folded over her chest, looking more annoyed than stunned. I don't think I would have been that brave if a blade was coming right at me. I would have flinched, screamed, and buckled to the ground in fear. But Toggs just bends, yanking it out of the hard-wood flooring, and walks it back over to him. It must be because she's from here. Maybe she knew it was coming, just like she knew the answers from the other tests.

"I will call out in order from best to last. When you hear your name, come up and receive your new lifeline."

Hutch is called first, and I can understand why. He is the fastest out of all of us and when Bear hands him a life-line, the room bellows with a loud, "Hoorah!" Next Toggy. I nudge Lou, knowing she has to be next. But when he calls my name instead, I am utterly flabbergasted. I thought for sure Lou would be next. She was the last to test, but it seemed as if she was as fast as Hutch. I step forward and when Bear hands me my lifeline, I grip it tightly, expecting it to be heavier. But, instead of examining it, I glance over my shoulder at Lou with a proud smile. Perhaps I can do this on my own. For the last few years, I have depended on her for mostly everything and now that I am stronger, mentally and physically, perhaps she can begin to lean on me for once.

"Hoorah," Bear says, and I turn back to him with a full smile, but the sound of glass shattering next to me makes my mouth go completely dry.

I look over at Yak, and he has his pistol aimed out in front of him. *Oh my goodness, who did he fail?* I slowly turn and for a moment, it doesn't seem real. Except the more my eyes dart from Yak's pistol to Lou on the ground, I realize it is. And a scream rips out of me, raw and loud. I rush forward, but before I can reach her, Bear wraps his arms around my waist, stopping me.

"It's okay. There's nothing to fear," he says in a soothing tone. "Just breathe."

My breath vibrates wildly as I struggle against him. I kick and scratch and fight, but he's too strong. I can't get out of his hold. *Why won't he let me go to her?* At least let me be with her until the end. I need her to know she isn't alone.

Through blurry vision, Alex bolts forward and Hyena grabs him like Bear is me.

"I gotta be helping her! Let go!" he shouts. I skim the others, and no one from our group is concerned about Lou, not even Hutch. Only me and Alex. All Lou's done since arriving has been protecting and helping the others. Alex was right from the beginning. It is everyone for themselves.

My grief weaves into a wild rage as I cut my gaze back at Alex. He looks right at me with desperation and hurt in his eyes. And I know that look. He wants me to do something, but what? I grip the blade tighter, trying to read his expression, and it hits me. He wants me to do what Lou did in the mining caverns. But I've never killed anyone before. That was always Lou, not me. And she only did it to save one of us.

I stare at her lifeless form and my soul feels empty. *How can I go on without her? How can I take all these lives . . . for her?*

"Do something!" Alex screams.

I lift my eyes to him, knowing I have to at least try. It's what she would do for us. I swallow my feelings like it's my last breath because I know what I'm about to do will kill me. I squeeze my eyes shut, trying to find Lou's courage, and hear her voice, "Cower and he'll let go." With a deep inhale, I open my eyes, relax my shoulders, and cower into myself.

"Are you okay?" Bear asks.

With another nod and shrinking into myself even more, I grip the blade tight and wait for him to think I'm weak and not a threat.

"Okay."

He loosens his hold on me, and I quickly twist out of his arms. I lunge at their leader, forcing my blade into his neck, hard and swift, but the light in his eyes isn't draining, nor does he look hurt. If anything, he looks irritated and furious. I glance at the blade embedded in his neck and there isn't any blood, either. It isn't a real blade. It's a fake one that slides into itself, and my lips part at my mistake.

Movement catches my eyes. All the Naturals from above jump down, fists clenched, and stride toward me. I wet my lips with my stomach spinning and not the good kind when you're happy. Not like I was earlier, but the kind that makes you go still and non-responsive in defeat. I no longer care what happens to me or if they send me back. At least I'll be with Lou.

I inch away, dropping the fake blade, but it's too late. Yak grabs me in a rough manner, forcing me to the floor with my cheek pressed against the cold flooring. He leans closer to my ear with his knee digging into my back, and pain slices through me.

"I am not your enemy, girl. Attack me again and you will be gone."

He pushes off me, and I close my eyes, waiting for him to pull his pistol, but he doesn't. *Why? How can I be with Lou if he doesn't fail me, too?* A helplessness washes over me, and I roll into a tight ball with a violent sob as Lou is dragged out of the room. I know Alex is at my side, but he cannot comfort me this time, and I pull away from his reassurance. He tugs on my arm, forcing me to listen.

"Hey, don't be halting now. We almost to the end." He leans closer with his voice hopeless, but stern. "Now get right."

How? Lou wasn't just my protection. She was my very best friend. My lifeline, and now she is gone.

"I can't," I rasp. Without Lou, loss and despair are pulling me under. I press my fingers into my eyes with my chin trembling uncontrollably, willing the darkness to take me.

"Please, be bricky one last time." The desperation in his voice is hard to ignore, for I know I am all he has left. Lou wasn't just my best friend; she was his too. He grabs my hand, clinging to it in a firm grip. "Don't give. Not today."

His words cut through my misery. This isn't the first time he's asked me to get up or hold on another day. In the mining caverns, there's a special spot for the exhausted to sleep. It's for those who don't want to be bothered or awakened and can quietly fade away in the night. I used to stare at that spot, asking myself, "Why am I fighting for a life filled with so much pain and suffering when I could simply end it all?" But every night before I could muster the energy to crawl over there, Alex would say, "Not today. Tomorrow."

"If ye give, ye know I will, too. I can't be doing this wit' out ye. Please, for us."

I squeeze my eyes shut with a deep inhale, for I know he's right. He will follow me. Alex has walked with me and Lou for so long now, I fear he might not know how to survive without one of us. I cannot allow him to fail or leave him alone with these people. So, for Alex, I pick myself off the floor and drag my feet in line with the others.

DECEPTION

|||| |||| |||| ///

I spent all night crying over the loss of Lou, and even though I feel like my heart has been ripped out, Alex is right. We cannot let this hinder our goal. If we want to know what is happening to the failed Forgotten, so we can find and save Lou, we have to continue. We must be part of the three at the end of phase four. Which shouldn't be too hard. After my altercation with Yak, he failed the others that didn't have the modifications. There's only six of us left now. *But what if I'm not as strong as I thought? What if Lou was the one that brought that side out in me?*

"Eyes on me." Yak gestures to the door on our right. "This is where we will be training today," he tells us. "It's one of our weapons rooms." He glares down the line and meets my eyes. "And there are no harmful weapons in here, so don't get any ideas."

I lift my chin with confidence. I know I shouldn't antagonize him, but the sheer thought of him failing Alex next has my shoulders straightening with courage.

He forces air out of his nose with annoyance and turns back to the door like I'm not a threat. And I'm not. At least not yet. He presses his palm against a silver box attached to the wall, and a white light rolls under his hand. Seconds later, the door makes a strange sound, like all the air is being sucked inside, and he pushes the door open.

We enter the room and most of the walls, except the one in the back, are covered with all sorts of toys. Small ones. Big ones. And some I even recognize from my childhood. *How can any of these be weapons?* I ignore the tall glass box near the empty wall as I move farther into the room and push my anger aside, paying attention to their leader.

"To know how to use these weapons properly, first you must know what they do." He pulls a pair of bulky spectacles from the wall and, when he puts them on, I am completely fascinated. They are nothing like my father's spectacles. There isn't any framework that rests on the ears; instead, he slides these straps over his head, fastening them on from the back. And the lenses aren't clear. They are dark gold and when he moves his head, they shimmer.

He turns back to the wall and grabs a piece of cloth. I watch intently as he wraps the material around the lower half of his face. When he speaks again, his voice is muffled, and I realize it isn't a normal piece of cloth. There's something attached on the inside of it.

"This is what is inside our disguise and as long as you are wearing one, these weapons will not affect you." He reaches for one of the toys and it looks like a small red ball I used to play jacks with as a child, but I know that's not what it is. It is a weapon and I protectively step in front of Alex.

Yak cocks his head with a mean grin. "That won't protect him," he says and, without warning, he tosses the ball right at me. It bounces a few times, releasing a loud exploding sound with every leap, and comes to a halt before me. I turn to Alex, but my vision is twisted, and, with each step, I feel as if I'm about to fall over with this loud ringing in my ears. Jumbled voices and groans are heard all around. I look up and their leader is walking straight for us, and then he splits into two figures.

I don't know which one is truly him as both figures pass by, one on each side of me. I start to turn, searching for the real one, and his arm wraps around my shoulders. He's trying to shove something inside my mouth, but I fight against him, and he grips my forehead tight, forcing my head back. He pries my lips open, and a burst of air invades my mouth.

He releases me with a hard shove, and I stumble forward, shaking my head. The effects are wearing off, and fast. I stretch my eyes and Yak is doing the same thing to the others, except they aren't pushing him away. If anything, they are eager for his help. When he finishes with everyone, he walks back over to the wall, yanking off the spectacles, and grabs another weapon.

"What you experienced is a weapon we call 'Mary Jane', and it is only the first part of the weapon. Mary." He raises his palm, showing us the jacks. "This is the second half, Jane. It's what you throw next, after your enemy is disoriented."

I inch backward with a quick glance over my shoulder and then face Yak, bracing for the impact. But when he releases them, nothing happens. They just slide across the floor like normal jacks.

"It takes a minute for it to react. It's why we use Mary

first," he tells us and, within moments, the jacks slowly start jumping to life.

One leaps near Alex's foot, and he yelps away from it as the other jacks start bouncing, merging into one big silver sludge. I step away from it, but like a whip, part of it slings itself at me. The silver sludge wraps around my ankles, and, with a hard yank, it pulls me to the ground. The more I struggle, the tighter it forms, crawling up my legs.

"It detects movement," Toggy says as it starts, cocooning her legs like a massive spider web, and I instantly stop moving.

"Just our feet or—" The second Alex sticks his arm out, the sludge stretches, yanking him to the ground. "It be anything," he squeals.

"How long it be?" Hutch asks, struggling against the sludge.

"About twenty minutes," Yak answers. He starts toward us, spraying the sludge with a cloud of white dust. It immediately starts shrinking and pulling away from our legs until there's nothing left but a pile of white powder.

"What that be?" Alex asks.

"Fire extinguisher." Yak sprays the silver sludge a few more times before heading back over to the wall and reaching for a blue ball. It's not as small as the red one but small enough that it fits perfectly in his palm. "This is called 'Simon'. And for this one, I'll need a volunteer to step into the glass box."

I tug on Alex's shoulder, and he steps back with me as the rest of the recruits follow suit. Everyone except Caleb. The boy Toggy stabbed with a fork.

"Alright, Pup, in you go."

"What? I didn't offer," Caleb argues.

"Looks like you did."

Caleb does a double take over his shoulder. "What the . . . really?" He turns all the way around and squints at us on his way to the box. "You bunch are some sorry bunks."

"Better ye than us," Hutch chuckles, and everyone but me joins in his laughter. I lower my head with an ache in my chest. *How can any of them be jolly and carefree with Lou gone? She is the reason most of them are still here today.*

"Alright, enough," Yak says. I lift my head just as he opens the glass door.

Caleb enters, pushing blond bangs out of his blue eyes, and then turns, pointing right at Jack. The boy that I went up against in the last phase. The one I nearly killed.

Caleb drags a thumb across his neck.

"What? I ain't done nothing," Jack complains.

"Exactly. Ya should be having my back."

"The only back I be having is my own," Jack says, whipping his head over to me. His deep blue eyes, almost purple, are heavy with anger and I know from experience how mean his fists are. "And ya best be remembering that."

"Aye," Hutch says, moving in front of me and into Jack's personal space. "But ye forget how she dropped yer ass. She almost be ending ye."

"Enough," Yak says again and closes the door on Caleb. "Are you ready?" Yak asks, but he doesn't wait for a response; he opens a small hatch on the top. "Fire in the hole." He lets the ball drop from his fingers and quickly closes the hatch, stepping back to join us. It bounces around Caleb's legs, releasing small spurts of smoke with each bounce. Caleb bends with a fitful cough as the box fills with purple smoke until we can no longer see him. Moments later, his hand presses against the glass like he's trying to steady himself, and I glance up at Yak. He has an arrogant look, like he's impressed with himself, and my stomach rolls with hatred once more.

"What's happening to him isn't harmful. It's a special mist that, when inhaled, will knock you unconscious, causing memory loss." He turns and addresses us. "The other day when some of you woke from those pods, confused on how you ended up there, it's because Bear used this on you." He points at the glass box. "And we only use Simon when we aren't on an island to hurt anyone. Only subdue them. And when they wake up, we can fill in the gaps, giving them any story we want."

He touches the pistol on his hip. "It's the same type of substance that's in here. It doesn't kill you, just knocks you unconscious. Except this one won't erase your memory. Sometimes we fill in the gap right away, but most of the time, we just wait for it to wear off on its own and you remember when you're ready."

"So, all those Forgotten that be failing, they ain't gone?" Hutch asks. Yak nods slightly, and my mouth parts. I now have confirmation that Lou isn't dead.

"Correct. But the difference between the pistol and the ball is the ball can inflict a huge group of individuals at once and only lasts about five minutes. Whereas the pistol can only hit one person at a time, and it can last up to an hour. Now, if the pistol is used and we still want them to forget . . . " Yak slices his cold eyes on me. "We have ways of erasing their memory, just like Simon."

"So, where they be?" Hutch asks.

"They are sent home." Yak moves closer to the glass box, presses a button, and all the mist in the box swirls high into a large tube connected to the ceiling.

My chest vibrates with tears threatening because they

didn't find us at home port. We were in the mining cavern, which means they must have sent Lou back there.

"Do it harm ye? The pistol," Hutch asks.

"I'm not going to lie; it hurts like a bitch. It's why they convulse like they do."

"Why are they all called names like Mary Jane and Simon?" Toggy asks.

"Well, sometimes when we dock, we are only there for information, not to harm anyone, so not everyone will be together. We will be scattered on the island."

He pulls a small device from his ear. It's so small I can barely see it in his hand. "This is called 'an earpiece' and all those that leave the ship for a mission wear one." He gestures to his bracelet. "With this and the earpiece, this is how we communicate with each other." Yak shifts his stance, folding his arms over his chest. "Now, let's say you are alone trying to gather information from folks and come across a large group that starts threatening you. A group you cannot take on by yourself, not without revealing who you are. Because when we are only there for information, we go as ourselves, not in our disguise. It's also why some of the Naturals have long hair and some do not. We never know if we need to pose as a Forgotten or a Spoon."

Yak waves his hand as if dismissing the last statement. "Anyway, you can't just come out and say, 'I'm being threatened and I'm at the saloon'. Instead, you would say something like, 'How about a round of ale for my pals'. Now we know where you are. At the saloon. This is also an attempt to settle the misfits, while at the same time warning us this group could cause a problem.

"Now, if you aren't able to settle them down, then you would say something like, 'Hey fellas, I'm not here to start any trouble, just here to see my girl, Jill', or Jack. Now, we know how dangerous the situation is without warning them, because Jack and Jill are actual pistols that will harm them. But don't worry, you will learn all this in training." He walks over to the table and comes back with one of those skin-pricking pistols. "Now, how about we wake up Caleb and carry on? We have a lot to cover today."

He opens the glass door and squats in front of Caleb, pressing the pistol against his neck. Caleb lurches up with a loud gasp and clutches at his chest. "Wh . . . what be happening?" He looks up at the glass box and then at us. "Where we be?"

I can see the confusion on his face, and I turn to Alex, knowing I have experienced the same confusion every time I have awoken in one of those strange beds. *But why are they wiping our memories? And how many times have they used it on us? On me.*

HOORAH

|||| |||| |||| ||||

The last few weeks, all we've done is train. In the mornings, we practice physical combat skills with Bear and Fox. In the afternoons, we practice weapons with Hyena and the younger trainer, Owl—the one that asked if I could learn when I first arrived. In the evenings, as a team, we study the new weapons. What they are, how they work, and which ones are the harmful ones. Those we aren't allowed to touch. Instead, we practice on the same type, only they are fake, like our lifeline blades.

But tomorrow is the last week of phase three and I can't sleep. My stomach is in knots with worry for Alex. If this test involves weapons, I know I'll pass. Bear has said I am the best pup in weaponry, but Alex isn't. I flop onto my side and punch my pillow, trying to find a comfortable spot just as a loud blast pierces the hallway. I sit straight up in bed, straining my ears, listening to Bear's voice howling down the hallway.

"You have two minutes to dress and stand at attention."

Alex and I soar out of bed, practically jumping into our new uniform. Ever since Lou failed, Alex has been staying with me. I don't know if the trainers have noticed or if they don't care. I'm just grateful he's with me in the evenings again. I don't know what I would do if I lost him too.

Alex sits on the edge of the bed, pushing his feet into heavy black boots. "I'm glad they be showing us how to wear all this last night."

I sit next to him, lacing up my own boots, and he lifts off the bed, shaking his legs out one at a time. "Everything be fittin' a lil' too snug, 'specially the boots. Why they gotta be so tight? I can already be feeling the soft parts forming."

I lift off the bed, joining him by the door, agreeing. All of us are going to have blisters before the day is over. I shove the black blouse inside my matching-colored trousers. And once everyone is at their door and standing at attention, Yak leads us down a flight of stairs. We stop at the lowest level and enter, following him down another long hallway with two closed doors on each side of the corridor.

We enter the first door on our right and our boots clomp along a metal staircase as we descend another flight of stairs. Inside, the room is massive, with a large trench filled with sand. On the far wall, spilling out, is a man-made ocean rolling toward a false shoreline. And dug into the sand is a pull-up bar we used in phase one. I step off the last rung and see the rest of the trainers underneath the staircase, standing at attention.

"Hell Week is not only to test your endurance, but to also find your strength and/or your weakness. Not everyone will pass Hell Week," Yak says, and I wring my hands behind my back. My heart is beating so fast all I can hear is the blood pounding in my ears. It's only the first day. No, only minutes into Hell Week and I already feel like throwing up. If Alex fumbles, how will I save him in time? It's not like I can rush to his side and take the hit for him. That pistol is a lot faster than me.

"Begin."

Crap! Everyone's scattering, and I wasn't listening. What are we supposed to do? And then I see everyone moving toward the trainers. Toggy steps around Owl and reaches for the bag behind him and I realize I need to grab a bag, too. I approach one of the bags, but just as I reach for it, Hyena shouts, "Not that one!" I flinch my hand back, moving backward, and he follows me, screaming a hair away from my nose. "Are you stupid, Pup? Do you not know who your trainer is? Were you not listening when Yak assigned you idiots?"

I glance around and everyone has their bag but me. Not only that, but the only bag left is behind Bear. With a hard gulp, I step around Hyena for my bag, and he marches over to Alex. I bend for the straps and my fingers slip. Whatever is in here is heavier than me. It must be twice my body weight. And right on cue, Bear turns and starts on me, picking up where Hyena left off, shouting in my ear.

"I'd say ring out, but I think you might be too stupid to find the bell. Move, Pup!"

I swallow whatever emotion wants to spill out of me and drag the bag in line with the others. Again, I thought once I managed to get it there, Bear would stop yelling or, at the very least, step away from my face, but it only gets worse. Especially after Yak tells us the bags represent an injured Natural and to get down on all fours, holstering the strap around our shoulders, where the bag hangs in front of our belly, and bear crawl it through the waves. And for some reason, by the time I have mine on, the waves are higher and rolling faster. I can barely see, much less breathe, as the waves crash against me, nearly toppling me over.

"What are you doing, Pup? You're out in the open. If you don't move, both of you will die. Dig those heels in and move your ass!" Bear shouts, walking beside me.

By the time I finally make my way back to the sandy shoreline for the tenth time, I roll onto my back, worn out and gasping for air. If that were truly an injured Natural, both of us would have bled out long ago, seeing how I am the last one to finish. And being last is possibly the worst thing to be; there's no time to catch your breath. No time to rest your muscles or recover because afterward, Yak has us lying on our backs doing all sorts of physical activities while the waves crash into us, yet again.

Now, we're hanging on the pull-up bar. And to my surprise, this is a lot easier than it was during phase one. So, when Yak says, "up," everyone lifts their chins above the bar with ease, and we are able to stay in this position a lot longer than before, too. When he says, "down," no one drops like before either. We all hang with our knees bent, never touching the ground. All while the trainers yell at us. I'm starting to think they just enjoy the sound of their own voice because one of them is always yelling at someone.

It's been at least five minutes and Alex is starting to struggle. His fingers keep slipping and every time he falls, Hyena is hollering at him. I don't know how to help him other than pulling the attention onto me. I fall into the sand, landing on my knees, and Bear whips his head at me.

"What are you doing, Pup? Get up!"

I slowly push to my feet, clapping sand off my hands, and Bear lifts his chin with a slight nod, stepping away from me. I jump for the bar, but I allow my fingers to slip, and Yak strides toward me, fast and mean.

"What's wrong with you? Yesterday, you were my number one recruit and now you're dead last." He moves close to my ear. "I don't know what you're up to, but you'd better get your ass on that bar. Now!" He turns to Bear. "If she falls again, fail them all. I'm done with this shit."

Number one recruit. How is that? I thought Hutch was.

"You heard him. Up!"

After what felt like a hundred hours of pull-ups and push-ups and whatever else Bear could think of, trying to break us, we stop for lunch. But even then, we weren't eating fast enough or the right way. And since everyone here has grown accustomed to being called "Pup", whenever a trainer shouts out, "Hey Pup," we all turn around. I don't think they even know who they're calling for or why; they just want to know which one of us will turn, so they'll have someone to yell at even more.

After lunch, we are escorted to another room with tables scattered throughout, and on each table is a pistol. Beside it is the cleaning equipment for it. I pick the table next to Alex with Hutch on the other side of him. I eagerly bounce my chair closer to the table. Finally, something I am good at. Not that the others aren't, it's just weapons are the one thing I really excel at. Like Jack has become the best at physical altercations. Hutch is the fastest when we run the obstacle courses. Toggy, she's the smartest, and Alex, he's good at everything, just a few steps behind the rest of us. And Caleb, well, he's really good at running his mouth. I haven't seen him stand out in anything but just filling the room with insults. I ignore him, but Hutch and the others, they engage.

"Hey," Alex taps Hutch on the arm, "I ain't really mindin' during this phase." He pinches the firing pin between his fingers and lifts it off the table like it's covered in boogers. "What this be?"

Hutch gives him an easy grin. "When ye ever be paying mind?" He chuckles and before he can tell Alex what it is, Yak enters.

"Before we begin the next task, you will be timed on how long it takes to clean and assemble your weapon. Afterward, you will be escorted to the firing range and be tested with your practice weapon."

Excitement leaps into my throat at the mention of practice weapons. It's one of my favorite things to do. They aren't real weapons; I mean, they look real, but the ammo is paint. The first time we used them, we didn't know the ammo was paint. And when Bear stepped out for a moment, Toggy accidentally shot Hutch, and chaos erupted. I thought he was going to kill her, but once he figured out it was paint, he shot her back, and a playful war began. Bear returned and, of course, he wasn't happy. Paint was everywhere and on everyone. That was the one and only time he left us alone.

I glance around the room, and everyone is grinning ear to ear. It's everyone's favorite. But all my excitement fades when Yak strides toward me like he means me harm. *Why?* He stops, standing right next to me, not saying anything, and I reach for my weapon. I fumble, almost dropping it back onto the table, but I grip it tight with a deep inhale. I can do this. I just can't let him get to me. He places one hand on the edge of the table and the other on the back of my chair, and fear vibrates down my back. I lift my eyes to him and one corner of his mouth curls.

"I've seen you in training. I know you excel with

weapons, so don't pretend to be weak now, or I will fail everyone here. Starting with the little one you're so fond of." He straightens with his palm resting on the pistol holstered on his thigh. And then lifts his other hand, holding a small device, and bellows out, "Go!"

When I finish with no mistakes, I give him the same smile he gave me, and he folds his arms over his chest. "Again, but faster," he orders. After the second time with no mistakes, he growls, "Again." Except this time, he snatches up the pistol and takes it apart for me. But he doesn't place them together in a neat line; instead, he mixes all the parts up and scatters them on the cloth. He turns to Alex and orders him to move, then he drags the table to sit directly in front of me.

"Fox, come here," Yak tells him, and then faces me. "Fox is the best we have with weapons. I want to see how well you measure up against him." He dismantles Fox's pistol like he did mine. While Fox sits directly in front of me, everyone shifts in their seats. A cold sweat shoots through me as they turn around to watch.

"Bear, you take Fox and I'll take her."

"With pleasure," Bear says with a dark smile and rubbing his hands viciously together.

Yak hands Bear something, but whatever it is, it's super small because I never see it. "Everyone up and pick a side. The winner's team gets a bar of chocolate."

Chocolate! That's extravagant. I had always heard about that, but never had it before coming here. It's also Alex's favorite. Now, I have to win. I dry my palms along my trousers as Alex, Hutch, and Toggy move behind me, with Caleb and Jack standing behind Fox.

"Now, this isn't your normal 'who is faster' in a nice quiet space," he reveals with a smile. "This will be sort of like it is out there. Bullets flying. Swords charging. And chaos all around, with no time to think. So, I want everyone to make some noise. Stomp your feet. Slam a chair and yell as loud as you can. Let's make it as distracting as we can." Yak sneers down at me. "Are you ready, Pup?" I nod, and he adds, "First one to raise their pistol wins. Go!"

The second I reach for the main part of the pistol; a scream slices the air and I fumble for the parts. Bear pokes Fox in the back and Fox jerks sideways with a moan.

"His crew is gaining ground. They're climbing aboard the ship. Bang, a bullet hits you." Yak presses his thumb into my shoulder. Except I don't believe it was just his thumb because an electrical current bolts down my arm. I shake the numbness out, and Fox grins at me. This must be what Bear did to him. A distraction.

"Faster," Alex says behind me, and my pulse races.

"Bang," Bear says, and I glimpse up just in time to see Fox fumble with his pin. It slips from his hand, but before it hits the floor, he reaches for it with fast reflexes and continues on. His hands are patient but fast and if not for his fumbling, he might have won.

Instead, we both stand at the same time with our pistols inches from each other's foreheads. The only difference between us is I slid my finger into the trigger and pulled. He didn't. He winked at me with his mouth curled, making a clicking sound with his cheek. The same one Lou used to make when she was leading her horse into the barn, and just the thought of her brings tears to my eyes.

"The Pup wins," Yak announces, and my team celebrates behind me, but my heart isn't in it as we are led out of the room. I miss Lou so much my heart feels empty without her.

EVERYONE HAS SECRETS

Day one of Hell Week was not at all what I expected. Now sleep, that was a different story. We weren't allowed back to our own quarters. Instead, they had us piled up in the mess hall, sleeping together, and it was freezing. Whatever cooling fan they had above us must have been on high blast. It was loud and so cold my teeth chattered the entire night. But again, that wasn't the bad part. In the caverns, Alex, Lou, and I used to huddle against one another for warmth because we never had pillows or blankets. The bad part was the loud explosions startling us awake every hour. It was almost like someone was shooting a pistol nearby, but rapidly, like all the pistols in this place were going off at the same time.

So, given the fact none of us had much sleep, I imagine today will be harder. Especially when Yak tells us we will be performing water tasks and to be in our bathing attire. We walk into their indoor swimming hole and stand at attention, waiting for Yak. Beside me, Toggy inhales deeply and the expression on her face tells me everything I need to know. Dread.

She looks at me with a hard swallow and then leans close. "Whatever happens, don't panic, okay?"

I give her an understanding nod as the trainers enter behind Yak, and the trainers are wearing some sort of black, skintight attire. The only flesh showing is their hands, feet, and face. Even their hair is tucked inside this strange get-up. They stop across from us at the edge of the man-made pond, and just as I am going through every possible scenario that could make me panic once I'm in the water, a group of older Naturals, maybe in their twenties, enter the room. Except they aren't wearing the strange get-up, they are in normal wear. Well, normal for these people, anyway. Snug trousers, rolled slightly above the ankle, with holes or rips in the knees. And their tops are somewhat loose with strange symbols or portraits painted on them.

"Today, you will use all the techniques you learned in phase one," Yak begins telling us. "Bobbing, floating, and traveling. Except this time, you will not be able to use your hands or feet." He gestures to the older Naturals, and they start toward us with thin strands of rope. "As a Natural, if you ever find yourself tangled in kelp or rope, I need you to be comfortable in the water until help arrives."

Alex shoots his hand in the air, and Yak grins at him. "Yes, you will have help if needed today. And no, you will not fail if you are assisted. It is how you learn." Alex lowers his hand, and Yak's smile turns almost bitter as he paces along the edge of the pond across from us.

"However, if you panic and go into a fearful frenzy, then yes, you will fail. Being a Natural means having a nerve of steel and never allowing fear or panic to overtake you. Now, don't get me wrong, being flustered is completely different than a complete breakdown. It's why you are being tested today. Someone that is not comfortable in the water, particularly in a dire state, can not only harm themselves but the person trying to help them. Those that can remain calm will pass today."

Now it's my turn to swallow in alarm. I look to my right and Hutch's jaw is clenched tight. I know he can swim. He passed the first test during phase one, but at the same time, he isn't a strong swimmer. I want to reach out and give him a "you'll be okay" reassurance, but I can't. My hands are already tied behind my back. I cut my gaze across the pond and the trainers shove something clear in their mouth. But it doesn't go all the way in, it's too big and half of it covers their lips.

Yak lifts his chin, and the trainers jump into the water while the older Naturals guide us closer to the edge. I stare at my toes hanging over the edge as someone binds my ankles and my entire body starts to shake. *What if Alex fails?* My pulse quickens more. *What if I fail?*

"Three. Two," and before Yak says, "one," a hand shoves me forward. I splash into the water and, the second my feet touch the bottom, I push myself to the surface. When I break through, I gulp for air before sinking back down. As I do, I blow all the air out, so I can reach the bottom and push myself back to the top again.

I continue to bob up and down as the trainers stay under, watching us. I see Bear each time I sink down, and he gives me a thumbs up, but I don't focus on him. Instead, I focus on the bubbles trickling from his mouthpiece. That must be how they breathe underwater. I try to stay in sync with the bubbles. When they float up, so do I, and it seems to work because my confidence is coming back. I can do this as long as I continue at this pace. Not too slow. Not too fast. And most importantly, staying calm.

After about twenty bobs, Bear reaches out and grabs my ankles, spinning me over and over. The water is churning like boiling water and now I'm confused and disoriented. I don't know which way is up or down and then I remember the dolphin kick my father taught me. Except in training, Bear called it "traveling". I kick my ankles the best I can with them bound together and force my body out of the gurgling water. When I see the ball of light dancing on the water, I thrust my body toward it and start bobbing all over again.

The tenth time I break the surface, I hear Yak say, "Float." I sink, relaxing my muscles, allowing myself to float back to the top. But once I'm there, it's hard to stay afloat and not panic. Everyone is trying to position themselves at the top. Same as me, and it's stirring water, forcing it over my face. I'm trying not to be rattled by it, but the small sips of air I'm able to take are making me nervous. Not because I might fail, but because I might actually drown.

I'm no longer in a pass or fail situation; now I'm fighting for my life and panic has replaced my nervousness. I'm struggling against the ropes, trying to reach the surface, but it's no use. Every time I reach the top, I'm gulping in more water than air, and my lungs are on fire. The sheer thought of never breathing again sends me farther under the water, but not enough to reach the bottom. I'm unable to push myself back to the top. My chest squeezes painfully, and I know I'm in trouble and should dolphin-kick my way to the top, but fear has overpowered panic, and I'm struggling even more. I need help, but no one is offering. Bear is feet from me, but his eyes aren't on me. He is watching Toggy, who is also struggling near the surface.

And just as the last of my air slips from my mouth, a blur spins me around, forcing something into my mouth. I latch onto the hard, chewy piece and lock eyes with Hyena as bursts of air fill my lungs. He gives me a thumbs up and I nod, thankful he was watching me. And before I can truly catch my breath, he wraps an arm around my waist, and we glide through the water. When I reach the surface, I float near the side and he reaches for the mouthpiece. He clamps his mouth onto it and then swiftly maneuvers through the water, toward Jack. Just as I am wondering what I'm supposed to do next, strong hands pull me out of the water. I sit on the edge as someone cuts my restraints.

"Pass," I hear Yak say. I look to my right, and he's pacing along the pond, watching everyone struggling. A towel is draped over my shoulders and then a hand ruffles my wet head. I pull the towel closer and glance behind me.

"You did good, Pup," one of the older Naturals tells me.

"Fail," Yak says again. I turn back to the pond with my heart lodged in my throat as Caleb is pulled out of the water. He isn't breathing. I pull the towel up to my mouth, pressing it against my lips as the one that pulled me out quickly goes into action. He kneels next to Caleb, pressing his hands hard on Caleb's chest, and my eyes widen. *What is he doing?* If Caleb isn't dead, that sure enough will kill him.

"Pass," Yak says, but I can't pull my gaze off Caleb. The Natural stops and pinches Caleb's nose as he leans close, blowing into Caleb's mouth.

"Pass."

"Thank you," I hear Toggy say, keeping my focus on Caleb. The Natural stops blowing and goes back to pressing on Caleb's chest.

"Pass."

"Jeebers. I thought I be a goner," Alex says.

I cut my eyes at him and then lift my chin at Caleb. The Natural pinches his nose again, blowing, and Caleb's body jerks upward, spitting water and coughing. And I finally breathe, patting at my own chest. That was amazing. He just saved his life. *How? Better question, why did they allow it to go that far, that they needed to save him?*

Yak lifts his chin at the Natural bent over Caleb and the Natural nods his head. *Does that mean Caleb failed? If so, I fear what our next challenge will be? What tomorrow will bring?* It wasn't Caleb's fault he almost died.

"Pass."

I run the towel against my nose as Hutch is pulled out of the water. The older Natural helps Caleb out of the room and Yak instructs us to get back into the swimming hole.

I don't know how long we were in the water, but my muscles are screaming with fatigue and my teeth are chattering. All I want right now is a blanket and food, but the day isn't over because now we are being escorted to another room dressed in full gear. Heavy boots and bulky black attire. I just hope whatever we are about to endure, it isn't anything physical but has food afterward. Lots and lots of food. I am completely drained.

I sit at one of the small tables in the same room we tested our pistols in, except there are no pistols. Just a strange-looking green ball with various shaped holes punctured all around it. And by the looks of it, the colorful objects that fit into those shapes are stuck inside the ball.

"What be this?" Hutch asks, pulling out the chair in front of me.

"It's a puzzle and you aren't to touch it until Yak arrives," Bear replies.

"Umm, when we be eatin'?" Alex asks, sitting at the desk to my right.

"Not until later," Bear replies as the rest of the trainers walk in and stand at attention in front of us.

"But I be clammin," Alex moans.

"What is clammin'?" Owl asks.

"Starving," Bear replies.

Owl puffs out air, shaking his head slightly. "Then eat air, Pup."

"Okay." Alex shrugs and begins gulping and sucking in air as we wait for Yak. "Crap. I think I be eating too much." He bends over, holding himself. "Me belly hurts. I think I'm gonna heave." He peeks up at me with a mischievous grin and then straightens with the loudest belch I've ever heard. The room bellows with laughter, including the trainers. Well, everyone but Owl.

He leans forward with one dark eyebrow raised. "And he's supposed to be one of your best recruits? Wow." He straightens with a hard eye roll. "No wonder the other Naturals are watching us."

"I'm sorry. How many recruits do you have left? That's right, none." Bear gives a slight shrug. "So maybe it's you they're watching."

"Enough bickering," Yak says behind us. He joins the trainers at the front of the room. "You may begin."

I look at Toggy sitting on my left, hoping for one of those hints she likes to give, but she doesn't offer one. She doesn't even look my way. She just picks up the ball and begins spinning the punctured shapes around until a piece slides through the opening. I turn back to my own ball, and Alex jumps out of his seat.

"Done. Now, can us be eatin'?"

The room squawks with confusion because Alex is never done first. He's always dead last. I glance over at Yak and his lips quirk up as he reaches for a small wooden block and walks it over to Alex. "Now do this one."

Alex finishes it before I can manage my third piece out, and Yak walks over, giving Alex another puzzle. Everyone lifts out of their seats, ignoring their own puzzle as we watch how quickly Alex assembles each puzzle Yak offers him.

"This be fun." Alex grins, finishing another puzzle. "But how many I gotta do before us can eat?"

"This one, and then you may eat," Yak says, placing a colorful cube in front of Alex.

Owl moves closer, watching over Hutch's shoulder. "I believe we have finally found something this pup is good at." He chuckles. He leans back and speaks to Bear, "I get it now, but how did you know?"

"During phase one, I thought I saw hints of intellect hidden in that brain of his, but every time I thought I had him pegged, he'd do something that made me second guess myself. Like eating air. It's why I wanted to do this test," Bear says.

"Ye mean this be a test?" Alex asks and then looks at me with a grimace. I know what he's thinking. Neither of us wanted the others to know how smart he is in fear of them separating us.

"Yes," Yak replies, reaching for the puzzle on Alex's desk. "Not many can solve a Rubik's Cube and definitely not in the time frame you did it. You might just be the smartest one here."

The room puffs with all sorts of questions, some at Alex

and others at Yak. But the silence from Hutch and the look on his face, I know he isn't pleased Alex kept this from him.

"Alright, calm down. Time for dinner," Yak informs us.

Knowing I need to keep my eye on Hutch, I start to follow him to the mess hall, and Alex hurries toward us.

"Hey, there be a reason I didn't want no one to knows." He glances over his shoulder at the trainers talking with Yak and then back at Hutch. "But it ain't cos I—"

"Hey, everyone be having secrets," Hutch says with a shrug. He looks at me and then back at Alex with a smile. "Ye be allowed to have your own secrets and reasons. I be having secrets, too. Don't mean we ain't mates, yeah?"

"Yeah." Alex nods with a lopsided grin.

"Alright." Hutch pulls him into a headlock, scrubbing the top of his head with his knuckles as we make our way to the mess hall.

I can't help but wonder what secrets Hutch is hiding and why his demeanor changed? Better question, why did he look at me that way? Does he know something about me? *Crap! Does he know who I am?*

WE ALL HAVE SCARS

After our bellies are full and ready to pop, everyone huddles together in the mess hall, away from the cooling fan, fast asleep. But a door slightly clicking open bolts me upright. I peer into the darkness, trying to see who it is, and a hand clamps over my mouth from behind.

"I need you to come with me. There's something you need to see. It's important," Toggy says. I hesitate a moment, remembering the last time they wanted to sneak out, and she leans closer. "Trust me, you're going to want to know this. It's about you."

My heart skips a beat, and I look over at Alex's sleeping form.

"He can't come. Just you," she says and tugs on my arm. I force a dry, hard swallow down and when I stand with her, I notice a hint of light shining from her hand. But it isn't like the cylinder she had in the secret tunnels. This one is so small it doesn't even look like she's holding anything. She opens the door leading into the hallway, and I squint at the brightness as I follow her. She stops me at the end of the hallway and presses the coin-sized light into my palm.

"This is a pinch light. Just push the middle and it will come on." She hesitates a moment with a quick look over my shoulder and then adds, "I give you my word. You are safe. Just . . . please don't run." She opens the door to our left, but she doesn't enter. Instead, she pokes her head inside, making a strange animal noise, and my hands grow cold and sweaty when I see Bear's profile.

"You have two hours before Yak returns," she whispers and shoves me through the doorway.

What is going on? Where are they taking me? The door closes behind us and I turn in the darkness. *Why isn't Toggy coming with us? Is she coming back?*

"We don't have much time. Follow me," Bear says, lightly tugging on my fingertips, and I jerk my hand back. "Hey, I know it's scary and you don't trust us. And I get it. I've been there, remember? But this is important. And if we don't go now, we might not have this chance again."

His voice is calm and reassuring, but the reasoning of why I have been brought to him without Yak's permission still has not been said. I want to ask. No, demand answers. *Why do I need to follow him anywhere? Why can't he just tell me what it is here? And why the heck won't he look at me?* But I know I can't ask or demand anything. Too much time has passed for me to speak now. If I do, there's no telling what they will do to me.

"Please," Bear says with his head down. "I promise I won't let anything bad happen to you."

My stomach rolls with a strong desire to run, but the intrigue of what is so urgent consumes me more than running. Plus, if I needed to, I think I could take him. He might be big, but he isn't as fast as me. I just can't let him behind me.

I pinch the small device and follow him up a flight of stairs, waving the light across the numbers painted on the walls. We finally stop at the top of the stairs and Bear opens the door near the number five. He peeks inside, looking left and right, and then gestures for me to follow him. We hurry into the hallway, rushing into an empty room with small glowing bulbs pulsating on the floor. It doesn't give off much light. More like a small fire, pulsing in a hearth, and I stop pinching the side of my light.

I look behind me and when I turn back to Bear, panic rolls down my back as he reveals a hidden door on the back wall. It's just like the one Toggy showed me, but on a different floor. *How many of these tunnels do they have? And where does this one go? Most importantly, why is Bear taking me in there?* Fear and distrust gnaw in my gut, and I step away from him.

He turns, finally looking at me, and my fear is heightened more than ever before. I fumble the pinch light up, shuffling backward with my heart painfully pumping against my chest. *What's wrong with his eyes?* He moves closer, and I steal another step away from his glowing, feral eyes with a hard pant. I will my feet to run, but my heavy, numb limbs won't move. I am completely frozen in terror. *Is this why he refused to look at me?*

"Please don't run. I understand trust is earned with you. Believe me, I get it." He lowers his head like he's the one frightened of me. "I've seen your scars. All of them. Even the ones you think no one can see. I see them." He lifts his cat-like eyes to me, and I remember those eyes. My mouth goes dry with my fear penetrating every cell in my body. Those are the same eyes I saw in the trainers' quarters the evening I snuck out with Toggy. "I carry the same night-mares as you."

He turns his back on me and, just as I step forward to attack, he lifts the tail end of his shirt, and I stop. My jaw tightens at the deep, pink slashes across his back, and I press my fingers in my lips with my back burning with the same memory. I have only felt the painful ripping of flesh once. It was right after we were transferred to our second cavern. The next day, Lou swore she'd never allow them to hurt me again. And she didn't. She always received mine and Alex's punishment and sometimes the younger prisoners, too.

I step aside, hugging myself, and he tugs his shirt back in place. I avoid any kind of eye contact, for I know how difficult that was. To allow someone to truly see you. He takes a step closer with his hand up, slowly inching my way, and I shake my head, mentally asking him to stop, and he does.

"Okay. I get it. Just let me show you this one thing and afterward, if you still don't trust me, I'll walk you to the back door and unlock it myself. I'll even help you and Alex with a boat, and you two can go wherever you want. You can disappear."

I look over my shoulder at the open doorway with a thick throat. It could be a trick. I flick my eyes back onto him, and I can't help but wonder if he was sent as a diversion or a ruse to lower my guard. The same kind our wardens have used against us before. Except Bear isn't a prisoner pretending to be hurt. He is a Natural. My enemy, pretending to be like me, and that could be a lot more dangerous. I lower my head, pinching the light on and off as my brain spins with every possible scheme and outcome if I follow him. *Is this what Toggy was waiting for? To get me alone and sabotage me.* I look over my shoulder again. But the chance of freedom. The very thing Alex and I are desperate for, how can I not? Plus, I need to know where Lou is. Maybe if I go with him, he will tell me. I turn back to Bear with hope driving me forward and give him a quick nod.

Once we enter the secret passage, he walks slowly in front of me. "Before the world went to shit," he says over his shoulder, "the Naturals knew what was coming. It's why they came here and built this place. It was supposed to be the one place Mother Nature wasn't going to hit, and it was. Back then, this was a safe haven for those that believed them. Of course, not many did."

We hit a T in the tunnels, and he touches my arm like he's making sure I'm still with him as he guides me to the left. I swing the light behind me, at another long tunnel, and my pulse races. Perhaps I've made a grave mistake by following him because I might not be able to find my way out if the need to run arises.

"Two years later, they ventured out to see if anyone survived and needed help. But all they found was pure evilness, wreaking havoc. Where people were killing each other over food and water, and, over the years, it's only gotten worse. However, some of the Naturals believed not everyone out there was evil. Some believed good people were still out there but in hiding. They just couldn't find them. It wasn't until a few years later they finally found an island full of good people, but they were struggling. Some came back with them, some stayed promising loyalty if the Naturals helped with medicine and food. And the Naturals did. Once a year, the Naturals would return, treating injuries and sickness and giving crates full of food and medicine for another year, and then continuing their journey, searching for more people."

We turn left at another fork and then directly right and I know now my fate rests in his hands. I have no other choice but to trust him if I want to get out of here. If I want to get back to Alex.

"But it seemed impossible to reach everyone that needed help. So, they posted signs and clues for those in hiding, hoping they would come forward. Around that time, pirates learned of this place. They wanted it for themselves and started hunting for it. So, when word got back to the Naturals, fear spread through the island. It's why they created these tunnels. They wanted a place they could hide if they were ever attacked.

"Not that they ever were. Pirates are evil, after all, and anytime one of them came close to figuring out the clues, another pirate killed them for their information before knowing what the clue held. And over the years, with no education and most not knowing how to read, the fear of them finding this place was slim. Not that the Naturals stopped worrying about it. They didn't. They even created this wall around the island that, to the normal eye, looks as if the world ends right here, so most turn back. Crow and his team have even started making new clues and hiding them just like before, in the hope of reaching more people."

He stops and faces me. "I'm only telling you all this because I want you to know that the Naturals are good people." He presses his palms against his chest. "We are good people. We don't just save the Forgotten. We save all those that need our help. Even Spoons."

I flinch at the word "Spoon". *Does he know who I am?* I shine the light through the darkness, knowing I should run, but where? I don't even know how to find my way out of here. I am completely lost.

"Hey." He touches my arm, and I flinch again. "It's

okay. I'm not going to hurt you. I just want to show you something." He faces the wall to our right and presses his hand against it, revealing another hidden door. Against my better judgment, I follow him inside, but the second I see the Wolfman, my heart thunders in my chest. *Where has he been this entire time? Here.* I look around the small area. There's a settee pushed against the wall to my right and above it is one of those black portraits we have in our training room. Next to the settee is a bookcase filled with boxes.

"Don't worry. Wolf won't hurt you," Bear says, and I turn my attention to them. Wolf is standing under a dim light, shuffling through a stack of parchment scattered on a desk, with Bear standing next to him. Both looking for something.

I pry my eyes off of them and focus on the large chart above the desk. I dare a step closer, trying to make sense of the chaos. Red yarn is weaved around articles and gossip pinned to the chart. But the door opening behind me cuts through my confusion. The rest of the trainers are entering, and I hug myself with my shoulders hunched, trying to make myself smaller. *What are they doing here?* They brush past me, moving to the back wall. Fox and Owl sit on a worn and faded settee with Hyena perched on the arm.

"Don't worry. They aren't going to hurt you, either. Okay?" Bear says, turning slightly to lean against the desk.

I give a slight nod, still refusing to make eye contact with any of them, and Bear continues.

"Anyway, what I was saying was, the Naturals have had alliances with other islands for years now. This way, if something ever went wrong, we would have a place to go. And in return, like I was telling you, we supply their people with food and medicine every year. But over the years, those safe havens have been destroyed by pirates, leaving only a few islands left. And one of those islands is Capra Horn."

My head snaps up with my pulse pounding in my ears. That's where I'm from.

"Here it is." Wolf turns and hands me a strange illustration where the texture is smooth and glossy, not coarse from ink or paint. I stare at the boy hanging upside down from a tree and then peer up at the trainers, staring back at me. I focus back at the portrait, at me and Lou hanging next to the boy. All the blood drains from my face as Wolf asks, "Do you remember him?"

I give another nod and thumb my cousin's face with a trembling chin. *Who made this?* I turn the portrait over, wondering how did I not know about it? And how do the Naturals have it?

"The boy in the picture is me," Wolf says, and my eyes shoot up, searching for hints of Ford in him. I look at the pale brown eye to the dark one and then back to the scar. If this is Ford, which I seriously doubt, what happened to him?

"It's true," he continues. "It's the only picture I have of us. The second I was back on the sub, I stole this from Mom's photo album and joined the Naturals. Well, I didn't just join. I had to go through the same phases, like everyone else. I even talked Hyena and the others into joining."

"Yeah," Fox begins, "he filled our heads with all sorts of adventure and heroism until we agreed to join."

I look over at the back wall and Owl stands. "I'm sorry for being so harsh with you that day. Truly I am." He starts forward. "If I had known you—"

"Hu-uh," Bear interrupts, bolting off the edge of the desk and inserting himself between us. "Not yet, Owl."

Owl looks at me and then back at Bear like he's fearful of him, and then lowers himself back down.

"Anyway," Fox says with a quick glance at Bear like he's afraid of him, too. "Once we became full-fledged members, the other Naturals learned of what we were up to, and we had more in our secret group. Before we knew it, every Natural here was joining us in the search for you."

"Of course, we hid it from Yak," Hyena begins, folding his arms over his chest. "If he ever found out, he would have put a stop to it. Not that he didn't want to search for you, he did; it just wasn't his main goal. He only looked for you when we had free time. At least, that's what we thought, but a few hours ago, we learned that the Alpha Team has been searching for you this entire time. It has been their only mission for the last six years, but no one knew about it. Not even Wolf."

Wolf takes the portrait from me and looks at it. "I never gave up on you, Tippy."

He said my name. He knows who I am. A cold sweat drenches me with my stomach churning with nausea. I need to get out of here before something bad happens to me. I slowly take a cautious step backward.

"Hell, I was still searching for you with you sitting in the next room." Wolf moves closer, and I take another inch backward. "I didn't know you were here, and I still wouldn't have known if I hadn't overheard them talking about it." He takes another step, but Bear shoots his hand out before he can reach me, and I'm thankful he stopped him. "Yak made sure our team didn't know because he knew I'd tell you."

"That we would tell you," Bear corrects and then looks right at me. "And with you being the best recruit Yak's had in a long time, he didn't want anything to delay your training."

Hyena pushes to his feet, and I flinch backward, nearly bolting out the door. "Whoa, no need to be skittish. I'm not after you," he says, halting in place. "I was just going to say, it's why Yak didn't fail you the day when you attacked him during the modification testing. Every Natural here would have turned on him. It's why they jumped down like they did. It was for your protection. Not his."

I rub at my sweaty brow and look over my shoulder with a hard pant, weighing my options. Should I run or stay? If I stay and do as I'm told, maybe Bear will keep his word and Alex and I can leave. We can be free. But every fiber in me is telling me to run. That they are lying to me. I bite my lip; running isn't an option. If I run, where would I go? I could become lost here. I could die in these strange tunnels. It would be just like the mining caverns. Dark, scared, and alone. I turn back to them with the only option I have, and hope Bear keeps his word.

"Tippy, I'm sorry I didn't—" Wolf starts toward me, and Bear stops him again, holding his arm in a tight hold. "Bear, if you grab at me one more time, I'm going to put you on the floor."

"Then read the room. Can't you see she is utterly terrified and confused. Hell, she probably isn't even registering half of what you're saying."

"She's not scared of me. She knows me," Wolf says with a hard jerk, freeing his arm.

Bear yanks him back again. "And you don't look anything like the boy in that picture. Not since your accident. If you push this, it could break her."

I press my fingers to my lips while Bear and Wolf argue, feeling trapped and seconds away from shutting down. I need air and room to run, but knowing I may never have either makes my throat constrict, nearly closing. I squeeze my eyes shut, wishing Alex was here. He would know what to do.

"Tippy," Wolf says softly, and I cautiously open my eyes. "I know you believe Uncle Potro isn't with us anymore, but he is." He looks over his shoulder. "And if I can reach him, you'll—"

My heart slams against my chest. "Papa's alive?" I ask breathlessly and turn for the door. "He's here? Where?"

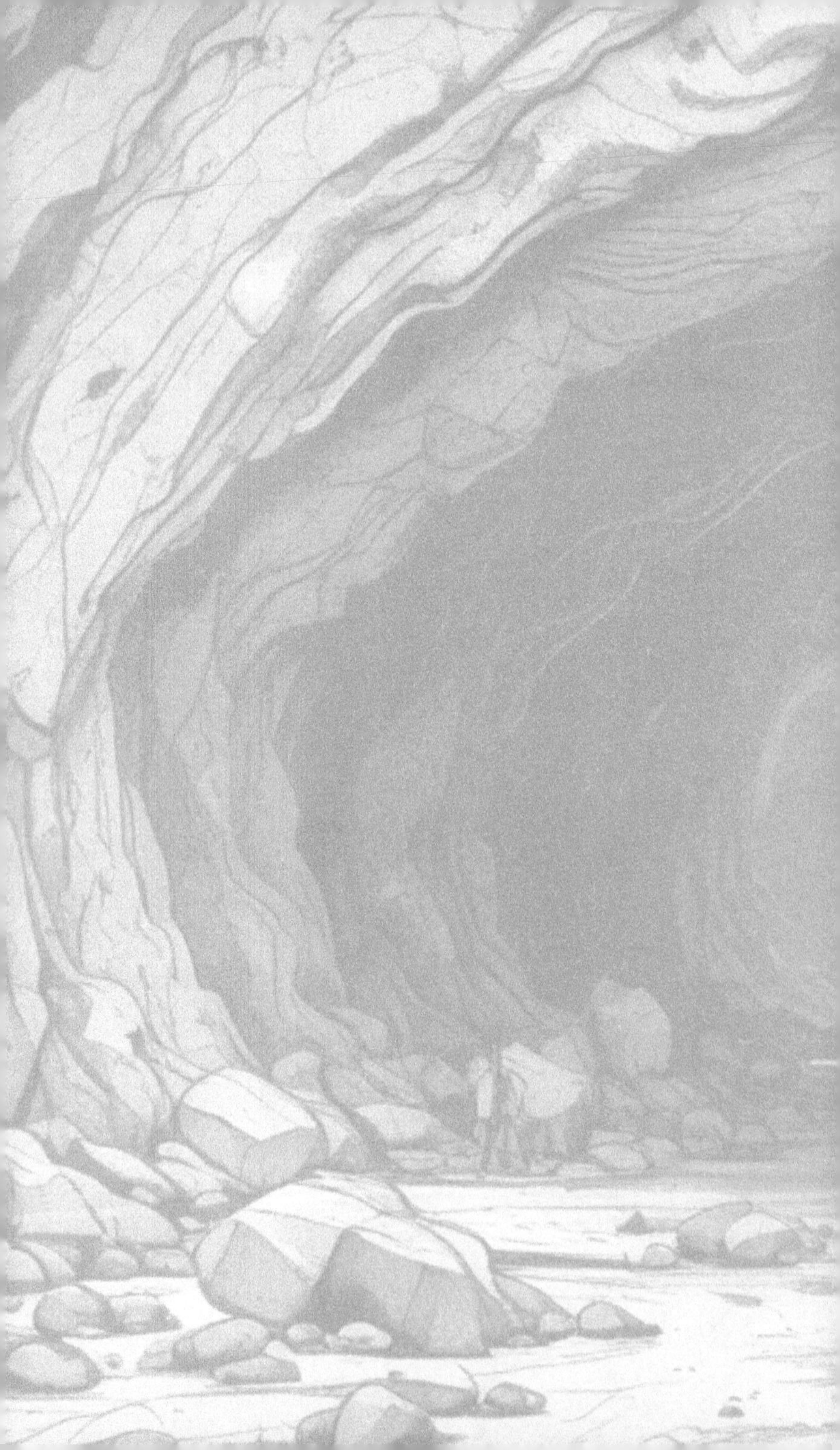

THE REFUSAL OF HIS WORDS

~~HHHH~~ ~~HHHH~~ ~~HHHH~~ ~~HHHH~~
//

"No, Tippy. He's not here."

I stop a breath away from the door and lean into it as the night I was sentenced burst behind my eyes. The captain's laugh. Papa's desperate pleas. And Father's scream. I clench my jaw, forcing the memory away. *No. He cannot be alive. No one could have survived that night.*

But what did he mean by if *I can reach him*. My chin trembles with disappointment and foolishness as the realization starts to form. It's just a trick. Another way to fool me into trusting them. Just as Wolf is trying to fool me into believing he is my cousin. Not only that, but they deceived me into speaking. I shake my head, but Wolf knows Papa's name and mine. *How?* My shoulders slump, because what happened to me and Lou is legendary. It would be easy to go to Capra Horn and ask about me. Anyone could find that information.

My chest squeezes painfully because even though I hate

admitting it, my heart wants this to be true. But my brain is telling me not to trust them. Not to listen to my heart because the last time I did, they tricked me. I lowered my guard and trusted them, and when I wasn't looking, Yak reminded me exactly who was in charge by taking Lou. It's just another way of telling me who has the power. But I must know what their plan is. *Why are they playing with me? What do they want or believe they will achieve by fooling me?*

"Tippy, Uncle Potro still resides at the Lopez Estate, and if I can reach him, you'll be able to speak to him. Tonight," Wolf tells me.

I inhale deeply because Wolf is good. He's not once said dead or alive. He has chosen his words very carefully. But to know what they want from me, I must continue with their ruse. And perhaps, at the very least, I can find out what happened to Lou.

I turn fully around with a thick swallow. "How?"

"With that." He points at a bulky contraption on the desk. I know exactly what it is. It's a Ham Radio. I move closer to the desk and stare at the same model my papa had. I glide my fingertip along the top, remembering all the times I used to talk to Ford. *But where is the black box that goes with it? Do they think I don't know how they work?*

"But before we do this, I need you to know we can only speak in code. If you say anything that isn't code, you will be placing everyone in danger, especially Uncle Potro." He flips a switch, and the front brightens. *Hmm. That's right. They have electricity. They don't need the black box. So, I guess they win that one.*

Bear pulls the chair out from behind the desk, offering me to sit, and I lower into it. Wolf picks up the handheld radio and it makes a high frequency noise. He begins to speak into it, spouting out numbers and letters.

"Anybody monitoring, I'm looking to sell or barter wolverine pelts."

He lets go of the button on the handheld and speaks directly to me. "Wolverine was your mom's Natural name, and this message is for anyone friends with Uncle Potro. Now, they will know this conversation will be about you and whoever picks up knows they will need to speak in code."

I nearly laugh at his words. Now, I know he is lying because if he really was my cousin, he would know my mother died from pneumonia when I was a baby. And her brother, my papa, took me in and raised me as his own. Wolf just shot himself in the foot.

"Wolverine was one of the best Naturals," Bear begins and the way he moves closer, slowly with his hand up, I can tell he is the only one here that understands me. "Just the name Wolverine is legendary around here. The older Naturals, the ones that knew your mom, say we've not had anyone as fierce and sympathetic to our cause as her. It's why after your procedure, all the Naturals were there. They wanted to see if you had any of your mom in you." He flashes me his dimple. "And you did not disappoint." He turns his attention to his friends on the settee. "Hoorah!"

"Hoorah!" they return.

I mash my lips together, desperately trying to keep myself from smiling. They must think I'm really dumb. I start to act the part and a voice rings out from the box, rambling more numbers and letters, and I turn my attention to it. And it's definitely not my papa's voice. Whoever this is has a nasal tone with a thick southern drawl.

"I might have a friend willing to take them off your

hands. How much are you asking?" the voice responds with a yawn.

Wolf squints at the others, and the way he drops his head, I can tell it's not who he wanted to answer. I close my eyes, shaking my head slightly. He really should be in the theater with those acting skills.

"I was hoping for three gold for the pair," Wolf responds.

Bear grabs my attention by perching on the edge of the desk, on the other side of me, and I scoot my chair away from him. "Three gold is the time Wolf wants to speak to him. And since there is a time difference between here and Capra Horn, a pair of pelts is the time it is here."

My mouth parts. *Time difference. How far out are we?* A loud snort rings through the box, and I turn my focus back to Wolf.

"Three? I don't know if he'll pay that much. Maybe one, and that's if you're lucky," the gentleman says with a chuckle.

Wolf rubs his jaw and speaks right at me. "He doesn't know if he can reach Uncle Potro in time. It's one in the afternoon there and it will take some time to run him down." He pushes the button on the side and talks into the handheld. "If your friend knows pelts, he knows what I'm asking for is peanuts compared to the ports that sell them."

Again, Wolf speaks to me instead of into the handheld. "Peanut is your code name. Now he knows it's you that wants to speak to him. So, he'll try harder to find him. Especially since I'm guessing Uncle Potro doesn't know we have you yet."

A lump forms in my throat at the nickname. It's the same one my father used to call me and hope swells in my chest. Maybe this isn't a trick after all. I shake my head. No, it has to be. My mother was never a Natural. She was a farmer on Husk Bay.

"Alright, I'll ask and get back to you." Static hisses and then the gentleman speaks again. "And if this is the same no-good clown that was here a few years back, just know we don't take kindly to cheats and liars around here. You'll have trouble at your feet the second you dock."

The gentleman on the other end doesn't trust him and that in itself tells me everything I need to know. He's lying.

"Wouldn't expect any less," Wolf responds, rubbing the back of his neck.

"You have a nice day now," the gentleman replies, and they both end the conversation, rattling off their numbers and letters again.

Once everyone settles back comfortably, Wolf desperately tries to engage me in small talk, asking if I remember this or that from when we were kids, but I never engage. Not verbally. Only a nod or a shake of my head, and I must admit, he is better than I thought. He knows more than he should for someone that isn't my cousin.

Twenty minutes later, I decide I'm done playing their game and push to my feet. I'm tired and I want to go to bed. Plus, aren't they afraid of their leader? If Yak finds out I'm gone, there's no telling what he'll do, and I'm not looking to be on his bad side. At least not today. So, whatever they have planned for me, it will need to wait until morning. I clear my throat and stand.

"Bear, I know you're not going to keep your word, so will you please just take me back to the mess hall?"

"What?" Wolf asks. "Don't you want to speak to Uncle Potro?"

"No, I do not."

"Why?"

"Because I know this ruse." I dip my chin. "Well, maybe not this exact one, but the outcome is still the same. Papa won't make contact and you'll say, 'we can try again in a couple of days'. And for the next few days, you'll expect me to walk the line. To be on my best behavior and if not, you'll take this opportunity away from me. But I'm not stupid. Not the way you lot think. I know he is dead."

"But he's not," Wolf says softly, pushing off the desk.

I lift my chin with disdain, burning the back of my throat. "Yes, he is. I was there. You bunch weren't. You don't know what we did that night. But we do. We are reminded every day of what we did, and what the punishment was for breaking the law. We are the reason the wounded and dead bled into one another. No one else. Just us. All because we believed those stupid stories my cousin used to tell us. How the Naturals help all those that help the Forgotten." I step closer to Wolf with anger and disgust swimming in my belly.

"So, if you truly are him, where were the Naturals that night, huh? Where was our help? Our protection? Nowhere, that's where. Because you are not my cousin." I sling my arm at the trainers sitting on the settee. "And you bunch are no different from pirates or Spoons. With all your rules and lessons, and the consequences of breaking them. And you wonder why Spoons refuse to help. Well, this is exactly why." I turn my attention back to Wolf.

"We are the lesson that is told to every Spoon and why no Spoon will ever lift a finger to help again. Because the consequences of breaking our law are a lot more damaging than yours. So, trust me, Mr. Wolf, when I say no one could have survived that night, no one did. The second the sheriff allowed Sammy to give out our punishment, she did. But we weren't the only ones she punished. Everyone on Capra

Horn was. Even Ford." I wipe spit and snot and tears from my face, hard and fast, no longer caring about the consequences of speaking out of turn. "And you bunch failed Lou. You sent her back or killed her, I don't know."

The radio cracks, and Wolf turns toward the strained and heavy panting, chattering out numbers. I clamp both hands over my mouth with an unexpected feeling of joy and fear swelling in my chest. I can't seem to breathe or move. I'm afraid if I do, my papa's voice will fade and I'll wake up, and still be a prisoner of my undoing.

"Tippy, did you hear me?"

With a tight grip over my mouth, I finally inhale through my nose and shake my head.

"He wants to know how you're doing. Come here and I'll help you reply safely."

But the night I was taken invades me like a nightmare I cannot wake from, and layers of shame blankets me with guilt. *How can I speak to Papa knowing what I did?* I shake my head again with a backward step, refusing the one thing I have fantasized about for years.

Wolf looks right at me and responds for me, "There's a little scarring, but not noticeable unless you're looking for it. Otherwise, the pelts are in good condition."

"And I'd rather inspect them for myself."

My mouth dries at my papa's tone. *Is that anger and disappointment in his voice?* I take another step backward with a whimpering hiccup. *What if he doesn't want me back, and he's cross with Wolf for finding me?* I lower my head, thankful my papa is alive, and a thought occurs to me. *What if there are other survivors? Maybe we didn't kill as many as we thought.* With that, my belly swims with a sickness. *If there are more that survived, that means the sheriff could be too? Did I imagine his death as I did Papa's? If so, what will he do to me? Will he send me back? Hang me?* I stagger on my feet, nearly falling over, and Bear catches me.

"Don't touch me!" I shriek, jerking away from him. "I hate you. I hate all of you."

"I was only trying to help," Bear says, backing away from me with his hands up.

"Yeah, well, if you really want to help me, bring Lou back," I cry and hug my middle, staring at my feet. "Please. Just give her back."

"Enough of this nonsense. Take this." I look up and Wolf is handing Hyena the handheld. "I thought if you spoke to Uncle Potro, you'd stop with this." He marches toward me and before I can react, Wolf grabs my shoulders. "Whoever this Lou is, she isn't here."

"Because you took her," I seethe and restrain myself from spitting in his face.

"No." Wolf squeezes my arms painfully.

"Wolf, stop," Bear forces through his teeth.

"She needs to know," Wolf says over his shoulder and then looks back at me. "Lou is not here. Only you. You are Lou."

WE ALL HAVE LIMITS

//// //// //// ////
///

"No. No. No," I repeat, jerking out of Wolf's firm grip and lean against the door. My chest aches and my skin feels raw and tight, like I've been scrubbing myself with sand for days.

"I didn't believe it either. Not until I went back and watched the footage. Bear, show her."

"Wolf, I don't think this is a good idea. I think we should get Doctor Lawson," Bear says.

"And we will, but first she needs to know," Wolf says. "She needs to see it firsthand. Like I did. Now, do it, Bear. Show her what I saw."

Bear lifts his arm and slides his finger across the top of his bracelet. Within seconds, the black portrait hanging above the settee flicks on, and Hyena turns, pointing at it with a stiff finger.

"This is your first day here. Watch."

I clutch at my throat, staring at the moving

portraits. *What is this and how is it working? And the sound. How are there voices coming out of it?* The uncertainty of how this is working has me moving closer as I focus on the portrait.

"I say leave shit alone." That's our old top dog.

"Whoa, she be wobbled." My breath hitches at my voice coming through the black box. I'm the one talking to the top dog, not Lou. *Where is she?* Before I can search the black box for her, the pictures roll again, but at a rapid pace. I can't keep up with them until they slow down. It stops on the second day, right after our first test, with the stands and everyone is in line behind the butterfly. Wolf enters, lunging at a small Forgotten, and it isn't Lou that punches him. It's me. I instantly reach up, massaging the front of my neck with a dry swallow as I watch Wolf on the black box, shouting at me.

"Know your place, Pup."

I feel like I'm losing my mind. Like I'm no longer pretending to be a wobbler and I hug myself, forcing the nausea down.

"And this is you in the mess hall, meeting the other recruits," Bear says next to me, and the portraits roll again. When it stops, I see myself race around the table, grabbing food off trays and tossing them into the trash can. My upper lip beads with sweat, and my pulse races out of control. I'm the one Hyena is chasing, not Lou. I move as close as I can to the black box, searching all the faces for Lou, but she isn't among them. I can only see Alex. *Where is she?*

"And this is you the other day. Right after your modifications and you received your lifeline."

The portraits start again, and my breathing is rapid and wild. I can feel my wrist vibrating out of control, but I ignore my bracelet. The portrait shows a loud scream pushing out of me as Bear holds me against him. I wet my dry lips, waiting to see Lou on the ground in a trembling fit, but she isn't there. Only the other Forgotten, and they're facing me with worry and fear. And Yak, he doesn't even have his pistol out. Everyone looks confused at why I'm screaming. But what has my brows pinched and tears threatening is Alex.

"Let go! I need to be helping her."

He isn't talking about Lou. He's talking about me. All that worry and fear is for me, not Lou. I turn away from the black box, shaking my hands out in front of me as a darkness moves over my eyes and I lose my peripheral vision. I cup my head, squeezing as hard as I can with my breathing doubled. I feel sick all over. *Is any of this real? Or are they trying to trick me again?*

"It's okay," Wolf says, moving in front of me. "You don't need Lou anymore. I'm here. You're safe now."

I step around him, stumbling sideways with anger and panic lacing through me. I have to get out of here. I can't breathe. The room spins like I'm trapped inside a tornado, but instead of debris swirling around me, it's voices . . . *I told you not to* . . . I start for the door, and something bumps into me . . . *Fuck you, Bear* . . . I grip the edge of the desk for support and, with each churning swirl, I hear a calm voice in the midst . . . *Just breathe* . . . I search for an exit, but the door is so far away . . . *Take that shit outside* . . . I waver, trying to blink the dark spots away . . . *That's it, Tippy. In and out, deep breath now* . . .

I'm trying to do what Hyena's soothing voice is urging, but the tornado is fierce and becoming more powerful with each passing turn. I lean against the desk, but the harder I try to stabilize myself, the darker it becomes. I shake my head, stretching my eyes wide and swallow the salty saliva back down. And right when I think I'm about to lose my dinner, I fall to my knees and darkness swallows me.

My eyes flutter at the voices nearby.

"Hey, she be awake." I sit straight up, and Alex throws himself on the bed, hugging me tight. "Ye be right?"

I nod, taking in my view. I'm back in my quarters. *How?* My stomach hardens as everything Wolf revealed rushes back to me, and a hollowness fills my chest. Fear threatens the back of my throat as my eyes land on a female figure standing at the door. Whoever it is, their back is to me and they're in a heated conversation with someone on the other side. Her blonde, nearly white hair is rolled into a tight bun and she's wearing a gentleman's navy-colored suit, but it's shiny like silk. *Who is this? I've not seen a woman like this since my arrival here.*

"Being the leader gives me the right to know what's going on with her. To know if—"

The voice on the other side of the door is Yak, and I slowly pull away from Alex. I start to swing my legs over the side of the cot and a hand touches my shoulder. It's Wolf. *What is he doing here?*

"Don't worry, it's just mom arguing with Yak. You're safe. She won't let anyone in here unless you say it's okay, including Yak."

I turn back to the door, seconds away from a panic attack, and scoot to the edge of the cot. *Can that really be Aunt Amy?* I look back at Wolf. *Can that really be Ford?*

"And I am her guardian while she is here. When it comes to her, what I say goes. Not yours, but mine. And that includes pulling her from the program if I so choose."

"Amy, I understand, but she is one of our best recruits. If you can just wait until she finishes the program, she'll get the help she needs. We need her."

"I do not give a damn what you need. Only what she needs. You should have told me she was here the second you learned it. Now, please remove your foot or so help me, David, I will remove it for you."

"At least ask her what she wants before making any rash decisions. It's her life. Her decision to make."

With that, the door shuts and the second she turns, my heart swells into my throat with my chin trembling uncontrollably. I push to my feet with my head lowered in shame and go to her with whimpering apologies.

"There is nothing to apologize for, Tippy." She pulls me in for a tight embrace and I cling to her. "What happened that night is not your fault."

I pull away slightly, keeping my fingers balled into her silk top, fearful if I let go, she will disappear.

"It is my fault," I say with a tight throat. "Father died because of me. How many other kids lost their parents because of what we did?" My chest tightens at the thought of Lou. *Where is she? Did she survive that night? Or was she punished with me, and I lost her somewhere along the way?* I look over at Wolf and shake my head; no, Ford. "Was Lou . . . " I shake my head again. "I mean, was Mable captured that night, too? Or was it just me and Alex?"

"Holy shit!" Ford soars to his feet so fast, I stumble backward, colliding into the sink.

"Ford. Language," Aunt Amy stresses, stepping between us.

"Sorry," he tells his momma and looks at me like he's cross with me. "Is that who Lou is?" He looks at Alex and then back at me. "Mable."

"Yes," I reply softly. "So, was she captured with us?"

"No," Alex says, staring at the floor. "It be just ye and I. Always."

His admission hits me like a ton of bricks. *He knew this whole time, and he never said anything. Or did he?* I open my mouth to ask and Aunt Amy cups my face, forcing my eyes to her misty blue ones. "Mable is doing great. She is actually living with your dad. When her grandmother had fallen ill, Potro stepped in and moved them both into his house."

My heart swells into my throat with a wide smile. "She's alive?" I say, wiping my wet cheeks.

Ford looks at me with his face twisted in anger. "Yeah, and if you thought she was mean before." He eyes his momma and then looks at me, rubbing his jaw. "Let's just say, she isn't the fun, loving girl you two remember. And Cotton Wayne, he isn't the same, either."

"What they be like, then?" Alex asks.

"Mean as a rattlesnake. Both of them."

I ignore Ford's comment because he doesn't understand the loss of a parent. I don't even think he knows what loss is. How it can break you down and make you feel empty inside. Not only that, but he doesn't know how awful Mable's grandmother is. If she is on Capra Horn and taking care of her, Mable is struggling. Mrs. Miller will not allow her to be her true self. She will force her to be someone she isn't, and another wave of guilt settles in my stomach. She's been alone this entire time with no one to love her. Not the way I did. I look over at Alex with my chin quivering. At least I had Alex. He loves me the same way I love Mable. Unconditionally with no judgement. I wipe my snotty nose with my sleeve.

"My actions hurt so many that night and if not for—"

"No, Tippy," Aunt Amy hushes, pulling me close. "All you did is exactly what the Nat—"

"Mom, now is not the time," Ford interjects.

"Then when?" she asks in a harsh voice. "After everything Tippy and Alex have been through and witnessed, they have the right to know exactly what we do and how we do it."

"Because if they choose to continue with the program, they—"

"Continue?" Aunt Amy roars, stepping away from me. "Tippy has literally given the skin off her back to help the Forgotten. She does not need to give more of herself. And as far as Alex goes, he is far too young to even be in the program. I can't believe Yak allowed it."

"We had to let him in." Ford slings his hand at me. "Or she—"

"I don't care why. All I care about is their wellbeing."

Ford inches backward, clearing his throat. "And like Yak said, it is not your decision to make. It is hers. After all, this was her dream." He looks down at Alex, still sitting on the bed, looking terrified. "All of ours." Ford faces his mom again. "And now, they're here, together, in the midst of our dreams coming true, like we planned. I can't allow you to take that away from us. It has to be their choice."

"Ford is right," Aunt Amy's bracelet says. She's wearing the same type Ford and the other trainers wear.

"It's your Uncle Pablo," Aunt Amy says, lifting her wrist. "He wanted to come in person, but we both agreed it might be too hard on you if you saw him. At least for now. But he can hear everything we are saying and is able to speak to us through this."

I nod my head, staring at the device on her wrist, ignoring the fact that everything is moving too fast. But she is right. Uncle Pablo and Papa are twins, and seeing him might have sent me into another episode. My chest vibrates as tears flood my vision. I grope for my aunt's hand, fearful I might already be having one and, if so, I never want it to end. I want all of this to be true even if I can never return home.

"Tippy," Uncle Pablo begins, "I'm not trying to persuade you one way or the other, but all those children you and Mable hid away and saved from previous raids . . . before Sammy punished you . . . " His voice trembles slightly and he clears his throat. "A few of those children are now Naturals. One of our best, Elk, he is a Natural now. You might not have been able to save those children on that particular night, but you and Mable saved more than you think. You've always been a Natural at heart."

I think back to when I was young. To all those times Mable and I took turns hiding them, and then to what I know now of the Naturals. How they gather the Forgotten, bringing them here, and he's right. I never paid much mind to it then because it was normal for a Forgotten to sneak a ride on a cargo ship and go somewhere else. Somewhere with fewer orphans to fight over food. It's why I never wondered what happened to them when they disappeared. I always assumed they were looking for a better place to live and hoped they did. And knowing some of those children or teenagers are here and are now exactly what I was pretending to be all those years, a Natural, closes my throat completely.

"So, if this is something you truly want, you will need to finish the program," Uncle Pablo says. "But, in doing so, just know your dad will not be happy about this. He did not want you to follow in our footsteps. So, if you choose this path, we will not be the ones to tell him. It must come from you."

I lower my head, wringing my hands, because there is so much to consider before I decide. More questions and information about this place, these people. *And what of the failed Forgotten? What happens to them? And Papa, how can I speak to him after everything Lou has done?* My chin trembles and I press it into my chest. *What I have done.*

"Tippy, it be right." Alex brushes his arm across his nose, staring at the floor. "I can be going back. It be right."

"No," I say and go to him. I squat in front of him and reach for his hands. "Wherever I go, you go, remember?"

"Aye, but . . . " His voice drops and cracks. "These be yer blood. Not us." He looks up at me and my throat tightens at his bloodshot, tearful eyes. He's trying so hard not to cry.

With an uncontrollable chin, I say, "True, but you are my family, too, Alex. You are the most important person to me. I will never leave you. Ever," I stress with a tight squeeze of his hands. "Okay?"

"Right." He nods, brushing his nose again.

I wipe my cheeks dry. "Now, what would you like to do?"

"I wanna be joining, but she say I can't. I be too young."

"You can still join if you want," Uncle Pablo says. "I can make that happen. I mean, you still have to go through the program, but I can talk to Yak."

"Pablo," Aunt Amy says through her teeth.

I twist around to sit next to Alex, and I grab his hand. "I want to join too," I say, before Aunt Amy can argue with Uncle Pablo.

"I do not think this is a good idea," she stresses.

"Why?" Ford asks, dropping on to the other side of

Alex. "You and Dad didn't mind when I joined at thirteen. That's only a year older than him. Not that much of a difference."

"Ford does have a point," Uncle Pablo says.

"Yes, but . . . " She presses her lips into a thin line, hesitating, and then asks, "Are you sure?" I give a quick nod. "Very well. *However*, if you pass this last phase, you—"

"Once they pass," Ford corrects.

"Once you pass this last phase, you will be evaluated. Both of you. I want to make sure you are healthy, mentally and physically. Do we have an understanding?"

I draw in a deep breath and nod in agreement. "Thank you," I croak.

"Aye, thanks." Alex grins.

"Do not thank me yet. A lot can happen before then. Including what your dad will do to us when you tell him."

"Still, thank you." I push to my feet, full of hope. "You do not know—"

She pulls me in for a tight embrace. "No, I do not," she says in a thick voice. "And I sure as hell do not know how you two survived as long as you did." She reaches past me and pulls Alex to join in the hug.

I wanted to say because of Lou, because even if she truly wasn't there, she was. She is the reason me and Alex are here today. But instead, I hold my aunt tighter, knowing I no longer need to look for ways of escape. Or have that overwhelming feeling for us to run. For this is the safest place for us.

She pulls away and cups my face. "I have given you something to help with the identity. You should not see Lou unless you are in extreme fear. But it will not last long, only a few days."

I nod again, and she opens the door, walking out, and I hug myself, hoping all of this is not just in my head.

"Tomorrow is testing day, so—" Ford says, invading my thoughts.

"Wait." I wipe my tears away and turn to him. "I thought there were three more days of Hell Week left."

"Yeah, about that," Ford begins, rubbing the back of his neck. "Mom kept you under for a couple of days. She said you needed the rest."

"Wait. Is everyone still in the program? Do they know who I am? Hutch?"

"Yes. Yes, and yes." Ford grins, crossing his arms. "When Yak told them who you two are, you should have seen their faces."

"They be heavy?" Alex asks. "Hutch be heavy?"

"Not at all. He said he figured it out right after phase one. Why? Has he been giving you two trouble?"

"No." I look over at Alex and then back at Ford. "We just want to know what we are walking into," I tell him.

Ford tilts his head, eyeing us, and then says, "Okay." He starts for the door. "Well, tomorrow, during testing, I want you both to stick close to Bear and Hyena."

"Wait. Why? Aren't you going to be there? I thought you were part of their team."

"I am, but since most of them think I failed, I can't go back. Not until the end."

"Why?"

"It's part of the process. One trainer always fails in phase one. It shows the Forgotten no one is above a punishment." He opens the door and turns slightly to look at us. "Do exactly what Bear and Hyena say. They're my best friends. They'll make sure you both pass."

"Isn't that cheating?" I ask.

"Most definitely." He grins and shuts the door behind him.

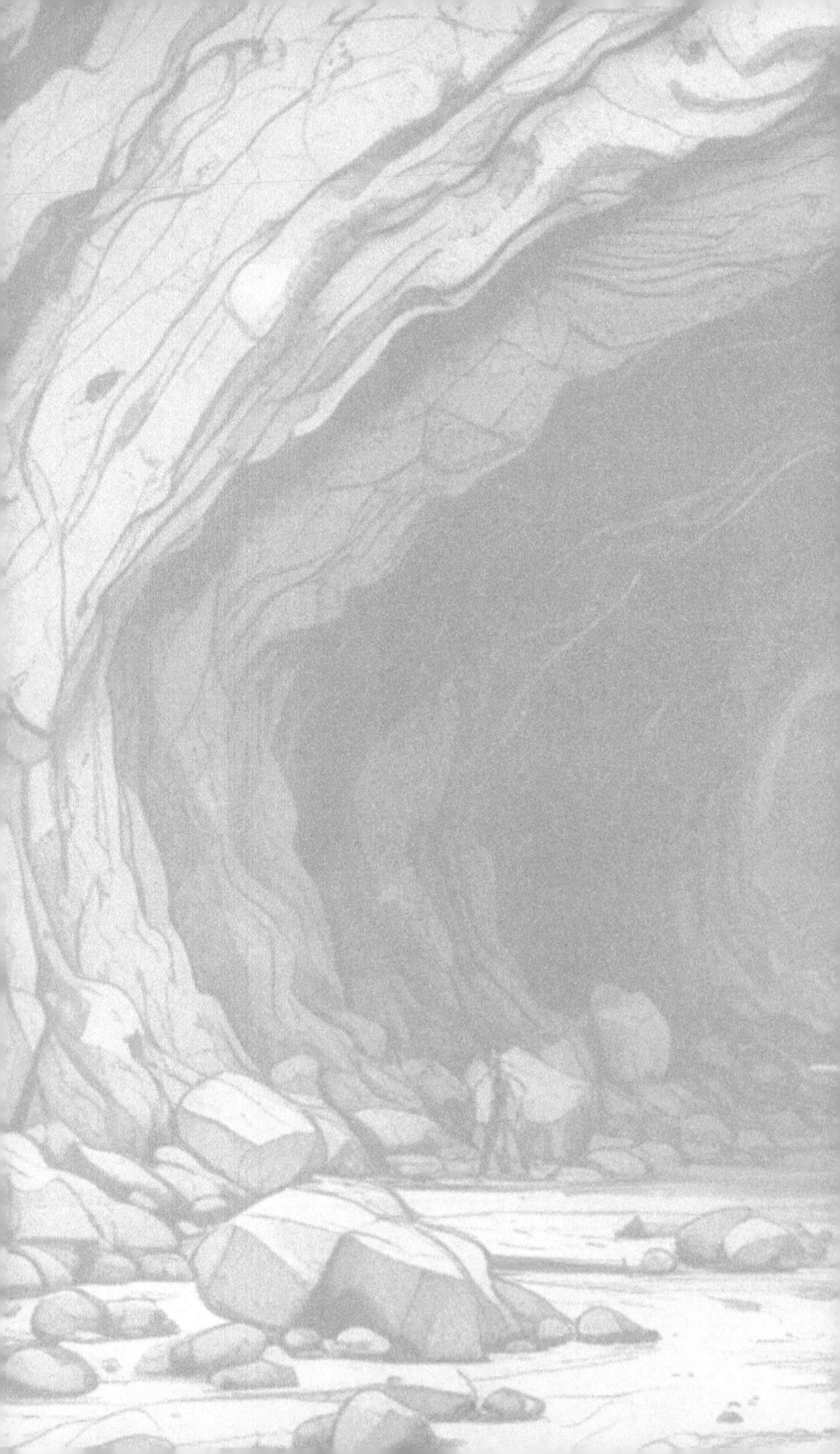

DO NOT FALL

The next morning, we are lined up against the wall in the hallway, waiting for our turn to test. And since it's testing day, we aren't dressed in full gear and heavy boots. Instead, they have us in black trousers, and a matching sweater and sneakers. I can't help but wonder why we haven't been wearing this attire the whole time. These are a lot more comfortable than the other garments they've given us. These are soft and loose and warm.

I lean my head against the wall, wondering who will be next to test. Hutch and Jack have both entered, but neither have come out. It's just me and Toggy in the hallway and neither of us are talking. I strain my ears, trying to hear Alex testing inside, but all I can hear is my own breathing. I rub the back of my head and stare at the floor, waiting and listening and worrying until my stomach is sick. I stretch my legs out just as the door opens and Yak and Fox walk out. I crane my neck, trying to see past Toggy. *Where are they going? And where is Alex? Did he fail?* The door opens again and Bear gestures to me.

"You're next. Hurry up," he tells me.

I push to my feet and step around Toggy to enter behind Bear. He walks up to a table in the center of the room, and it's filled with weapons. *Where did they take Alex?* I skim the empty white walls to a smaller table against the back wall and next to it is a door. *Is that where they took him?* Hyena clears his throat and I see him off in a corner, standing next to a strange contraption. The door on the back wall opens and an older Natural walks through it, joining Bear at the larger table. His face is kind, almost angelic as he smiles. He stops behind the large table directly across from me.

"I'm Elk." He smiles. Tears threaten at the name and before I can ask if he is one of the Forgotten I saved, he speaks again. "I will be in charge of your testing today. Are you ready?" I clear my throat with a firm nod, and he points at the table filled with weapons. "I will call out four weapons and you will pick up the weapon you believe it to be. Let's begin. Billy."

I browse the table for the small solid piece of metal that Yak called a "Billy Club" in training. When I find it among the other weapons, I reach for it and then carefully place it back onto the table. But he grabs it and hands it to Bear. I mash my lips together and watch as Bear walks it over to the small table by the back door. *Why did he remove it? Did I get it wrong?*

Before I can think more of it, he calls out, "Mary."

I quickly reach for the small red ball, leaving the jacks on the table, and his mouth twitches as he hands it to Bear. "I told you; she wouldn't need my help," Elk says.

Bear eyes me a moment and then says, "We'll see."

"Kyle."

Sweat forms on my brow because that's one of the harmful weapons. I wipe at my forehead before handing Bear the return stick, and Elk calls out, "Jack and Jill."

I pick up the two pistols on the table and they both scatter into action. I have no idea what is happening. *Did I pass or fail?* All I know is the one in charge is urging me toward the small table that has the weapons I chose on it.

"Drink this," Elk tells me and hands me a small vial of green liquid.

"What is it?" I ask.

"It's for the simulation." He points at the contraption Hyena is standing at. "It isn't harmful. I promise."

I look at Bear, and he gives me a quick nod. "It's part of the process. Everyone goes through the same thing. Even I drank it when I went through the program. It's completely safe."

I do as I'm told, and I'm surprised at the taste. It's sweet and sour at the same time.

"Now, put these on," Elk tells me, and I take the weapon holster he offers me.

Once I have them on, Bear and Elk are shoving the weapons I named into them.

"And put these in your ears. It's for the next test."

I push the earpieces carefully into both of my ears. The same way Yak taught us a few weeks ago. Seconds later, Elk is slipping some strange-looking headgear over my head, and it blocks my vision completely. *How am I supposed to know what to do if I can't see or hear?*

He secures the headpiece tighter on my head and pain radiates in my temples like there are needles attached to it. And then I hear a crackling in my ear, followed by Hyena's voice. "Can you hear me?" I give a quick nod and then flinch as a hand squeezes my shoulder. "That's only Bear. He's going to help you into the next room and then we will start the second part of your test, okay?"

I nod again and allow Bear to guide me forward. We take a few steps, and he tugs on my shoulder slightly, and I stop as his hand slides off me.

"Okay," Hyena begins, "all you have to do is finish the test without help and you will pass, okay? Now, I'm about to turn on your vision, but what you are about to see is not real. It is only a simulation to start you on a path. Once you are on it, you will be in control of what comes next." There's a long pause as I wait. "And Tippy, I need you to understand that whatever you bring into the simulation, it cannot hurt you. You are in complete control. Here we go. Three. Two."

It's completely dark still. I turn my head slightly and still nothing, but when I face forward again, I see a small flame dancing inside a lantern a few feet from me. My pulse races and I wet my lips because it looks as if it's floating in the air. I start toward it but stop as the flooring groans angrily. I look down and my heart slams against my chest at the water sloshing back and forth over my shoes. I lift my head just as water spits over the dancing flame and the ship slowly begins to reveal herself. It creaks and moans as it dips over waves. I turn in a tight circle, scanning the area, and my stomach churns with the sea. I can feel the sea's anger and I thrust my hands out, trying to keep steady as she spits her distaste of being ridden onto the deck. *Whose ship is this?* I look up at the black flag and my heart drops. It's a pirate ship. I spin in a circle again.

An explosion erupts behind me, and I instantly cower, looking for the enemy. Instead, all that's behind me is another ship off in the distance with lanterns swaying on that ship, too. I straighten. *Where is everyone? Where is the crew that is running this ship? Or is that what I'm here for? I really hope not. I don't know anything about ships.* I turn again and a figure appears on the upper deck.

"Come abou' and ready the guns!"

Whoa. Are we chasing that other ship? I take a step closer, straining in the darkness, and a pirate emerges a few feet in front of me. He's dressed in faded and worn tan trousers and a billowy stained shirt. He has tattoos covering every inch of his face in the design of the dead. I know that face. It's the same one that tried to take me and Alex. Except Ford stabbed him and we ran.

"Aye, Captain," he hollers. He strides toward me, and I scurry out of his way, hiding behind a large wooden barrel.

"Git ready for 'em to broadside. An' no matter what, don't be letting 'em board."

"Aye, Captain," the Pirates reply again. He pulls a pistol from his waistband and aims it at the ship in the distance.

With my heart beating out of control, I watch the captain pace on the upper deck and if not for the quick violent strides, I'd believe this is a woman. But I can't see the captain's face to be sure it's a man. I hunker farther down, away from who I assume is the captain's first mate, and the destruction blooms into life. A crew of at least a hundred pirates is revealed, and their actions are quick and organized as they carry out their captain's orders. They are wearing the same tattooed design on their face.

I peek over the rim of the barrel, away from the madness, just as a second ship swiftly maneuvers right up next to this one. And that crew is throwing iron claws tied to ropes, but just as fast as the claws are hooked and digging into the wood, the crew on this ship is hacking and sawing at the ropes. Before I know it, longboards drop across the two ships. *What is going on? What am I supposed to do?*

Men. Women. And even children are walking or jumping onto this ship with pistols and swords drawn. Bullets cut through the frenzy, zinging over my head. I lower myself even farther and hear a voice behind me.

"They be coming. We gotta hide them." I force a glance over my shoulder and Lou is tugging on my arm. *Why is Lou here?*

Still hunkered, I turn fully around, but it isn't the sixteen-year-old Lou I've been seeing. She's eleven and in her nightdress. "Hurry. We gotta go," she stresses. She holds her sword up and gestures for me to follow. I peek over the barrel and when I turn back, her form disappears like a shadow blending into the night.

"Tippy. Answer me. Are you okay?" I hear Hyena ask me.

I wet my lips, not knowing how long he's been talking to me. But the urgency in his voice and frantic words tell me a while. I scan the area one more time, searching for her, but she's gone. I turn back around, and everything is gone. Including the ship. All that is left is the single lantern floating nearby.

"Yeah, just a little frazzled, but I'm good," I croak out and push to my feet.

"Okay," Hyena says with uncertainty in his voice.

I straighten my shoulders, proving I'm okay, and a small dark figure materializes in front of me. The same way Lou left seconds ago. "Hello," I call. "Lou, is that you?" I move closer and the figure grows, revealing her true self. She turns abruptly with a nasty snarl and aims a pistol right at me.

"End 'em all!"

I instantly buckle with a whimper. It's the Commodore. My entire body goes numb. *Why is she here?* I slam my eyes shut, trying to force the memory away, but the tighter I squeeze my eyes, the more visual the memory forms. I bravely peek one eye open, and the memory of that night grows stronger.

The darkness swirls into something else. Something awful and horrifying, just like the pirate standing in front of me. And before I can stop the nightmare from fully forming and block that night out, like I've always been able to do, I'm standing inside Papa's library. I'm sent back to the night I was sentenced. Where pistols demand attention. Panicked screams obey commands. And a loud voice calling order. The raid that belongs to Sammy "The Terror".

I REMEMBER YOU

ⵤ ⵤ ⵤ ⵤ ⵤ

I rush into my parents' library and close the door behind me. I'm scared. I press my forehead against the smooth wood, desperately trying to swallow my fear. But this rescue mission isn't like the other times. This one is all wrong, starting with the pirate chasing us. Pirates don't pursue Spoons. They ignore us. So why now?

"Hey, ye sure this be safe?" Alex asks.

"Yeah, we've done this loads of times," Mable says.

With a hiccupping breath, I wipe hot tears from my cheeks and force myself to face what I started. I made a promise to Alex, and I must keep it. I must be brave, like Mable.

I face forward and Lou is standing in front of my parents' bookcase, holding a lantern high. And ghostly images crawl along the walls. I blink the eerie images away and smile at Alex. "It will be okay," I reassure him. "I promise." With a dry, hard swallow, I tiptoe farther inside, guiding him closer to Mable.

"I barely got 'em here," Lou says. She moves closer to the secret bunker. "But I think I got 'em all." Alex goes down the steps first and then me. But instead of following Alex, I turn to Mable for the lantern.

"Please be safe."

"Always." She hooks her pinky with mine and we both kiss our fists. "Love you."

"Love you too." I hesitate for a moment. My belly hurts. "Mable, I think—"

"We'll talk later, okay?" She urges me down the steps, and I oblige with my belly twisting in sickness.

She closes the hatch on me, and I can hear the chair grinding back in place as I lock the hatch. I hurry down the steps and hang my lantern on the back wall, and I'm bombarded with questions from the Forgotten. One's I do not have the answers to. Most of the Forgotten down here are older than me.

Ruckus sounds above us, and I know it isn't Mable. Even when we aren't up to no good, she's quiet. It's someone else. And with each striking step, dust sprinkles onto our cheeks, and I hope, with all my might, Mable snuck out safely. I scan the Forgotten with a lump lodged in my throat. If these are pirates and they find us, how can I tell the Forgotten I won't be big enough or strong enough to save them? I think of Ford and Cotton Wayne. They are the strongest boys I know, and they didn't stand a chance against one pirate. There must be at least five above me. My chin trembles uncontrollably as I lock eyes with Alex. I'll have to allow the others down here to be taken. I cannot help them.

"Find what be mine!"

I look up, peering through the floorboards. I can feel the captain's fury. Her voice is loud and violent, just like the blood pumping inside my veins. I side-step, trying to follow the shadows moving along the slates, and then I lose sight of them. Wherever they are, I can hear them tearing the place up. *What are they looking for?* I move along the Forgotten, trying to find them, and Alex pulls on my arm. He points at the small flame in the lantern, and I close my eyes at my mistake. Before I can reach it, a voice cackles out, "Found ye." When I look up, there's an eyeball peeking through the flooring and a primal scream rips out of every single one of us.

"Come outta der, or me burn ye ou'," the captain demands. She moves and the light from above peers through the slates, shining on Alex. Defeat, fear, and sadness are summarized in one look. I have failed him. He reaches through the darkness for my hand.

"It be right."

My heart shatters and my knees nearly buckle me. *How can I give up so easily?*

"It be right," another Forgotten tells me.

Would Mable give up so quickly? Cotton Wayne? No, they wouldn't, so neither can I.

The captain paces above us and I look up at the locked hatch. As long as we are down here, they can't get to us. Maybe we can wait them out until Papa comes. He will save us. He's stronger than anyone.

I lift my chin and bravely shout, "No!"

"Come ou'!" she threatens, followed by the sound of glass shattering.

"Everyone to the back corner," I tell them, forcing them away from the stench dripping through the cracks. But the bunker is so small, we only move a few feet away from the hatch.

"Las' warnin'.'"

"No," I defy again and swallow the bile rising in the back of my throat. *Hurry, Papa! Please hurry!*

Moments later, the sound of a match striking sends panic down my back, and within seconds, a burning inferno threatens the staircase. "Cover your face," I instruct, pulling the end of my nightdress up. But it doesn't really help. The smoldering air is like sharp claws shredding my throat with each swallow. I bend with the others in a coughing fit. It's getting harder to breathe, and I know if we don't do as we are told, we will all die down here. The one thing I'm trying to keep the Forgotten from: a long and painful death.

"Let us out," a Forgotten pleads, pushing his way blindly through. And then another plea and another. Their requests are hard to deny, especially when a small girl falls at my feet, choking.

"Okay. We're . . . we're coming out," I cough.

I move to the stairs and as I open the hatch, smoke swirls in with flames twisting and crawling toward me like one of Mable's winged reptiles, spewing fire. I squint and cough, trying to find my way out when something cold and wet drenches me. More smoke pours in as I'm yanked through the swirling embers. I rub the sting from my eyes as I start for the front door, but a hand seizes my freedom.

He forces me around and I shout, "I'm not a Forgotten. I'm a Spoon. You cannot take me." I kick the ugly pirate in the shin with all my might. And when he releases me with a yelp, I race out of the room. I fly down the hall and out the front door.

"Tippy!"

"Father!" I soar off the porch steps and slam into him. "I had to help. I just had to. And you always say we should help all those in need," I blubber.

"I know, Peanut," he says, lifting me into his arms. "But not this time. This time we cannot help."

"Why?" I wail, just as strong fingers dig painfully into my arms.

"Let go, Jonah," the sheriff tells my father. "She broke the law. She must be punished."

I turn away from the sheriff and reach for Papa, standing next to us. But Father holds me tighter. And when the sheriff reaches for me again, Papa inserts himself between the sheriff and Father, holding me.

"No!" my papa demands. "She meant no harm. She is only a child. She does not understand the rules."

"Nonetheless, Potro, all should follow them. Even children," the sheriff grumbles.

"And I said no. Touch her again, I will end you where you stand." Papa's voice is mean and growly. I've never heard him that cross before and I twist in Father's arms. Papa has a pistol aimed at the sheriff, forcing him to back off.

"Sheriff." I cut my gaze to the house. Marching down the porch is the captain, towing Alex behind her in a rough manner. "She ain't the only one that be needin' to be punished." She pulls her pistol with a black smile, and I turn my gaze away. "Take this one, an' burn 'em all!"

"Wait!" I hear the sheriff shout and I cling to Father's neck. "We had a deal. You can't punish all of us. Look. I'm giving her over." Fingers dig into my arm again.

"No!" Father screams, holding me tighter.

"Jonah, stop! Give her—"

A gunshot sounds behind me, and Father buries my face into his shoulder. "Don't look, Peanut."

"Take another step and you're next, Sammy," Papa says. "Jonah, run."

Before Father can pick up speed to run, another shot is heard behind us.

"Grab that Spoon!"

Father stops and turns back to the house with his chest vibrating against mine. "Potro!" I start to turn and look, and a loud explosion pains my ears. Within seconds, I feel myself falling.

Before I hit the ground, my headgear is yanked off my head.

"It's okay. It is only a memory. You're safe," Bear tells me.

But it feels real. It even looks real. The wall in front of me has images rolling across it and my breath hitches in painful hiccups. A younger me is screaming and kicking while a pirate drags me off of Father. Bear cups my face, forcing my eyes off the rolling portraits. But I can still see parts of my home port burning.

"Just breathe."

I pull in a deep vibrating breath, straining my eyes at the wall. Parts of the memory are bubbled and blistered, like someone lit a match to it, until the entire thing singes into nothing.

"Good. Again. Another deep breath," he says.

I do as Bear asks and hear hushed whispers from above. I look above Bear's head. My throat constricts and a chill runs down my back at all the Naturals watching. Bear wasn't the only one that saw what happened to me that night. I start to lower my chin and the oldest Natural in the group, maybe late twenties, slowly pushes to his feet. *Is he disappointed in what I did that night? At how many lives I killed because of my actions?*

He pats at his chest, slow and hard, three times and then says, "My blood."

I clench my teeth, forcing my emotions down as the others follow his lead. *What does that mean? And why is he pulling his pistol?* I look at Bear and then back at the Natural, and that's when it hits me. I have failed my test. I face Bear with a thick throat.

"Please give my apologies to Ford. I really thought I could do it."

"No. No. No. No." Bear brushes tears off my cheeks with his thumbs. "You did good," he tells me in a broken voice. "Better than good. Then and now. Your bravery that night is well beyond any Natural here. In my eyes, you are already a Natural."

My chin trembles, and I lean into him. He cups the back of my head, holding me tight, and the door opens beside us.

"Let go."

"I can't, Elk," Bear mutters. "I promised Wolf I'd—"

"Yes. We all did. And if you don't let go of her, Yak will know she didn't finish her test." He grabs Bear roughly by the arm, and before Elk can address Bear again, I pull away.

"It's okay." I force a smile. "Ford will understand just as I do. Please, before Yak returns, let me fail. Let me join Alex." I dry my cheeks with another smile. "We both know I wouldn't have gone on without him, anyway."

Bear wipes his nose with a firm nod, and I move to the center of the room, feeling completely exposed. *Is this what happened to the others before me? For Alex?* I look up at the Natural that has a pistol aimed at me. *Did the others plead with him? Did they ask for another chance?* With a deep inhale, I straighten my shoulders and stand tall. *Or did they accept their fate like me?* I bravely lift my chin and, after he nods back at me, the sound of glass is heard loud and clear as I wait for the hot current.

A PRISON FOR ALL

~~HHH HHH HHH HHH~~
~~HHH~~ I

A bitter chill slithering along my skin wakes me and I lift off the cold floor in confusion. I stagger forward, smoothing away the goosebumps as a freezing fog cloaks my vision. I'm only able to walk a few feet before colliding into an ice wall. I turn in a small circle. *Am I in a closed room?* A shadow moves on the other side, and I vigorously start melting the thin layer of frost with my sleeve. Once I have a small hole to peer through, I no longer see the shadowy figure. I blow warmth into my hands and chatter out, "Hello?"

The figure hits the wall with a loud wail, and I flinch backward as it hurls itself against the ice once again. I glance over my shoulder with a jittery pant, and my breath mingles with the icy, cold atmosphere. The shadow throws itself against the wall again and I rush to the other side, gliding my hands along the cold surface, searching for a way out. But there's no way to free myself. I'm trapped. I move along the walls, banging and screaming for help, but that only woke whatever is on the left side of my glass-made prison.

Within seconds, wailing and screaming surrounds me and it sounds as if there are more than just two. Their cries are loud and fierce as they howl and scream, forcing themselves against the barriers. I squat, hugging myself with intense fear spreading through me. *Is this real? Or is this all inside my head?* I cup the back of my neck, rocking slightly.

"It's not real," I say continuously and, little by little, the voices come to a stop.

I sit in the center of the room and keep watch on the shadows lurking nearby. *Where am I? How did I get here?* I hug my knees tighter. *Did I die? Is this the afterlife?* The way this place looks like a wispy cloud, it would make sense. A shadow screams and lunges, bouncing off the wall. Maybe this isn't Heaven. Maybe this is the between place. The place you go when God doesn't know if you're good or bad. I lower my head onto my knees, knowing where I'll go if I'm not already there. With everything I've done in the caverns, I'm not good. Not anymore.

I sit on my rear, rubbing warmth into my thick wool socks. My fingers and toes are stiffening, almost going numb from the cold. *Wait. Isn't Hell supposed to be hot? Like really hot. Am I not dead?* I squeeze my eyes shut and try to remember my last moment. The last thing I remember, and it hits me. I failed my test.

I push to my feet, pacing and blowing warmth into my hands. Bear didn't want me to fail. He tried to stop it, but I wouldn't let him. I accepted my failure. I stop walking. *Where is Alex? Did he fail, too?*

"Mute!"

"Alex!" I turn my head slightly. "Where are you?" I ask with hope driving me forward. I jog along the walls, searching for his voice. The shadows stir awake again, but this time, I ignore them. I need to find Alex.

"Here."

I stop with my ears perked. I can't tell which direction Alex is in with the others screaming and banging.

"Talk to me so I can find you, Alex."

"Over here," he says, followed by a loud bang against the wall.

I rush toward the sound, searching, as he continues guiding me to him. Once I think I'm in the right spot, I blow hot air against the wall and then rub my sleeve on it, creating a hole to see through. The second I see him, my heart swells into my throat. "Please tell me you can get me out!"

"Umm . . . I can be trying!" Alex voices.

I hug myself with a shiver, and Alex pushes away from the wall. "Don't leave me. Please don't leave me, Alex."

"I ain't." He points at something to our right. "There be buttons there, an' I ain't sure which one be freeing ye. And Yak say I only get a single chance."

"So, this is another test?"

"No, it be the same test," Alex replies, pressing himself against the glass. "We ain't finished yet. And if we don't be choosing wisely, he say we both fail."

Relief. Hope, and desperation take over and I push my face against the window, too. "Okay, do the buttons have words on them?" I ask.

"Yeah, but ye know I can't read."

"Yes, I know, but you can describe the letters to me. We can figure out what the words are together."

"Yeah. Right." Alex smiles. "The top button be having something like a bubble." He lifts his hand and forms a circle. "The next one be having a line with a bubble next to it, like this." He raises his index finger and forms a circle with his other hand, bringing them together. "This one, I don't know how to say. It be having a bunch of lines. It be like this . . ."

Before he can give a hand motion, I force out, "Open. You're spelling open. Press that one."

"Ye be sure? Cos there be others trapped like ye and they ain't good." He looks left and right and then back at me. "I ain't wanting to be releasing them toos. This be the only section with buttons. What if I get it wrong?"

"Okay. What do the other buttons say? Explain them, please."

He motions "closed" and then "locked", and I know it has to be "open". It is the only one that can free me. Plus, if this is a test, then maybe they've used this prison before. Perhaps this is their testing box. With a fearful swallow, I peer through the glass.

"Alex, if I'm wrong, then please forgive me, but I can't stay in here much longer. We have to chance it. Please, press the top button."

"Ye sure?" he asks with his brows pinched together.

"No," I frown, "but if we don't, I'm going to freeze to death."

Seconds after he presses it, the door releases with a low sucking sound and the frozen vapor quickly disappears. When I step out, all I see is a hallway lined with glass. Floor to ceiling with more glass blocks dividing each room. I look to my right, at the one connected with mine, and it isn't filled with cold air. None of them are. I study the gentleman, slapping his head and talking to himself, and my heart skips a beat. The plaque printed next to his door says, Benny "The Frenzied".

I turn and all the doors have a pirate name printed on

them. *What is this place? And why are they holding pirates prisoners?* I scan all the glass-made prisons and a few pirates are confused, like the one muttering to himself. But most are pressed against the glass, looking right at us.

"Ay', come 'ere."

I turn, keeping Alex protectively behind me, and see an elderly gentleman sitting on a cot. Haven "The Deceiver": First Mate to the Butcher. His long white hair matches his jumpsuit. And on the inside of his forearms, he has tattoos. A pirate ship on his left and an eagle on his right. But what's unnerving is that this one doesn't look scared, not like the confused ones. If anything, he looks amused. I eye the door at the end of the hallway, to the other pirates locked inside their own glass-made prisons, and then back at him. *Could this be another test? A Natural pretending to be a pirate. Perhaps to see how we react to pirates.*

He rests his barefoot on the edge of the cot and balances his elbow on his knee, gesturing us closer. "Don't be jolted. I can't be hurtin' ye," he says with a sly grin.

Nope. That's a real pirate. We need to get out of here. And fast.

"I don't like it here. Let's be gittin'," Alex urges, plastered to my back.

"Tsk. Tsk," the pirate sounds, staring right at us. "Don't be lettin' the others hear ye or ye'll be joinin' us sooner than ye think." He leans forward with his grin blooming into a full, black smile. "But if ye be lettin' us out, I can 'elp ye. We can take this here place o'er. What'd ye say? Wanna be me first mate, yarr. An' run 'em through."

"Run 'em through!" a pirate voices behind me.

"Run 'em through!" The others repeat over and over.

My heart drops and I fly down the hallway, practically

dragging Alex behind me. Once I'm on the other side and the door is safely secured shut, I turn to Alex.

"Wh . . . why do they have them locked up like that?" I chatter and look up at the warm air blowing on me.

"Yak says cos they be holding answers to meaner pirates."

"Oh," I mutter, rubbing warmth into my arms. "What now?"

"We wait for the next," he says, pointing at his bracelet.

"Next?"

"Yeah, everyone be trapped like ye and we gotta be freeing em'. Like I did with ye. An' Yak say we wait here and no move till we get the ping."

"Ping?" I ask, lifting my face to the warm air.

"No idea, but Yak says we'll knows."

I face Alex. "Will there be clues or something?"

Alex shrugs. "Ye want me hoodie," he asks, lifting the hem of his black sweater.

"No." I stop him. "I'm starting to warm up. Thank you, though."

Minutes later, my bracelet flashes Hutch's name, but only for a second, and then a countdown begins. I peek up at Alex and his face is scrunched, trying to read what it says.

"It says Hutch, and we have thirty minutes to find and free him," I reply.

"I know where he be." He grabs my arm. "Let's git. This place be giving us the creepies." He turns, walking forward, and talks to me over his shoulder. "This whole place be a jumble of looking glass and since I be the one to start the test, Yak be letting me walk it. He say I be needing to know where everyone be and I only get a single chance. That I should be doing the maze more times." He looks over at me with a proud smile. "But I didn't need to. I know where everyone be, single go."

THE TEST OF ALL TESTS

//// //// //// ////
//// //

Alex leads me into a room that looks like a dungeon. The walls and flooring are made of dark red bricks, and hanging from the ceiling are all sorts of chains. Small. Wide. Long. Short. And in the center of the room is Hutch. He is in a box, too, but he hasn't woken up yet. His head is hanging with his arms stretched above his head, tied to the top corners. And his feet are shackled to the bottom, too. We start to go to him and a strange noise echoes above us. I look up and gears are grinding against each other, lifting the box high into the air. Once it stops, a copper tube shoots down, and water gushes out of it, straight into Hutch's box.

"Hutch!" Alex hollers.

Hutch lifts his head, a little groggy, but as soon as the water hits his head, he awakens fully and begins fighting against the restraints.

"Hutch!" Alex shouts again, and Hutch's wild green eyes land on us.

"Hey, get me outta here!"

"We wills. Just . . . just hold yerself," Alex says, moving away from me.

I move closer, inspecting Hutch's box as he pleads for our help. Water is pouring into his box at a fast rate. How are we going to get him down and out of that before it fills to the top? I scan the ceiling where chains are hanging, draped throughout, and then I see it. There's a red and white target near the left corner of the room and it's hidden behind one of the larger chains. The target is so small, I almost missed it.

"Alex, there's a target over there."

"Then, this mean this be all ye." Alex races back over and holds up a pistol in front of my face.

I take it from him and turn it over in my hand. It isn't a working pistol. It's only the base of one. "Where did you get this?" I ask him.

"Over there." He points. I follow his finger and then race over to the baskets lined against the wall. Each basket is filled to the rim with pistols and ammo. But as I get closer, I see that they aren't working pistols at all. They are only parts and not all fit together. Some are for shotguns and some for rifles, but none are for the one in my hand. I look over my shoulder at the target and I immediately know that is how I free him. My chest squeezes because Alex is right. This is all me. I ranked highest on weapons, and Hutch's life depends solely on me.

"Hurry!" Hutch hollers, struggling against the shackles. I turn back to the baskets, pulling the only weapon out that is partially put together, and begin searching for the missing pieces.

My hands shake at seeing Hutch already knee-deep, and none of these pieces are the ones I need. I move to the next basket and dump it onto the ground, skimming all the parts, and when my eye catches the charging handle, I snatch it up. I move to the next basket, but I can't find what I'm looking for. I glance at the other basket and see Alex standing under Hutch, breathing heavily with his hands griped tightly together.

"Ye gotta hurry, Mute."

"I know, and you shouldn't stand there," I tell him.

"Why? He needs to be knowing he ain't alone."

I glance up at Hutch and then back at Alex. "I'm not asking you to leave him. Just move a little farther away, so you aren't standing directly under him."

Silence hovers between us as I continue searching for the next part, and Alex quietly moves away from Hutch. But not far, just enough that if I fail, the box doesn't land on him.

"What she be saying!" Hutch hollers.

"Not to be standing under ye!"

"Why? What's gonna be happening?"

"Nothing."

"Does she not be thinking she can do it?" Hutch squeals, struggling against the restraints even more.

I reach for the bolt carrier group and see Alex shrug.

"Alex, stop talking to him. You're only scaring him. And I can do this. I just need everyone, including myself, to remain calm."

Alex races over to me with his eyes wild and fierce. "Mute, ye gotta hurry. Like now!"

My hand soars up like a viper, fast and mean, as I yank him to me. "Ya think I don't know that. He be my mate, too." I hear my voice. The way Lou used to speak, and I uncurl my fingers from his shirt, gently pushing him away. "My apologies, Alex." I focus back at the task at hand. "I didn't mean to grab at you and speak like I did. I need a firing pin. Will you please help me find it?"

He squats down, combing thoroughly through the parts with me. "It be right. I be jolted too. I be . . . find it."

Alex hands it to me and I insert the pin with a quick glance up at Hutch. The water has stopped with Hutch's lips puckered right at the waterline, sucking in air. I soar to my feet, rushing over to the other wall, and rummage through all the magazines and clips. And when I find the one I need, I shove it into place and move to the center of the room.

I aim the pistol at the target and then blow out a steady breath as I pull the trigger. The small yellow paint pellet hits the target, and Hutch's right arm is released. My mouth parts with my heart racing. That's only the first one. Where are the other three? Luckily, Hutch remembered the technique Bear taught us in phase one and he cups his hand over his mouth, creating a larger hole to breathe through.

"Alex, help me find the other three targets."

"Sure, what they look like?"

I point at the one I shot, and he nods.

"Yeah, I seen one over there when we come in."

I follow his finger and to the left, under a low hanging chain, is another target. I side-step for a better shot and pull the trigger. Hutch's leg releases and his toe grazes the bottom, but not enough to bob up for more air. I quickly scan the room again.

"Over here."

Alex rushes over, dragging the basket I knocked over to the side, and I pull the trigger. Hutch's other arm releases, and to my surprise, Hutch still remains calm. He uses both hands as an air pocket, while his big toe keeps him steady.

"We gotta hurry. Where it be?" Alex asks, pulling at his hair and moving in a small circle.

"I don't know, but you need to calm down. Close your eyes and think. Did you see any targets when we first entered? Or while you were talking to him. Was there anything out of place?"

He closes his eyes for a moment and then they pop open. "Jeepers! I should have been knowing. We gotta work as a team, always." He runs over to the back wall and points at the discolored brick. "This be different." But instead of asking me to shoot it, he presses the brick into the wall. Within seconds, a plug at the bottom of the box drops. As the water leaks out, Hutch gulps for air. It isn't draining fast enough, we still need to release his other leg so he can climb out.

"Mute, there."

Alex points and hanging at the bottom of the box is the last target. The final shackle springs free and Hutch quickly jumps onto the edge of the box. He soars over the ledge and lands perfectly on his bare feet. When he straightens, he slings water off his face and then looks at me. "Ye be cutting it a little close, yeah?"

I open my mouth to apologize, and our bracelets vibrate, flashing a new name.

"Toggy's next," I tell them.

"I know where she be."

We rely on Alex since he's been through this mirror maze and knows exactly where he is going. But this time, Alex doesn't take us to another room. Instead, he stops at the edge of the hall and points left.

"She be down there."

I step in front of Alex and there she is, on the other side

of the long tunnel, strapped to a chair. Hutch starts forward and I grab his arm, stopping him.

"Alex, check the area and make sure it's safe." Before the words are completely out of me, the tunnel walls move and shift as objects swing and dart outward.

"Ain't nothing safe about that," Alex blusters, slinging his hand at the long tunnel.

"Yes, but maybe there's something here, like the false brick, to stop it or slow it down." I scan the area. "There must be something."

"There ain't," Alex says, dragging his hands down his face.

I turn to Hutch with a grim face. "Which means, you'll need to get through that to turn those off. Otherwise, Toggy is stuck in there." Hutch looks at me like it's my fault. Like I'm the one that created this . . . thing. "You can do this. You're the best out of all of us."

"Let's be trusting so, yeah?" Hutch says, bouncing on his toes and shaking his hands out, slinging water everywhere.

"Wait." I pull my top off, leaving my undershirt on, and hand it to him. "We need to get you dry so your footing is better." I shimmy off my trousers until I'm standing in my short long johns. "Here, take mine."

"Yeah, good thinking."

While he changes into my warm, dry clothes, I move aside, and Alex joins me against the wall.

"Bonus," Alex says.

"I ain't needing no bonus," Hutch says, poking his head through the sweater. "This be all skill." He cracks his neck. "Watch and learn, Pup." But his voice isn't as strong as it usually is, and my heart goes out to him.

"Hutch, would you like for me to go instead?"

"Naw, I got this," he tells me with a wink. And then faces the tunnel, rubbing his hands viciously together, and darts forward.

Alex grabs my hand as Hutch jumps and ducks and squeezes himself down the dark tunnel. All while avoiding swords and arrows darting from the sides with a huge boulder swinging lower and lower above his head. The second he's through, Toggy mouths something and Hutch disappears.

I move closer, trying to see down the dark hall and the tunnel walls shift as the deadly objects move back into place. Before they're fully aligned, I'm making my way through to help Hutch with Toggy. But as I join him, my bracelet vibrates, flashing Jack's name.

THE COMPLETION OF TRANSFORMATION

IIII IIII IIII IIII

IIII III

After the five of us finish our test, Yak and all the trainers escort us to a small room with six egg-shaped beds in the center. The soft glow of light pulsing from the flooring reminds me of the night I learned the truth about myself. Except now, as I enter the same room, I'm not afraid. I follow behind Toggy, careful not to step on the circular light, and stand at attention against the wall. Bear and the other trainers follow suit, standing directly across from us on the other wall as Yak halts between two beds.

"You have successfully passed phase three, and out of seventy-eight recruits, you five are all that remain. Congratulations."

"Hoorah!" the trainers bellow.

"If you thought phase three was hard, it's nothing compared to phase four. The next phase is all about fear, trust, and hesitation. First, I want to explain what you are about to experience and why." Yak looks right at me. "This is your last procedure and with this one, we will be altering your vision and hearing. When you awaken, you will be able to see in the dark and your hearing will be improved. You will be able to hear a whisper ten feet away." The room squawks with delight and Yak raises a hand, hushing everyone.

"Yes, it's exciting. However, you will also have a longer recovery than the last procedure. Once you are unconscious, you will be out for nearly a week." He gestures to a bell hanging by the door. "So, if phase three was too difficult for you, please feel free to ring out."

I skim the others, waiting to see who or if anyone will ring out, but no one does. Everyone here wants to become a full-fledged Natural, and to my surprise, that includes me. I don't feel as if this is something I must do in order to be safe or free. If they truly are saving and helping others, then I want to be a part of that. I want my life to have meaning. Something I never believed I would feel or have again. I only wish there was time to sort it all out. To understand what all has transpired, especially with my papa. If he really was a Natural, why did he never tell me? I have so many questions.

"Good. Let's begin." Yak moves out of the way and gestures to the beds. "Please pick a pod and enter."

A warm palm slides into mine. "Ye be right?"

I look over at Hutch with my heart full of love and admiration. I don't know how long we have truly been friends, or if it matters, I'm just grateful we are now. Perhaps one day I can show him the same kindness he has shown me. Not just anyone would willingly stand by a wobbler, and without fear. And Hutch did.

"Hoorah," I chuckle and allow him to guide me to a pod.

I sit on the edge and sink into the mattress with my legs hanging off the side.

"I be here, yeah?"

I give a firm nod and Alex points at the pod to my left.

"An' I be here."

I give another nod and Yak steps between us.

"He'll be fine. I promise. I'll be watching over Alex myself during this procedure. As for you, are you doing okay? Scared? Anxious?"

"A little," I admit and watch as the trainers shut Toggy, Hutch, and Jack inside their pods.

"Would you like something to help with your nerves? I can give you something to relax you."

"No," I clamp a hand over my bracelet, "I need to do this. I just . . . it might take a few minutes longer, is all."

"Take all the time you need. But if you change your mind, Bear is your trainer. He'll be the one watching over you." Yak gestures to a short, stocky gentleman entering the room. "Along with Dr. Carl. Just say the word and he will give you something."

"Okay." I nod.

"Let's go slow," Bear says beside me. "How about we start with swinging your legs around and onto the bed, okay?"

I lift my legs onto the bed and so does Alex.

"Here, you can use my key ring." I look up and Bear is offering me his rawhide. The same one he braided during phase two when he sat with me while I recuperated. "This helps me when I'm feeling nervous. It allows me to focus on braiding it and not worrying about what is happening around me."

"Thank you." I take the silver ring with three strands of rawhide attached to it. But I don't braid it; I slip the ring on my index finger, and it swallows me, allowing me to twist it continuously as I look over at Alex.

"Where's me toy?" he asks Yak with his palm up.

I can't help but smile as I slowly lower myself down and Bear moves closer.

"That's not a toy and you don't need one. You'll be fine," Yak tells him.

"I don't know. I be feeling woozy," Alex says, swaying slightly, and then shoots his arm upward, showing Yak his bracelet. "And look, me charm be runnin' fast."

"It's barely blinking." Yak swats his hand away. "Your heart rate is slower than mine."

"Exactly," Alex says, wide-eyed. "I might be fadin'."

"Jesus," Yak says and looks over at Bear. "Is this the kind of crap you've been dealing with?"

"Pretty much, yeah. Fox and Owl think it's hilarious. They've even given him a name. Honey Badger."

Yak looks down at Alex. "Yes, that certainly fits," he says, and I notice Bear has been slowly closing my hatch.

Instinct forces my arms and legs up, holding the hatch in place.

"Are you sure you're okay?" Yak asks.

"Yes, just . . . " I lower my arm and say, "I'm fine. You can close it."

"Are you sure?" Bear asks.

"Yes."

The hatch closes and I twist the ring faster, staring at the purple glow above me.

"Can you hear me?"

My heart rate quickens with my eyes darting back and forth at Bear's voice. "Yes."

"Good. I'm going to walk you through this. But if you

start feeling sick or scared, just let me know and I'll open it back up, okay?"

"Okay," I say with a deep inhale, trying to calm myself.

"In a moment, I'm going to release a mist that will help you fall asleep, okay?"

"Okay." I tighten my thumb against the silver ring. "Is this the same stuff that's in the blue ball Simon?"

"Sort of, except it won't erase your memory and it won't come out in small lingering smoke trails. Think of this one like someone just sneezed in your face." Right as he says it, I flinch at the warm substance. "Gross, huh?"

"Yes." I grin, and my shoulders relax.

"Now, I'm going to count backward from ten. Here we go. Nine." A calmness spreads through me. "Eight." A giggle escapes me. "Seven." I feel like I'm floating. "Six." It's hard to keep my eyes awake. "Five."

I peel my groggy eyes open and instantly know something is wrong with my vision. It's as if someone sucked all the color out of the room with a dark haze around everything. I lift up and press my fingers to my eyes, trying to clear away the sleep. But when I open them again, it's still the same. I swing my legs over the edge with my skin slicked with fear.

"Hey, you're up earlier than I thought."

I turn my head around to Bear's voice.

"Whoa." He stutters to a stop with his face twisted in worry and then rounds the pod, slow and cautious. "Your eyes have been altered so you can see in the dark, remember?" He squats near me but is careful not to come too close. "Everything you are experiencing is completely normal."

I draw in a deep breath and slow my words and

thoughts as I scan the other pods behind me. "Alex and Hutch . . . is everyone, okay?"

"Yes. You are the first one awake. Would you like to return to your room or stay with—" He shakes his head with a funny face. "That was a dumb question. Of course, you want to stay with Alex." He lifts to his feet and scans the room. "Let me hunt down a chair and you can sit with him until he wakes up. Oh, and Wolf's here. Do you want me to get him?"

"Yes, please. That would be great."

While we wait, Ford, Bear, and Hyena sit with me. And I can't help but stare at Ford's face. I want to know what happened, but I also know what it's like for others to pry. I hated it when anyone asked Lou—I mean, me—about my scars. Instead, I ask, "How long has it been since you've seen Lou? I mean, Mable."

Ford crosses his arms and slumps into the chair. "I don't know. Long time."

"Oh, he knows." Hyena grins, mirroring Ford's posture. Except Hyena isn't sitting directly in front of me. He's sitting to my left. "Every time Wolf would come back from visiting you, it was Mable this and Mable that." Hyena turns his head slightly to look at me. "And it only got worse when they were together."

My eyes nearly pop out of my head as I lean forward, asking, "You went steady with Mable? For how long and why did it end? I want to know everything." I lean back, forgetting my own words about prying. "My apologies, Ford. I didn't mean to pry."

"It's no big deal. And yeah, we went steady for like a hot minute, but it wasn't anything serious. It just ran its course."

"Not serious?" Bear laughs, throwing a thumb at Ford. "Hell, he'd still be with her if he hadn't taken the hit for me and ruined his perfect little face." Bear pats Hyena's shoulder with the back of his hand, asking, "What was it he said when he saw his scar?"

Hyena smiles wide, showing all his teeth, and then shifts in his seat with a sniff. He wipes at the corners of his mouth, slow and exaggerated, forcing the grin down. "She wouldn't want no mangled lookin' fella like me," Hyena says pitifully. And then Bear and Hyena roar with laughter as Ford sucks air through his front teeth, annoyed.

"You know she wouldn't have cared. She isn't like that," I say to Ford.

"Yeah, that's what I thought, too. But right after this happened," he points at his face, "I was supposed to go see her, but I couldn't. I couldn't face her like this. Not until my scar healed a little more and my eye was fixed. So I—"

"Wait. Why not use the same medicine that I had . . . those Nano things?"

"Because this happened off the sub. Out there, there is no medicine like that. If you're hurt off the sub, you're patched up the old-fashioned way until you're back on the sub. And by the time I got back, the damage was done. The only thing they could fix was my eye. Even then, they couldn't fix it, fix it. Not like it was. I mean, I can see out of it, but the color, that's gone." He pauses a moment and shifts in his seat.

"Anyway, I called her on the ham, used Mom as an excuse. Said I needed more time with my family and to sort things out before I return. And she practically jumped at the chance to end things." He shifts uncomfortably again. "So, it's not like I'm the one that ended it. It was her."

"What was her reason for ending things?" I ask.

"She didn't give me one." Ford shrugs. "She ended the

call and all communication. I haven't seen or spoken to her since. And that was three years ago."

"Hmm." I settle back into my chair. "That doesn't sound like Mable. There must have been a reason."

"Yeah, and like I told you before, she's different now. Meaner."

"How would you know if you haven't seen or spoken to her since?" I ask, trying not to sound defensive, but a sliver is still heard behind my words.

"I just do. And I'm done talking about this with you." He pushes to his feet, ending the conversation by walking away.

A NATURAL NAME

꒰꒰꒰ ꒱꒱꒱

Phase four is about to start and, according to Bear, it's a big deal because those that pass become a true Natural. I blow out a steady breath to slow my beating heart, but it doesn't help. The five of us left are lined against a wall as we wait for Yak and our trainers. The tension and silence hanging in the air is overwhelming, making my stomach sick with nerves. Finally, Yak strides down the hall and I straighten my shoulders.

"Let's ramble!" Yak calls, and the energy turns wild and fierce.

The trainers are racing down the hallway, aggressively, making animal calls like they're about to go to battle and sweat forms under my arms. I don't know if it's because of the winter gear I have on, or how they are reacting to going outdoors, but it has my stomach knotting. I pull in another deep breath and Bear steps into my view.

"You're with me," he says and hands me a pair of thick, mirror-like eyewear along with a heavy bag.

Hyena shoulders through us and then bends to Alex's level. "No silliness or clowning around. You must take this seriously. Got it?"

He hands him the same gear, and Alex looks up at me with a scrunched face. "Yeah, Pup. No fooling about. This be serious," he says sternly, mocking Hyena. "Nah, us just foolin'. This gonna be clean, yeah?" He grins with excitement.

"Nope, I'm switching," Hyena grouches and snatches the back of Alex's coat.

"Hey! Hands off the goods. This be fresh," Alex blusters on his tippy toes.

"Hyena, stop fooling around and help Alex hook up," Yak orders.

"Yeah, Hyena," Alex sasses, pulling his eyewear over his eyes.

"Hold up. I don't think you have those on the right way. Here, let me help." Hyena pulls Alex's eyewear an inch from his face and releases them with a hard snap.

Alex bends with a yelp, yanking his eyewear off his head, and quickly straightens. "Ye wanna be playing? Welp, it be on."

"Me already be bringing it," Hyena taunts.

"Enough. Both of you. Now, open the door," Yak orders.

Hutch nudges me and then leans close to my ear. "It be nice to see them getting an ear bashing instead of us, yeah?"

"Yes," I agree, returning his smile, and shoulder Bear's bag over my winter coat. It's heavier than I thought. I adjust the weight and whatever is in his bag clinks together like jars knocking against each other. I carefully face forward in line, hoping I don't break what's in here.

The door slides into the wall and a gust of wind sends snowflakes swirling inside, and I welcome it. It's been so long since I've seen snow; my lips spread into a wide grin.

"Here," Bear says, raising his voice over the howling gust. "Put this harness on."

I accept the strange-looking straps as Hyena orders the same to Alex. Except he didn't offer the harness to Alex like Bear did with me. Instead, Hyena and the other trainers point behind us, at all the straps hanging on the wall.

"How?" Alex asks.

"Like this," Hyena says, and we all watch as he steps into the holster, demonstrating how it goes around both of his legs. And then pulls and fastens it on for a tighter fit around his shoulders.

"Why? What it be for?" Alex asks. "I thought we be going outside."

"We are. It's so you won't fall to your death, but if you'd rather just hope for the best, we can do that." Hyena leans outside the door, peering down, and then glances over his shoulder at Alex with a shrug. "Maybe the snow will break your fall."

Alex peeks over the edge and then shuffles closer to me. "There ain't no ground." He reaches for the straps off the wall, and everyone follows suit. Once mine are on, Bear steps in front of me, tightening my straps with a hard yank and then moves behind me. He's close. Too close and I step forward, but I can't move. I'm attached to something. I look behind me and we are linked together.

"I hope you aren't afraid of heights, because that's mostly what phase four is all about. Heights and endurance with a couple of things in between," he tells me. "The good thing about phase four is it's only a few days long, instead of weeks."

"Oh, okay," I mutter and face the open doorway, but I can't see anything. It's completely white. I inch closer, about to look over Alex's shoulder, and Hyena touches my arm.

"Excuse me, please." He squeezes between me and Alex, linking himself with Alex. And then clips something similar to a child-sized bracelet onto the wire above us, and I hear the same snapping sound behind me. I reach up and it moves freely along the wire.

"What that be?" Alex asks.

"It's what your harness is attached to. It will keep you from plummeting to your death." Hyena bends his knees, bouncing and swinging freely underneath the wire. What-ever that bracelet is, it's holding his weight and I gulp at the small size. "Yep, mine works," he says, pushing Alex's closer to the edge.

"Whoa, wait. I ain't tested us yet."

"Don't worry, it will be over before you know it. Espe-cially if yours doesn't work." Before Alex can reply back, Hyena pushes them both off the side.

A scream rips out of Alex, and I inch closer to the edge with a dizziness spinning in my belly. I grip the sides of the frame in a firm hold and peer down, but I can't see them. The storm is carrying so much snow, I can only see about three feet down before everything turns white. I've never seen anything like this. I mean, I've had winters before, but nothing like this. Not where the snow blankets the world, hiding wildlife and vegetation.

"I won't let you fall. I have you," Bear says and wraps an arm around my waist. "Put your goggles on." The second I pull them down, and before I can prepare myself for the fall, he pushes us off the edge, too. I cling to his arm with a sharp scream, but quickly shut my mouth. The vicious air is cutting my throat like I'm inhaling knives. I tuck my chin, zooming through the air, and seconds later, I hear Bear's voice. It's loud and demanding. "Lift your legs!"

I do as I'm told, and as we slow, he digs his heels into the snow. When we come to a stop, a blur reaches out and clips me to them. "Ziplining is fun, huh?" Hyena chuckles.

"It be mind buzzing," Alex replies. "I wanna go again."

"Yes, it was fearful, but in a thrilling way." I agree with a grin and step aside for Hutch and Fox.

Once everyone is on solid ground and clipped together, Yak takes the lead, and we follow along a wire with the wind whistling between us. I can barely see Alex in front of me, much less any trees or wildlife, but I can hear them swaying and howling nearby and in the distance.

Hours later, as the sun begins to set and the snow slows to a flurry, we reach a flat plane. Yak stops us near a group of small huts covered in snow and I bend over to catch my breath, massaging my thighs as he faces us.

"This is where phase four will begin. The most dangerous of all phases. Here, we cannot control the weather, animals, or the circumstances. Do not wander off alone. Always stay with your trainer. If another whiteout hits or you encounter a wild animal, we will not find you until it is too late. Now, please get with your trainer and help set up camp for the evening."

I walk over to Bear, and he guides me to one of the huts. "This is us." He points. I hunch my shoulders, following him inside and remove my eyewear. And my vision is nearly drained of all colors.

Bear tosses his bag onto a sturdy slab of wood shoved against the wall. I carefully slide his heavy bag off, placing it under the table as he grabs a broom from the corner. He pokes the handle into the small opening in the ceiling, creating a larger hole. And the second sunlight peers through the opening, my eyes instantly pool with tears at the brightness.

"Want to brush some of this snow out while I make a fire?" he asks, offering me the small broom.

Before I start sweeping, I stretch my eyes with a hard blink, trying to adjust my vision that is tinting with color again, and ask, "It's strange, isn't it?"

"What?"

"Never losing your vision, only the color."

"Yes, but what's really staggering is how your eyes look in the dark. Yesterday, when I saw them, I nearly fell over. I didn't say anything then because I didn't want to scare you, but later, I asked Yak, and he said it's normal." He points at me. "Yours and Alex's eyes are different from ours in the dark. They don't have a small shimmer to them like the rest of us. Yours are brighter, like the end of the pinch light."

"Pinch light?"

"Yeah, remember the small light Toggy gave you when we were in the tunnels."

"Oh, pinch light. Yes, I remember." I turn back to my sweeping. "So, how did you receive the name Bear? Is it a name you picked? Or one you were given, like Fox gave Alex, with Honey Badger."

"No. It picked me."

I face him. "What do you mean, it picked you?"

His face softens, sliding into a full grin as he walks toward me. "You'll find out in the morning," he says and then bends swiftly, walking out the door.

As Bear and I rest for the night, I toss and turn in my sleeping bag. My nerves are on edge and being this close to the fire; I'm hot all over. I quietly crawl out of my bag and tiptoe over to the door. With a quick peek over my shoulder, I step into the snow and my wool socks soak with moisture. The cold air instantly calms me as I move farther away from the huts and closer to the snow-covered forest.

I lift my chin to the moon, peeking out from a cloud with a smile. This is the closest I've been to freedom since my sentencing and I throw my arms in the air, twirling among the dancing snow until I'm dizzy with pleasure. The same way I would when I was kid. Not that we ever had heavy winters like this, where the snow is almost knee deep, but we did have enough for snowballs. And, on occasion, there was plenty of snow to build small snowmen or tiny forts in a playful snowball fight.

A blur invades my vision and I stagger to a stop, staring wide-eyed at the animal in front of me. Whatever it is, it hunkers slightly and my heart slams against my chest. I back away with a shudder and its yellow eyes silently follow. Another step backward, but it doesn't follow me this time. Instead, it dips its head and moves to the right like it wants to get behind me. I suck in air and the chill slices my throat raw as I glance at the huts behind me. I'm too far away. It will have me in his teeth before I can make it back. I don't know what to do. Yak was right. I shouldn't have left Bear's side, not even for a moment.

The snow melts on my cheeks like hot tears as I side-step closer to the huts, but this time, I bump into something solid. I go still all over with my pulse thundering in my ears.

"Easy now," Bear says, stepping in front of me with a pistol aimed at the animal. The pistol pops loudly, and Bear quickly turns to me, shoving the pistol into my hands. "You killed it. Got it?" he tells me as Yak bolts out of his hut.

"What's going on?" he demands.

I swallow with unease as everyone slowly begins to crawl out of their huts. I look over at Bear with confusion. *Why does he want me to lie and say I killed it?* He glances at me for a moment and then back at Yak. "We came out for some fresh air and the lynx snuck up on us, but she handled it," he lied.

Yak walks over to it and lifts the animal's head, examining it. He lets the head drop and then looks right at me. "Come meet her and embrace your Natural name."

This is what he meant by "I didn't choose it, it chose me." I hesitate with another look at Bear. It doesn't feel right to accept a name I did not earn, but he gives me a slight nod just as the trainers start chanting, "Lynx."

I wet my sore and chapped lips and walk toward it with a quick, false smile. But as I squat beside the animal, my breath hitches as I glide a shaky hand along its brown, furry coat. "I have never seen anything as beautiful as her," I say in a soft voice.

"Yeah, she be," Alex agrees, kneeling next to me.

"Alright." Yak pushes to his feet. "Since everyone is up and raring to go, let's get this day started." Yak points at me and Bear. "You two pack this up for the butcher and taxidermy. The rest of you team up with your trainer and grab your gear. We're going hunting. The animal that comes to you will be your Natural name. Kill it and bring it back so you will have a disguise."

"What if one doesn't come?" Toggy asks.

"If one does not appear, then you will hunt again, but on a different island," Yak responds flatly. "And if you are given a name that is already taken, for instance, Bear, yours will have the color before it. You would be known as Black Bear or Brown Bear. However, we do prefer you to find your name here. Not only are you searching for your spirit animal, but you are also thinning an overly populated area. That is why we start the hunt here." Yak moves forward, gesturing for everyone to gather their things. "Now, let's get moving. We have a lot to cover today."

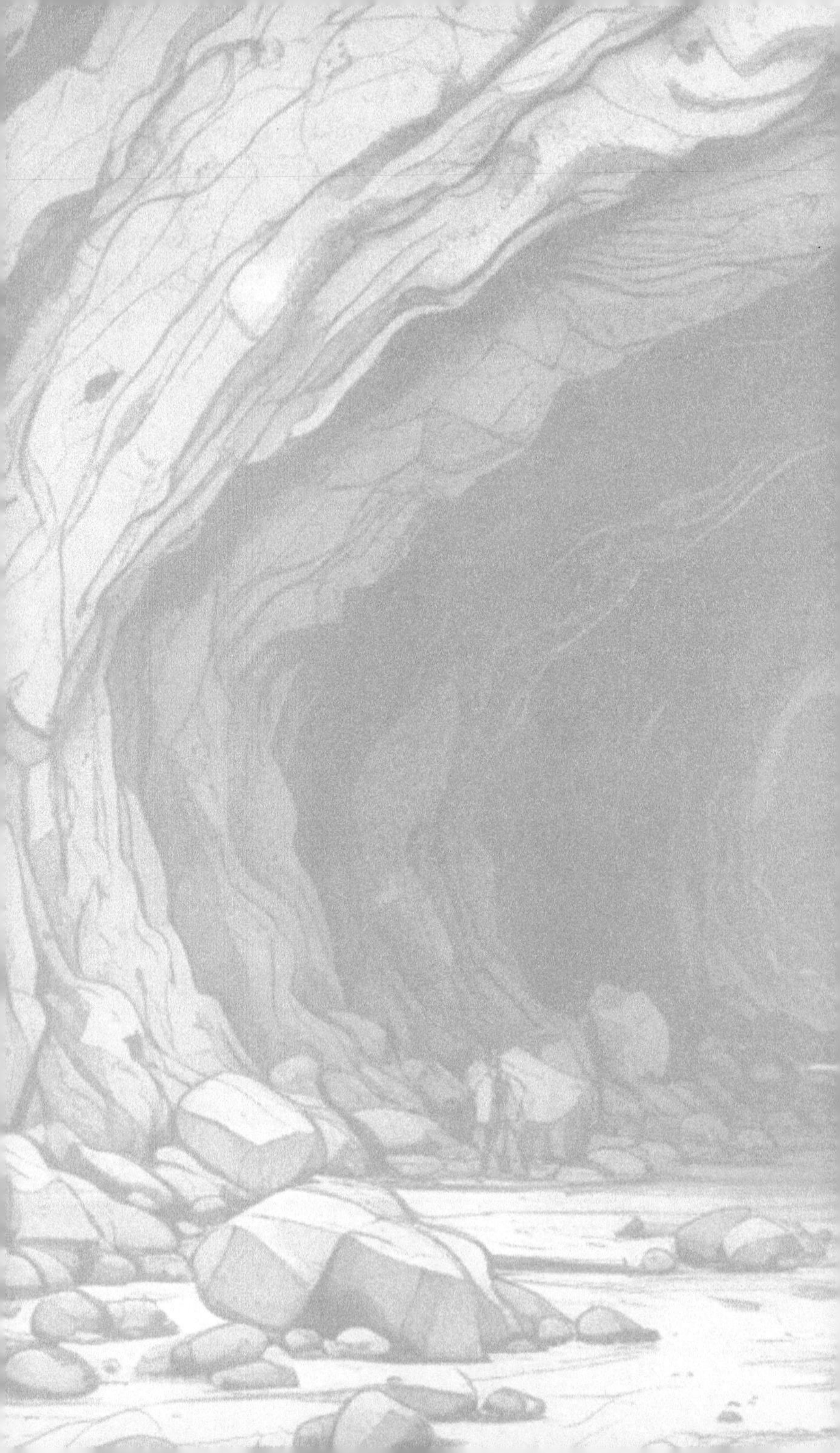

WHEN HEALING BEGINS

Bear starts toward me, and I rub the cold off my arms. He stops in front of me with a quick glance over his shoulder and then back at me.

"Same thing happened to me during my last phase." He bends for the lynx, cradling it, and then turns as we both head to our hut. "We were out here fooling around when the bear came. I didn't kill mine, either. Wolf did. At the time, I didn't know what it meant, just like you. Why would he want me to lie and say I did it? But knowing what I do now, I understand why. Bear matches me more and Wolf matches him perfectly."

Bear hunkers, entering the hut, and lowers the lynx next to his gear on a wooden table. "You can take a few minutes to warm up first before we begin."

"Thank you," I say, pulling my day clothes over my long johns. "Are you close with the rest of your team?"

"Yes." He turns and leans against the table. "Our whole

team is close. Sometimes too close." He folds his arms over his chest. "When you eat, sleep, and train with the same people every day, that can lead to bickering or worse. But at the same time, there isn't anything we wouldn't do for each other."

I sit on my sleeping bag, moving closer to the fire, and gaze through the hole in the roof. "The night sky is magnificent. I could stare at this view for hours and never get bored. Even with the gloomy sky. When you've been locked up as long as I have, it's the small things, like watching the sky or the freedom to daydream, that captivate you." I close my eyes and inhale deeply, absorbing this moment.

"I miss daydreaming. I never had the time or luxury to dream about anything when I was sentenced." I open my eyes and stare at the sky. "I spent all my time planning and when the days move slow like those clouds, you have plenty of time to think. My brain was in constant chaos, making plans and how to execute them. There wasn't a single moment when I wasn't prepared for any situation. Even when I came here, I was looking for a way out. A way to free us." I lower my gaze and look at Bear.

"This is the first time in years I'm not thinking about my next move. It's just like those days we spent together in my quarters while I recuperated after phase two. I didn't feel like a prisoner. I wasn't looking for an escape. I felt safe. I think that's why I let Lou go. I knew, in a way, I didn't need her anymore. I could protect myself."

Bear grins and moves closer to the fire. "I pretty much told the others the same thing after it happened. I think I'm the only one that truly understands you because I've been there. I was just like you when I first arrived." He squats and warms his hands, staring into the fire.

"The first couple of days during our phases, no one even

noticed I was off. Most of the time, I was myself with the others. Mainly with Wolf, since we were in the same room. We didn't know Hyena and the others at the time. They were in a different room. We didn't start connecting with them until we were one small group like yours now. But Wolf and I became close right away, like we were brothers separated by birth. But when we began phase two, that's when Wolf said I was different. The phases were getting harder and anytime I thought Wolf might fail, he said I'd turn into my brother, Jason. I never meant to harm Wolf or the other recruits, only the trainers. So, Wolf never feared me, at least not like the other recruits did."

He lifts his gaze to me. "Just like you and Alex." Bear grins, shaking his head slightly. "When Yak told him you wouldn't be back, he went nuts, tearing the mess hall apart. He wouldn't listen to reason. No one could control him or even settle him down. Finally, Yak pulled his pistol, and it took two shots to put Alex down. The first one he took like a champ. I don't know if it was because his adrenaline was so high, and he fought through it, or what. But he just kept going after Yak, shaking his arms and legs like he was walking it off. Scared the crap out of Yak and the rest of us." He looks up, drinking in the view through the hole. "You two have a bond so strong; we've never seen anything like it before."

"Is that why you never failed us, because we remind you of what Ford has with you?" I ask.

"Partly," he answers, and pushes to his feet, moving to the wooden table. "Now, how about we get this dressed."

Shortly after I helped Bear clean up our area, I see Hutch and Fox walking back into camp. And as I'm walking toward them, I notice he doesn't have an animal with him. But then again, it could be smaller than mine and perhaps packed into his bag.

"Hey," Hutch smiles wide and proud, "I got a big one. Too big to bring." He turns to Fox, asking, "What it be again?"

"A bison."

"Yeah, a bison, and Yak say he gonna need more Naturals to haul it back."

I open my mouth to congratulate him, and Alex races up to us full of energy and nearly out of breath.

"Yer not gonna believe what I git." He leans close, cupping his mouth. "Well, what Hyena git," he whispers.

"Little shit nearly got me killed," Hyena growls. He drops a large animal covered in white fur with thick horns.

"So, what is it? What's your Natural name, Alex?"

"It be a Dall Sheep."

"It be a pain in my ass. It nearly rammed me off the cliff." Hyena grabs Alex by the scruff and forces him toward us. "Please trade with me."

"No one is trading," Yak says in the distance. "You are paired together for a reason."

Hyena looks over his shoulder and then back like he wants to hit something. Instead, he leans close to Alex's ear. "Next time I tell you to take the shot. Take the fucking shot!" And then marches back into his hut.

Alex bends for the sheep's leg. "I think that one be rabid," Alex says.

"I think you might be right." Bear chuckles and bends with Alex to help him with the sheep.

Once the sun is fully up and everyone is ready for another day of trekking, I put on my eyewear to block the blinding glare bouncing off the white ground. Bear links us to another long rope attached to the side of the mountain, and we hike along a ridge, trekking higher. In fact, we are so high now, when I look to my right, I can see the ocean. It's vast and empty, stretching as far as the eye can see. Not even another island is nearby. On Capra Horn, my home port, there isn't a spot on the island where you can't see another mass of land. And here, it's just like Bear said while I followed him in the tunnels. Like the world ends here. Wherever *here* is.

I continue following behind Alex with Bear on my tail, and after hours of hiking, I realize Yak was right; this phase is much more grueling. My legs are on fire, and I can't catch a proper breath. Not to mention the hunger pains and dry mouth. I understand the reasoning of us being attached to the rope now. I'm starting to feel off balance. Every step I take, my legs shake uncontrollably and just when I think my legs are going to fail me, we stop at another flat plane. Except this one doesn't have small huts. Only a snow-covered area. Yak shoulders off his bag and addresses us.

"We'll take a short break for lunch. Check vitals and then continue on."

After Bear unlinks me, I walk over to the center of the area and fall into the snow. And to my surprise, I'm not the only one struggling. The other recruits are also out of breath and massaging their legs next to their trainers.

"Why are you not drinking your water?" Bear asks, squatting in front of me.

I squirm off his heavy bag with disappointment. I didn't ration my water jug properly and I'm almost out, which I'm surprised at. I should have known better with how I've lived these past few years.

"I'm not really thirsty," I say with a dry and hoarse throat.

He reaches behind me and drags his heavy bag between his knees, opening it. "Lynx," he snaps, pulling out five full jugs of water, "you're not drinking nearly enough water. You should have gone through most of these already. Why are you saving your water?" He looks up at me with concern heavy in his throat. "Are you planning on running?"

I turn away from his probing eyes; my cheeks burning with embarrassment. "No. I didn't know they were mine. I thought I was carrying your bag, and I didn't want you to be cross with me for taking something that isn't mine."

"Hey," he says, tapping me on the knee, "look at me." I brush a tear off my cheek and face him. "From here on, what's mine is yours, okay?"

I nod with a weak smile.

He slides his hand into the bag with one side of his lips quirking up. "But that also goes both ways. What's yours is mine and I believe I saw Elk sneak you a peanut bar." He pulls it out and twists around to sit next to me while I grab one of the water jugs, downing most of it.

"These are rare now, and I've not had one in months." He peels open the outer package and rips it in half, taking a small nibble off one piece, savoring the taste. Fox guides Hutch and Alex to us, and I look over at Hyena, wondering why he isn't with Alex.

"Hyena will be helping Yak with vitals," Fox says, dropping next to me. "So, we are to watch Alex and make sure he drinks his water and that." He leans back, holding himself up on his elbow, and looks over at Bear. "Ahh, you have the good stuff. Give me some," he says with his hand out.

"Pound sand. This is ours," Bear says, offering me the other half.

"What be 'pound sand'?" Hutch asks, sitting next to Fox while Alex drops in the snow directly in front of me.

"It's a polite way of saying fuck off." Fox grins. Alex looks over his shoulder and Bear nudges him in the knee.

"Hey, if you say that to Hyena, he'll give you a proper what for."

I sit up straighter at the phrase. It's the same one Lou used to say to Ford right before they landed in the dirt in a mean altercation. The first time she said it, he asked what it was, and instead of Lou explaining it, she gave him a demonstration by slapping him hard across the cheek. I look at Bear with a smile, knowing Ford must have told him what it is, and my smile grows, wondering if he did the same thing to Bear.

"A what for?" Hutch asks with a scrunched face.

Alex peeks up at me with a sly grin.

"Don't," I say, but Alex ignores me and leans forward, slapping Hutch.

He soars to his feet, wide-eyed, and holding his cheek. "Why'd ye do that for? I ain't done nothing . . . wait. I be gettin' it." He grins, dropping back into the snow. "I be liking that one."

"So does the rest of our team, especially Wolf," Fox adds.

"Who be Wolf?" Hutch asks.

"You'll see," Fox replies.

I offer Alex and Hutch part of my peanut bar and Fox makes a grab for the one I offered to Alex.

"He can't have that," he says, shoving the hunk into his mouth.

"Oh, ye about to git a what for, fer sure now," Alex threatens with a raised fist.

"Why?" Fox asks with a mouthful. "I just saved your life. You're deathly allergic."

"What'd ye call us?"

"I didn't call you anything." Fox laughs. "Allergic means you'll die if you eat it. You have an allergy to peanuts."

Alex looks at Bear for confirmation. "Really?"

"Yes. You're the reason peanuts are now off the menu for us."

"An' the others, they be heavy cos of it?"

"No," Fox says, swinging his legs up and wrapping them around Alex's upper body, and then pulls him down into the snow, holding him in place. "We aren't complete assholes. We actually like you and never want any harm to come to you."

Bear leans forward, shoving Alex's face halfway into the snow. "Ye be me blood," he says with a wide grin.

"I've heard that before. When I . . . " I stop talking, remembering they didn't want Yak to know anything about my test. And with him having hearing like he does, I change my words, only asking, "What does it mean? My blood."

"It means you are my family, and I shall protect you as such," Fox replies.

A smile blooms from both me and Alex as Yak drops a bag behind Hutch.

"Alright, you knuckleheads. Who wants to go first?" Yak asks, and Alex shoots his heavy, coated arm in the air.

After our vitals are taken, we begin hiking again, but not nearly as long as before. Maybe an hour and Yak stops us, telling everyone to unhook from the rope attached to the side of the mountain wall. When I turn, following the others, my eyes are instantly drawn to the long row of red cylinders mounted on wooden stakes. *Are we about to be done with phase four? Am I finally going to see where the Naturals live? Where Ford lives.*

Yak addresses us with soft features and a genuine smile. "We are close to our community and should arrive by nightfall. Where your last test will occur." He turns, gesturing to the row of cylinders. "And on our way, we spin the mani wheels, sending prayers to the heavens. Sacred words and prayers are written and coiled inside each wheel and are only to be spun clockwise like this," he demonstrates. "Now, come along and spin the prayer wheels as we continue."

Everyone walks in a single line, silently rotating the prayer wheels, and when we come to the end of them, there is a long bridge made solely of rope. On the other side of this bridge is another flat plane, as if mirroring this one.

"Only one team at a time will cross. Owl, you and Weasel will go first," Yak says.

Owl, the dark-headed trainer, guides Jack closer to the edge, but just as they are about to cross, Jack stops and turns around. "I can't."

"Yes, you can. It's all in your head. I'll be right behind you," Owl says encouragingly.

Jack glances over the edge and then back at Owl with his face pale and sickly looking. "I can't. I can't," he repeats with a slight stumble, and Yak yanks him away from the edge right before his knees buckle, and he passes out.

"Well, that's a shame. Owl, take him back," Yak says.

Owl bends, tossing Jack over his shoulder. "See you on

the other side." Owl turns, carrying Jack back down the mountain.

"What will be happening to him?" Hutch asks.

"He'll join the other failed recruits," Yak answers. "Now, let's get moving. Daylight's burning." Yak helps Toggy across, making the walk look effortless. Once he returns to our group, he looks at Alex. "Alright, Hyena, you and Sheep are up."

Alex steps forward, and Hyena yanks him back.

"Hold up." He turns Alex around and bends to his level. "Don't be goofing around out there. You—"

"Yeah, yeah, I be hearing ye the first time ye say it. Ye ain't gotta keep telling us every time we be doing somethin'."

They start for the bridge, and I hear hushed voices beside me. I pry my eyes off Alex and see Fox speaking to Hutch encouragingly. I lift my eyes up to Bear.

"Like I said before. I hope you're not afraid of heights," he says with a grin.

I turn my attention back to Alex, and Bear leans close to my ear. "Don't worry, I will be right behind you every step of the way. I won't let you fall."

Alex wobbles on the rope halfway across, but not by accident. "Whooahh," he laughs, shaking the rope.

"Knock it off," Hyena hollers in a forceful tone.

"Why? Ye be jolted of heights?" Alex giggles.

"No," Hyena states, slapping Alex on the back of the head. "Now, shut up and go."

"Alright, dang," Alex snickers and shuffles along the rope.

After Hutch and Fox cross, Yak turns to me. "Alright, Bear, you and Lynx are up."

The second I grip the rope and step onto the thin cord, the entire bridge starts to sway. I glance down before taking another step, and my heart drops. We must be at least a hundred feet up, if not more. I wet my lips and force my other foot forward, and the bridge sways even more. I stop and steady my breathing and watch below as the ocean slides up and over the shoreline in huge chunks of ice.

"Don't focus on what's below you. Just focus on putting one foot in front of the other."

I slide my gloved hand along the rope and force another foot forward. "You're doing great." Another step and then another. "Just like that, keep going. You're almost there." I peek up and he's wrong. I still have a long way to go. I look back down and my head spins, swirling and churning all the way down to my toes. "Calm your breathing. You're fine. I won't let anything happen to you. Just breathe."

I grip the rope so tight my hands are stiff and my thighs on fire, but I power through with my feet steady on the cord.

"Ye got this," I hear Alex shout.

I take another step with a quick glance up and Hutch is hunkered next to Alex with everyone behind them, encouraging me forward. Something about their encouraging voices steadies my footing, until I'm at the last step. I shakily reach out for the wooden stake to pull myself up and Hyena grabs the front of my coat, yanking me forward.

I fall onto my hands and knees, crawling away from the side with my entire body shaking while everyone congratulates me. I stop and sit on my heels, stretching my fingers out, but they won't move; they are stuck in the same position as if I'm still out there struggling with the rope.

"Someone be jolted of heights, yeah?" Alex chuckles, and I give a quick nod. "Here, let us be helping." He reaches for my hand and gently starts massaging my gloved palms until my fingers start to relax, but before I can calm my heart completely, Hutch's high-pitched voice has me on my feet and moving toward him.

"Ye mean it be another test?" Hutch asks.

I peek over the edge and the hundred-foot drop is gone. Instead, it's only a trench, and Yak is walking across it, proving there was nothing to fear.

"Yes. It was only an illusion," Yak says proudly. "I needed to know who is terrified of heights and who is scared of them. Being terrified until you pass out, like Jack, you cannot overcome. But if you are only scared and still cross, you can overcome that fear with training." He lifts himself out of the trench and waves us forward. "Come along. We're almost there."

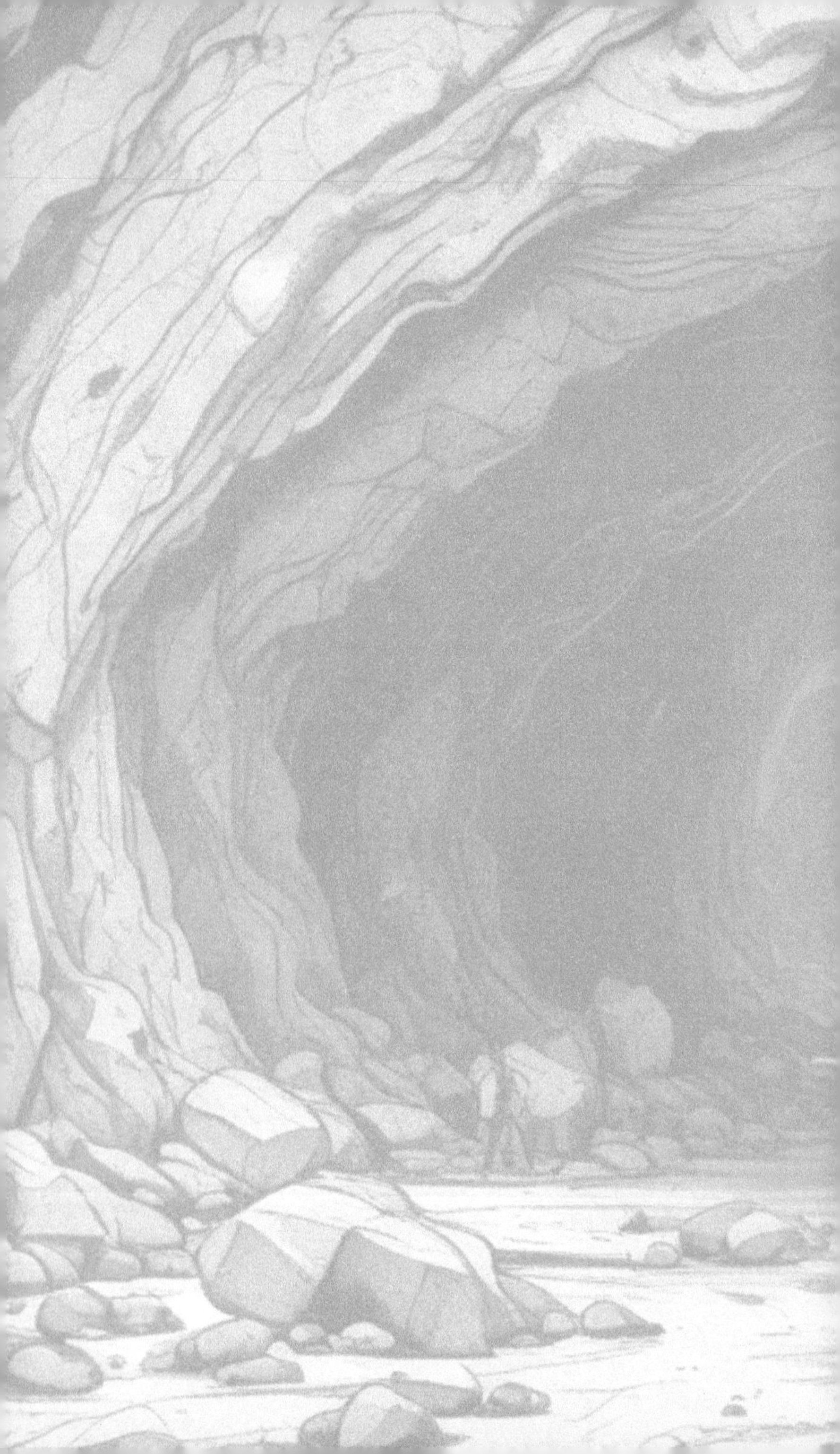

A NATURAL HOME

We stop at another bend, and before we round the curve, Yak turns to us.

"We are about to pass through the Peak of Crosses." He slides his bag off his shoulder. "It is where we remember those that have fallen in our resistance. Now, please do not be alarmed, and remember, we have been doing this for over fifty years. And in the beginning, the Naturals were not as solid as we are now. We have learned from our fallen brethren." He pulls out a small cross, and from the size and color, I assume it is the wooden block he has been whittling.

He smiles, but it doesn't reach his eyes as he gestures for us to continue. I follow behind Toggy, and when the Peak of Crosses comes into view, my mouth parts with a gasp. I slow my steps, barely moving, as I take in the scene. Before us is a staggering amount of crosses. Big. Small. Plain. Decorative. And directly in the middle of this massive grave of crosses is a path. Yak brushes by us and stops along the path, tossing a cross into the mix, and then looks up to the sky.

"Hold it down up there until we get there. Rest in peace, Racoon."

Alex looks up at me. "This be the flattest thing me ever sees."

I open my mouth to agree, and Hutch squeezes between us, hanging his arms over our shoulders. "Yeah, it be." He stares out in front of him and clears his throat, adding, "I want ye both to know, ye'll be known by us."

My breath hitches as he pulls away and starts down the path. A Forgotten doesn't use the phrase "I love you". Instead, it's "you will be known by me" or "I know you". It's the same meaning as the Naturals "my blood". And the Forgotten never say I know you, unless they truly feel it and know they have found their person. The first time Alex said it to me, my throat closed with tears threatening. Just like now.

"Hutch." He turns around, walking backward, and I add, "I know you, too."

"Me blood," Alex says, patting his chest.

Hutch looks skyward with his chin trembling, and before he can control his emotions, I rush forward. I hug him tight. The same way I used to hug Lou. Alex joins me in hugging Hutch, too.

"I ain't never had a family like this before," Hutch says.

"And now you do. A very big family too," Yak says, joining us. Not in our group hug, but standing next to us. "We are all family, and you are now a part of it." We pull away from each other and Yak gestures for us to follow. "Just a little farther now."

We walk through the Peak of Crosses, around another curve, and before us is a dark, wooden structure, nestled against the mountain, standing tall and intimidating. A massive wooden statue of a lion guards the left side with an equally large-sized bird watching the right. And as beautiful as it is, that's not what's eye-catching. It's the small bridge or walkway, if you will, leading toward it. Wood carvings line the bridge from dragon heads to warriors holding spears and shields.

I start forward, gliding a hand over one of the rolling flames tucked between a dragon and a spear, and the wood is smooth like silk. It reminds me of Papa's desk back home. It, too, was made out of a dark wood with a soft finish. I walk up the steps, slow and careful, taking in the view before coming to a stop in front of the tallest door I've ever seen.

Yak pulls on the door, but not easily. He puts his entire weight behind it. The door scratches against what I assume is their porch, and the melody and low chanting inside have a tranquil effect on me. My eyes mist with a lump forming and I resist the urge to hug everyone here. Instead, I enter behind Alex, and I'm completely in awe of the building's sharp arches and elaborate carvings. And the ceiling, it's so high I have to fully expose my neck to see it. It's almost as if the entire building was carved out of one massive chunk of wood. In the center of the room is another statue, and for the life of me, I have no idea what it is or what she is supposed to represent.

"This is the Buddhist Goddess Guanyin," Yak begins in a soft whisper. "She represents compassion and mercy."

"Why she got so many arms?" Hutch asks in the same soft tone.

"It shows her ability to help many people at once," Yak says.

"This be yer God?" Alex asks.

"It is for some, but we have many religions here. No one is forced into one. We allow everyone to choose the one that pulls to their soul. Or none at all. The choice is yours."

An elderly gentleman starts toward us, and Yak turns his attention to him. He's wearing something similar to a thick red blanket draped over his left shoulder, with his right shoulder bare. He stops in front of Yak, pressing his hands together in prayer, and bows his bald head slightly. "Namaste," he says.

Yak greets the man in the same warm fashion, and then Yak turns to us, gesturing for us to follow him. As we do, I notice the trainers are stopping to greet this gentleman in the same fashion. Even Toggy greets him, and I instantly feel ashamed. I tug on Alex and Hutch's coat and then start back toward the gentleman.

"Namaste," we greet, and the gentleman grins proudly before returning our greeting.

Yak clears his throat, and we hurry back to him as he guides us toward the left wing. From here, there are more of these gentlemen sitting on pillows and small benches, singing or praying; I can't be certain. But whatever it is, it's absolutely beautiful.

We walk down a gloomy hall lined with closed doors, and I glide a finger along the gold-leafed wall until we are standing under a dark alcove. Yak opens the door, and we walk into a room painted red with gold leaves etched on the ceiling. He instructs everyone to take off their winter gear. As I hang my heavy coat next to Bears, I turn to Yak's voice.

"This is the last part of phase four. It's not a test but a loyalty oath. If you choose to join us and give your life for our cause, you will receive a tattoo."

I instantly look at Toggy, removing her coat. She has a

tattoo, just like trainers do. *Is this what it is? Is she already in a team? If so, why is she here?*

"But this isn't a normal tattoo." Yak's voice pulls my attention onto him. "This will bind you and your team together as one. You will not be able to stray too far from this connection without your team knowing. If you do, the one with your name inked onto their leg will turn to stone and he or she will not be able to walk properly until your group is brought back together. It's how we know if someone is missing and to not sail without them."

He gestures for us to take our seats by a bald gentleman sitting on a gold pillow. He's dressed the same as the one that greeted us, except this one is holding an object that looks like a giant needle. Toggy moves forward, taking a seat, and fear slicks my skin. I want to scream, cry, and run, all rolled into one. Instead, instinct kicks in. I move in front of Hutch and pull Alex protectively against me. I inch away from everyone with my palms sweating. I thought we were free, but if that tattoo really binds us together, then we aren't. We'll never be able to go or do whatever we want. We'll still be prisoners, just in a different way.

"This is your last chance to back out." Yak points to a bell hanging beside him.

Alex turns slightly to look up at me, and I know what he's asking without needing to say the words. I press my fingers into my lips and stare at the small, golden bell by the door. *What should we do? Should we give? Or continue with no freewill?*

BINDING BLOOD

卌 卌 卌 卌
卌 卌 ||

"Relax, the hard part is over," Hyena says to Alex.

"No, it ain't," Alex begins with fear vibrating in his voice. "This be like the digging pits, waiting for our fresh mark."

Yak steps around Hyena, and Hutch plants himself between Yak and us.

"Whoa." Yak raises his hands and backs away. "I was only going to say, this isn't the same." His voice is calm, almost a whisper. "This is supposed to be a proud moment. A mark of accomplishment. One that promises to save all those that are like you. And no one will rush you or force you to do something you do not want to do or be a part of. This is why we give you a choice."

"Just be giving us a tick, yeah?" Hutch asks.

"Take all the time you need. When, or if, you decide to join us, you may." Yak walks over to a small forge behind the gentleman as the trainers stand against a wall next to the forge.

Hutch pulls us deeper into the corner. "So, what we doing? We joinin' or givin'? Cos, I ain't joining without ye."

"Search us. If we give, do that mean we be out? Do this be another test? I don't know what to do," Alex says, dragging his hands down his face.

Hutch looks over his shoulder, chewing on his nails. "Mr. Yak, can we still be joinin' and not get the tattoo thingy?"

"Well," Yak begins, shoving his hands deep into his front pockets and, before he can answer, I step forward.

"If the tattoo links us all together . . . " I start with a quick look at Alex and then back at Yak. "It's like you are shackling us all over again." I lift my wrist, showing him my bracelet. "It's the same as this. If we pry it off, the heart will stop blinking, and you will know we aren't here. But again, we could pry it off if we truly wanted to. A tattoo is permanent, just like this." I shove my black sleeve up to my elbow, exposing my brands. "We will never be free, not truly."

Bear sucks in a loud breath. "I never thought of that," he says with anger thick in his voice. "I should have known better." He lifts his chin, staring at the gold painted ceiling. "Why didn't I think of that?" he mutters to himself.

"It's not your fault, Bear," Yak tells him. "This is how we learn."

A crackling sound comes from the back wall and when I look that way, a light brightens the darkness. And within seconds, the wall disappears with a tall Asian gentleman, maybe in his forties, standing near the corner of the window. Behind him, in the shadows, is someone else.

"Since Alex and Tippy survived the mining caverns longer than any recruit we have had," he begins, and I immediately know he isn't like the other Naturals. His back is straight as a board and his words, and the tone of his voice, are polished like he comes from wealth. "They would know better than anyone what to expect, or what future recruits would fear. Perhaps it is best if they are in charge of all future recruits that come from prison."

"I agree," Yak says, and then asks, "All those in favor?"

"Hoorah!" the trainers echo.

The gentleman looks over his shoulder, at the person behind him, and then back at us, and the crackling noise sounds again. "I would also like to add, if their team agrees, to allow Hutch, Alex, and Tippy one month before receiving their tattoo. For this will grant them the ability to witness exactly what and how we operate among our family."

"An' if we be refusing at the end?" Hutch asks.

"Then you shall fail," the gentleman replies sternly.

Alex looks up at me and, again, I know that look.

"We shall wait and see," I tell Alex, and he gives me a firm nod, knowing exactly what I mean.

"All in favor?" Yak asks.

"Hoorah," the trainers agree.

"Alright, looks like we are done here, then."

"But what about Toggy?" Hutch asks. "Ain't she gonna be tattooed?"

"Nope. Toggy is part of our team," Hyena says, rocking on his heels like he's clever.

"Then what team we be with then?" Alex asks.

"Us," Bear says. "Three of our brothers quit last year. Said it was too hard, so we were looking for three replacements to complete our team. It's why Toggy was placed in the program with you. We wanted the best, and we got the best."

"Wait," Alex blusters, shaking his hands out in front of him. "Let's be getting back to the oath thingy. Ye telling us, we can give even after the tattoo thingy?"

"Of course. Why do you think all the Naturals are so young?"

"So, the tattoo thing can be removed?" Hutch asks, still chewing on his nails.

"Yes. The link and all your enhancements are removed before you are sent home."

"Why ye not say all dis first? Why everythin' gotta be a test?" Alex says, dragging his hands down his face again.

"Honestly," Yak begins, folding his arms across his chest, "we tried that once, and the Forgotten ran right over us. We couldn't control them long enough to teach them anything. We ended up having to send every single one of them home. So, the following year, we went back to the old ways. And sadly, the old way works."

"An' home be where ye find us?" Alex asks.

Yak's lips turn up in a sly grin. "Follow us and you shall see."

A WEAKNESS FOR HOME

‖‖ ‖‖ ‖‖ ‖‖
‖‖ ‖‖ ///

Yak leads us through the door and down a dimly lit tunnel, brightened by torches, where passageways fork and curve deeper into this maze-like channel. We go up steps, walk straight, and then head down steps. We round corners so many times, my brain can't seem to wrap around how far we truly are inside this tunnel. I glance over my shoulder as we turn another corner and Hutch reaches out, stopping me from colliding into Alex.

"Before we enter," Yak begins, "I want you to see and understand firsthand what you have signed up for and what you are fighting to save. Take it all in, fill your heart with it because one day while you're out there, you'll be so exhausted, you'll believe you cannot go on. Or your eyes are so heavy with sleep, you don't think you can stay awake. And when that time comes, because it will, I want you to remember this day, this moment, and know you can, and you will, because you are not fighting for the Naturals. You are a Natural fighting for the Forgotten."

"Hoorah!" the trainers holler.

Yak turns, opening the door, and light filters into the tunnel, casting shadows on the clay-like walls, and my breath hitches. They look just like the shadows I saw in my parents' library when I led Alex to Papa's secret bunker.

Will I always be reminded of that night? Will every shadow plague me with what I did? The shadow moves as if answering my question and I flinch at Hutch's hand on my shoulder.

"My bad." Instead of removing his hand like he normally does, he squeezes my shoulder with a welcoming smile. "We be moving forward, but we can be waiting if ye need."

"No. I'm good." I reach up and squeeze his hand. "Thank you." I return his smile and then move forward.

The room is circular, with another statue in the center. Except this one isn't nearly as large as the other ones. This one is slightly taller than me. I move closer, inspecting the green woman with her arm raised high, holding a torch. In fact, the entire room is painted green, but not with a brush. It looks like someone came in and painted the whole place with just their hands. There are handprints everywhere, apart from one spot. I move around the statue and there's writing on the wall.

Give me your tired. Your poor. Your huddled masses yearning to breathe free. The wretched refuse of your teeming shore. Send these. The homeless . . .

A powerful rawness stretches in my throat, burning all the way down into my belly. I press my hands to my middle with rapid breaths. Alex walks up to me, clutching onto my wrist.

"What be wrong?" Alex asks me.

I try forcing the thick lump down, but I can't. It's growing larger. Instead, I just stare at Alex and Hutch because I know they can't read what's on the wall. They aren't where I am emotionally, not yet.

"Help her! She can't be breathin'," Alex hollers.

"She's fine. Just emotional," Yak says, clamping a hand on my shoulder. "Are you okay?"

I nod continuously, shaking my hands out in front of me with slow sips of air. Yak moves closer to the written words and, with his voice low, but deep, he reads the message.

Afterward, Hutch lifts his chin with a long exhale and then bends, holding his knees. "That be hittin' us hard."

"Yeah, it be," Alex says, rubbing at his mouth with strong forceful motions and when he blinks, tears roll down his cheeks. "A lil' warnin' next time, yeah?"

"This isn't even the best part," Bear says.

"It ain't," Alex asks, drying his cheeks.

"No." Bear folds his arms over his chest with a welcoming smile. "So, prepare yourself. What you are about to see will hit you harder than this. At least it did for me."

"Come along." Yak turns for the green door. "One more stop and then we go home."

As we follow Yak through the door, I'm surprised when we don't step into another tunnel. Instead, we come out on the other side of the mountain and into clean, fresh air. And there's a crowd facing us, cheering loudly. There are so many, I can't see past them.

Who are they? Are there more Naturals than I thought?

A small, thin girl with fiery red hair pushes through the crowd, and I stagger backward with my throat raw and swollen. That's our old top dog and then I see Christopher among them. The first Forgotten that failed and I anchor my blurry vision at Yak.

"You didn't return them? You kept them?"

"Every last one," he says, smiling down at a young boy next to him. "They have a home. A family. They go to school. And when they grow up, they learn a trade. Some marry, some don't, but most become a part of this community. Or begin a life out there. Like your dad did."

I pat at my chest, forcing my emotions back down. "The Naturals really are the savior of the Forgotten?" I croak.

"Of course, and they're all here to welcome you all home."

"Yeah, we be watching, and Tippy, ya be the brickiest one," a tall, blonde Forgotten says. "I nearly dropped when Hyena be chasing ya in the food room."

I give a slight nod and inch backward, not feeling like the bravest one.

"Nu-uh, it be Hutch. Didn't ya see how he be runnin' past all them swords and such," a short, dark-headed girl adds and then turns back to Hutch with her cheeks a golden-red. "Ya got clean skills."

"Yeah, but my favorite be Alex," a lean teenager behind her adds. "The way ya took two shots and nearly walked it off." He shakes his head slightly with a grin. "It be wicked clean, yo."

I wipe at my wet eyes as they slowly start to surround us. And after about ten minutes of questions and congratulations, Yak raises his hands. "Alright, that's enough. You'll have plenty of time to speak more tonight."

The crowd moans with disappointment as they drift away, and I finally get a glimpse of the village. In the summer season, when Ford would visit, he would tell me tales of the Naturals and how they lived. And his stories always started the same way. I've heard it so many times, I practically have the beginning memorized. I inch forward, taking it all in, and I can hear Ford's voice. I can even see him moving along with the story as he performed each verse.

Once upon a time, in a far-off land, a group of people formed a clan called the Naturals. And their palace sat on top of the highest mountain in the world, surrounded by trees. In fact, there were so many trees, they couldn't cut enough down to build, so they built their village around them. Trade stations had trees sprouted from the rooftops. Homes were built high above, sturdy and solid on the branches, that not even a quake could shake them. With a boardwalk that twisted and curved in every direction. Up. Down. Sideways. No matter where you were, the boardwalk would lead you to your destination. And, higher in the sky, floats a protection barrier. Like a fairy flew overhead, sprinkling her protecting dust over their world.

I lift my chin skyward at the evening sky, and it shimmers slightly, just like Ford described.

"Let's get you home and settled, shall we?" Yak says, interrupting my thoughts, and I realize I'm the only one still standing at the top of the steps.

"So, what that be?" Hutch asks with his chin lifted, looking up.

"It's a dome. It's sort of like a ceiling. Without it, everyone would be wearing layers and trudging through snow. In the spring and summer seasons, we open it so we can feel the air."

"Super clean," Alex mutters, gazing up at the dome.

We follow behind Yak and the trainers on a path that

looks like liquid trees until we come to a stop. I bend down to touch its glass-like bark, and Yak gestures to our left. Outside the shop are two small stands filled to the brim with fruits and vegetables.

"This is Fresh Picks." Yak looks down at Alex. "And no, they are not free. Please do not take anything from these shops unless you plan on purchasing it." He points to our right. "That is Freedom Bank. It's where we keep our coins and yes, each of you will have your own account, but you'll learn more about that later."

We walk farther along the path as Yak tells us what each shop is and, sadly, all are closed today. He goes on saying, normally when they are open, the village is bursting with energy. He explains there's a coffee shop, ice cream parlor, bakery, hair salon, and a clothing shop. And that's the one that grabs my attention. I instantly move closer to the window, leaning against my cupped hands for a better view. Inside, there is no display box filled with different patterns to choose from or colorful material lined against a wall. Instead, the outfits are already sewed together for you and there are so many stylish ones. Whoever owns this shop must have a fast hand.

"Come along, Lynx. We have a celebration to attend."

I push off the window, jogging to catch up with everyone, and Alex repeats, "Celebration?"

"Yes. Every year there's a big festival to welcome the new Naturals."

"Wait. What be happening to phase four?" Hutch asks.

"You finished it," Bear says.

"But we didn't do nothing," Hutch states.

Bear talks over his shoulder with a smile. "But you did. We learned quite a bit about you three. That hike up here is challenging. A lot of people can't make that trek. Not without complaining or needing help, and none of you did."

"Then how the failed Forgotten be getting here?" Hutch asks.

"The tram," Yak replies as he begins motioning with his hands. "It's a huge box that can fit five or six people. It's suspended high in the air by these cables and, with a push of a button, it zooms through the sky."

"Do we git to be using it?" Alex asks with excitement.

"No. Naturals don't normally use the tram unless it's an emergency."

"What we use is called a 'zipline'," Bear says. "It's the same thing you went down a few days ago. Except this one takes you straight here, not just to the bottom of the building."

Yak guides us to the right, toward the only home that is not in the trees and, from its size, I can understand why. It's huge, maybe three stories high. The front is framed in a sharp arch with so many large windows that if there weren't logs separating them, one would think it was just a massive window. And the orange glow thriving inside looks like a colossal-sized fireplace burns deep within the walls. We walk over a small bridge with a stream gurgling under it. I lift my eyes and to the left of the home is a tall waterfall.

"This be our home?" Alex asks in awe.

"Yes," Yak replies as he guides us to the right side of the house and stops in front of a door. "This is you. Go ahead inside. Jamie is waiting for you." Yak pats Alex on the shoulder. "Good luck. You're going to need it." He chuckles and walks away with quick strides.

"Who be Jamie?" Hutch asks.

"Ohhh," Bear says with wide, frightful eyes, "you'll see."

The trainers are backing away from us, slow and cautious. Even Toggy looks like she's about to turn and run.

"You'll all see," Hyena says sinisterly, but there's a grin in his eyes. And then the trainers turn, running in all directions like they just stole something.

"I don't be liking that," Hutch says.

"Us neither, 'specially if Hyena be jolted. He ain't jolted of anyone."

"They're probably just picking on us like a prank or something." I turn to Alex and Hutch. "What can possibly be worse than what we've already been through with Bear? Come on." I reach for the doorknob. "I'll even go first."

The second I walk through the door, the scent of lemon and pine catches my attention as we are greeted by a bunch of adults. They are all dressed in what looks to be their Sunday best. Tan trousers. A pressed, long-sleeved white top. Fancy brown buckled shoes. Even their hair is sleeked back to perfection. The gentleman that asked Yak if we could wait one month before receiving our tattoos steps forward.

"Welcome, I am Mr. Jamie." He gestures to the other adults behind him. "We are den parents and tutors. Each of us belongs to a team. And I am your main den parent." He lifts his chin, staring at Alex. "While you are in our charge, you will learn everything you would if you attended school, including how to behave with your peers. You will attend speech therapy once a day with me and proper dining etiquette with Mr. Paul." He gestures to a short, stocky gentleman with light hair and dark eyes. Mr. Jamie goes on about cooking and cleaning, on who does this and that, but I'm not really listening.

I cut my eyes behind Mr. Paul. I've not seen anything like this kitchen before. Especially one with all the objects sitting along the back of the countertops. It's packed full of canisters and herbs and there's even a clear jar filled with cookies. A kettle whistling draws my eyes back to the center of the room, and Mr. Paul pulls a kettle off the cooker. I am utterly flabbergasted on how it's working. The cooker is flat on the countertop and it's right in the center of the kitchen with no fire underneath to cook it. He turns and opens one of the many cupboards lined above the sink, pulling one of the cups crammed inside it.

Mr. Jamie grabs a long switch off the counter, and I protectively move in front of Alex and Hutch.

"Do not be alarmed. This is only used to grab one's attention. With so many Naturals in such a large home, it can be difficult to speak over all the commotion. One swift hit on a countertop or wall can make quite a sound."

A thin, dark-headed gentleman lifts his own switch higher and looks at it like it's his prized possession. A smirk breaks his tight lips. "Although I have used this on my team. The ones we consider adults. The Alpha Team." He turns those stern, gray eyes onto us with his switch pointed in our direction. "And I understand they have taken a liking to you three. So please, heed my warning and do not do as they do. Do not allow them to talk you into foolishness and tomfoolery. Follow the rules and you will not have your property taken away as a punishment."

"And the rules are simple," Mr. Jamie says. He moves away from the others, toward an arched doorway. He stops and points his switch at a long parchment hanging by the kitchen doorframe with rules written in perfect penmanship. "Respect others and their property. No cursing. No drinking. No hanky panky. No sneaking out after curfew. Curfew is twelve o'clock sharp for sixteen and older, and nine o'clock for the younger ones." He pivots, facing us. "Now, follow me and I shall show you to your rooms."

He escorts us to what I assume is their library, where the scent of pine is strong. Two red settees are in the middle and even the carved wood along the material is polished to a shine. And there's a rug focused in the middle of the room. It's big and green with a stitching of a lion in the center. Along the walls are shelves with every space filled with books, and a smile spreads across my lips. I do hope those are available for everyone. When I was younger, I used to love to read. It was my favorite thing to do.

We continue through the library and under an elaborate archway, all sorts of animals are carved into the wood. In the front parlor, the walls are covered with framed portraits, each one with a different face with their Natural name engraved on a golden plaque. All placed wherever space could be found. In the center of the room is the largest settee I've ever seen. Its coloring is a dark gray, nearly black, and it's curved like a giant horseshoe. And lazily slumped in it are three younger Naturals, watching a smaller version of those black boxes with moving portraits.

I lift my chin at the decoration hanging from the tall ceiling and my lips curve at the lights sprouting from the horns. This must be what brightens the outside windows in a soft glow. An uproar of voices and commotion pulls my eyes to the wide, coiled staircase snaking its way up three levels. And from the sounds of it, chaos is minutes away from something or someone exploding.

"Whoa! What be that?"

I pull my gaze off the staircase and onto the three younger Naturals on the settee.

"It's a tablet," Mr. Jamie says. "Tomorrow, each of you will receive your own device. On it, you can listen to music, read books, or watch movies. Whatever your heart desires. However, if you break a rule, I will turn your service off for the day, week, or month. It all depends on which rule you have broken. All you shall have on it is your studies."

He turns on his heel, gesturing for us to follow him up the staircase. When we reach the second landing, he addresses us. "This is the male's quarters. No females are allowed. If you dare try, I shall know, and you will be punished. Same goes for the female quarters. Now, Lynx, please stay here while I show the boys to their room."

Alex glances over his shoulder at me and I press my lips into a thin line, willing myself not to follow. *How can I protect him and Hutch if I'm not allowed on this floor?*

"We be right." Alex grins.

"Yeah, I'll be watching him," Hutch says, and I uncurl my fists, stretching my stiff fingers out.

They turn to follow Mr. Jamie and voices above have me leaning over the railing, looking up at the third floor.

"Hurry before he comes up here." A girl giggles.

I strain over the railing with my chin lifted to the voices, and then back down the hall at Mr. Jamie. He's yanking a tall boy out of a room with string hanging out of his mouth. "Go floss somewhere else." He turns to Alex and Hutch. "This is where you will wash. Everyone shares, so you will need to get with the other boys for a schedule."

I start to lean back over the railing, and notice Owl is standing on the step below me.

"Elk is gonna get it," Owl teases in a chuckle, and then strains over the railing, making a strange animal noise. He leans back and smiles at me. "All the den parents used to be Naturals, and that was Mr. Jamie's animal call. A panther. It's how we warn the others. Although, it rarely works. The den parents are the only adults besides Yak that still have all their enhancements. No one's ever been able to sneak by or outrun them. They are fast and super smart. They know all our tricks. And if, by some small chance, you think you've fooled them and got away with it," he shakes his head, "you haven't. They just think whatever you did at the time isn't worth the headache. But trust me, they keep notes of everything and then when you do something again, bam! They have that handy-dandy notebook ready and start reading off all the shit you've done and use it against you."

I glance down the hall, and Mr. Jamie is striding toward us with liquid smooth movements. I can see it now. He walks just like Yak and the trainers. Full of confidence and charm, with a touch of danger behind each step. Mr. Jamie stops near us, slicing his brown eyes on Owl.

"Honestly, do you truly believe I do not know my own call?" He doesn't give Owl a chance to reply. Mr. Jamie starts up the stairs, flicking his wrist like he's warming up the switch as Elk comes to a skidding stop on the first step.

"Whoa," Elk chuckles and thrusts his hands out, "easy now," he says with a lopsided grin.

They both stand, staring at each other like they're waiting for the other to make the first move. And when Elk, ever so slowly, reaches for the banister, Mr. Jamie lunges. Elk soars over the railing, landing on the second floor right in front of me.

"Hey. What's good," he says with red paint smeared on top of his grin. Mr. Jamie lands right behind him and Elk looks over his shoulder and then back at me. "Catch ya later." He grins and bolts down the staircase with Mr. Jamie chasing after him, viciously swinging the switch.

"I'm going. I'm going," Elk laughs, trying to block each hit.

Mr. Jamie turns, marching back up the staircase with

his switch aimed at a girl leaning over the railing. "You're next, Rabbit."

The girl gives the same quick laugh Elk did and then turns. A door slams shut with a laughing screech before Mr. Jamie can take another step.

I look down at the first landing, and Elk smiles up at me. "Worth every mark." He winks, wiping the red paint off his mouth.

I inhale deeply with mixed emotions. In the Spoon world, this is normal. I've seen many of my friends get the switch when I was younger. Not like that, of course. Maybe one or two licks behind the barn. Especially Mable: she was forever in trouble with her mother. But the way Mr. Jamie was swinging it triggers a memory of our last night in the caverns. I didn't go to sleep next to Alex before the Naturals attacked. I was in the punishing box for being the ringleader of a well-planned escape. At least, I thought it was.

But with no food for days and barely any water, I wasn't thinking straight. I didn't consider a snitch. I figured every kid there would want out, but that wasn't the case. While we were spreading the word of escape, he was running back and telling the guards what we were up to. And when we reached the top level, the warden and all his guards were waiting for us.

"Hey, what'd I miss?" Alex asks, and I push the painful memory away.

"Elk getting a whooping," Fox replies.

Mr. Jamie clears his throat and I eye his switch a moment before shakily following him to the female floor.

YOU ARE NOT HERE

||||| ||||| ||||| |||||

||||| ||||| ||||

Mr. Jamie walks me to my room, and I'm surprised when he tells me I won't be sharing one with anyone. Since there are only thirteen female Naturals, there is plenty of room on the third floor. He opens the door for me and, as I enter, he walks by me to a smaller door.

"While you are here, you are allowed to wear whatever you want. No more uniforms." He opens the closet and gestures to the clothes hanging inside. "Mrs. Lopez took the liberty of shopping for you." He closes the door and turns to me with a genuine smile. "You may decorate your room however you want. Free speech is always welcomed and encouraged."

I swing my hands behind my back, nervously wringing them as I scan the room. I already have everything I need. A bed, a bureau, a long mirror hanging on the back door of the closet. Heck, I even have clothes. It's just like back home.

What else would I need for decoration? I'm no longer a child and have no need for a toy box.

I think back to my parents, how their room looked. Maybe a few candles that smell like flowers. Father always had some of those. He said they brightened the room and his spirits. I lift my chin to the circular globe above and then to the strange lantern on the bedside table. I guess I don't need candles. Perhaps a quilt or nice stitching or . . . I catch myself. *What am I thinking? I'm a Natural now. I don't quilt or stitch. I train, protect, and help.*

"Do not worry. I'm sure the other females will eagerly help with the decorations."

I give a quick nod and he starts for the door, but before he walks through it, he adds, "Tonight is supposed to be fun. Do try and have some." He hesitates with his features softening. "You, of all, deserve it most."

He shuts the door quietly behind him, leaving me alone with my own thoughts. *Crap. I forgot about the celebration.* I sit on the edge of the bed and wipe beads of sweat off my forehead. *Have fun. How?* I haven't even had time to absorb everything. This place. My training. Papa alive. Who my mother was. Everything is moving too fast. Perhaps I shouldn't go tonight. I squeeze my hands tightly together in my lap. But Alex and Hutch will want me to go, and neither will go without me. I wipe my sweaty palms on my trousers; so I shall.

What kind of celebration is it? Is it like a tea party or an all-out ball? I've been to a tea party once back home and even though it was a bunch of us younger girls, Father said it was similar to the adult ones. And that one wasn't too bad, even Mable enjoyed herself. But a ball. I push to my feet and pace in a small circle, suddenly nauseous. I've never been to a ball before. Nor have I been taught how to act at one. If everyone here knows I used to be a Spoon, they will expect me to know most of this. And I don't.

What if I make a fool of myself? What if everyone laughs at me because I don't know the proper etiquette or dance?

My chest squeezes painfully with a shortness of breath, and I drop back onto the bed, forcing myself to breathe. The same way Bear and Hyena tell me when I'm having trouble breathing. Deep breath. In and out.

"This be quite the setup, yeah?"

My breath catches in my throat at seeing Mable perched on top of the bureau. I hug myself, rocking back and forth on the bed. "Go away. You aren't real."

"Then why ya keep seeing me, huh?" She grins and kicks her legs out, hopping down to move around the room. "I don't get it. Ya got your own room in a big ol' house." She turns, jabbing a fist into her hip. "Ya even got a governess to tend to ya every need. It's like ya never left The Horn." She moves closer, bracing her hands on her knees, and leans close to my face. "So, why ya sad, Tiptoe?" She tilts her head. "Or is it Mute or Lynx now?" She straightens with a dismissive wave. "I can't keep up."

I cup my head, squeezing my eyes shut, forcing her from my thoughts.

"Ya'll need to be picking one soon. They'll all be watching," she mutters.

"Go away!" I screech.

"Whoa, I get that you're upset, but there's no reason to scream at me."

Hearing Ford's voice, instead of Mable's, forms tears, pooling. "My apologies, Ford, but . . . " I glimpse up at the bureau. "I thought you were her," I respond weakly and hug myself tighter. "Since my sentencing, I have transformed into many versions of myself in order to survive. And the very thought of which version of me will appear tonight, or even in the future, forms a sour taste in the back of my throat."

"Bear said this might happen. He told me to give you this until you can see Doctor Lawson tomorrow." I glance up, and he's holding a small tablet and a water jug. "But—"

I toss the tablet in my mouth, reaching for his jug, and throw my head back with a long swig. Fire burns the back of my throat, forcing a violent cough out of me. "That . . . is not water," I choke.

"No shit," he chuckles, snatching the jug from me. "And if you had let me finish, you would have known that," he adds, dropping onto the bed next to me with a long swig of his own. "The pill you swallowed is called a 'Topper'. It's the same thing Mom gave you last week, but it was in liquid form, and you were out. But the pill is what you will begin tomorrow. It's what Bear takes to help ward off those feelings and thoughts. It won't make them disappear completely. You'll still have them every now and again. Bear does, but he says it helps not to see them as often." He offers me his jug. "And this is vodka. It will calm your nerves for tonight."

I wave the jug away. "I don't think I should go tonight?"

"Yes, you should," he states, downing another swig.

"But I don't even have a proper dress."

"What do you think those are for?" he says, gesturing at the dresses hanging over the closet door. My throat goes dry at the stylish dresses, and I instantly press my fingers into my lips. This most certainly is not a tea party.

"Mom wasn't sure which one you'd like, so she had me bring over three different—"

The bedroom door opens. "Eww," Toggy says with

disgust and then glares at Ford, throwing a thumb over her shoulder. "Out."

"Wow, I think someone needs a lesson in manners." He chuckles, pushing to his feet. "Maybe I'll go have a word with Mr. Jamie about it now."

"Yeah," Toggy steps forward, "and I'll be sure to tell him you were up here in a girl's room."

"Like I care. I'm not scared of him," Ford snorts. She opens her mouth, but before she can yell, Ford is on her with a hand clamped over her lips. "Alright. But I'll remember this the next time you want me to cover for you, so you can sneak out and see Derek." Toggy squints at him, mumbling under Ford's hand. "What?" he chuckles, leaning his ear closer to her trapped mouth. "I can't hear you."

She yanks his hand away. "I said, OKAY."

"Yeah, that's what I thought." Ford turns to me with a satisfied grin. "Now, personally I like the—"

Before he can finish, Toggy grabs his right arm in a tight hold, twisting it behind his back, and forces him toward the door. With a hard shove, she pushes him out, asking, "What'cha gonna do now, Bish?"

"Ohh," Ford chuckles angrily, "about to whoop your ass."

"Please," she snorts and slams the door in his face as he steps forward.

She spins toward me with her hands clasped together in excitement. "Time to try on dresses." She pulls me to my feet. "Your aunt was supposed to be here, but she isn't finished with all the event stuff downstairs yet and asked me to take over until she's done. Which I was going to do, anyway." She grins and then turns to the dresses. She reaches for the simple, sheer dress and holds the sunshine-colored material against my front. "Umm." She cocks her head. "I don't know. Maybe." She tosses it on the bed and then holds up a midnight blue one. "Perfect. Try it on."

"Why?" I ask, refusing to take the dress. At least what she's calling a dress. There's hardly any material. If I weren't already planning on not attending, this outfit alone would have stopped me. There's no way I would go out in public wearing that, yet alone to a ball.

"So, we can see how it fits, silly."

"I understand how this works. What I'm asking is, why would I try it on if I will not be attending?"

"What?" she puffs. "But everyone goes. Well, maybe not everyone. Bear only went our first year, but only because Yak forced him to."

"So, it is required?" I ask.

"First year, yes."

"Fine," I sigh. "I'll try on the green one."

"Are you sure? Because it's god-awful. And how will you find a hottie to kiss at the end of the night if you wear it?"

"Yes, I am sure. It has sleeves and a back, so it will cover most of my scars. And it's long enough to cover my ankles." I reach for the dress, avoiding eye contact. I know most girls my age have a romantic tie or at least are interested in someone. But for me, I just can't imagine having one. I don't even know who I am anymore, much less being interested in someone in a romantic way. I begin removing my outer clothing, leaving my long johns on.

"My apologies, Toggy, but none of that interests me." I step into the dress, pulling it over my hips. "I just want to get this night over with and get on with my training." I spin around, throwing a thumb over my shoulder. "Will you button me up, please?"

"Nothing to apologize for," she says, buttoning my

dress. She steps into my view with a wide grin. "It looks better than I thought it would. Now, I'm going to hit the shower. Wanna come?"

"No, thank you. Not yet."

"Okay. But come tell me when you're out of the shower so I can do your hair and makeup."

"Makeup. What is that?"

Her grin grows even bigger. "You'll see. Oh, and your shoes are in that box over there." She points. "You might want to put them on now, so your feet can adjust to them."

She leaves the room, and I step closer to the mirror, admiring the elegance of the dress. I run a hand down the front of the silky material and tears threaten. I squeeze my eyes shut, inhaling deeply, and I can almost smell Father's lavender soap fluttering around me while he and Papa prepared for a social event like this one back home.

I was much too young to attend back then, but how I used to dream of the day when I could. And now that I am, neither are here with me. This isn't how I imagined my first social event would be. They are supposed to be here. To help me pick out the pattern and material and ease the painful processes of sewing my first dress. And when the day came, Father was supposed to tie my hair back in a matching ribbon, and afterward, Papa would tell me I'm beautiful. But they aren't here and it's all because of me. I lower my head with shame and guilt just as the door creaks open with a knock.

"Tippy, may I come in?"

I turn and, the instant I see my aunt, I lift my dress and rush toward her, wrapping my arms around her waist. I hold on tight and cry into her shoulder while she soothes away all my thoughts and misgivings.

NOT THE WALTZ I KNOW

Three hours later, I'm standing alone in front of the mirror, staring at Aunt Amy and Toggy's work. Well, mostly Toggy's work. My legs, eyebrows, and armpits are on fire from all the waxing. And these shoes are already pinching my toes painfully. I press the emerald and gold butterfly clip holding the left side of my bangs back, and it digs into my scalp. My eyelids are painted a shimmery gold, along with something called a "batwing look". And every time I blink, it feels like my eyelashes are going to stick together with so much goo on them.

I tug at my snug, long sleeves, moving closer to the mirror, and I don't look like me. I reach up, wiping most of the mauve-colored paint on my lips across my sleeve, and it smears against the corner of my mouth. *Crap.* I move closer to the mirror, rubbing at it so hard. I can't tell if it's paint or rawness now.

"Hey, it's time," Toggy says from the doorway. I turn

around, thumbing the corner of my mouth, and I freeze in place. She's in the most outlandish dress I've ever seen. It's tight, knee-length, and black with a long slit going up the left side, revealing her entire leg. Her left shoulder is bare with her bosom pushed high, nearly to her throat, with her right shoulder in a long sleeve.

"Too much, huh? Well, I can fix it." She starts forward on red heels resembling a long spike. And as she moves closer, I notice it isn't a black dress, not really. It's made out of fringe and as she walks, the black fringe sways, revealing a devil-red undercoat. She pulls a handkerchief from her red clutch and goes to work, blotting, swooping, and rubbing at my face. She smells like a rose garden. This is not the Toggy I know.

"I've been the only female on our team for so long that I was so excited to get ready with another girl and I went a little overboard. Sorry," she says with a grin.

"Do you not spend any time with the other female Naturals?"

"I do, but sometimes I feel out of place. When you spend fifteen hours a day with just your team . . . " She stops blotting and gives me a bleak look. "And ours is full of dumb boys." Toggy begins on my face again. "You start to act like them and that makes it hard connecting with the other girls. Sometimes, my playfulness comes off all wrong or too harsh." She turns me to the mirror, asking, "Is that okay, or would you like me to remove more?"

"It's a lot better, thank you."

"Good, because I don't think I could have taken off much more." She grins and hooks her arm with mine, studying me in the mirror. "You are fire," she says with a wide smile, and I secretly say the word under my breath, trying to remember all the new words she used while we were preparing for the event. "Are you ready?"

"No," I simply state, and she laughs, pulling me to the door.

"I can't wait for you to meet Derek. He's the eldest son of Chancellor Gibson, and the hottie I'll be kissing tonight," she says with a playful nudge.

We start down the staircase with the other females, and they are dressed just as outlandish as Toggy. I press a hand against my silk dress, thankful mine covers all my lady parts, and that my shoes aren't like the other girls. Mine still have a small heel, but nothing like those spikes. At the bottom landing, stand all the males dressed in their best attire, including Bear.

I lean close to Toggy, asking, "I thought you said Bear doesn't attend these functions."

"He doesn't. Which makes this very interesting," she replies, skimming the females behind us.

I step off the bottom step and Alex reaches up, tousling the top of my head. "Ain't ye pretty?" he says, and my butterfly clip wiggles free.

"Why? Why would you do that?" Toggy gasps in disbelief and quickly snaps it back into place.

"What? All I be doing is this." Alex shoots his hand up to Toggy's hair.

"Touch me and die, turd." She flinches, slapping his hand away from her brown curls.

"You never touch a lady's hair. Especially before an event," Hyena informs him.

Alex grimaces an apology as Yak enters the front parlor, squeezing through the crowd of Naturals.

"Alex, it's fine," I tell him.

"Still, I should be knowing better." He frowns.

"Honestly. I don't care. See." I reach up, pulling the clip out, and tousle my hair into a tangled mess.

"Thanks," Alex says shyly.

"Always." I smile, and Toggy gives me an annoyed look. "My apologies, but I'm not really into all this."

"It's fine," she says, pulling me into the crook of her arm. "This is exactly why we wanted you on our team."

"Thank you."

Ford pushes through the crowd, planting himself right in front of me, smiling. "So, what do you think of this place so far?"

"It's extravagant," I say as the room bellows with laughter and chatter. Ford cups his ear and I repeat myself.

"Yes, it is." He grins.

"Yo, Wolf," Fox calls, and when Ford turns, I skim over his shoulder, wondering why we aren't entering the ball-room. Then I see that Yak and Mr. Paul are only allowing certain people inside, and Yak is calling two people at a time, forming a long line toward the back of the house. I lift onto my toes and Hutch is at the front with a pretty female on his arm. Yak calls Alex and another female Natural, and then Ford.

"Hey." Toggy clamps a hand on my shoulder and leans close to my ear. "I think I know why he's here now. Fifty bucks, he's an escort. Probably yours."

Mr. Paul snaps his fingers in the air, calling for Bear, and I ask, "What?"

"What?" she asks, lifting her voice over the crowd.

My name is called, but I ignore Yak. In the last three hours, while Toggy helped me get ready, she used so many terms, like "bet" or "bussin'", that I had no idea what she was saying most of the time. It wasn't until Aunt Amy told her I was confused with her word choices that Toggy slowed down and explained all of them to me. And since I need to know what this new word "buck" means, I ask, "What is—"

"Let's go," Yak says, roughly forcing me into the line behind Hyena.

Without knowing all their lingo, or how to act here, I fidget in place, hoping I don't make a fool out of myself tonight.

"Hey," Fox says next to me. "If you'd feel more comfortable with someone else as your escort, I'm sure Yak would understand if we switched." He starts to reach over Hyena's shoulder for Ford, and I stop him.

"No-no-no, it's not that at all. I enjoy your company. I just . . . Toggy used a term I'm not familiar with and I didn't get a chance to ask her what it means. May I ask you?"

"Sure," he responds as Ford enters the ballroom, followed by loud cheering.

"What's a buck? Is it—"

Fox chokes on a cough, and the tall blonde next to Hyena turns to look at us.

"I'm fine, just swallowed wrong," he tells her and coughs again.

"Are you sure? Your face is turning purple," she voices.

Fox clears his throat, and I lean forward, asking Hyena. "Toggy said, fifty bucks Bear would be an escort. Is a buck a form of currency here or is it something else?"

"Ohhh. A buck," Fox repeats. "I thought you asked me something completely different," he laughs, patting his chest. "Jesus."

Hyena laughs over his shoulder. "Yes. She was gambling." He turns slightly. "And he was supposed to be your escort, but Mr. Paul needed him for something else."

"Ohh. Wait?" I face Fox. "What did you think I asked you?"

"Trust me, you do not want to know," Hyena replies with another grin and then turns back around just in time to enter with his escort.

We move forward, and Mr. Paul stops us at the edge of the doorway. "Wait," he tells me and then gestures for me to smile. I press a hand to my belly with a deep inhale and force a smile as the crowd inside cheers loudly for Hyena and his escort. Fox tucks strands of long blond hair behind his ears and adjusts his bun. *Is he as nervous as me?*

"Now," Mr. Paul tells us.

We step into the ballroom, and the joyous murmurs fill the room with exhilaration as Fox and I are introduced. This is a lot more lavish than any ball I could have conjured in my daydreams. My heels sink into the plush, red carpet flowing down a staircase. I lift my chin to the chandeliers sparkling in the soft light and my ankle wobbles in these shoes. Thankfully, Fox braced his arm or else I would have tripped. To the left of the room is a large, long table filled with Naturals and Mr. Jamie is sitting at the head of it. Fox guides me to the right, toward the smaller tables filled with adults and those that are not Naturals.

We stop at a round table decorated with silver-edged china and polished silverware. Fox moves in front of me and pulls out my chair.

"Ain't this clean?" Alex says, sitting next to Hutch.

"Yes," I agree before carefully sitting next to Ford, feeling completely out of sorts. "Thank you, Fox."

"Yep." After helping me sit, Fox turns, walking to another table with two adults, probably his parents.

From the looks of it, those that were born here are sitting with their families on this side of the room. With all the Naturals on the other side of the room, sitting with the den parents. I look back at Alex and Hutch sitting with us and my chest warms at knowing that someone considered them as my family. I glance at Ford with a strong emotion pulling at my throat. *Was it him?*

"Tippy, it is so good to see you."

I turn my head and my heart leaps into my throat. I shakily lift out of my chair and start to lean into him, but then I remember Papa isn't here. It's Uncle Pablo, Ford's father. "It is so good to see you, too," I say with my throat nearly closing, and Uncle Pablo pulls me close.

"I am so proud of you, Tippy."

"Thank you," I say softly, and notice the ballroom is eerily quiet.

I pull away, and all eyes are on us. I gracefully take my seat as the room quickly turns into whispering gossip again. I scan the table, trying to find my bearings, and notice two empty chairs. One to my left, with Aunt Amy on the other side of it and another empty seat on Ford's right. Then Hutch, Alex, and Uncle Pablo. I look over at the empty chair next to me, trying to control my emotions as a white-gloved gentleman pours golden bubbles into dainty glasses. *Is that liquor? Perhaps the same kind Ford gave me earlier. If so, I do not want to drink it.* I press a hand to my chest, eyeing the table.

"You do not have to drink that," Uncle Pablo tells me and then addresses the other white-gloved man pouring fizzy drinks.

"But you can, and you should," Ford says with a knowing look, before taking a small sip of his own.

"Nonetheless, you may, and you ought to," his mama corrects. "Furthermore, do we need another lesson in etiquette with Mr. Paul?"

"No, ma'am," Ford says with a lopsided grin, sliding his elbows off the table.

"Although, I believe Sheep needs one," Aunt Amy replies with a quick lift of her chin at Alex.

"For Pete's sake," Uncle Pablo says, taking the fizzy glass out of Alex's hand.

"What? Mr. Jamie say we can partake anything that be on the table," he says with the same snooty tone as Mr. Jamie. "And that be on the table."

"Yes, but not this. I know this place is different from out there, but we do not allow twelve-year-olds to drink alcohol," Uncle Pablo says, placing the glass farther away from his reach.

"Hey," Ford says, leaning close to my ear. "It's the only night out of the year we are allowed to drink, and we only get one glass, so it's okay if you do. No one will judge you for it." He pulls back, flashing me a wide grin and a wink as he takes another sip of his own.

"Alex," Aunt Amy grins, "you remind me of Benji when he first arrived."

"What about me?" Bear asks, lowering himself into the empty chair next to me.

"I was just saying how Alex reminds me of you when you first arrived," my aunt admits.

"Probably worse." Hyena chuckles, lowering himself into the chair next to Ford.

Bear moves his chair closer to the table, and I am very aware of his knee brushing against mine. I secretly scoot to the other side of my chair, closer to Ford.

"Tippy, how are you settling in?" Uncle Pablo asks.

"Fine, thank you," I reply and reach for my napkin, careful not to allow the gold-circular ring slip from the middle. I place the napkin in my lap, wondering how I am to use this without it falling off.

"If you aren't happy with the wardrobe I picked out for

you, we can go shopping tomorrow," my aunt adds, sliding the ring off the napkin, and I secretly pull mine off under the table, placing it onto the table like she did.

"Thank you, but there is no need. They are lovely," I reply, and my knee begins to bounce nervously as a gentleman serves the table with food. Ford slides his hand under the table and places his hand on my knee, and I stop at once.

"Whoa. What this be?" Alex asks with amusement.

"It's a lobster tail," Hyena tells him.

"Do me pick it up and gnaw at it like a chicken bone?"

"No," Uncle Pablo laughs as everyone cheerfully helps Hutch and Alex. And my heart aches at the cheerful chatter. The last time I was at a dinner table, it was the night I was sentenced, and Mable was there, and it was also in joyous conversation. I lower my head with my jaw clenched. I miss her and my parents immensely. And again, Ford stops my knee from bouncing.

I peek up at Uncle Pablo and desperately want to speak to Papa. But I'm terrified. *What if he doesn't understand all the bad things I did in the caverns? What if he doesn't like the person I have become?* My stomach churns at the thoughts because I don't even know who I am anymore.

I push my food around and, by the time the last course is finished, I'm eager for the evening to be done and over with. I'm ready to go back to my room and take off these painful shoes. I start to push my chair out and Bear soars to his feet to help me.

"Thank you."

"You're welcome."

"Ford," Aunt Amy begins, and Uncle Pablo helps her with her chair. "Please be on your best behavior tonight. Make good choices."

I turn around, wondering where Ford is going after this. *Is there more to this evening? Gosh, I hope not.*

"When am I not?" Ford snorts.

"The second you met him." Uncle Pablo chuckles, aiming his bubbly drink at Bear, before gulping it down in one swift swallow.

"What? I'm not the bad influence. He is," Bear declares, lifting his chin at Hyena.

Hyena turns his head with an easy grin. "What? Yeah, I'll be right there," he says, pretending to be called away and walks over to Toggy's table. The trainers are completely different people here. Playful and nicer. I almost feel silly now for fearing them as I did.

"We be done?" Alex asks.

"Yes. Go have fun," Uncle Pablo says.

Hutch and Alex eye me a moment, and I quickly add, "Go. I'll be fine." I smile.

"Ye sure?"

"Yes. Go."

They both start toward Toggy's table and my aunt moves closer to me. "If you need anything, let me know. I'm only minutes away, okay?" I nod, and she pats my cheek. "Do try and have some fun tonight, dear. Before you know it, you will be back on the submarine and in training. I should know. I was once a Natural, too."

"Oh, don't you worry, Mom. We will," Ford says, hooking his arm around my neck and pulling me close. It's the same playful gesture we used to do as kids, except it was me usually hooking my arm around his neck and pulling him closer, right before we landed ourselves in trouble.

"Hmm," she moans, squinting at Ford. "Maybe I should stay for Tippy."

"Sorry, no adults allowed except for den parents." Ford grins.

"Don't worry, Mrs. Lopez. I'll keep him in check," Bear states.

"Thank you. It's good to know Ford has good people watching over him." She turns to me, giving me another hug. "Good night, dear."

"Ford, not too much fun." Uncle Pablo points at me with a silly grin. "You either."

I give a quick nod and, the second they are gone, I turn to Ford. "I'm going to head back upstairs," I voice.

"What? The night hasn't even begun," Ford complains. "There's so much more to tonight."

"I understand there might be more to this evening, but—"

"Oh my God, you won't believe what Otter did," Fox interrupts. "Mr. Wess is going to lose his shit." He reaches for my untouched drink. "Are you finished with this?" he asks, but he doesn't bother to wait for a reply. He throws his head back, downing the entire drink.

He lowers the glass and reaches for another one, and while he has Ford and Bear's attention, I quietly step away from them. But just as I reach the double doors, a group of young girls rush over to me, and the room grows hot with so many huddled this close. They are speaking rapidly and non-stop that I can't keep up with their questions. My muscles tense as I search for a way out, but someone latches a hand around my wrist.

"O.M.G. he came," one of the girls says. "He's the chancellor's son, and he never comes to these things. He must be here to see you." The small, honey-blonde girl tightens her grip on my arm. "Let me introduce you. It'll give me a reason to talk to him."

"I'd really rather not."

"Yes. You have to," she emphasizes, dragging me behind her. "Everyone's been talking about you for days. If I'm the one to make the introductions, I'll definitely be on his radar."

I can't keep up in these shoes or with her rambling, and when she stops suddenly, I bump into her. I straighten myself, wobbling slightly, trying to remember if I courtesy and then make eye contact or before. So, I keep my eyes lowered.

"Lynx, this is Derek." I start to courtesy and the girl gasps, yanking on my arm. "O.M.G. What are you doing?" she asks through her teeth.

I stagger into her, still refusing to make eye contact with him, for I don't want to make matters worse. I really wish I knew their customs here. "Greeting, Mr. Derek," I reply, feeling small.

"Well, stop. We don't courtesy here. We just say hello," she says in a snotty tone. Her friends crowd around us, snickering, and I shrink even smaller. I can tell by her sharp tongue she is cross with me, and I honestly don't know how to fix it.

"Gina, stop being a bitch."

I look over my shoulder, and Hyena and Toggy are both right behind me.

"Come on, let's get a drink," Hyena says, guiding me away by the elbow.

"Thank you, but I think it would be best if I just went back upstairs."

"I'm not asking," he says and tightens his grip, guiding me along the polished hardwood floor, lifting untouched drinks to his lips as we go. Behind me, I hear Toggy's heated voice, and I glance over my shoulder. The girl named Gina is near tears, and I feel bad for her. It isn't her fault I don't understand their ways. I start to pull away and go to her defense, but Hyena yanks me back.

"Nope, Gina gets what she deserves and more if Minx has anything to say about it." I glance over my shoulder, forgetting that Toggy's Natural name is Minx. It will take some getting used to.

"Trust me," Hyena says, hurrying me along. "No one messes with her when she's pissed. Not even Bear. Her fists hit harder than yours."

"But—"

"No buts," he says, and we stop at a table full of drinks. He hands me a dainty glass full of red liquid and asks, "So, what do you think of this place so far?"

"It's different," I mutter, watching Gina race up the stairs in tears. I press a hand to my belly as Toggy and Mr. Derek turn toward us, holding hands. *Please don't bring him over here.*

Hyena leans close, invading my air. "Minx, huh?" He straightens and flashes me a proud grin. "That's cool. No judgment here if you like girls. I like them, too. Maybe more than you. Eh, eh," he chuckles, nudging me in the arm.

I sidestep, trying to balance my drink from sloshing over the rim, and my entire face burns with embarrassment as Toggy joins us. Thankfully, without Mr. Derek.

"Whoa. What did you say to her?" Toggy chuckles.

Hyena throws me an evil grin, like he's about to embarrass me further. Luckily, I don't have to tell him I'm not interested in anyone. Female or male. Because a tall female in a long, flowy pink dress plants herself right in front of him.

"You are disgusting. And to think I waited eight months

for your return," she complains and ends the conversation with a hard slap across his jaw.

"Jessica, wait!" Hyena hollers, chasing after her.

"And I thought tonight would be boring." Bear chuckles, sliding into Hyena's spot next to me.

"Why is she cross with him? He isn't wearing her ribbon," I ask.

Toggy dips her chin. "Her what?"

The confusion etched across her face clearly tells me they do not have this custom here and heat crawls along my skin. "Nothing," I reply and turn, placing my drink onto the table. "I don't belong here."

"Yes, you do. More than most," Toggy says and grabs my shoulder, spinning me around. "And you're not going anywhere. Tell me what this ribbon thing is."

I pull my shoulder free from her as more Naturals start to crowd around us. "You will only laugh," I say, rubbing at my forehead.

"I won't laugh. I promise." Toggy points at the circle closing me in. "And anyone that does, I'll smack that shit out of you." She faces me with a big grin. "Go on."

I wet my lips with more heat crawling up my back. "Well, when a couple has been courting for a while and the boy is about to leave the island for higher learning or an apprenticeship, whatever you call it here, the girl will tie her favorite hair ribbon onto his wrist the day of his departure. When he returns, and the ribbon is frayed and faded from wear, the girl will know he is an honorable gentleman worthy of marriage. If he returns without the ribbon or the ribbon is like new, then the girl will know he had removed it so no one would know he was taken, and she will gracefully find another suiter."

"Oh, I'm definitely getting a ribbon for Derek tomorrow."

"You don't think it's stupid?"

"Not at all."

"Does it always have to be a girl? Or can a guy give something to a girl?"

"Fox, I don't think there are enough ribbons on the island for all the girls you and Hyena date," Ford chuckles, joining the group.

Fox cocks his head and opens his mouth like he's about to say something mean, and I interject before he can. "If you truly like a girl, it's not unheard of for a boy to give their favorite tie or something they wear every day. If the girl accepts it, they will bind their schoolbooks with it. This way, the community will know who it belongs to, and that she is taken."

"Wait," Toggy begins, "we're only here for a few weeks. How will anyone know it belongs to me?"

"It can be anything," Ford replies and lifts his chin. "Like Bear's keyring. He's always braiding it. So, if he gave that to the girl he likes, and she carried it around, everyone would know she is taken and by whom."

"So, it just needs to be something I'm known for? Yeah, I can do that." She grins proudly.

"I don't think you can give Derek your snarl." Ford chuckles and raises his drink to his lips.

"Yeah, well, who asked you?" she snaps and bops the end of his glass, staining the front of his crisp white shirt red.

"Minx! A word," Mr. Jamie calls.

"HA!" Ford points in her face.

She slaps his hand away with a squint, mouthing a very bad word to him, and then joins Mr. Jamie in the corner.

"Whoa. What happened to you?" Hyena asks, rejoining the group.

"Minx," Ford responds, dabbing a cloth against his front.

"Been there," Hyena admits just as the lights go out and the ballroom roars with excitement.

"Kick it!" a voice demands, and the lights flash on and off in all sorts of colors. I lift onto my toes, searching over Ford's shoulder. Elk is on a platform, standing in front of a table and moving his hand efficiently over something on top of it. Within seconds, strange music pierces the air, loud and violent, as the crowd moves excitedly to the center of the room.

"What type of music is that?" I ask. "And where are the instruments?"

"Ohh, you're about to learn all kinds of music tonight." Ford chuckles.

"I don't know." I start to pull away and Ford stops me.

"Nu-uh, we do everything as a team, and we aren't ready to leave yet."

"Yes, but these shoes. My feet hurt."

"Then take them off."

"What?" I squeal in a harsh whisper. "I cannot do that. This is a fancy event."

"Yeah, well, it's about to get unfancy." Ford laughs, toeing off his shoes.

And before I can stop him, he tosses me over his shoulder as he removes my shoes. He carries me toward the crowd and then drops me next to Alex. And the floor vibrates under my feet as everyone jumps up and down.

"Hey, looks here, what Musk show us," Alex hollers over the music. He's kicking one leg out while punching the air with his arm, and I can't help but smile. "Ye try it."

"No, thank you. I'm going to go to my room. But you stay and enjoy yourself."

"Can't." Alex stops and looks up at me. "Not if ye ain't here. Where ye go, I go. Member?"

I hesitate a moment, not wanting to stay, and Ford raises an eyebrow at me.

"Are you really going to make him leave?" Ford asks.

"Okay." I lift my index finger with a small grin. "One dance."

"Heck yeah." Alex smiles and he and Ford demonstrate the dance once more.

Within minutes, I'm in tune with them, but not for long. Hutch slides toward us on his socks with a wild grin. "This be sic, yeah?"

"If ye gonna be heavin', do it over der," Alex tells him.

"Ain't that kind of sick." Hutch laughs. "It be their word for 'clean'."

"Oh, I be liking that one." Alex lifts his chin with his entire body strained with glee. "This be sic!" he shouts, and I can't help but be pulled into the joyous event.

WHICH ONE IS THE TRUE ME?

HHH HHH HHH HHH
HHH HHH HHH I

I laughed so much last night my cheeks still hurt this morning. I ended up staying the entire time and, for the first time since my sentencing, I had a wonderful time. Dr. Lawson, my counselor, said the Topper helped, but I don't believe that was even a factor. If I only see Lou when I'm scared or anxious, then I wouldn't have needed a Topper last night because once we began dancing, I was neither. Of course, she says I still need to take it every morning at breakfast and that Mr. Jamie will help me to remember. And that I must continue seeing her twice a week, and at the end of our holiday, she will give me my evaluation on whether I am healthy enough to stay in the program.

Now, I'm sitting at a small table with Alex and Hutch as we wait for Mr. Jamie. Whatever room this is, it quickly becomes my favorite. There's a huge window directly in front of us that nearly swallows the wall. The scenery alone is magnificent. This room faces the waterfall cascading into a small pool of water with trees and flowers everywhere. To the left of the room is a wide bookcase filled with all sorts of games, but the one that catches my eye is the chessboard. I've already asked Alex to play with me and I do hope we are allowed to play it in this room.

"What do ye think he wants us for?" Hutch asks, sitting to my right.

I turn my attention onto Hutch, and he's chewing on his nails.

"Search us." Alex shrugs. "I ain't done nothing." He winks at me. "Not that he be knowing."

"Ye think we be in trouble then?"

"Good morning."

Hutch nearly jumps out of his chair at Mr. Jamie's voice, and I can't help but wonder what he did to be this paranoid.

"Good morning." Alex and I return.

Mr. Jamie rounds the table to stand in front of us and then drops a thin leather bag on the surface. "I only have a few things to go over and explain, and then you may have your day back. Shall we begin?" He doesn't wait for a response. He goes straight into a long lecture on how to treat one another from this point forward. Followed by a list of rules we are to obey while on holiday. Afterward, he hands us each a device called a "tablet", and then demonstrates how they work, like what options to click for music or books. There's even an option to click if we want to paint. He goes even further, telling us this is not just for entertainment, but we will also be doing all our schoolwork on it as well. And I am in awe of the device. I eagerly listen to every word, absorbing all the new information that by the time Mr. Jamie is ending our time, I can't believe an hour has flown by.

Mr. Jamie shuts down his tablet just as Ford and Hyena enter, both wearing a clever grin. Hyena eyes Alex a moment before they both acknowledge Mr. Jamie with a polite greeting.

"Sorry to interrupt, but may I speak with Lynx for a moment, please?" Ford asks.

"Yes, you may," Mr. Jamie informs him as he shoves his own tablet into his bag. "If you have any questions, please ask. I will be in the library."

I begin to stand, but Ford and Hyena swagger toward me, inserting themselves between me and Alex. "Mom and Dad want us over for dinner tonight," Ford begins, watching Mr. Jamie walk out the door. "We should be there around—"

The second Mr. Jamie is fully out, Hyena turns. He yanks Alex out of the chair by his collar and slams him against the wall, holding him up. I instantly stand, and Ford grabs my arm, shaking his head.

"Did you tell Jessica I caught a virus that turned my wang green, and it should be falling off any day now?" he asks in a low growl.

"Alex, you didn't?" I gasp, ignoring Hutch holding his belly in a hearty laugh.

"What? I don't even know a . . . what'cha say her name be?" Alex asks with confusion.

Mr. Jamie enters back into the room, marching toward them, and grabs Hyena by the ear.

"Release Sheep now," Mr. Jamie stresses. Alex drops to his feet, quickly shuffling away as Mr. Jamie pulls on Hyena's ear until he is bent over in pain. "Do you need another lesson on manners?"

"No, sir," Hyena growls.

"Good. Now, apologize."

"I'm sorry, Mr. Jamie."

"Not to me," Mr. Jamie says through his teeth, tugging harder on his ear.

"Alright, dang." With a low growl, Hyena snarls out, "I'm sorry, Sheep."

"For?" Mr. Jamie probs.

"For using my fists instead of my words."

"It be right." Alex grins proudly, drumming his fingers along the tabletop on his way to the door. "An' it ain't Jessica I be saying that to; it be her sister," he admits and bolts out the door before Mr. Jamie can correct his speech.

Hyena's eyes turn murderous, and I can tell it's taking everything he has not to chase Alex down and beat him bloody.

"I want to see both of you in the library. Now," Mr. Jamie stresses as he walks out the door.

"Damnit, Wolf. You were supposed to be watching for him," Hyena growls, rubbing at his sore ear.

"I was," Ford replies with a sly grin. "I watched him come in and bend your ear." Hyena makes a throaty sound as he strides to the door. "Well, what did you want me to do?" Ford begins, following him out. "Lay Mr. Jamie out so you could beat the snot out of Sheep? Who, by the way, used his words instead of his fists to get the better of you."

Hutch slings an arm over my shoulder. "I don't know who be scarier. Mr. Jamie or our team." He grins. I look at Hutch and we both say, "Mr. Jamie," at the same time.

Once Ford and I arrived at his parents' home, I willingly helped Aunt Amy and Uncle Pablo with dinner. Ford, on the other hand, sat on a stool behind a counter, watching and laughing at all my questions. I thought for sure they would laugh along with Ford, or maybe be annoyed with me. Instead, they answered every question with as much enthusiasm as I did in asking.

Most of the kitchen gadgets fascinated me, from the rice cooker, juice blender, can opener, to all the different mixing bowls and utensils and pots and pans. Back home, all we had was a large boiling pot, used for water and stews, and a smaller one for vegetables. A frying pan for fish or chicken, and an oven pan, used for casseroles or pies and cakes.

Then, there was the microwave and fryer that cooked food in minutes. And to clean everything, they put all the dishware in a wild box called a "dishwasher". But the one magical thing that blew me away were the solar panels and windmills that Uncle Pablo told me about.

By the time we sit down for supper, I am no longer hungry. I only want to go have a look at these energy sources. Instead, I take my place next to Ford, hoping there will be time after dinner.

Aunt Amy places a roasted chicken with vegetables surrounding it in the center of the table as I skim the dining room. There's no china cabinet or fireplace like back home. There's not even a door dividing any of the rooms. Instead, it sits right next to the kitchen with an open view of the rest of the home. I can see all the way into the front parlor. Where a tall tree stands directly in the middle of the room. From there, two bedrooms and a powder room spread farther into the home.

"Is this the same style of home you and Papa grew up in?" I ask Uncle Pablo.

"Yes. I know you were really young when my mom and dad passed, but do you remember your grandparents?"

"My apologies, Uncle Pablo, but no, I do not," I admit,

taking in the differences between the two households, mine back home, and the kind Papa grew up in. It makes me wonder if I ever really knew Papa. *And what about Father? Is everything I know about him a lie, too?* I turn my attention back to Uncle Pablo. "And Father, is he from here too?"

"No." Uncle Pablo begins, reaching over to carve a piece of chicken off the bone. "Potro met your father, Jonah, by accident. He wasn't even supposed to be on Husk Bay. Potro had just finished a mission and was supposed to be on down time. But Spider, our leader at the time, told Potro to go train the new recruits on how to mingle and purchase items from Spoons." He slices off a thin piece, placing it on Aunt Amy's plate.

"Thank you," she says with a sweet smile and then looks at me. "Jonah used to work on one of the fruit farms there, and the second Potro laid eyes on Jonah, he was smitten. But Jonah, on the other hand, it took nearly three years for him to come around to Potro. Your dad was persistent."

Uncle Pablo takes his seat with a wide grin. "Jonah once told me before they were married that he thought Potro's been in a room too long, smelling his own farts because he thinks his shit doesn't stink."

"Pablo, language," Aunt Amy says.

"Sorry." He winks at Aunt Amy and then faces me. "Anyway, Jonah looked me dead in the eye and said, 'And it does stink. Something awful too.' I nearly fell over because he had my brother pegged." Uncle Pablo shakes his head, digging into his meal. "Potro always did think he was better than everyone else. It wasn't until Jonah saw you on Potro's hip that he changed his mind. After he learned about your mom, he—" Aunt Amy reaches over, squeezing Uncle Pablo's arm, silencing him.

"Tippy, your parents have told you about your mother, yes?"

"Yes." I pull the silver ring off the napkin and carefully press the napkin on my lap. "But how do I know if what they told me about her is true? I mean . . . I didn't know Papa was a Natural, or that Father worked on a farm." I turn my attention to Uncle Pablo. "Is my mother really your sister and did she die from pneumonia?"

"Yes and no," he says, full of sorrow. "Yes, your mother was our older sister, Maria. It's where your middle name comes from."

"Yes. Papa told me that."

"But no, Maria did not die from pneumonia." He shifts in his seat and points his fork at me again. "I see a lot of her in you. How protective you are with Alex. She was the same way with me and Potro. She never wanted us to join the program. Said it was too dangerous and why Maria retired when we came of age to join the program. She wanted us to join her in the Naturals' Red Cross missions. The submarine that travels all over, helping rebuild homes and giving aid in whatever the island needs."

"The Naturals have two submarines?" I ask with surprise.

"Yes, but not many know about it. The one the Naturals use now is a newer version of the older one. It's spacious with a lot more tech on it. The older and smaller one is used for our Red Cross positions, and they are filled with retired Naturals. It's hard to get into. Plus, they are gone for years at a time sometimes, not just six or eight months out of the year. They travel farther out than we do." He forks a carrot.

"Anyway, her team was dropped off on Drow Inlet, rebuilding after a hard hit from Dalton, 'The Grizzly'. He completely demolished the place. Thankfully, no one was hurt, and Maria and her team were able to swoop in and get right to work. Six months later, our submarine received a distress call from a member of Maria's team, saying they were being attacked again. At the time, we didn't know who this pirate was. He was new and trying to make a name for himself, and he did. He quickly became 'The Butcher'. He didn't follow pirate rules. He did what he wanted." Uncle Pablo squeezes his fork, staring at his food. "We still haven't been able to catch him."

Aunt Amy reaches over, gently touching his hand before pushing to her feet and leaving the table.

"We did get his first mate, though," Ford says between bites.

"You did?" Uncle Pablo's head snaps up. "When?"

"About a month before we came back. He's down in the hold right now."

"That's good. Has he given Yak any information about his captain?"

"No. Yak hasn't interrogated him yet. He was waiting until after boot camp so he could take Walrus with him. Yak's been teaching him everything he needs to know so he can take his place as our leader next year."

"Walrus is a good choice," Uncle Pablo says, and then turns his attention back to me. "Anyway, by the time we arrived, 'The Butcher' and his crew were gone. There was nothing we could do but help those that survived, and not many did. Only a handful of Spoons and only one guy from Maria's team, Jamie. Your den parent. He's the one that made the call. And when we got there, he was holding an infant in his arms. At first, we thought you belonged to someone from the village and then Jamie handed you to Potro, saying you belonged to Maria. We didn't even know Maria and Vance were expecting when they shipped out."

Aunt Amy enters back into the room, holding something close to her chest. "Maria's death hit us hard, Potro more. He took you straight to the sub and when we finally joined him, he wouldn't let go of you. No one was allowed to hold or feed you or even watch you while he slept. Not even Pablo. Potro kept you close the entire time. And when we returned, he informed us he was retiring and moving to Capra Horn. I tried to talk him out of it, so you could grow up here. But he wouldn't listen."

"We both did," Uncle Pablo adds. "But he said he was going to build a life with you and Jonah away from all of this, and he did."

Aunt Amy hands me a square frame. "This is your mother."

I hold the silver edges with shaky hands, staring at the woman I'm named after. She's standing between Papa and Uncle Pablo, and my chest squeezes painfully. I instantly reach up, smoothing down my big curls. I always thought I had Papa's hair, just not as curly. I thumb the dimple on her chin. The same one I have. But she's not the one I know. Papa is and seeing him again makes my throat tight and my chest ache. I start to hand Aunt Amy her frame back and she stops me.

"You may keep it," she says with a smile. "We have more. I can get them all out after dinner if you want."

"Yes, that would be lovely, thank you, but I'd rather have one of Papa," I respond, carefully placing the frame back on the table. I look over at Uncle Pablo, not wanting to hurt his feelings. "I know she was your sister and my mother, but I do not know her. Not like I know Papa." I lower my head shamefully. "And—"

"No need to feel bad, Tippy," Uncle Pablo begins. "I understand."

I look up, and my chest warms at his smile. "We have loads of Potro. You can have as many as you want. After dinner, we can get the photo albums out and you can pick which ones you want."

"That would be lovely, thank you," I say with excitement.

"Sorry to interrupt all this, but we don't have time for that. Not tonight," Ford says, shoving food into his mouth and in a hurry. "We have a game to get to, remember?"

"Ford, don't speak with your mouth full," Aunt Amy says.

I swallow the food in my mouth and wipe the corners of my lips before asking, "Game? Like chess or cards?"

"No." Ford grins wickedly, also wiping at his mouth, but with a lot more force. "This is a physical game."

Uncle Pablo smiles wide. "It's what they used to play back in the old days called 'Roller Derby', but over time, the Naturals have tweaked it a bit to make it harder with their abilities."

"And it's sort of a big deal because we only get to play it for the few weeks we're here. And we're going to be late if we don't leave now." He looks over at his mother. "May we be excused?"

"Yes, you may." She reaches over and squeezes my arm. "Have fun."

I press my lips together, hesitating as Ford stands. "Will Alex be there?" I ask him.

"Probably." Ford pushes his chair in. "Everyone goes," he says, reaching for his glass of water and gulping the rest down.

"Can we go by the Naturals' home and see?"

"No need. Check this out." Ford pulls out a small rectangular device. The same one I've seen Mr. Jamie use.

He taps the front and the face of it brightens with all sorts of small, colorful boxes. Each one with a different design on it.

"May I ask what that is?"

Ford peeks up at me with a lazy grin. "It's a phone." He moves closer, leaning over my shoulder so I can have a better look at it. "It's our version of a ham radio. If we want to speak to someone that isn't nearby, we use this." He thumbs the green box, and it expands, revealing a list of names. "I can click on any of these names, and it will instantly allow me to communicate with them. I can speak to them through this, what we call a 'phone call', or I can text them. I prefer texting." He picks Mr. Paul's name with his portrait next to it.

"All I have to do is type in what I want to ask and, within seconds, he'll reply back. But not everyone answers as quickly as he does. That's why I'm asking him. He's pretty good at replying right back." He uses his thumb, working the letters, fast and efficiently, that he must do this a lot to be this good at it, and with just one hand.

Have you seen Bison or Sheep?

Seconds later, like magic, words appear.

Yes, they are with me at the game. And will you please bring Lynx, so these two will stop asking me if she is done eating?

OMW!

"What is OMW?" I ask.

"It means 'on my way'," he tells me, pulling my chair

out. "Don't worry, you'll learn all that when you get your own phone."

"I'm going to get one, too?" I ask with excitement.

"Of course," Uncle Pablo tells me, reaching for his water and then points a finger at Aunt Amy. "This one will want to know where you are at all times. And she'll probably call or text every five minutes, so you might want to learn it fast." He chuckles.

"And if you don't, she'll send Mr. Jamie, and trust me, that's worse than Mom knowing your business."

"Hey," Aunt Amy says, "I'm not that bad."

"Yes, you are," Ford and Uncle Pablo say at the same time.

"Come on, let's go," Ford says, practically dragging me out of the room.

A COMPETITION AT ITS FINEST

||||| ||||| ||||| |||||
||||| ||||| ||||| //

Instead of going back to town, where most of the shops are, Ford guides me to the right, where a majority of the trees are. Next to one of the larger trees is a tall building off on its own, with groups of people moving toward it. Above the double-glass doors is a large sign, brightened with lights.

Shrek – 6:00. Fifth Element – 9:00.

We follow everyone inside, and I'm instantly hit with a smell that makes my mouth water.

Ford says something, but I'm not listening. I'm more interested in why everyone in front of us stops. I lean to my right, watching everyone huddling closer to a long glass countertop, shouting orders at two teenagers working strange contraptions behind it.

"That's the concession. Drinks. Popcorn. Snacks. Do you want anything?"

"No," I mutter, straining my eyes around the crowd, watching a teenager fill a cup with brown liquid. If I didn't know how magical this place was, I would think there was a leak in their watering well.

"Good. Let's go." He tugs on my arm and guides me down a dimly lit hall with large portraits on both sides. We turn right and there's a wide staircase leading farther down. Once we reach the bottom, we start through another set of double doors and it's a whole new world down here, but darker. This is no sunny fairytale atmosphere like it is up top. This has a more dangerous feel to it.

There are small twinkly lights, flashing on and off, as if they're the music notes to the bells and whistles ringing. And the voices, it's almost terrifying. I can hear every whoop and holler from everyone bustling around. The atmosphere alone is thrilling.

"This is an arcade," Ford says, raising his voice. "It's Owl's favorite place. I'm sure he'll want to bring you and the others tomorrow or the next day."

I shoulder through the crowd with Ford and raise my own voice. "It's so loud."

"I know. It's the hearing thing, but you'll get used to it. And just think, we haven't even made it inside yet."

"What?"

"The arena," he replies, and pulls me away from the mob. All while explaining to me what an arcade is and pizza and how to win toys through tickets. When we finally reach the arena, I am completely in awe of this place. We stop right next to a gentleman standing by the entrance, and Ford pulls out some sort of green parchment from his pocket.

"This is our form of currency here." He looks at me with a lopsided grin, holding one up. "This is a buck." He laughs, handing the gentleman a bunch of bucks. "Hyena told me what happened, so just remember there are no secrets with our team. No matter what it is, if one of them sees or hears about it, it's bound to be told to the rest, and you'll be teased forever about it."

We follow the crowd into another large area and, up ahead, I can see another doorway.

"Like the way they tease you about what happened with Mable?" I ask, lifting onto my toes, searching over shoulders and heads.

"Exactly, and that was years ago." When we enter, my eyes nearly pop out of my head at the large space. There are so many people packed in chairs, sitting along the edges of a massive, circular platform.

"We're down there," Ford says with a lift of his chin. We push through a row of people and then stop next to Mr. Paul, with Hutch and Alex on his right.

"Hey," Alex says, leaning over the railing with a wide grin. "This be sic, yeah?"

I start to reply back, but Mr. Paul interjects, correcting his speech. Hutch gives me a playful grimace and I can't help but return it.

"So, what do you think?" Ford asks me.

"It's nothing like I've seen back home. I mean, we have games, like marbles and hopscotch, you know that. But those are played by children, and the adults never sit nearby, watching and cheering them on. It's marvelous. This whole place is a dime."

"Look at you trying out new words," he says with a nudge. "I knew you would like it." Ford leans over the railing, inhaling deeply. "Plus, we've got the best seats in the house. You can actually smell the sweat and energy as they skate by."

"Skate?" I ask, ignoring Alex moaning and arguing with Mr. Paul.

"It's sneakers with wheels on the bottom. That's the track they skate on, there." He points. "And the large hole in the middle, that's out of bounds. It's the one place you don't want to go because that means you're out of the game." My eyes widen slightly, and he grins. "Don't worry. If they fall into it, there's a large net to catch them. That's not what can hurt them. It's the obstacles that rise out of the track, which, again, aren't a big deal with their reflexes. They can duck and slide or jump over them, all while trying to avoid the other players, pushing or tripping them toward the obstacles, or into the hole in the middle. All that, with an illusion of the last winner's animal chasing them. If it catches you, it sends a bolt through you, freezing you in place. That way, no one can argue it didn't touch them. The last player still skating is the winner."

"Sounds barbaric." I frown. This doesn't seem like a playful game at all and I'm not sure if this is something I want to watch.

"It is." He grins. "I usually play, but since this is your first game, I wanted to watch it with you. Here they come." He smiles, drumming his hands on the railing.

A strong voice cuts through the noise, announcing each player, while the crowd bellows with their favorite player's animal call. Ford cups his mouth, releasing a loud barking sound as Hyena rolls by. And then Fox, Owl, and Bear. Even Toggy is playing. Each player is wearing the same type of athletic clothing we wore in training, except they have their animal printed on the back of their shirts.

After the Naturals are introduced, a gunshot pierces the air, and I nearly buckle. The sound alone is disturbing. But the crowd bellows with excitement as the track ripples up and down, with obstacles shooting out of the flooring. Minutes later, a massive, rabid-looking Elk rises from the middle, and I stumble backward with wide, fearful eyes, falling into my seat with a hard pant.

"It isn't real, just an illusion." Ford chuckles and grabs my wrist, pulling me back to the railing.

I wet my lips and watch as the animal maneuvers around the obstacles, chasing the players at a remarkable speed. Toggy, the only female playing, is dead last and my stomach lurches into my throat as it gains on her. I know it's only a visualization, but it looks so real that I clutch onto Ford's arm. She throws a shoulder into the player next to her, passing him, and a new obstacle shoots up. He slams into it, falling face first onto the track as the animal performs the act of swallowing him whole.

A teenage Natural, not in the game, jumps over the railing, snapping something onto the back of the statue-like player, and then races back. And just before the players round the curve again, the losing player is yanked high in the air, off the track.

Five more players fall in the middle or are frozen in place, and each time I think this is the end for Toggy, she out maneuvers the others, slipping just out of the animal's reach. And when she finally goes down, I dig my nails into Ford's arm.

"You have got to let go." He laughs, prying his fingers under mine.

"My apologies," I say with a dry swallow. "It's just so . . . intense."

"But fun, huh?"

"Yes," I admit to my surprise, wiping my sweaty palms down the front of my trousers. "A part of me wants to play." I grin.

"I thought you would. We can even team up and take on Elk and Bear. Whenever those two play, no one else wins, whether it's solo or teams." He grins. "But next year, you and I are going to dominate."

Bear skates by, and I join Ford in growling and cheering for him, that by the time it's down to him and Elk, my throat is raw and sore. I grip the railing tight when Elk slams into him, bouncing sideways like he hit a tree. Elk wobbles along the edge of the pit with his left skate grinding against the side of the track, near the hole, trying to stabilize himself. And I can see the grin in Bear's eyes as the mean-looking animal gains speed on him. If Bear can come back around and nudge Elk into the hole before the illusion catches him, he can win.

I lean close to Ford's ear. "What does he win?"

"A date with any girl here."

"Seriously?"

"Yes. Not that he needs to win to get a date. Bear can practically get any girl he wants."

Elk rights himself off the edge just as Bear rounds the curve, gaining speed. They are nearly side-by-side with the vicious animal on their heels, but instead of pushing faster, Elk slows himself and throws his arm out to push Bear into an obstacle shooting out of the track. Bear soars over it and the illusion catches Elk instead, freezing him in place.

"Hell yeah!" Ford hollers as Bear is announced the winner.

Hutch raises a black scarf high in the air and Alex roars out his animal call. Bear slows his speed, tossing his mouth guard into the crowd, and the females go silly, clutching the air and knocking into each other, trying to catch it. Bear skates over to the loser's box, opening it, and our team congratulates him as they skate toward us.

"Grats." Ford leans over the railing to bump fists with Bear. "Elk would have won if he hadn't tried to take you out."

"I know. He should have just passed me," Bear says with a smile and then turns his attention to me. "Hey Lynx, are you going out with us tonight?"

Before I can answer, Alex squeezes through us. "Wow, that be buzzin' me mind," he says rapidly. "Do ye think us can play?"

"I don't see why not." Bear shrugs.

"Sheep, you can barely walk and talk. How are you going to skate?" Hyena asks, rolling toward us.

Alex opens his mouth just as Mr. Paul calls for him. "Sheep! Curfew."

"Yeah. Yeah, me comin', Dizzy."

"Alex!" I gasp and yank him to me. "You cannot call him that. It is Mr. Paul."

"What's a Dizzy?" Toggy asks, stopping herself with the railing.

"Old man," Bear chuckles.

"Ohhh. You're going to get it," Hyena teases, wetting the tip of his finger and then reaching over the railing to shove his finger into Alex's ear.

"Ye 'bout to git it," Alex bristles, lifting a shoulder to wipe away the slobber.

"Wait," Hutch begins, "how ye know what Dizzy be?"

"Because I used to be a cabin boy," Bear admits.

"Yeah, some of our best Naturals used to be with a pirate crew, like Bear," Ford says.

"Only because we appreciate it more. Being a cabin boy isn't easy," Bear tells Ford and then looks at me. "It's damn near as bad as being a prisoner." He turns his attention back to Ford. "We'd go days without food or water, working our ass off. And if we didn't fetch something or clean their shit fast enough, we'd get a lashing. So, when someone from a pirate crew comes here, it's paradise."

"Ain't that the truth," Hutch says, shoving his hands deep into his trousers. Curiosity gnaws in my belly as I watch the other Naturals moving through the crowd. *How many used to be with a pirate crew? And which ones? Were any of them with Sammy's crew?*

"Sheep! Now," Mr. Paul calls, and I pull my attention back to my team.

"Yeah, I be comin'," Alex hollers back, pushing past us, and then turns to Hyena. "Oh, I almost forget. Mia wants us to give ye this," he says, digging into his front pocket. When he pulls out his hand, he leans forward, slapping Hyena across the jaw.

Hyena soars over the railing with a growl, but I step into his path, blocking him from chasing Alex.

"No," I tell him. He looks me up and down with his jaw clenched before backing off. And I turn to Bear with a satisfied grin. "Congratulations. I do hope you have a wonderful time on your date tonight."

"What date?"

"The date you won for being the victor," I say and turn to Ford. "If you don't mind, I'm going to head back with Alex. We have a game of chess to finish."

"When did I win a date?" Bear asks again, and then he smiles wide and silly, pointing his water jug at me. "Is it with you?"

"No." Ford steps between us and leans against the railing, blocking Bear from me. "Yeah, I think that's best. See you in the morning."

I start to turn, and Hutch grabs my shoulder. "Hey, I'm gonna stay with 'em, yeah."

"Okay. Have fun," I add with a wave, and as I'm walking to the exit, commotion sounds behind me. I glance over my shoulder, and Ford has his fist balled into Bear's shirt, yanking him close in a heated conversation. I turn back to the exit, wondering what girl he's telling Bear to stay away from. I thought Ford still liked Mable.

SOMETIMES A BLACK HEART ISN'T BORN, IT'S CREATED

~~////~~ ~~////~~ ~~////~~ ~~////~~
~~////~~ ~~////~~ ~~////~~ ///

It's been two weeks since the game and Alex, Hutch, and I have been eating, seeing, and doing everything we can before our holiday is over. We've even gone to the three sister islands nearby, and we finally got to use the tram. We saw farms and greenhouses and science buildings. Everything the Naturals need is scattered among all four islands. The one thing I haven't done is speak to Papa and everyone is on me about it, even Doctor Lawson.

Every session I have with her, she tries to bring it up, but I've managed to change the subject and leave without talking about it. I don't need to speak with Papa to know how disappointed he would be with me. Or the shame I would bring to our family name if he knew how I turned out. It's bad enough I'm judged and watched at everything I do here.

Even now, sitting outside Doctor Lawson's office, I can feel judgmental eyes watching me. I look up just in time to see Bear pull his gaze off me, and he shifts in his seat. I hug myself tighter, but not because he's watching me. He's forever watching me like I'm about to go off at any moment. It's because today isn't just another session. Today is our last day of evaluation. In fact, we only have two days left on the island and I'm terrified we might fail.

I look over at Alex, knowing I'll be going first, and my stomach hardens. *What if we slip and say something we shouldn't? Or she can see that we are lying or holding something back.*

Before the door fully opens, I can smell Doctor Lawson's flowery scent and I force a smile, sitting up taller.

"Good morning," she greets. She's wearing the same outfit she had on yesterday when I saw her at the coffee shop. Except her cream-colored blouse isn't as smooth. It's wrinkled and there's a small brown stain near the second button. And her blonde hair isn't as full and flowing over her shoulders as usual. It's pulled back in a messy ponytail.

"Good morning," my team greets. Ford was right when he said we do everything as a team. And, apparently, that extends to therapy sessions. Thankfully, they don't go inside with me. They wait out here, in the waiting room, until I'm finished. But with our enhanced hearing, I know they can hear everything that is said.

"Looks like someone had a good night." Fox grins as I push to my feet. "I believe Mr. Jamie had a good night, too. In fact, I haven't seen him since dinner last night."

"Mind your business," she tells him, but I can hear the playfulness behind her words as I brush past her and into the office.

I sit on the edge of the brown leather chair, my usual spot, while Doctor Lawson sits directly in front of me in a matching chair. She crosses her legs, opening her tablet, and

I instantly feel nervous. I stare behind her at the two large portraits. One is of a lion, standing in a field, and the other one is an eagle soaring through the air. Against the wall, to my left, is her desk and it's filled with all sorts of gadgets and toys, along with jars of candy and chocolate. To my right is a cream-colored settee with tall plants on either side of it.

"How are you today, Tippy? Are you starting to connect with the people around you?"

"I believe so, yes. Thank you. Everyone, especially my team, has made me feel welcome and included."

This is where I use my distraction and direct the conversation to where I want it to go. Ford. It's how I've been able to avoid talking about Papa. I straighten my shoulders and force another smile, trying to seem well adjusted. Her words, not mine.

"I've been shopping with Toggy and Aunt Amy several times already. Even Fox has taken me to some of his favorite shops. I've been just about everywhere with Hyena. He has a lot of energy. He's silly and funny like Alex. And probably why Alex enjoys his company. Neither of them takes anything seriously. Hyena is probably the most surprising when it comes to first impressions and not at all like I first thought."

I pull in a deep breath before talking rapidly and non-stop. It's what I've seen everyone do, so it must be normal. I must be normal.

"Bear likes food and lots of it, so we go anywhere food is served." A genuine smile touches my lips. "I can see why he is so big. And Owl and Hutch get along well. They are practically joined at the hip now. But the one I've connected with the most is Ford." I grip my hands in my lap, preparing for what I need to say next.

"We both love to read, except I'm not as polished as

him. I can't read as fast and, sometimes, I have trouble reading the bigger words, but I'm learning and so are Alex and Hutch. And with everything I've done and seen here, Ford has been by my side the entire time. Not that I mind too much, it's nice having my cousin back. It's almost like it was when we were kids, especially with all the pranks that's been going on inside the Naturals' home."

Except without Mable. I miss her so much.

I force a big and bright smile, just like Toggy does, so I appear happy and normal.

"Yes, you have spoken quite a lot about Ford during our sessions. I can tell he means a great deal to you, but we are not here to talk about him. You agreed today we would talk about your dad and why you refuse to speak to him."

"I know, but I feel like there is more to unpack with Ford first," I say, hoping if I use the same words she's used on me, she will stay on topic, and I'll pass with flying colors.

"Yes, I understand, but I also know the root to everything is with your dad and we haven't even begun *unpacking* the anger you have for him."

Another forced smile. "I'm not cross with Papa."

"Are you sure about that?" she asks, gesturing to my lap.

I look down and my hands are balled into tight fists. "Okay, maybe a little cross, but not the way you think, and certainly not toward Papa. I understand why he kept this world a secret."

I have my own secrets. I uncurl my fists and rub my palms along my jeans with panic settling in my belly. She isn't staying on topic. I scan the small room, biting my lip, trying to figure out how I can direct her back. If we talk about anything else, I might slip up. I might fail.

"Tippy, the only way this works is if we talk about those uncomfortable feelings you're having."

"I do not have uncomfortable feelings," I say firmly. *Why won't she allow me to talk about Ford? If these sessions truly are about me, then shouldn't I have a say in what we discuss?*

"Okay, then what feelings do you have for your dad?"

I gaze down at the floor, searching for the right words, and notice she isn't wearing heels today; instead, she has on white sneakers. I shake my head, dismissing the thought. *Focus.*

"Tippy, are you still with me?"

"Yes," I reply, and lift my smile to her. "My apologies, and no, I'm not having an episode. Your medicine works very well. Thank you."

A little too well. With all the medication I'm on, I'm finally able to see clearer. I remember everything that happened to me and Alex during our time in the mining caverns. And there's so much bad; I understand why I blocked it all out. Why I needed Lou to hide behind and Alex to defend Lou's actions by telling me it was okay. It's how we survived.

"I no longer see Lou. I was only thinking of—"

"Of the right words to say, so you'll pass?" She smiles, crossing her legs again. "But that isn't how this works. This isn't boot camp. You will not fail because you gave the wrong answer. All you have to do is be honest with me and be willing to talk openly about your feelings. If you cannot do that now, then I cannot trust you will be honest with them later, once you are out in the field."

Sweat forms on my upper lip. *Is she about to fail me because I haven't been honest?* I wipe at my mouth with my brain spinning. I don't know what to say or how to act now. *What would Alex do?*

"So, I'll ask again."

Oh my goodness! What am I going to say? Or do?

"How are you feeling about—"

"Terrified," I blurt and quickly clamp a hand over my mouth. I didn't mean to say that. It just slipped out. This is why I rehearsed everything with Alex. Why I needed her to stay on topic. I'm not as good with lies and deceit as Alex is.

"It's okay to be scared of your feelings. It's even okay to have regrets, Tippy. You not only lost your father in the raid, but also yourself. And you have not had a chance to properly grieve for either."

"I don't regret what I did that night. I would do it all over again if it meant saving all those children in the caverns. It's just . . . " I lower my head. "I'm not the same person I was."

I am a bad person. I have hurt people. And worse.

"You have been through a very traumatic incident. No one expects you to be the same person."

"I will kindly disagree," I say, looking up at her. "Everyone keeps telling me to let go of the past. To stop holding on to it and eventually I will find my old self. But the Tippy they knew is gone. I am no longer the girl that believed she could save the world. I'm the girl that has seen the world and how awful it is, and the things I had to do . . . " I stop myself before I say too much and avoid eye contact.

"Is that why you refuse to speak openly about your feelings, or with your dad, because you think no one will understand the things you had to do in order to survive?"

Her choice of words surprises me. Not because I didn't do as she is saying I did. It's just that not all of my actions were for survival. Not even for Alex's. In the beginning, yes, but toward the end, that's when I became a bad person.

"If that is the case, then I am sorry to say you will not be able to join the program." She closes her tablet and places it on the table beside her. My head jerks up with my heart slamming against my chest. "To be in the program, Tippy, you must be able to talk freely about your missions. Otherwise, if we do not work through them, all those what ifs and ugly thoughts and emotions will destroy you, mentally and physically. It's why the Naturals depend on their council. Taking a life, or attacking pirate ships and invading coves, is not something any Natural enjoys. It's terrifying, but they do it, and afterward, they willingly come straight to us, so we can begin with the healing process." She leans forward slightly. "Now, would you like to start over and actually be honest and share your troubles?" She gestures to the tablet. "Or should I turn in my report as is?"

"But I can't be honest." I rub at my forehead. "Not about the mining caverns and everything I did while I was there."

"And why is that?" she asks, reaching for her tablet.

"Because if I am, then . . . " I stare at her tablet with my knee bouncing. "I just can't." I lower my eyes and stare at her sneakers. "I don't want to be sent back to prison," I mutter.

"Tippy, there is nothing you can tell me that would cause me to send you back. Now, or in the future. This is a safe place. Whatever you tell me, stays with me."

I glance over my shoulder at my team on the other side of the door and a tight ball forms in the pit of my stomach.

"Tippy, this room is soundproof. They cannot hear what is said in here." I face her and her smile is big. "Did you really think your team was that quiet?" She tilts her head. "Especially with Alex and Owl out there?" She chuckles. She pushes to her feet and walks over to the door, opening it, and their voices and laughter fill the room.

"Hey, did she pass?" Ford asks, and Doctor Lawson closes the door on him.

"Now, shall we start again?" She walks back to her chair, reaching for her tablet. "How about we start at the beginning?"

"The beginning, okay." I blow out a steady breath, hoping this will not be my downfall. "After I was handed to my first warden, he only gave me one year. He told me losing my parents was punishment enough, but in order to keep peace among Pirates and Spoons, I must still do prison time. But unlike the Forgotten, if I had grandparents or some family left that were willing to take me in afterward, I could still have a life. So, I should keep my head down, my mouth shut, and do as I'm told, and I'll be out of there in no time. That's when I stopped talking." I pull in another steady breath.

"It wasn't even a full month before I was sentenced another year. Alex was sick and every time he would throw up, it would wake the guard outside our cage. After the third violent heave, the guard entered and started beating on him, ordering him to be quiet. And something inside of me snapped. I shoved the guard off him, and he stumbled backward, landing in our mess bucket. His entire backside was covered in poop and all the prisoners laughed, especially the older ones. But instead of receiving a lashing for it, Alex and I were sent to the warden the next morning. When we arrived, the guard had a black eye, and his arm was in a sling. He lied to the warden. He said he caught us trying to escape, and that we beat him with a drilling tool. Which we certainly did not, but we were still moved to another cavern. One with more security and even nastier guards.

"And Alex, he was so little then . . . I told him to tell

everyone we were kin." I grip my knees and lift my chin to the ceiling. "I thought if everyone believed we were related, the guards and prisoners would leave him alone. Maybe give me his punishments, but I was wrong. The only way I could take his lashes for him was if I forced myself between him and the guard. Or whoever was hurting him because it wasn't always guards." I run my brown sleeve across my wet nose. "I did everything I could to help him and the younger ones, just like the night I was taken. But it always felt like no matter what I did, something worse happened to us."

"And do you always feel like something bad will replace the good?"

"Has it not?" I say with a touch of irritation. "After all those years of doing good on Capra Horn, bad finally caught up to me and I was sentenced. It wasn't until I turned just as mean as pirates that the odds turned in our favor and we were rescued. For that reason alone, is why I'm terrified. If anyone were to truly know me and what I am capable of, it wouldn't just be Papa that is ashamed of me, it would be everyone." I press my lips into a thin line. *Crap. I shouldn't have said that.*

"Are you saying you must do a little bad to even the playing field for good?"

"No," I reply, thankful she didn't catch that last part and push to my feet. I walk over to her desk, reaching for a flat, blue-colored rock. "All I'm saying is there's bad in this world." I turn, leaning against her desk, and begin rubbing my thumb against its smooth surface. "It's like a curse and there's no magic spell you can cast that will catch it or stop it. Not like I thought we could as kids. All one can do is accept that bad things can happen to good people. And I have. I know I cannot stop every bad thing that happens, but I can be vigilant and not become too comfortable or lower my guard again. I can stop the past from repeating itself."

Doctor Lawson doesn't say anything to me; instead, she writes something on her tablet. *Did I say something wrong? Did I fail? Or worse, is she going to put me on more medication?* Just the thought of adding more makes my stomach churn. She looks up at me, putting her rock back onto her desk.

"I can certainly understand that," she says with another smile. "I can even understand your hesitation in speaking to your dad." She closes her tablet and leans back in her chair. "So, for now, let's just focus on learning who Tippy is. This isn't the first time you've mentioned you aren't the same person, and you don't really know who you are anymore. Tippy, Mute, Lou, and now Lynx. So, let's figure that out first."

My heart drops. "Does that mean I failed my evaluation?"

"No. It means the root of all your worry is not with your dad, but with yourself. If you cannot accept and forgive yourself for what happened, then you will never be happy. But, in order to forgive yourself, you need to know who you are and that's what we are going to focus on. For the next few sessions, instead of me asking how you're feeling, let's talk about what you like and dislike. Let's figure out who Tippy Lopez is today, not who she was or who your dad or team or even Yak want you to be, but you. How does that sound?"

"That sounds wonderful," I say with a real smile. "Does that mean I can stay in the program?"

"Yes, for now. But only if you continue to be honest with yourself and me. And I want to see you three times a week, okay?"

"Thank you." I nod. "I will. I promise. I'll come every day if I must."

"Alright." She smiles and pushes to her feet, moving toward the door. "Let's go tell your team."

She walks back over to the door, and I can already feel the tension in my shoulders relaxing. Not only did I pass, but I found someone I can trust and talk to about my past that isn't Alex. Because not even Alex knows some of the stuff I've done or endured in order to protect him and the others. And I don't believe he should know.

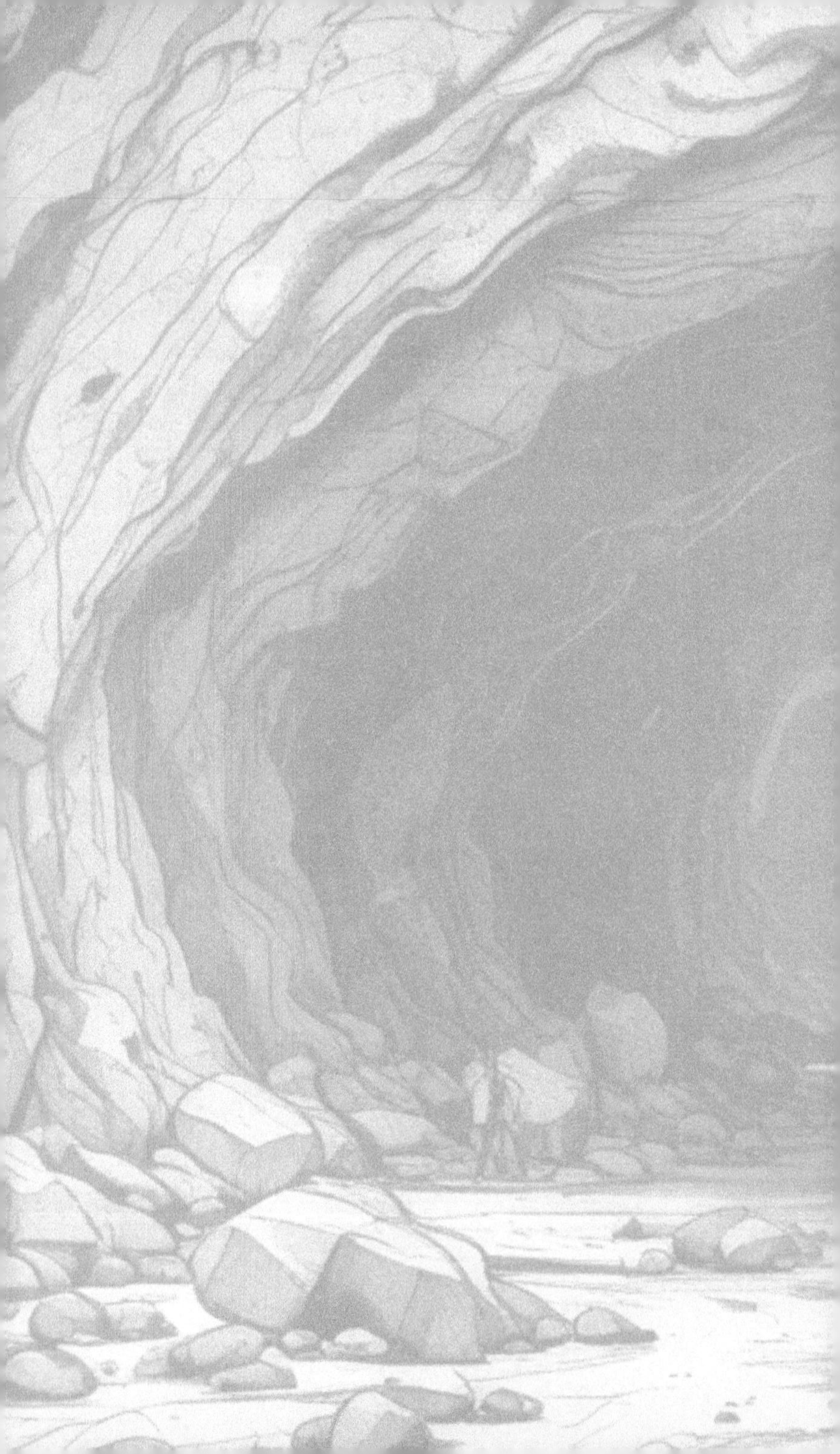

LIKE ME

The next morning, I take my usual spot in the dining hall for breakfast. And the normal chaotic sounds swirling around all the small tables makes me feel at home. Like I've finally found my place in this world. I sit at our team's table, across from Bear, and he gives me a sleepy grin.

"How did you sleep?" he asks, as most of our team is in hushed whispers with one another.

"Good, thank you for asking." A genuine smile spreads across my lips as I smooth the napkin neatly in my lap. "And you? How was your evening, Bear?"

"Restless." He leans back as Mr. Jamie lowers a small cup of tablets in front of him. Thankfully, I'm not the only one that has to take medication. Bear also has to take the same amount as I do. Including a Topper. Mr. Jamie lowers my cup of tablets and then takes his seat at the head of our table. He eyes the empty chair to my left and then looks directly at me.

"Where is Sheep?" he asks.

I glance at the chair Alex is usually in and then back at him. "I'm not sure. Would you like for me to go and find him?"

"No," Mr. Jamie states and snaps his napkin out, placing it neatly on his lap. "He knows the rules." He reaches for a platter of biscuits and then eyes me with a knowing look before handing the platter to Bear. "Do not sneak him food, Lynx."

"Yes, sir," I respond. But we both know I will.

Halfway through breakfast, a door from upstairs slams shut, followed by squeaky footsteps hurrying down the staircase. Mr. Jamie pushes to his feet, throwing his napkin on the table as Alex enters, covered in some kind of green goo.

"There ye be." Alex squints at Hyena.

"I see you found your way out." Hyena grins, and the dining hall bellows with laughter.

"I'm gonna clobber ye," Alex hisses, and races through the tables scattered throughout the dining hall.

"Sheep!" Mr. Jamie commands, reaching for his switch. "This is not the time."

But Alex ignores him and lunges, and the dining hall bellows with chatter and laughter. The first strike upon the table makes me jump. I look across the table at Bear, and his body is tense with his knuckles white around his fork, staring right through me. Another prominent whack hits the table, and I can see fear vibrating through him as he mutters, "Stop."

Mr. Jamie is triggering something in Bear, and I reach for his Topper. I lift it to him, but he isn't paying attention to me. "Bear, take this." Again, he doesn't acknowledge me and when Mr. Jamie raises the switch a third time, Bear pushes to his feet so fast, I flinch. His arm soars up with the fork poking into Mr. Jamie's neck.

"Ye ain't gonna be hurting him again."

The room falls silent with all eyes on Bear. Ford leaps from his chair and I clutch at my throat as every Natural in the room stands with him.

"Get back!" Bear hollers.

"You do not want to do this," Mr. Jamie says in an understanding voice. "Put the fork down." I lift out of my chair, wishing there was something I could do for Bear, but I've been there and when you're in that deep, no one can pull you out.

"Naw." Bear leans closer and drops of blood seep from under the fork. "I be seeing ye, Dizzy, an' what ye be doing. I know who ye be."

Ford cautiously steps closer, lightly touching Bear's arm, and my chest squeezes painfully.

"He isn't who you think he is. It's Jamie. He wouldn't hurt you. He wouldn't hurt any of us."

I can see the confusion on Bear's face as his eyes dart from Ford to Mr. Jamie, and my heart goes out to him. And myself. *Is this what I look like when I turn into Lou? Am I this terrifying and mean?*

"Look at him," Ford says once more. "Really look at him, Benji. He is a good man."

Bear shifts on his feet with his eyes turning wet and frightful as the realization slowly hits him. His mouth opens, with no words escaping, as the fork slides from his hand. He scans the room, slowly backing away, before dropping into a heap on the floor. Ford quickly kneels behind him, wrapping his arms around Bear's chest, rocking them both back and forth in a soothing motion.

"Fox, go get Doctor Lawson, and do try to be discreet.

Elk, you and your team guard the doors. This house stands strong today," Mr. Paul says sternly. That simple phrase had every Natural scattering into action, pushing tables and chairs against the walls and then forming a tight circle around Bear.

"I'm so sorry, Mr. Jamie," Bear says in a heartrending voice. "Please don't defect me. It won't happen again. I swear it."

"No need for apologies," Mr. Jamie says, dabbing a cloth at his wound. "Everyone has bad days." He squats next to him. "Just breathe. That's good. In and out. Calm your heart, Benji," he says, breathing with him. But when Bear looks up and sees the blood on the cloth, he wails again. "No. Stay with me. Look past the incident. Take control," Mr. Jamie says, pressing a hand against his chest. "You are not alone." Mr. Jamie gestures for everyone to gather closer. "Feel the strength and love surrounding you, Benji."

Hyena reaches over Ford and places his hand on Bear's shoulder. "My blood," he says.

My chin trembles with my throat painfully tight as one by one a Natural whispers, "My blood," while they position their hands on Bear. I stretch my arm out, joining them, and Alex locks eyes with me, placing a gooey green hand on top of mine. "My blood," we both say.

Minutes later, Fox is urging Doctor Lawson toward us, and everyone peels away from Bear, making room for her. She squats next to him with her best smile. "Hi, Benji. Would you like to go talk in the library?"

"Yes," he croaks, wiping at his wet nose. "But I don't want a private session. Not yet. I need a team session first, please."

"That's fine, whatever you want." Doctor Lawson

straightens and then addresses Mr. Jamie. "Could we please have some hot tea, sunflower seeds, and chocolate?"

"Of course."

Mr. Jamie turns for the kitchen as I follow everyone into the library. I didn't know they had group sessions like this and I'm not at all prepared for it. *Why would Bear want us to hear his personal thoughts?*

I quietly sit in one of the cushioned chairs near the open door. Alex drops on the floor at my feet, wiping a napkin across his face and arms, trying to remove the green goo, while the rest of the team gathers close together on the two settees mirroring each other. Even Hutch squeezes himself between Toggy and Owl as Doctor Lawson stands next to me, reaching inside her bag.

"I was planning on handing these out once we were on the submarine, but I think now works better." She pulls out a thin red-looking bracelet and hands it to Alex. "A rubber band for you."

"Hey, this be like the one I see in yer office," he says with a smile.

"Yes, it is, and it's yours now."

"Wow. Thanks."

"You are most welcome. I want you to wear it with your Fitbit and anytime you feel nervous or overwhelmed, I want you to pull on it, but not too hard, or it will hurt when it snaps back." She digs into her bag again and then hands me the same flat blue rock I picked up in her office. "A worry stone for you, and the same applies." She walks over to Hutch. "And a fidget spinner for you." She turns around, taking her seat at the other end of the two settees, facing me and Alex, and pulls out her tablet.

"Now, before we begin, I would like to explain how a team session goes. We do not use Natural names. After all, each of you are real people with real feelings and sometimes when we use a person's given name, it helps to remember that. Also, in a team session, I normally do not speak or ask a lot of questions. I am mostly here to keep everyone calm while the team openly expresses their troubles or concerns. Any time you feel upset or attacked, please do not shout or attack back; instead, use the tools I have given you and calm your heart before you speak. If that does not work, you may excuse yourself and come back when you are calmer."

Behind me, Mr. Jamie walks in carrying a silver tray filled with everything Doctor Lawson asked for, and quietly places it on the long, short table between the two settees.

"Thank you, Jamie," Doctor Lawson says. He gives a quick nod and then turns, closing the double doors behind him as he leaves. Ford reaches for the hot tea as Bear pulls out his rawhide. Hyena grabs two small white cups. Toggy reaches inside her pocket for a yellow-looking worm. Fox rolls two silver marbles in his palm while Owl places a small bowl of chocolate chips in his lap.

"Now that everyone has their tools, we may begin." Doctor Lawson opens her tablet. "Benji, would you care to start us off?"

"Okay," he begins, braiding his rawhide, "I guess it's time to explain why I've been so stressed lately and perhaps why I had an episode." Bear looks directly at me and Alex. "With you two here, and seeing how close you are, it triggered me. Not that it's a bad thing. I'm grateful to have you two here and on my team. Every time I look at you, I'm reminded of what we are fighting for. It's just . . . I started thinking about my brother and how I lost him." He looks at Doctor Lawson and lifts a hand before she can reply. "And I know I should have come to you, but I thought I could handle it. I didn't know it was affecting me the way that it was."

"It's perfectly fine. We are here now, and we can discuss all that during our one on one later."

"Thank you." Bear unbraids the rawhide and then turns his attention back to us. "But that isn't what is bothering me." He begins braiding it again. "When part of our team bailed before we could even have our first solo mission, I wasn't even mad about it. I never thought they meshed well with us. I was ready to find replacements long before they quit. It's why we sent Togangela in, so we could find three people we actually liked, and hopefully, we'd have the perfect team, like Elk's team." He leans back against the settee with a quick wipe at his mouth.

"I guess what I'm trying to say is, I'm scared you two are going to bail on us, too, but without any notice or a goodbye. I'm just going to wake up one morning and you two will be gone." He looks right at me. "And it will gut me if you do."

"Same," Fox agrees, rotating the silver marbles in his palm.

"Yep," Hyena adds, spitting into his cup.

Why is he spitting his food out?

"I've thought it," Hutch admits, watching his charm spin freely.

"It's one of the reasons I've been on your ass about your dad," Ford says, and I pull my gaze off Hyena. Ford balances his teacup on his knee, holding onto the rim, avoiding eye contact. "I never wanted to come out and ask because I didn't want to pressure you. But since everyone is thinking along the same lines as me, I feel like I need to now." He turns his attention to me. "Is that why you refuse to call your dad and tell him you want to be a Natural, because you know you're going to run the first chance you get?"

"We ain't runnin'," Alex says, and then looks over his shoulder at me. "Aye?"

"See, that right there is what's scary," Bear says, gesturing at us. "Even if Alex wanted to stay, and you didn't, he wouldn't. He wouldn't even pack his shit. He'd just say, 'Let's get' and never bat an eye at it."

Hyena spits into the cup. "Or us."

"No," I tell Alex and then say to the group, "We aren't running. I like it here."

"Then why is it like pulling teeth to get you to do anything with us?" Ford asks. "Even the other night, when we pranked Benji, you did it, but it felt more like you had to do it than something you wanted to do. And when we were kids, you lived for this stuff."

"And," Hyena adds, tossing more food into his mouth, which I don't understand if he isn't going to eat it. "No matter where we are or what we're doing, you two always sit farther away from us, like now."

I glance over my shoulder at the closed door, and then back at the group.

"And even though you're here, you're not," Bear says, as I watch Alex snap his rubber band against his wrist. "Not mentally, and that makes me think about what we talked about during phase four. When you said, back in the mines, your brain was constantly spinning for ways of escape."

"Plus, you never say home," Toggy adds, stretching her worm, and I see Alex's wrist turning red. "It's always the Naturals' home, like it isn't yours, too."

"And what about your—" Owl begins.

"Stop attackin' her!" Alex roars, jumping to his feet. "Ye

ain't been through what she be through and why she be doing the stuff she do. Ye ain't—"

"Alex, it's okay," I tell him, placing a hand on his shoulder.

He turns to me, visibly shaking. "But it ain't. An' this stupid thing ain't working," he says, and I stop him from pulling it off his wrist.

"Look at me." I grab hold of his fists before he turns and acts on his anger. "They don't understand us, not like we do each other. And you're right. They don't know what we've done. And yes, it might not have been the right way to ask me, but they do have the right to know why I do them." I angle my head. "Unless you do not want them to be a part of our family and if that's the case, we can leave right now and go somewhere new. It's up to you."

"I ain't wanting to leave. I be liking it here."

"Me too. Which means, if we're staying, it won't just be me and you anymore."

"Yeah," he says, popping his knuckles. "I know. I gotta have their backs, too."

"And we'll have to answer all their questions, and any they have in the future. Otherwise, we aren't giving them the chance to know us like we know each other, okay?"

"Yeah, I be hearing ye." He turns, lowering himself back on the floor, loosely hugging his knees.

I look over at our team and rub the tension in my neck. "A few weeks ago, Yak explained why the Naturals instill fear in boot camp and the reasoning behind it. And I understand that because I also have my reasons why I do certain things. I've already told Doctor Lawson most of what I'm about to say and I do hope my truth doesn't send me back. Or worse, your prison." I think back to the prison the Naturals have.

"Like I said before, no one is going to send you back. You are safe to speak freely here," Doctor Lawson says and closes her tablet. She nods at me with an easy smile, and I can feel her encouragement all the way to my toes.

"Thank you." I nod and wet my lips. "Like I told Doctor Lawson, my sentence started out only needing to finish one year, but Alex was being mistreated and I had to do something. I had to help, and I did, but in doing so, I was given another year." I lean forward, bracing myself on my knees, and stare at the floor. "Year after year, as my hatred for the guards and the system grew, so did my sentencing. If no one, including the older prisoners, were going to help the younger ones, then I was." I squeeze Alex's shoulder. "With Alex's help, I was able to intervene in every mishap and abuse, and before I knew it, we were being transferred to the hardest carven. The one where they send the really bad criminals. Those that have taken a life and why Alex and I were there." I slide my hand off Alex's shoulder and clasp my hands.

"I don't know how old we were. Time is different in prison. But we were young, the only kids there, and I knew the only way we stood a chance was if I took down the top dog prisoner, and I did. But I also had to stay top dog, which meant in order for me to keep my title, I had to do the same as the previous top dog. I had to instill fear the same way he did, and I did." I stare at the moose etched into the rug under the table and hope I am not looked upon differently. "It was the only way I could protect the weaker prisoners. Just because they weren't children didn't mean they weren't mistreated. A lot of them were. It wasn't until we were sold to a private owner, the one the Naturals found me and Alex in, that I stopped . . . hurting others." I blink the dead away and focus on Ford's kind face. "So, how can I speak to Papa, or anyone for that matter, of what I've done, when I'm the very thing the Naturals are trying to stop."

"But don't you see, you aren't anything like a pirate." Ford puts his teacup on the table and moves to the edge of the settee, looking at me. "You protected the weak. The very definition of a Natural."

"Maybe, but . . . " I go back to staring at the rug. "That's not the only reason I don't want to speak to Papa." I peek up at Doctor Lawson and she gives me another encouraging smile. I calm my emotions with a deep inhale and slowly exhale. "I know he will try to talk me out of becoming a Natural. If Papa never wanted this life for me, he will want me to return home and honestly, I don't feel like Capra Horn is my home anymore." I look at Toggy and wipe at my wet cheeks.

"I love everything about this place and what the Naturals represent, but I would rather not claim any land as my home port, especially one as magical as this one. The last time I did good for others, that's when bad things happened and not just to me, but everyone that lived there. And I never want any harm to come to this land and these people. Not claiming a home is my way of protecting this place." I turn my attention to Hyena, sitting next to Bear.

"In the mining caverns, we always sat near the door or stood at the end of the line because that was the only freedom we had. Plus, it gave us room to run if needed. But now, I sit by the door or farther away from everyone in case anything threatens the team, and hopefully, I can stop it." I brush my sleeve against my snotty nose and cut my gaze to Bear.

"Yes, sometimes I'm in my own head, but it isn't because I'm planning an escape. It's because I actually have the freedom to daydream. To think about the person I want to become or perhaps do all this new stuff that's here. Everyone has taken me to their favorite spots, but no one has asked me what I'm interested in. What I would like to do or see. So, instead of asking, because I'm scared I won't fit in, I try and imagine what it would be like to do those things.

"My apologies if our bond scares you." I scan the group. "Any of you, but we can't instantly trust and form bonds with just anyone. We've been tricked too many times. It's how we ended up where we did. So, yes, sometimes Alex joins in on your fun while I sit back and watch. I need to see if what you are saying to us is true by your actions. And yes, maybe that's the wrong way to go about it and we shouldn't test you and the others like we've done in the past, but it's how we've survived as long as we have." I shift slightly and focus on Doctor Lawson.

"I know I agreed to find myself, but I don't believe I can do that. Not until I make things right with my past first. Otherwise, that night will forever haunt me. I need to face what I did. I need to apologize for my actions and what came afterward." I lower my gaze with my throat tight and press my thumb into the rock. "Even if talking to Papa brings shame and disappointment, it's what I need to do." I force my emotions down and look up at Doctor Lawson. "If it's possible, I'd like to call him in the morning. I'd like to start my new life with a clean slate, so perhaps one day, I can forgive myself."

"I can make that happen." She nods happily.

I look at my team with knots forming in my belly. "And perhaps my team could be there . . . for support? I might forget how to breathe when I hear his voice again."

"Of course," my team agrees.

"Does anyone else have anything to add?" Doctor Lawson asks.

"Not from me," Bear says. "They put all my fears to rest. At least for now."

Doctor Lawson addresses the rest of our team. "Anyone else?"

"No," the team agrees.

"Then let's end the session with love."

Our team stands and head toward us, wearing big, wide grins.

"Group hug," Hyena says, lifting Alex off his feet.

"I ain't liking this." Alex squirms, and my chest warms at the love they all have for Alex.

I start to join and Hyena turns from the group. "You're next. Bring it in," he says, and I nearly suffocate with so many arms around me. Once everyone starts to peel off me, Ford hangs onto my back. He tightens his arm around my neck and leans close to my ear.

"It's good to hear the confidence returning in your voice. Always speak your truth, and don't go shrinking back into your shell, okay? If you need to talk, I'm here. No judgment. Ever."

"Okay," I grip his arm and look up at him, "but you also have to speak your truth, too. Starting with talking to Mable."

"Maybe. We'll see." He grins and quickly forces me into a headlock, scrubbing his knuckles on the top of my head.

MY BLOOD

||||| ||||| ||||| |||||

||||| ||||| ||||| |||||

It's been a long, exhausting day, and my bed is calling me. After Bear's private session, we celebrated our last day together as a team. We did all the things Alex and I wanted to do. We went for coffee, skating, to the movies, and the arcade. Then, we had dinner at Tammy's Diner. I had so much pie and soda, my belly still hurts. But the best part of the day was at the end of the evening, when we were supposed to be packing to leave. The Natural's doorbell rang non-stop and no one got anything done.

Every male and female teenager that wasn't a Natural seemed to stop by and give their favorite Natural a ribbon or bracelet. It was amazing. I couldn't believe I was able to bring something from my world to this one. I had so much fun sitting in the front parlor, watching as one by one someone was called to the door. And within an hour, every Natural here, even the older ones, were sitting with me, waiting to see if someone would come calling for them. It was the most I have laughed and enjoyed myself since I've been here. I already can't wait to return in eight months.

At curfew, Mr. Paul calls, "lights out," and I nosedive into my bed. I roll onto my side with a yawn to twist the lamp off, and Alex pops out from the side of the bed.

"Roar!" he whispers.

I nearly jump out of my skin, reaching for the pillow and bombarding him with it. "You scared the crap out of me." I silently giggle.

"I knows," he laughs quietly, blocking the hits, and then grabs it, yanking the pillow from me. He jumps on the bed, standing above me, smacking me right back. "I don't knows what ye be doing in the latrine, but I almost fall asleep on the floor, waiting for ye."

"Girl stuff."

"Eww." He stops at once and falls onto the bed, wiggling under the covers. "I still can't believe I ain't been caught sneaking up here to sleep, or ain't no one heard us whispering at night."

"Same," I yawn, shoving the pillow under my head. "Are you ready to become a true Natural tomorrow?"

He shares my pillow, facing me. "Ye mean the tattoo thingy? Yeah, I guess." He shrugs. "Are ye really gonna call yer dad tomorrow? Or are ye just telling Doc what she wanna be hearing?"

"He's my dad, and he has the right to know I'm not coming home. Plus, Yak says I can't join if I don't tell him, but you'll be with me, right?"

"Where ye go, I go," he says with a lopsided grin. "Night, Tippy. Don't be letting the bedbugs bite."

I slide a hand under my cheek with a smile. "But if they do, I'll grab a shoe and beat them black and blue."

"Yeah, ye wills." He moves his head around, looking for

a comfortable spot, and then closes his eyes. "Know ye," he yawns.

"Know you too."

At eight o'clock the next morning, everyone's bag is stacked and piled near the front door, ready to be moved to the submarine. Luckily, we don't have to carry it down the mountain. Mr. Paul says they have them transported by the tram. But for now, Papa is waiting for my call, and I am so nervous. *What if he isn't truly happy to hear from me, like Uncle Pablo says?*

I take a seat on one of the settees in the library and my uncle lowers onto the coffee table, facing me. He places the ham radio next to him as Mr. Jamie hooks it up. I rub my palms along my jeans as Alex sits close to my left. Ford drops to my right while the rest of our team stands by the door, like they're guarding it. And a part of me is grateful. Not only did they listen, they seem to understand me. Even if it's only a little.

"Do you remember when you and Ford used to talk on these?" Uncle Pablo asks me, and I give a quick nod. "Good. It's just like that. A normal call to a family member you haven't spoken to in a while. The only thing I ask is to not use any Natural names, okay?"

I give another nod, and he picks up the handheld receiver to make contact. It makes a high frequency noise and my stomach churns. It feels like I've gone back in time and I'm sitting in my room, waiting for Papa to come in and scold me. I press a hand to my belly with a slow, steady breath, hoping I can keep my breakfast down.

"Ye be right?" Alex asks, reaching for my hand.

"Yes. I'm just really nervous."

He squeezes my hand. "I be right here, yeah?"

"Thank you."

Papa's voice rings through the radio and my heart beats painfully against my chest. Uncle Pablo offers me the hand-held and my hand shakes uncontrollably as I take it.

"You only have ten minutes before his battery runs out," Uncle Pablo tells me. He lays his cell phone on the table with a timer already counting down.

I press the button on the side, muttering, "Hello."

"Hola Mija. It's good to hear your voice."

My chin trembles at the endearment with tears pooling under my eyes. "Yours too," I croak, and Ford squeezes my shoulder.

"¿Cómo estás?"

"I'm good, gracias. How are you?" I ask and slide off the settee and onto the floor.

"Oh, you know. Old and rickety," he says, and I can hear the smile through the radio. I brush at my wet cheeks and a box of tissues slide across the table. "¿Te están tratando bien?"

"Sí, Papa. They are treating me very well." I smile and pluck a tissue from the box. I run it across my nose with a deep inhale. "I have made lots of new friends."

"Muy bien." I can hear the strain in his voice. "That's real good, Mija. Does that mean you will be staying?"

Even though Papa doesn't sound disappointed or cross with me, I fear my answer will produce one or both of those emotions from him. I pull my legs into my chest with a hard swallow. "I would very much like to, Papa." And again, I feel like a small child, waiting for the angry "no," and him demanding I come home immediately.

"I know, and it's okay." A warmth spreads through my

chest at his reply. "Jonah and I always knew the day would come when you left us for a better life. Su vida. I understand more than you know."

The sadness in Papa's voice when he says Father's name has guilt dropping heavily in my belly like an anchor sinking. I bury my head in my knees, blocking the world out, and clutch the handheld tightly against my lips. "Por favor perdóname, Papa. I didn't mean to hurt anyone. Especially Father." I suck in the last word with a painful sob and the air thickens, hot and heavy around me.

"Don't cry, Mija," Papa rasps. "There's nothing to forgive. I'm proud of how brave you were." His voice cracks. "How valiente you've been since." He pauses a moment and then adds, "I should have been honest with you about our family. I always meant to tell you, but I thought you were too young to understand the privacy needed. Had I known what you were up to and how well you truly understood the world, I would have explained sooner. Maybe we could have . . . " He pauses, and my chest tightens at the sorrow in his voice. "Por favor perdóname, for not protecting you better." The words vibrate out of him and a stab of pain shoots through my heart.

"It's okay, Papa," I snivel. "I understand more than you know. We both had secrets and reasons for them."

There's another long pause, and Ford squeezes my shoulder again.

"Te extrano, Mija," Papa says with a loud sniff. "The house isn't the same without you."

"I miss you too, Papa."

A chair creaking sounds through the radio. "¿Eso significa que vas a venir a visitarme?"

"Yes. I would like to come visit very much, Papa." I

finally lift my head to dry my cheeks and my entire team is huddled close around me. "May I bring my new family?"

"Of course," Papa chuckles.

I focus my attention on Uncle Pablo's phone and my heart aches at the time. Forty-five seconds. Ten minutes is not nearly enough time. I grip the handheld tighter, staring at the seconds ticking by.

"Papa, I have to go."

"I know, but we'll talk again soon."

"I hope so."

"Te amo, Mija."

"I love you too, Papa."

Uncle Pablo starts toward me, and I unwillingly give the handheld to him. I press my fingers into my lips, fearful I might not have said enough. Or perhaps said the wrong thing, in the wrong tone. *Does he know how much I miss and love him? Did my words come off as that, or were they accusing?* My brain works overtime, analyzing the conversation, and it stops on his apology. *Does he think I blame him? Is that why he asked for my forgiveness?*

"Wait." I push to my feet, wrapping a tight hand around Uncle Pablo's wrist. "I have to tell him it isn't his fault." My voice is desperate and high as I fumble for the handheld and pull it close to my lips. "Papa, I need you to know I don't blame you. I never did. Not once. Okay?"

"And I never blamed you, either. Not once."

So many emotions spill out of me. Joy, relief, sadness, irritation, and hope. I lean into Uncle Pablo with a sob, and he wraps one arm around me as he ends the call.

"I want to see him. I miss him so much," I say into his shoulder.

"I know and you will." Uncle Pablo pulls back and cups my face. "And you can call him as much as you want once we are on the sub." He wipes my tears with his thumbs. "But you might have to fight or bribe your way through the line." He smiles and my heart aches at seeing Papa in him. "You aren't the only one that has loved ones not on the submarine."

"Okay," I sniff. Uncle Pablo pulls away and heads to Aunt Amy.

"You can have all of mine," Hyena says, wiping his eyes dry.

"Mine too," Toggy says, blowing her nose.

"Same," I hear from the front parlor. My heart swells even more as, one by one, a Natural from all the other teams agrees to give me their time.

A MARK OF HONOR

After my call to Papa, Yak is eager for us to receive our tattoos. I sit on one of the red pillows, nervously watching Yak and our team move about the room. I glance over at the back wall, where the rest of the Naturals are sitting behind the window, and Elk waves at me. I give a quick wave back and then face the gentleman sitting directly across from me. He slides a long needle along a cloth and my heart beats out of control.

Alex nudges me and lifts his chin at Bear, who is moving toward a small forge behind the gentleman. The second it bursts into flames, Alex grabs my hand and I squeeze with reassurance, leaning close to his ear.

"It's okay. Remember, this isn't like the caverns."

He huddles close to me. "Yeah, but it still gonna hurt," he says with a loud exhale.

"Yes," I squeeze his hand again, "but we have felt worse."

"But I don't wanna cry out or be looking like a baby."

"You won't, I promise. I'll even go first and tell you how bad it is, okay?"

"Their bond is so freaking sic." I look over at the window and Elk leans forward to speak to his team. "Yo, we gotta step up our game."

"I agree," his teammate adds, "but I'm also not sleeping in the same bunk as any of you. I like my space."

"No one is sleeping in the same bed," Elk's den parent, Mr. Jacob, says.

"Then why do you allow those two?" a Natural sitting behind Elk asks, lifting his chin at us.

"Circumstances are different. They are family," Mr. Jamie adds.

"So are we," Elk scoffs.

Mr. Jacob's straight posture leans forward slightly. "Then you most differently should not be having coitus with Rabbit, your sister."

"Touché." Elk grins with a nod.

"Know ye." Mr. Jacob smiles.

"Know ye two." Elk chuckles.

Alex nudges me, and when I turn to him, his eyes are wide and full of concern. I start to tell him it's okay. That if we were in trouble, Mr. Jamie would have disciplined us already, but Bear squats in front of Alex.

"I need to collect your blood. Give me your finger."

"Wait. She be going first," Alex says.

"I know. That's why I need your blood."

Alex looks at me with his lips pressed into a thin line and then back at Bear. He lifts his arm and Bear cradles his hand while he pricks Alex's finger with a small needle. A drop of blood forms on his index finger, and Bear reaches for a small, clear cylinder. He squeezes Alex's finger, forcing drops of blood into the tube. After five drops, he hands Alex a band aid and then walks back over to the forge.

"That ain't bad," Alex says, struggling with his bandage.

"Good," I say, knowing I should help him, but I can't seem to force my attention off Bear at the forge. *What is he doing?*

He grabs something similar to a dropper my father used to use when I was ill and adds three drops of something into Alex's blood. Except that doesn't look like medicine. It looks more like liquid metal. He shakes the cylinder, mixing the two together, and my breath stops briefly when he places it into a loud contraption above the forge.

Yak walks in front of me and squats, gesturing for my leg. "I need to clean the area." I stretch out my leg and he immediately starts smearing a strong smelling cloth along my ankle. When he's done, I start to lean forward and dry it with my sleeve and Yak swats at my hand. "What are you doing? I just cleaned that. Don't touch it."

"Okay," I say with a grimace. Yak stands and Bear pulls the cylinder from the forge. He hands it to Yak, who walks it over to the gentleman that will be performing our tattoos.

"Wait, that's his," I say, throwing a thumb at Alex.

"I know," Yak says. "Bison's blood belongs to Sheep. Sheep's blood belongs to you and yours to . . . " He stops talking and looks to my right, at the empty pillow next to me, and then to the rest of our team, sitting on a nearby bench. Everyone but Ford and he was just there. *Where did he go?*

"Where is Wolf?" Yak asks.

"In the latrine," Toggy says with her lips mashed together like she's trying not to laugh and swinging her legs out in front of her on the bench.

"He's got the back door trots," Hyena says, looking up at the ceiling and wiping at his mouth.

"Because of Minx and her stupid pranks," we hear Ford's voice echo from somewhere else, and the Naturals behind the window roar in laughter. I can't believe I was so scared of these people when we first arrived. They might pretend to be scary and tough, but they certainly are not.

"You bunch have got to stop with the pranks," Yak says sternly.

"Yes, sir," they agree.

Ford comes striding in with a hard squint at Toggy and sits next to me, yanking off his shoe and sock.

"Come closer," the gentleman gestures to me, and I scoot closer to him. He presses a thin, wet piece of cloth against my ankle and when he removes it, five horizontal lines made of strange symbols are printed against my skin. He points at each line and tells me what they say. "Protection. Kindness. Luck. Success. Alex."

I press a hand to my chest with a deep, calming breath. "It's beautiful."

The gentleman smiles with a firm nod and then dips the long metal needle into the cylinder. And with quick, rapid taps, he pushes the needle into my skin. I wince, and Alex scoots closer.

"How bad it be?" he asks with a hand on my shoulder.

"Umm, do you remember when we first arrived, and they injected us with all that medicine?" He nods. "Well, more painful than that, but not so bad you can't take it."

"Right." He smiles. "I be thinking it be real bad. Like a lashing. Cos on me old ship, one of the cabin boys, he hollered real loud when he get his."

"Well," Bear begins, moving closer to collect Hutch's

blood, "that could be because of the location. Where did he get it?"

"It be a wrap thingy and when the needle get here," Alex points under his bicep, "he hollered and say stop."

"That's why," Bear says, smiling. "Most aren't that bad." He raises his short-sleeve shirt, revealing all the tattoos of his team on his arm. He points at one under his bicep. "But this one, the sheep, it had me gritting my teeth, hard."

"Ye added us to yer ink?"

"Of course. This is my way of showing we're family."

"Ye have Tippy and Hutch's?"

"Lynx and Bison," Yak corrects. "You three really need to start using your Natural names."

"No, not yet. I didn't have enough money for all three, but it will be the first thing I do when we return in the fall."

"Oof," Ford breathes out. He shoots to his feet, running to the bathroom, and holding his rear. "I don't think I'm going to make it this time." He giggles, and everyone roars with laughter. Even Yak.

SHIPPING OUT

IIII IIII IIII IIII IIII
IIII IIII IIII IIII
II

When we climb into the submarine, Mr. Jamie is quick to give us a tour before we can even settle our feet. He shows us all the places we are allowed to go. Top floor, this is the part of the sub I remember, and it isn't at all as intimidating as I recall. He walks us farther along the corridor, to our quarters, and thankfully Alex's room is next door to mine. And then to the mess hall. On the second floor is the fitness room. A lounge where we can relax and where most of the ham radio calls are made. Plus, this is also where all the doctors and den parents' quarters are, including Yak's.

And then he tells us all the places we aren't allowed to go unless we have been invited. The lower level. That's where the control room is. And according to Mr. Jamie, there's a team of Naturals that run the submarine. Their entire job is piloting the sub from island to island. Plus, they are the only ones that know how to return home. Not even Yak knows the coordinates. Mr. Jamie says, this way if anyone is ever caught off the sub, they can't be interrogated and reveal their home port because the Naturals that run that room never leave the sub. And lastly, the lowest level and the most important room of all, is the weapons and war room. Where Yak and a team go over missions. It's nothing like I remember. Probably because I had my head down most of the time.

But now, as I'm back in my quarters, trying to settle in, worry roots in my belly as we sail away from the island. To leave the safety of Bliss Island brings a twinge of alarm. Maybe that's why the ship is so quiet. Perhaps everyone can feel the gloom in the air.

"Are you okay?" Toggy asks me, digging into her locker.

"Yes. I was just thinking," I reply, shifting on my bunk right beneath hers.

Rabbit, one of the Naturals from the Alpha Team, is laying on the top bunk of her bed, directly across from ours. She rolls onto her side. "You know, Lynx, that's part of your problem. You think too much," she says and twists slightly, reaching behind her back, and then offers me a flask. "Here, drink this. It will help. It's vodka."

"No, thank you," I say, waving it away. "I've had that before, and I didn't particularly care for it."

"You've had vodka before?" She eyes me for a moment, and her green eyes feel like they can see into my soul. "When?" I shift again, but this time uncomfortably. "And who gave it to you?"

I know exactly when and who gave it to me, but like Alex would say, *I ain't no fink.* "It was at the celebration." I angle my head like I'm trying to picture a face and then reply, "I cannot remember who, though, my apologies."

"Good answer," Rabbit says with a smile and then takes a long swig of her flask. "But this room is soundproof. All the rooms are. It's so we can get some sleep at night." She lifts up, swinging her legs over the side. "So, whatever we say in here," she jumps down, "stays in here."

I can tell by her tone it's more of a threat than a statement, and I nod my head in agreement.

Rabbit pulls her black hair into a loose bun and then walks out the door.

"Don't worry about her." Toggy sits on the edge of Porcupine's bed. The one below Rabbit's. "She's just worried you'll tell on her about sneaking out at night to meet up with Elk." Toggy leans forward, looking out the door and then back at me. "It's Porcupine we have to worry about. I bunked with her last year and ugh." Toggy drops her shoulders with her chin lifted. "She's the worst. Talk about a snitch. The only good thing about it is we'll only be bunking with her for a few days. After we visit with your dad, we'll be dropped off for training."

"Wait. We will be training on another island. Not on the submarine."

"Yeah," she responds. "And not just one island. Each island holds a different type of training and to complete them all can take up to three years. The first one is a really intense martial arts program, and your uncle is in charge of that one. We'll stay there for about six months before the sub comes back for us. We go home for holiday break, then off we go to the next island, and this continues until we've finished all the training programs. And not everyone finishes them. I mean, it's really hard. Harder than anything we've done so far in boot camp." She pushes to her feet. "Now, how about I give you the real tour?"

"I would like that very much, thank you."

I stand with her, and she hooks her arm with mine. "Afterward, you can show Alex." We walk out the door and she leans close to my ear. "There's a few spots that are going to blow your mind, but it's also a few of the Naturals' favorite spots, so you might have to fight for one." She lets go of my arm with a mischievous smile and then bolts forward. "Race you to the mess hall."

"Cheater," I laugh, racing down the corridors, calling out "excuse me" and "apologies" as I bump into other Naturals, trying to keep up with her. I finally catch up just as we enter the mess hall, and Toggy sneaks into the kitchen area. My heart beats out of control as I follow her, remembering the last time she wanted to sneak around, and I wanted no part of it. And now, I can't help but follow her into the unknown, full of excitement.

She stops in front of a door and turns to me. "This one isn't really a secret because everyone knows about it, but it's quiet if you need time alone."

She opens a broom closet, walking into it, and when I join her, the cleaning supplies hanging on the back wall moves as she presses the wall forward. We walk down a flight of stairs, all the way to the lower level. The forbidden floor. The walkway is so tight, Toggy and I can no longer walk side-by-side like we were in the corridors. She turns, raising a finger to her lips as we pass a door with a handwritten warning painted on it. Control Room and, from the look of it, it was written a very long time ago. The edges are worn with the pieces torn off and the ink is faded. Farther down, we pass another door, and the same handwriting is on this one. War Room. We continue quietly, with more warnings on our way. Weapons. Electrical. Water. Solar.

We finally turn left, at the back end of the submarine, and Toggy stops, but I still can't see past her. She is so tall.

"Hey, what are you doing down here?" I hear Bear ask. I

lift onto my toes, peeking over Toggy's shoulder. He's sitting inside a large circular frame.

"Same as you," Toggy replies.

"I thought we had to be quiet," I whisper over her shoulder.

"Not in this spot." Bear points at the ceiling. "Right above us is your aunt's office and the soundproof dome falls right here."

Alex pokes his head out from the frame, and my heart warms at seeing him with Bear.

"Lynx, ye gotta see this," he says with excitement.

I squeeze past Toggy, and my jaw drops at the sea life swimming on the other side of the window. A group of small fish dart through the water with sharks circling below them. Among them are larger fish about the size of my arm, gliding slowly around, sucking in even tinier fish.

"Here." Bear stands, and I take his seat against the window. A large-looking seal with curved tusks, nearly as big as those sharks, swims by, and Bear leans over my shoulder. He taps on the glass and my heart nearly explodes. "That's a walrus."

"Is that safe?" I ask, wide-eyed, debating if I should move.

"A walrus?"

"No. Tapping on the glass like that. What if it breaks?"

"Oh, no," he chuckles. "It's totally safe." A large animal rolls playfully into the group of fish and then snatches one into its mouth. Bear taps on the glass again. "Now, that is a seal."

"Whoa. Those be great white down there. Are they gonna eat it?" Alex asks.

"No. Those are salmon sharks, but I guess if they're hungry enough, they might try."

"Shit," Toggy says behind us. I look over my shoulder, and she's growling at her bracelet. "Mr. Jamie needs to have a word with me," she huffs and then peeks up at Bear. "Can you show her the rest and make sure she gets back?"

"Yep."

"Blimey!" I turn back to the window, and Alex has his face pressed against the glass. "There be an underwater village over there." He points to his right.

"Yeah," Bear says, leaning over my shoulder again. "There are loads of those down here. You'll see a lot more the farther away from home we get." He leans closer. "I can try and explain what everything is, but since Wolf was practically raised on this ship, he would know better. But I can give it a go."

We glide closer and Bear points at a sign hanging halfway off the building with letters missing, Du_c_ Bro_, and it's covered in algae. Everything is. "That was a coffee shop," Bear says.

"What is that?" I ask, pointing at something similar to an "M" poking out of the sea floor.

"If I remember right, Wolf said it was a chicken joint or something."

"What be those?"

"Those are vehicles. Wolf says they used those instead of horses to get around back then, and they could trot faster than a horse." He points again. "And those bigger buildings, out there, those were apartments. It's where large groups of people would live together." He points at another tall building. One at least five times bigger than the apartments, and a strong voice clears their throat behind us.

"I thought I asked you not to bring her down here, that I wanted to be the one to show her all this," Ford says behind us, full of annoyance.

Bear straightens. "I didn't. Minx brought her, but now that you're here." He moves out of the way and gestures for Ford to take his spot.

Ford looks at Bear like he's not sure if he believes him or not before moving closer. And since he isn't as big as Bear, most of the Naturals aren't, he sits between us. It's a tight fit, but we don't mind because we are about to learn everything there is from our past. Not even the teachers back home can give us the type of history lesson we are about to experience.

A CONNECTION I DARE NOT SEE

卌 卌 卌 卌
卌 卌 卌 卌
///

The first couple of days were fun and exciting. We explored nearly every inch of the submarine. Played games. Sparred for fun. We've even pulled a few pranks on the other teams. I've become comfortable enough with my team that my guard has come down. Not all the way, mind you, but enough that I joke and tease the others. Just like I used to with Mable, Cotton Wayne, and Ford. Even Alex has become comfortable enough with everyone that he isn't with me all the time. He spends most of his time with Hyena. And every night, I end my day in the lounge to call Papa. Luckily, the row of ham radios is always empty, and I have all the privacy I need. Not that I need it; we don't talk about anything serious. It's mostly idle chit-chat. The kind Ford and I used to have about Mable.

Except now, it's me that can't stop asking questions about her. I can't wait to see her and Papa tomorrow night.

I'm filled to the brim with excitement. It's why I can't sleep. I only wish Papa would tell her I'm coming tomorrow night, so I could talk to her on the ham. But he says he wants to surprise her, and I get it. I do too. So, instead of tossing and turning in bed, I've come down to the lower level to watch the old world pass by.

I can see why this is such a popular spot. It's quiet and calming. It's the perfect place to daydream. I lean my head against the cool glass, thinking about Mable. A smile spreads across my lips at the thought of her in boot camp. If she's anything like she was when we were kids, I don't think Yak would be able to frighten her enough to listen. He would definitely have his hands full with her. Probably more than he did with Alex. Especially if she knew there was no risk of actually dying. Which I would definitely tell her.

"Hey." I look up, and Bear is standing next to me. "May I join you?"

"Of course." I pull my legs into my chest. "Why are you up so late?"

"I just got out of a private session." He joins me on the wide circular frame, facing me, and loosely hugs his knees. "And now, I can't sleep."

"My apologies, Bear. I didn't know you were with Doctor Lawson. I can give you some alone time." I start to get up, and he grabs my arm. But just as fast as he reached for me, he lets go, balling his hand into a fist.

"Sorry. I didn't mean to grab at you like that. You don't have to leave." His voice softens to almost a whisper. "Please stay."

"Only if you're sure," I say, scooting back.

"I'm sure." He pulls his hair tie out, combing his fingers

through his long hair. "After the session I've had, I don't want to be alone, but I don't want to talk about it either. Usually after a private, Wolf and Hyena are on me, trying to make me feel better, but it doesn't help. I know they mean well and it's coming from a good place, but sometimes I just need silence. Like now." He rests his head on the back of the circular frame and closes his eyes with a long sigh. "And you're the only one that knows how to sit still and just . . . be."

I hug my knees, trying to make myself smaller because I understand. In the mining caverns, there were plenty of days that Alex and I needed the presence of the other, but not their words. When one of us was hurting, whether it was physical or emotional pain, the other would sit in silence, holding their hand. And tonight, I can see the hurt and loneliness in Bear. After what he said about Ford and Hyena, I don't believe he has an Alex to just sit with him, and I would very much like to his person. I want him to know he is not alone. That he has someone that understands him.

I press my cheek onto my knee and look out the window, debating if I should reach for his hand. I don't want to upset him if that isn't something he wants. Especially if he's never truly had someone to lean on before. I genuinely don't know what to do. I turn my attention back to Bear, and his sorrow is visible. His head is bent, braced against his right palm with his left hand hanging between his knees, slightly shaking. Without thinking, I reach for his hand and turn my head back to the window.

Whatever his worry is, he is struggling with it, and I hope I've not added discomfort to it. It would pain me more than him if I made him feel uncomfortable. Or worse, he thought I saw him as weak. I know from experience with

Ford, he never wanted anyone to see him as weak. Especially with Mable. He never cried if he was physically hurt. Instead, he would pretend to be tough or lash out in anger if it was emotional hurt. Now that I'm thinking about it, perhaps I should pull away. Even leave. I shift slightly, about to pull away, and he curls my fingers into his palm, tightening his grip. My shoulders release. Perhaps my presence is helping. We sit in silence for nearly an hour as I watch the old world and he works through his pain.

A heavy sigh vibrates out of him, and he squeezes my hand. "Thank you."

I lift my head and smile. "You are very welcome."

"I'm glad you were here." He looks out the window, avoiding eye contact. "I think I needed that more than a session. With me being the biggest one on our team, everyone sees me as the strongest one, but I'm not. Not emotionally. But for them, I put on a brave face and continue to be the leader they've made me." He looks at me. "It's nice to know I can be vulnerable with you. Thank you."

"I get it. I used to be that way with Alex. There were times I didn't want him to see how truly scared I was or how painful my beatings were. I thought if I was brave, he would be too. I always protected him more than I protected myself."

"How about this?" He scoots down slightly so he can brace his bare feet onto the circular ledge next to me, and I pull my hand away. "After our sessions, we find each other and sit in silence and just . . . be."

"I like that." I smile. I slide closer to the window, nearly pressed against it now, so we can both adjust and get comfortable.

"Me too." He leans his head back with his eyes closed, and I join him in relaxing myself.

We sit in silence for a few minutes, and then Bear curses. "I am so sorry."

I glance up, and he jumps, moving away from the window. I look at him and around him, wondering what he is apologizing for.

"I wasn't even thinking." He grabs a handful of his hair, staring at his feet. "I had you blocked in. I am so sorry, Tippy. Please forgive me," he apologizes again.

My mouth parts. I was so concerned with him that I didn't even notice.

"Why didn't you say something?" He lifts his eyes to me. "I forgot for a moment. I'll try and do better next time." He wets his lips with concern heavy in his voice. "But you know you can always tell me to move when I forget. I won't be upset. Never."

"Yes, but I honestly didn't notice."

"Really?"

"Yes, really." I smile.

"That's good. It means you're starting to feel safe here." He returns to the ledge and gestures to the window. "Want me to take that side?"

"No. I'm good here, but thank you for asking."

He slowly leans against the frame. "So, does that mean you feel safe with me? I mean, the only person you let block you in is Alex."

"Not so much as safe, but confident."

"Hmm." He angles his head with his brows pinched together. "Care to explain what that means?"

My lips quirk up, and I shove my hands into the front pocket of my red hoodie. "If you tried anything, I'm confident I could take you." I kick my legs up, bracing my bare feet onto the ledge next to him.

"Is that so?" He grins, kicking his legs up, too. "You know those are sparring words." He rests his head back and closes his eyes. "But I'll let it slide this time."

I think back to my first day here and how terrified of him I was. How he used those same words on Christopher right before he shot him. *Is that so? This is not a game. I am hard, but fair. And when you start to hate me, and you will, just remember, no one is coming to save you. I am your savior.* Now, I'm sitting alone with him, not scared at all, comforting him. I lean forward, poking him in the cheek, right where his dimple is.

"Only because you know I would whoop you." I grin.

He rolls his head against the frame and looks at me with a lopsided grin. "Careful now, or I'll make you eat those words."

I match his grin. "Careful now, or you'll embarrass yourself."

"Ohh," he chuckles with an easy grin. "That's it. It's go time." He jumps up and faces me. "Let's go."

"Are you sure? Because I've been holding back with you this whole time. And if we do this . . . " I suck in air with a grimace. "I'm going to take your title and then I'll be top dog of our team," I say with a hidden grin.

"Ohh," he chuckles again. "Now it's really on. Up." He makes a clicking sound, gesturing for me to get up.

"Okay." I shuffle out and stand, facing him. I lift my chin slightly so I can look him in the eye. "This is not a game, Benji. I am small, but fast. And when you realize I'm better than you, and you will, just know . . . no one is coming to save you. I am your savior." I quickly turn before my face betrays me and he sees me smiling.

"Wow. It's like that, huh? Get in my head and lower my confidence," he says, walking behind me. "I'll admit, it almost worked."

I don't answer. Instead, I quicken my steps, hurrying toward the sparring room.

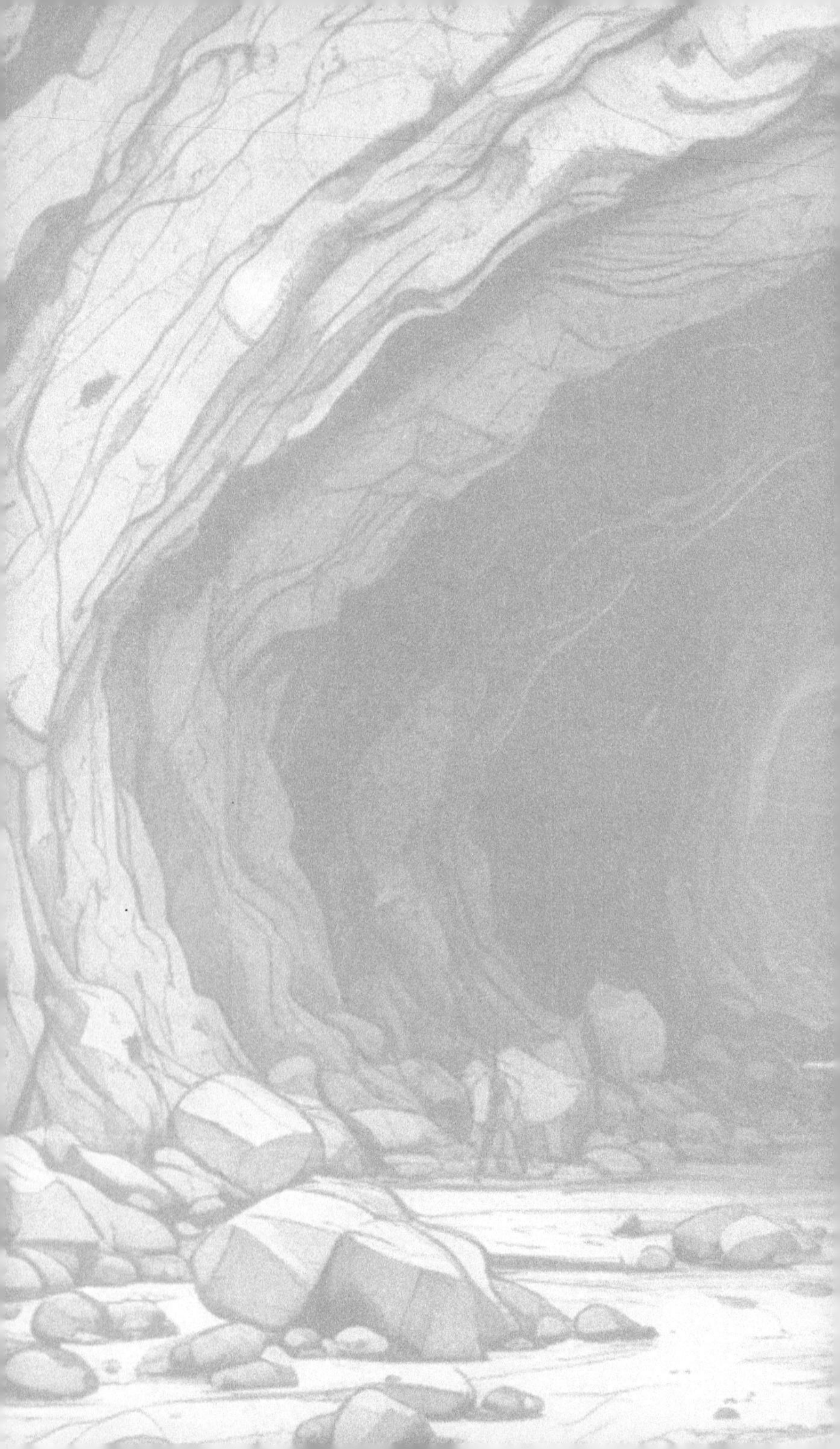

HOME AFTER ALL THIS TIME

~~卌 卌 卌 卌~~
~~卌 卌 卌 卌~~
////

At midnight, I stand behind Alex, waiting my turn to climb out of the submarine, and I have a flashback to the last time I was in this exact spot. I press a hand to my belly with the same apprehension. Except now, it isn't a fearful worry. My belly is spinning in dread. *What if I can't leave Papa once I see him? What if he asks me to stay and I can't bring myself to say no?*

"Hey." Bear slides up next to me and bumps his shoulder into mine. "Are you okay?"

"No, and yes. I'm a little nervous."

He bumps my shoulder again. "Well, if you want to sit and just be when you get back, I'm here. Okay?"

He starts to walk off, and I reach for his elbow. "Wait. Are you not coming with us?"

"No. This is more of a family thing. Plus, I've got some stuff to finish up here before we head out for training."

"Oh. Okay." I let go of him in confusion. *Family thing.*

How? The rest of our team is going, including Elk's team. They nearly jumped at the chance to come. I thought since Elk's team was the one that rescued me and Alex, they would want to see the reunion, and they did. Even Mr. Jamie and Yak are coming along. So why does Bear not want to go? *Are we not friends like I thought? Or is he secretly cross with me for beating him last night?* I look to my right and it's my turn to climb out, but I can't go. Not until I fix this first. I reach for him again.

"Bear, are you cross with me about last night? My apologies if you are, but it was all in good fun. You are still our team leader. I would never take that away from you."

"No. I'm not mad about that." He shoves his hands into the front pockets of his trousers. "I'm not mad at all. Why do you think I am?"

I open my mouth to reply, and Owl shouts out, "Bear! Are we doing this or what?"

Is he not coming either? Why?

"Hang on," Bear says over his shoulder, and then looks at me. "It's not that I don't want to come. I do. I just—"

"No. It's fine." I force a smile. "Go do what you need to do."

"You're sure?"

"Yes. Go." I give another fake smile and start to turn to the ladder.

"Hey." Bear touches my shoulder, stopping me. "You'll come find me when you get back, right?"

"Maybe." I shrug. "I might not need the sit silent thing," I say, hoping he can't hear the hurt in my voice.

He bends his knees with a growl and moves closer, whispering into my ear. "I'm planning something for you." He pulls back with a wide grin, flashing me his dimple.

"You are?" My eyes widen with excitement. "What are you planning?"

"If I told you that, it wouldn't be a surprise, now, would it?"

"I guess not."

"Tippy, let's go," Uncle Pablo shouts down at me.

"Now, go and have a great time. And when you get back, come find me," he says, urging me into the small area where the ladder is.

I grab hold of the ladder and then look over my shoulder just as Aunt Amy rushes by with an arm full of decorations. She stutters to stop and takes a step backward, looking right at me. "You didn't see anything. Got it?"

"Yes." I nod and turn back to the ladder, wondering what Bear and Aunt Amy could possibly be planning. I climb out with a smile, and I'm standing on a long, flat surface; the top of the submarine, and everyone is milling around, waiting. I look out into the distance and when I see lanterns brightening Capra Horn's pier, a raw, powerful lump forms in my throat.

"Are you ready?" Uncle Pablo asks, pulling me into the crook of his arm.

"Yes, and no. I have a mix of emotions right now. Excitement. Longing. A little anxious." I press a hand to my belly. "I feel like I'm going to throw up."

He kisses the top of my head. "You'll be fine. You'll see."

I inhale deeply as our transportation slowly emerges from under the water. Whatever those are, they slide up close to the submarine, and my stomach squirms.

"Whoa. What be those?" Alex asks, peeking over the edge a few feet from me.

"Jet skis. It's how we get to the island," Hyena responds, stepping onto one, and then gestures for Alex to join him.

Uncle Pablo squeezes me closer. "Now, we can't stay long. We need to be gone before sunrise. We have training—"

"I know." I grin. "We have training to get to."

"That's right. And don't think just because you're my favorite, I'll go easy on you."

"Umm, hello," Ford says, twisting on the jet ski. "Hurtful. Shouldn't I be your favorite?" Ford asks as Toggy joins him on the jet ski.

"You'd think so, huh?" Uncle Pablo teases, moving to his jet ski.

"Damn. Doubly hurtful," Elk chuckles, with Rabbit sitting behind him. His whole team is in their disguises. Rabbit's suggestion. She said it would be a great way for Mable to see a Natural in their full get-up, and I quickly agreed.

I step onto the jet ski, and it wobbles slightly as I adjust behind Uncle Pablo.

"Hang on to those bars, there." He points.

I grip the bars next to my thighs and hang on as our transportation roars to life. And within seconds, our ride jumps over choppy water, and I grip the handles tighter as my rear bounces me nearly off the seat. Water sprays into my face and I smile into it. It's so much fun, I can barely contain the joy spinning in my belly. But as we gain closer to the tall stone structure that surrounds Capra Horn, protecting it from fierce winds and the sea, my belly flips upside down. Especially when Uncle Pablo slows the jet ski, allowing it to float closer to the long dock. He pulls a cord out, tying it to the pier, and I carefully step onto the port. I rub the center of my chest with my eyes on the stairway leading up and onto the main island. I can't believe

I'm finally home after all this time. My heart is pounding out of control.

"That was the cleanest ride I've been on yet," Alex says with a full smile. He hops onto the port and turns to me. "Yeah?"

"Yes." I smile and drape my arm over his shoulder, pulling him close as we start up the staircase. "Are you ready to see Mable again?"

"Aye. But what if she be heavy? Ye know how she be. She don't like surprises," he asks at the top of the stairs.

"No, she doesn't. But I believe she will understand this one," I say, scanning the town square. Not that I can see much. Even with my eyes adjusted to the darkness. The town square, where all the shops are located, is at least thirty feet from us. All that I can see clearly are tall posts with candles burning inside them, casting shadows among the town. I take another step closer, and Ford squeezes between us.

"Oh, I don't think you have to worry. With me here, Mable won't have enough dislike for anyone else. When she sees me, all her meanness will be directed at me."

I start to argue the fact, but the building next to me closes my throat. The trade station that sits right near the stairs looks different. It no longer looks as if this is the postal office. Where everything delivered by ship comes here before it's delivered to the people of Capra Horn. I run a hand along the black soot stained into the wood and my chest aches at the memories of my actions. I step around the edge post office, closer to town, and everything looks just like this one. Burned and sad. Even the trade stations that once bloomed with life now sag with defeat.

"Mija."

I pull my gaze off the sorrow I caused so many years ago,

and there he is, my papa. And he, too, looks different. He isn't the clean-shaven man I remember. He has a beard now. Not long, just scruffy enough to know he doesn't shave every morning. And with the leather strap secured over his left eye, he looks rough. Cruel even. But as he starts toward me, my chest blooms with warmth and happiness because I know he is anything but cruel.

"Mija," he says again, wrapping his arms around me in a tight hold, lifting me off my feet. I bury my head into his shoulder, inhaling the hard work lingering from his skin and clothes. He smells the same as he did all those years ago and a knot forms in my throat. I never thought I would see him again, and in doing so now, big, ugly tears spill out of me.

"I wish I could bottle this moment up and take it with me," I cry into his shoulder.

"I know, but we will have many more." Before I'm ready, Papa lowers me back down and pulls away to hug Uncle Pablo. "Gracious."

"I told you we'd find her," Uncle Pablo says.

He pulls away from Papa to introduce the Alpha Team, and I stand aside. I lift onto my toes, searching through the Naturals crowding around Papa for Mable. The instant I see her, my heart feels nearly whole again. But without Father, a chunk will forever be missing.

She's on her toes, like me, and I don't think she recognizes me. Then again, I don't look the same as I did when we were kids. Just like she doesn't look like the Mable I used to know. Her hair isn't braided and hanging down her back. It's full and frames her pretty face. And she's wearing male clothing. Just like Papa. Black trousers with suspenders strapped over a long-sleeved white shirt. I cup my mouth with both hands and smile into them. She even has a rifle tucked under her arm. I'm so glad she's being herself. Even if it was without me. She finally sees me, and I race forward, nearly knocking her over as I slam into her.

"I'm so happy to see you, Mable. Oh, how I've missed you." I pull away and tears fall from her big brown eyes. "Don't cry. It's okay," I tell her and wipe away all her misgivings because I know she has them. I would. I only wish I could have spoken to her before now. I cup her small face and before she can speak, I say, "I'm okay. What happened, happened and we cannot change the past. We can only move forward." I smile big and happy, and for the first time, I truly understand Doctor Lawson's words. "And I hope we can do it together. Like we planned. As Naturals."

"Wait. Ain't ya staying here?" she asks in a gruff voice, and I press my forehead to hers. The same way we did when we were kids and one of us was hurt. Physically or emotionally. The same way I do with Alex now.

"No. I want you to come with me."

"Don't ye mean with us?" Alex asks and then clears his throat.

I pull away. "You remember Alex, yes?"

"Hey Mable?" Alex grins.

Her chin trembles as she yanks him roughly to her in a big hug. She looks up at me, over his shoulder. "How?"

"It's a long story, and I can't wait to tell you all about it once we are at the house. In the meantime, I have someone I want you to meet." I wave Hutch closer.

"Mable, this is Hutch. Hutch, Mable." I look over my shoulder at all the Naturals crowded around us. "This is our Lou."

Everyone speaks at once, and before Mable can greet anyone, another voice interrupts.

"We should take this back to the house before we wake the community. Dawn will be here before we know it," a tall elderly woman says, standing off to the side. For a moment, I don't recognize her. But then when she adds, "Mable Lou, come along. Now," in a harsh and demanding tone, I instantly know that's Mable's very strict grandmother.

I look at Mable, wondering how she is able to dress like a male and cut her hair with her grandmother here. I look over at Papa, speaking to Yak. *Is he the reason?*

"Mr. Lopez," Mrs. Miller says sternly.

I pull on Alex's arm, towing Hutch with me, and step wide around Mrs. Miller. Once we are farther away from her strict look, I stop and wait for Papa. He lifts a hand to me as he starts forward and all the misgivings I had fall away. But when he stops to talk to Mable, my heart aches for her. Her head is bent with her shoulders slumped, and I can tell she has her own mistrusts. *Is it about me?* I start to go to her and then stop when Papa cups her chin, and mine trembles out of control. Not because I'm jealous, but because I'm glad Mable had someone to love her while I was gone. I look over at Mrs. Miller, knowing she loves Mable, just not the way Mable needs it.

"This be where ye live, huh?" Hutch asks, and I turn my attention back to him.

Instead of moving up onto the boardwalk, like a lady should—like Mrs. Miller is—I walk along the beaten down dirt, packed into the ground. "Yes." I look past the shops, where homes and barns stand hidden behind the town square. "It seems so small now." The wind shifts, and the outhouses scattered near homes, raids my sense of smell. And my heart warms at the sense of familiarity, even if it smells awful. I shove my hands into the front pocket of my hoodie and eagerly share my old world with them. I point to my left. At the shops built close together, nearly on top of each other.

"That's the barbershop. Papa and Father used to go every Saturday while I played with the other kids over there." I turn slightly to point behind us, at a swing hanging from a tall tree near the church. I turn back to the barbershop. "And the building next to the barbershop is The Dancing Goat. The saloon. It belongs to Mable's family. Sometimes, if we were in really big trouble, our punishment was to wash all the dishes." I bounce on my toes, pointing at our favorite shop. "Oh, and that's the general store. We used to race along the boardwalk every afternoon after church, rushing inside to buy candy. She would get a butterscotch and I would get two peppermints. One for me and one for Alex. And Cotton Wayne would get a honey stick." I stop and look in the direction Cotton Wayne lives, wondering if I'll get a chance to see him while I'm here. He was a part of our group and a big part of my childhood. He wasn't just Mable's friend, he was mine, too. *Oh, I do hope I get the chance to say hi.*

"Look," Alex says, nudging me. He points above the schoolhouse in front of us, toward our secret spot. "That be where we meet up at night, and they give us food," he tells Hutch. Alex hurries his steps, talking to Hutch about the things he remembers here, but I slow mine.

I lift my eyes to the highest peak of Capra Horn, and the full moon shines brightly on our wishing tree. I look behind me, at Mable, and wonder if she and Cotton Wayne ever go there anymore. If they continued with our oath. To do one good deed a day for those in need. Or if they made new wishes without me.

Papa jogs to catch up and I look behind him. Mable is walking behind the post office, alone.

"Is Mable coming? Should I go to her?"

"She'll be along shortly. She just needs a few minutes to gather herself. You know how she is with feelings and all." Papa smiles.

"I understand." I turn, hooking my arm with Papa's as we walk, and lift my eyes once again to the tree that holds all our secrets. I should pay it a visit while I'm here. After all, it did grant me the one wish I asked for. To be a real Natural.

ACKNOWLEDGMENTS

I would like to thank my critique group. Heather, Andrea, Bree, and Robbin for all their feedback.

A special thank you to Branan for rereading so many chapters over and over, until I got them right.

To Brittany, for taking a simple idea and turning it into an amazing cover.

To Chelsea, for all the emails and phone calls and helping me bring this story to life.

To Cecilia, for all her emotional support, encouragement, and being able to bounce ideas around. Without her, I never would have had the courage to step out of my comfort zone and put myself out there. My story never would have reached an editor's hands and for that, I will forever be grateful.

Thank you!

ABOUT THE AUTHOR

Trena Cannon is a young adult dystopian/apocalyptic author. When not writing or spending time with her family, she can be found reading or in front of the Xbox gaming. Trena enjoys coffee, dark humor, and a good prank.